NO TURNING BACK

Michael stepped closer to Antonia. "You drive me to complete, utter distraction!"

Antonia stood her ground. "Oh? And just how distracted are you?"

Michael pulled her to him, staring into her eyes. He silently ran his thumb along the delicate outline of her slightly parted lips. Her chest heaved against his as she swallowed hard, aching to put an end to the heightening tension surrounding them. He raised her chin between his fingers, and lowered his hungry lips to hers.

His forceful kiss should have served as a warning, but Antonia felt a burning desire to know more of him, and she did not pull away.

Breathing heavily with passion, Michael held her from him. "I warn you, if you don't leave this cabin immediately, I'll not be responsible for my actions. You are more than one man can resist."

Antonia was locked in the binding spell of the moment, and had no other thought than satisfying her need for Michael as she gazed into his questioning eyes with unbridled longing.

"I do not want you to resist," she whispered . . .

THE BEST IN HISTORICAL ROMANCES

TIME-KEPT PROMISES   (2422, $3.95)
by Constance O'Day Flannery

Sean O'Mara froze when he saw his wife Christina standing before him. She had vanished and the news had been written about in all of the papers—he had even been charged with her murder! But now he had living proof of his innocence, and Sean was not about to let her get away. No matter that the woman was claiming to be someone named Kristine; she still caused his blood to boil.

PASSION'S PRISONER   (2573, $3.95)
by Casey Stewart

When Cassandra Lansing put on men's clothing and entered the Rawlings saloon she didn't expect to lose anything—in fact she was sure that she would win back her prized horse Rapscallion that her grandfather lost in a card game. She almost got a smug satisfaction at the thought of fooling the gamblers into believing that she was a man. But once she caught a glimpse of the virile Josh Rawlings, Cassandra wanted to be the woman in his embrace!

ANGEL HEART   (2426, $3.95)
by Victoria Thompson

Ever since Angelica's father died, Harlan Snyder had been angling to get his hands on her ranch, the Diamond R. And now, just when she had an important government contract to fulfill, she couldn't find a single cowhand to hire—all because of Snyder's threats. It was only a matter of time before the legendary gunfighter Kid Collins turned up on her doorstep, badly wounded. Angelica assessed his firmly muscled physique and stared into his startling blue eyes. Beneath all that blood and dirt he was the handsomest man she had ever seen, and the one person who could help beat Snyder at his own game.

DREAM'S DESIRE

GWEN CLEARY

ZEBRA BOOKS
KENSINGTON PUBLISHING CORP.

ZEBRA BOOKS

are published by

Kensington Publishing Corp.
475 Park Avenue South
New York, NY 10016

First printing: August, 1990

Printed in the United States of America

To Tammy
In loving memory

This book could only be dedicated to you, for your faithful companionship during the long hours of its creation.

You will always live on in my heart.

Sometimes when the night is still
I perch upon my window sill
And pretend a captain to be
Of a great ship upon the sea
Commanding it to carry me
To my
Dream's Desire

Chapter One

North of San Diego
Summer 1834

A deeply troubled expression shadowed Antonia's face. She still could not believe the turn her life had taken. In an attempt to put the distressing thoughts from her mind, she settled at the edge of a trickling stream, tucking her knees up beneath her skirt. Perched atop a granite boulder, she wistfully stared at a leaf as it sailed past the pebbles strewn about the stream. Studying the bit of greenery, Antonia imagined it a great ship taking her to exotic ports around the world and far away from the overwhelming problem facing her.

She reached out and grabbed the imaginary vessel. "I wish I could experience the feel of the sea beneath my feet aboard a ship, and visit all those places I have heard about since childhood," she said aloud. Thinking how her dream would never come true now, she crumbled the leaf and heaved a heavy sigh. "No. My fate is not to be so fortunate."

She caught sight of more foliage floating past her and a wry smile crossed her pert oval face as she rested a dimpled chin against her knees. She bit her lip and lowered long ebony lashes rimmed around brilliant green eyes flecked with amber.

With a deep sigh borne from unfulfilled longing, she allowed her thoughts to drift back to remembrances of sea adventures told to her by her *padre*. But it was long ago that her *padre* had bounced his only child on his knee, cuddling her close while he told of his travels and how he had been blessed to marry her *madre*. Dreamily, Antonia allowed her mind to conjure up the romantic tale . . .

James Winston had given up a rather dubious life as a sailor some two and a half decades ago, choosing to marry "a California lady" and join those of the *gente de razón*. James had been serving aboard the schooner *White Maiden* when it had put into the Porto de San Diego to replenish its stores of water.

"Ahoy, laddie," a weather-worn sailor hailed James. "Crane that neck of yours to shore. There be a beauty there that no man should miss."

While standing watch topside, the tall, yellow-haired sailor followed the old sea dog's instruction and caught sight of a vision on shore who had retired him from his bachelor days forever.

Señorita Rafaela del Rosario Ortega had been seated next to a shipment of *panocha,* enjoying the hard cone of sugar and patiently awaiting the return of her commandant *padre* from a routine inspection tour of the ships.

She had journeyed to the water's edge with her *padre* to watch the great-masted vessels while he conducted the affairs of state, and to bid good-bye to her beloved sister who sailed for Spain. Little did Rafaela know at the time that that journey would alter her life as well as that of her offspring many years later.

The daughter of an old established family, Señorita Rafaela had been betrothed as a child to the eldest son of a wealthy and powerful family, but had left the lovesick *novio* standing at the altar to run away with the dashing young James Winston a fortnight after the common sailor had been commissioned to paint a cameo of her.

Amidst accusations and violent protests, Rafaela and James returned to stand firm. After a month's objections, Rafaela's family finally came to realize the futility of opposition and hesitantly relented, giving their consent to legalize the union of love despite rancorous objections from her jilted *novio*'s family, who had sent their devastated son and a companion to Europe to heal his shattered heart.

James soon thereafter joined the Catholic Church, became a citizen of Spain, and settled into the life of a Californio. Eager to be accepted by his newfound family, James grasped the customs of Spanish culture with true alacrity. Hispanicizing his given name, the rechristened Diego adopted the prevailing speech and style of dress. It was the fruition of that union between a handsome, daring Englishman and a beautiful, dark, fiery señorita which brought Antonia Rafaela Winston y Ortega into this world some two years later.

"Convention be hanged," Antonia said to no one in particular as she snapped her thoughts from her parents' romance back to the present and her own plight.

She tugged at the crisp white peasant blouse until it draped past her shoulders just above the soft swell of her full breasts. Not yet satisfied, slender long-nailed fingers clamped on to the garment freeing it from her waistband to reveal a small waist. She then hiked the flowing checkered skirt up past her knees to expose long, slender thighs.

Just as the tension began to drain from her body and she settled back to revel in the peaceful privacy of her own daydreams, the moment was shattered by the pounding roar of hooves. Abruptly returned to the reality of her situation, she hurriedly smoothed her disheveled appearance.

"Señorita Antonia," the tall, wiry vaquero, Pedro Montoya, boomed. His bushy brows arched in disapproval as he surveyed the sight before him. "Your *padre* grows weary awaiting your presence. *Venga,* come so we may return to the rancho in time for you to ready yourself for your *novio's* arrival."

Antonia's brows spiked together and she glowered at the vaquero, which made him unthinkingly run his stubby fingers down the raised scar on his left cheek. He remembered too well the consequences of those amber-green eyes glaring with sheer rage above sensuously pouting full lips. Someday she'd pay for striking him across the face with that riding crop just because he had glimpsed her swimming at the lake five years ago.

"I have already given my *padre* my answer," she snapped. "I will not return with you. And I will not accept as my betrothed, let alone husband, that pompous, overstuffed swine chosen for me. If or when I wed it will not be to merge two empires."

"Señorita, I would not speak of your *novio* in such a way. He is a very powerful man and would not take kindly to such talk," Pedro advised.

"I shall speak of the man any way I please," she retorted, venting her frustrations on the vaquero.

"But your *padre*—"

"Need I remind you that I am fully grown and shall settle my own affairs?"

Even while she proudly boasted her independence of the rancho, she knew she would have to return to face her *padre* sooner or later. For although she bore her *padre*'s fair skin and hair, she had inherited her *madre*'s fiery temper and had no intention of going meekly as a lamb to the sacrificial altar.

"You know the future your *padre* has chosen for you, señorita."

"*Sí*. And you know that I have always dreamed of growing up to meet my own destiny — not one crafted for me. Even while my friends speculated about whom their families would choose as husbands for them, I remained on the fringes of the group. I did not share in their foolish pastimes then, and I will not be forced into marriage now; I have plans of my own." Her fierce pride would not allow her to be summoned like an errant servant. She would face her *padre*, but on her own terms and in her own time.

"Please señorita, we must be getting back."

"You will take back my message, not my person. Now leave me be or I may be forced to inform my *padre* exactly how you came by that scar," she boldly threatened. At that she dismissed the daunted vaquero with a flip of the back of her hand and returned her attention to another bit of foliage heading toward the sea.

"I will do as you request, but your *padre* will not be pleased, señorita." For a moment he thought of forcing her hand, but the infamous Winston determination chiseled coldly across her features made him think better of it. One permanent reminder on his cheek caused by that wildcat was enough.

She jutted out her chin. "That is none of your concern."

"As you wish." He gave a curt nod, hoping that one day he would have the opportunity to repay her for marring his face.

Furiously, he reined in his horse to retreat, sinking his spurs into the soft flesh of the already bloodied animal. It sprang into a full run. Again the long,

11

sharp rowels struck forcefully at the animal's flanks spearing it into flight. He threw one last backward glance at the willful young girl, and then disappeared around the bend in the trail.

No longer able to revel in the joys of simple fantasy, Antonia's repose ended. In her haste to leave the rancho early enough to catch the *carreta* carrying tallow to the coast, she had neglected to consider her return transportation. She exhaled a breath of resignation born from a life groomed for duty.

Sparing little time, she donned her sandals and tied her blond tresses back with a brightly colored kerchief. She rose to her feet to begin the long trek back to the rancho. She was determined to face her *padre* and be done once and for all with this proposed merger between the two neighboring families.

Climbing back up to the trail and trodding along the dusty path, she swung out her foot, kicking at rocks which littered her way. Anger continued to swell within her until she misjudged her distance and struck out viciously at a jagged stone before her. As her foot made contact with her surrogate foe, a surprised shriek escaped her lips. A sharp pain stabbed through her thigh, causing it to give way and sending her tumbling to the ground.

Momentarily stunned at her unexpected intimacy with the warm brown earth, she sat in the middle of the trail and cursed her plight. The pain of her wound and sight of the crimson-colored extremity brought a disgruntled moan to her lips before she looked up to see two dark figures mounted on horseback heading straight toward her.

Chapter Two

Mano reached out his left hand, encased in a tight black glove, and awoke his captain. Offering Captain Michael Domino a cool cloth for his head, Mano remarked, "You live a hard, fast life, my brother."

Michael draped the cloth across his forehead and groaned, "I take my pleasures where I find them."

"As you have since fate brought us together at the Mission San Diego de Alcalá. It was a most unusual pairing."

"Unusual?" Michael scoffed. "A seriously burned Digueño Indian and severely beaten English sailor dumped into the same room and not expected to live." Michael thought of the time they had spent convalescing at the mission and the lasting bond they had formed, which had spanned years and carried them many miles to faraway lands.

"But we fooled them all; we did live."

"True. We beat the odds, and finally we are about to repay a long overdue debt."

Mano, who had long ago come by the dubious Spanish name "Hand," due to the glove he wore to conceal his charred fingers, poured a glass of spirits for his captain and offered it to his friend.

"Ah, thank you," Michael said, throwing aside the

13

damp cloth and sitting up to take the glass.

"I believe a celebration is in order."

"We've labored long and hard to bring the negotiations with Dominguez to a successful close." Michael stretched and stifled a yawn.

"The credit is yours, my brother. El Señor Dominguez is a shrewd businessman. Your partnership will not be looked upon kindly by Mexico if you are found out."

"Yes, Mexico takes her independence from Spain very seriously. For the last twelve years the government has levied high import taxes at Monterey, California's only legal port of entry."

Michael's blue eyes sparked with a wicked gleam. He set his glass down, folded his arms behind his head, and gave a brief thought to his efforts along the coast before redirecting his attention back to his Indian companion.

"Dominguez has skillfully managed to circumvent the law," Mano observed.

"He has that. But we know how those regulations offered the man little in the way of the economic reward he sought. And our efforts to learn of his ways has shown he's never been a man to sit idly by and not reap the benefits he felt his due. He's done well for himself with a bribe here and there to the right officials, not to mention the other illegal ventures he's engaged in. I wonder just how well he'll do when we're finished with him." Michael's eyes slivered into hard, unforgiving slits.

"I look forward to that day."

"As do I." Michael's lips curled vengefully. "Investing the last few weeks bickering with Dominguez over our joint venture has not been wasted time. He has shown that greed will prove his downfall."

"I still do not know how you managed to get him to

accept two coins per hide or barrel of tallow," Mano stated.

"Not without a great deal of effort."

"Do you not mean skill?"

"More than likely it was his desire for the cargo we carry, since he'll use the price he gets for his hides to barter for our goods."

"The staples so highly valued in this remote part of the world removed from genteel European society, you mean."

"While English society may take comforts like coffee, sugar, spirits, bolts of fabric, and even shoes for granted, these people will pay dearly for them. Just look around the room. The man has obviously paid enormous sums for all the luxury he enjoys."

"But when you have finished with him, my brother, he will no longer wallow in luxuries purchased with the pain of others."

Michael lifted his glass high in toast. "I drink to that day."

Instead of returning to his ship in the harbor, Michael and the Indian had remained overnight at the enormous adobe hacienda belonging to El Señor Dominguez. As Michael's eyes trailed about the room, his companion could not mistake the icy glint of long-held hatred.

"Ah, yes," Michael said coldly, "a man could not help but be comfortable in such a palace. Even a bed such as this is sheer heaven when the beds we've usually been offered were little more than four legs laced together with leather strips." His gaze traced a path around the room again, and a strange, self-satisfied smile tugged at the corners of his lips.

"His hacienda impresses you, my brother?" the Indian asked.

"Who wouldn't be impressed? The walls are over a

foot thick. The sun is blazing outside and yet it is cool in here. Look at all the rich tapestries and European furnishings the man has surrounded himself with. There are few haciendas around to rival the vast Dominguez empire, except possibly that one we saw on our way out here." Michael crinkled his brows. "What was the name on that post?"

"Rancho de los Robles, I believe."

"Yes, that was it, Rancho de los Robles. I heard the man who owns it is equally as rich."

"So it is said."

In his mind Michael visualized both red-tiled, whitewashed adobe haciendas, which were enormous rambling structures built with sprawling spaciousness around vast garden verandas, dwarfing other more traditional cottagelike homes dotting California's scenic landscape.

The merchant captain was pleased with the successful undertaking. It was said that others rarely were victorious when dealing with El Señor Dominguez, for he did his bidding with the same vengeance with which he lived his life. Some even ventured to hint that the man held all mankind in ill repute, for nothing seemed to bring him more pleasure than the misfortune of others. Michael thought about how he had sought for the last two of his thirty-four years to negotiate an agreement with El Señor Dominguez, a huge foreboding figure of a man.

From the first day Michael had won the *Sea Squire* in a game of chance from the much bewildered son of an English lord twelve years ago, he had worked hard to earn the reputation he enjoyed as captain of the rechristened *Áureo Princesa*.

He had sailed California's waters first while it was under the flag of Spain, and now under that of Mexico. He knew that to his crew he appeared driven by

16

some demon in his relentless pursuit of this bargain with Dominguez, refusing to settle for anything less than success. His English crew was fiercely loyal to him, nonetheless he was aware that they wondered at his folly.

Although they knew that San Diego was the finest port at which to fill their hold with the hides they had been gathering for nearly two years, they had questioned why he insisted on returning to San Diego's shores again and again, constantly reminding him of the fact that no man made gain when dealing with El Señor Dominguez.

"It's a fine morning, my friend." Michael grinned, returning his attention to the present. "Pour another round and join me."

Mano, not always favorably inclined toward the spoken word, scooped up a glass from the nearby table and poured the rich amber contents into it. He then settled back on a plumply tufted chair.

"You drink and celebrate much, my brother. To celebrate the winning of a hard-fought battle, or that you are finally going to reap the revenge you seek?"

"I want Dominguez to get everything he deserves."

"Yes. It is time long-held demons are put to rest."

Mano watched Michael Domino's eyes harden to stone before he shifted his gaze and stared into his drink. With a shrug of his broad shoulders, Mano tilted his glass; the two men drank in the silent reflection of long sought-after revenge.

Captain Michael Domino finished the fiery liquid and rose from the rumpled bed, his heavily corded muscles rippling across a back toasted to a deep golden brown from the sun. A sardonic grin split his full masculine lips as his strong hands came to rest on his slender hips, and he stared down at the clothes strewn about the room.

He arched a thick dark brow. "Dominguez certainly knows how to celebrate in style, especially with those two wenches."

As Michael spoke, a thoughtful expression dropped over Mano's generally phlegmatic face. "You know they were not mere wenches but two of Dominguez's *putas*."

A glimmer of recognition twinkled into Michael's eyes and lit up his face with a lusty grin. "True, but they knew how to ease a man's needs and that's all that matters."

"For now, my brother," Mano replied, knowing well all the demons which drove his captain.

Time was of the essence in such business transactions as the captain had just completed, and there were more urgent matters to contemplate than desires of the flesh. Women held little fascination for Michael Domino other than meeting his physical needs. He had neither the time nor inclination for any type of involvement.

Michael shot a questioning glance at his companion's answer. He sensed a change in the Indian since they had landed on California's shores. But delving into the meanings behind each other's words was not generally their way.

He slid his breeches down well-turned, bronzed thighs and stepped to the hot steaming tub brought into his room before he awoke, sinking into the soothing waters. He took the soap into his hand, studying it for a moment before his lips slowly twisted at the corners into a strange, calculating grin. "Dominguez even has the finest of soaps." Turning his attention to the task at hand, he lathered the cloth into a fluffy cloud of suds and began to scrub.

His bath complete and straight-edged razor drawn across the strop several times to ensure it a smooth path, he wrapped a towel around his waist, settled into a chair, and wound hot, damp cloths over his face. After a moment to allow the towels time to soften the shadowy beginnings of a beard, he slowly scraped all trace of stubble from his handsomely tanned face. The task completed, Michael pushed himself up and spied his clothing. A dark frown overshadowed his face.

"Dammit! I've told you over and over again I'll take care of my own clothes. The next time I catch you laying out my things I'll slit your throat and leave you with an eternal smile from ear to ear to replace that infernal frown of yours. You know I don't believe in having others wait on me!"

As Michael was having his say, his Indian companion silently studied his face, noting the displeasure but also noticing the warmth disguised beneath the surface of those piercing blue eyes.

They had been together for many years and there was little of the captain that escaped Mano's observance. The Indian could read any man as well as the signs of the land, and his captain could cast little from his view. As words went, they were not always necessary. But a greater understanding existed between no men, for they had seen much together and had grown to be as brothers.

"You roar with the thunder of a lion. But the force of your protest carries with it the purr of a sleeping cat," Mano sagely replied.

"The cat sneaks up on its prey unobserved before it pounces. And when the time comes, it strikes with the deadly swiftness of the rattlesnake."

"The lessons of life have been harsh for you, my brother."

"But I have learned them well."

Michael pulled on his leather knee breeches, fastening the deep cuffs around his calves. Drawing his long arms through the billowy sleeves of the linen shirt, he buttoned the garment to the high collar, then he wrapped the neck cloth around his throat, knotting it but once. He donned a double-breasted, sleeveless waistcoat made of deep-blue percale and jammed on a pair of jockey boots.

Moving to the carved oaken dressing table, he adjusted the mirror to accommodate his height. At four inches above six feet he towered over most men. He pulled a brush through his thick sable hair, leaving it casually tousled. With heavy waves and bushy sideburns he gave the appearance of a fierce pirate about to do battle.

Groomed to his satisfaction, he placed the last of his belongings in his duffel bag, glanced around the room, and summoned his companion.

"Shall we partake of one last bit of Dominguez's hospitality before returning to the ship? I think it's fitting to enjoy the fruits of the man's labor."

"I shall accompany you out into the sun and then see to the horses," Mano replied, hefting the sailors' totes over his square shoulders.

Mano followed his captain from the room and down the elaborately furnished hall.

"*Desayunó* — breakfast — is being served on the veranda this morning, señores." The servant dipped his gray head, then led them through the enormous double doors. Once outside, Mano quietly disappeared into the shrubbery to enjoy his own repast of dried meats and biscuits and to keep a mindful eye out for his captain.

"*Buenas días,* Señor Capitán Domino. Join us." Dominguez motioned toward an empty chair next to him. "I do hope you rested well after the festivities and found the entertainment to be to your liking."

El Señor Dominguez threw Captain Domino a twisted, knowing grin. He hunched over the table in an elaborate cropped silk jacket, a shirt open at his thick neck. Short breeches strained at the ruby *bolero* wrapped about his rotund figure. His silk-stockinged feet, encased in dark-brown deer skin shoes, tapped impatiently. Dominguez was pleased with the image he presented, for he knew others held him in awe.

"You do me honor, señor, by allowing me to partake in such a fiesta. And yes, I found the entertainment most definitely to my liking." Michael cocked a brow and folded his large frame onto the chair. As he spoke the words in fraudulent innocence he snickered to himself, for he knew of Dominguez's particular perversity and expected that the show he had staged for him the night before with the two women had been enjoyed.

After bribing one of the *rancheros,* Michael had learned that Dominguez's rancho had been built to the strictest specifications of one who sought gratification through observing others engaged in lustful pursuits. Michael knew his performance had been delivered with all due finesse. His lips snipped into the faintest curl as he envisioned one particular portion of the scene.

He had lounged languidly on his back among soft satin pillows strewn about the bed while one woman wantonly teased at his long hard staff, her dark hair flying in twists of heavy curls. The other woman had fed him one carmel breast and then the other until he was buried within the undulating soft mountains before him.

While being the star performer before an unknown audience did not hold the same fascination for Michael Domino as it did for El Señor Dominguez, it did not unduly distress his mind either. Michael's thirsts usually had been quenched within the confines of the more private atmosphere of boudoirs or bordellos. No matter. Michael had logged the event for future reference should the need ever arise.

Once the thinly veiled greetings were concluded between the new associates, Michael paid his respects to the other guests seated beneath the vine-covered trellis and turned his attention to the morning's nourishment of heavy slabs of smoked pork, fresh eggs richly laced with cheese, tomatoes and peppers, warm tortillas dripping with newly churned golden butter, and an assortment of luscious fresh fruits — one of the blessings that the mild climate of San Diego offered. He washed down the feast with the much coveted mug of coffee.

"The coffee is to your liking, eh capitán?" Dominguez asked indifferently.

"Yes, it is. You most assuredly have the best of everything here," Michael replied, thinking of the decadent opulence with which the enormous man surrounded himself.

"I have been blessed to be allowed to enjoy the best that can be imported to this faraway corner of the world. Even such an expensive commodity as coffee." Dominguez feigned a humble sigh and lifted his cup.

Michael's brow arched slightly as he silently finished his meal, concentrating on his planned mission.

"I shall be returning to my ship to see that the hides are loaded," he announced. "Once again, I must thank you for your hospitality," Michael said innocently enough, yet his eyes bored deeply into Dominguez's.

"Of course, capitán." Dominguez smirked. "Oh, and capitán, do not forget the upcoming fiesta. I have arranged it in your honor."

"I wouldn't miss it," Michael answered.

With the demands of proper etiquette satisfied by all present, Michael left the gathering of Californios.

Upon reaching the tethered steeds, Michael was once again joined by his companion.

"Did you learn anything of interest, my brother?" questioned the Indian, who was leaning against the wooden rail.

"Nothing of any substance. It's obvious Dominguez enjoys a game of subtle innuendos. I wonder just how much he will enjoy it when he's not on the winning end."

"I look forward to that day."

"As do I, my friend," Michael said, bobbing his head. "As do I."

Mano had seen to the readiness of the two chestnut horses, which stood securely laced to the wooden post. They mounted and turned the animals away from the rancho.

Riding side by side, the sight of the two men was enough to tempt any woman so inclined. Although the Indian was not handsome, with his roughly hewn wide, flat features and deep-set, piercing eyes of the night, he neither lacked for female companionship nor for admirers of his powerful frame and shoulder-length hair. He was tall, but did not reach the towering height of the captain and was more squarely built in contrast to Michael Domino's immensely wide shoulders, flat stomach, and slim hips. Indeed, the two men cut dashing figures as they rode from the rancho.

Once reaching the main road leading back to the Porto de San Diego, they slowed their pace to a trot. They rode in silence for a long way before Michael broke the stillness.

"Well, my friend, at last we're going to see success in our mission," he boasted, shifting in the saddle.

The Indian only grunted. The gleam in his smoky eyes bespoke his understanding and required no more response.

Turning back to his own thoughts, Michael nudged at the horse's flanks, quickening the pace. He was anxious to return to his ship and finally put his long awaited plan into action.

Chapter Three

Michael was rounding a bend jagged with boulders, and so absorbed in the events of the last few days that the presence of what appeared to be a rather filthy-clad urchin sitting in the middle of the road nearly went unobserved until she appeared directly in front of the giant chestnut stallion.

"Watch out!" Mano yelled, noticing the impending disaster. He jerked hard on the reins of his horse, sending the mighty animal crashing into Michael's.

The force of the collision caused Michael to endure a nasty ride into the heavy brush as the horse careened wildly off the trail.

"Chrissake, man!" Michael's voice boomed off the solid wall of rock nearby. Cursing as he took command of the beast, he whipped out the sword attached to the saddle and slashed the tangled bushes.

After angrily returning to the trail he halted the great animal in front of the tittering young girl. He sheathed his sword, swung his leg over the saddle, and smoothly slid to the ground. His anger began to fade as he closely perused the slender figure he took to be the daughter of a *cholo*, one considered by the gente de razon to be an illiterate idler of little or no worth.

Laughing amber-green eyes momentarily met calculating blue ones; a strange undefinable twinge fluttered within Antonia's chest, and her gaze clung inordinately to the stranger's.

"My friend," Michael said to Mano in Spanish, "fortune appears to be smiling on me this day." He gestured to Antonia, who had ceased her amused giggling to slip into pensive thought.

Silently, she stared up at the giant of a man who stood over her. How unlike the usual parade of young men shoved at her, was this stranger.

"Even a delicious morsel such as this," he motioned again to Antonia, "has its due." At that he pointed to the needle-sharp thorns of the prickly pear cactus, which boldly protruded from his breeches.

His words caused Antonia to shift her gaze to the strong, manly thighs concealed within the tight breeches. Her cheeks flushed at the unbidden thoughts the man brought forth in her. The very idea unnerved her normally steady breathing, for she was unaccustomed to such unsparked attractions.

Antonia blinked several times in an attempt to banish the uninvited sensations rippling down her spine while he plucked the nasty thorns from his person. Then the words "delicious morsel" struck her with its full sobering impact.

"Oh, and what do I see before me but a mindless, overgrown buffoon undoubtedly preparing to provide entertainment for his like at some cheap tavern," she spat. She immediately regretted such a vicious, sharp-tongued attack but could not help but make comment on his reference to her as an edible tidbit.

Her fierce tongue had served her well in the past. Unwelcome suitors had soon been daunted by her quick wit and the intelligence with which it was applied. But it was that same quickness which often got her in trouble with her *padre*.

Unable to control herself, she added, *"Delicious morsel? . . . no señor. If you would but open your eyes you would realize the error of your ways, since I happen to reside at the Rancho de los Robles. And further . . ."*

Giving only scant thought to the content of the wench's words, Michael's eyes darkened and he glowered with amusement at this young woman who dared speak to him so boldly.

"One who wears peasant dress and exhibits the physical characteristics of an appetizing fieldhand in need of a good cleansing may reside at such a grand rancho but certainly not in the main house."

Did she not realize that with less provocation he had laid men permanently to rest? Not to be bested by some mere wisp of a female, whispery laugh lines drew out from around his eyes now of blue steel, and he grinned like a cat about to devour a bird.

"Why, I shall have you know—"

"I suggest you hold your tongue, señorita, before mine is forced to personally parry with that rapier poised behind those invitingly pouting lips."

"Indeed," Antonia said firmly. Her eyes came to rest on the sensual manly fullness of his grinning mouth, and she shook her head to regain her sensibilities.

"Yes. Indeed," he mimicked.

"You obviously do not realize to whom you are speaking."

"I think I realize quite well to whom I am speaking, señorita."

"You would not dare touch me," she sputtered.

Flames the color of a raging forest fire flickered into her amber-green eyes. She fully intended to enlighten him as to the error of his ways. She opened her mouth to retort and then snapped it shut. Maybe, just maybe, it might serve her purpose to go along with this unplanned turn of events. He was a man, the likes of which she had never encountered before, and in spite of their less than cordial meeting, she was strangely attracted to him.

"The wench doesn't believe I make it a practice to be true to my word." Michael threw his head back and gave a short laugh. "Let's get a better look at you."

In the heightening tension of the moment Michael failed to notice her wound. He was made aware of it when he clasped her wrist and roughly jerked her into his embrace.

"Ouch," she groaned. She instinctively drew back her hand to slap his face. But just as quickly she changed her mind and slipped her arm around his neck to steady her stance.

"You are indeed a spirited wench," he said.

Pleased with the sudden change in her demeanor, Michael answered Antonia's gesture with a quick reaction. Not letting the urge flee by, he swept her from the weight of her injured foot and held her tightly pressed against the hard wall of his chest. With eyes deepening to the desire of midnight blue, he left no question of what the next moment would hold.

"Señor, I beg you," she said, feeling the heat of his muscular arms through the thin fabric of her clothing.

"Señorita, a lady need never beg."

Antonia did not mistakenly read the man. He was going to kiss her. He was a total stranger. Probably some lowly sailor on shore leave from one of the large, white-masted vessels anchored off the coast. But, in spite of herself, she was experiencing an undeniable awakening of desire. What a life of sheltered experiences had not taught her, nature now provided. Without stopping to consider such a rash pursuit, she met his lips with eager anticipation.

What began as just another instance of Michael Domino taking his pleasure where he found it soon melted into a shared moment of tenderness.

Antonia felt weak as his lips explored hers. For the first time in her life she found herself responding willingly, envisioning what it might be like to experience more than just this all too brief glimpse of intimacy between a man and a woman.

Startled by his reaction to the eager innocence of the young señorita's kiss, Michael pulled away.

"That was a most inviting kiss," he stated flatly. Something about her had touched him, causing him to quickly drop the hardened veneer back into place before she affected him further.

"Sí, señor, it was," she said in no more than a mere whisper. She drew her fingers to her mouth, lightly outlining the tingling sensations lingering there.

"Who are you?" She attempted to swallow the dozen butterflies in her throat. Her lips remained parted, her gaze fastened to his grinning mouth.

"I, my beautiful señorita, am the lucky discoverer of a blossoming princess hidden beneath a layer of dust. But you may call me Michael."

"I am Antonia."

"My brother," Mano calmly placed a firm hand on Michael's arm, "the princess is in fact a wounded sparrow. Do not add to her injuries, my friend. It has never been your way to consider teaching the untried to soar."

Mano's words, perceptive beyond his thirty-three summers, brought reality crashing back. Michael lowered his eyes to the red, swollen foot, which did not resemble the other slender one aced within leather thongs. His eyes softened ever so slightly but quickly filled with a renewed severity.

29

"You're right. She is but a wounded fledgling. Her wings are yet to be fully tried. And besides, I do not make a habit of plucking the petals from an unopened flower."

Antonia pressed her lips into a tight line of frustration. She had been kissed one moment and rejected the next. She might not be well versed in the ways of the world, but he had activated a need in her; and she was used to having her needs met.

All of a sudden feelings entwined with her thoughts, and Antonia rashly finalized the decision that the situation in which she found herself might just prove to be a deterrent for the forced union awaiting her. Without giving it even so much as a moment of careful consideration, she mustered her most beguiling smile.

"Are you so certain of your expertise in matters of the heart that you know the type of bird you hold?" she crowed, arching her brow. If he reacted in the way she hoped, she would be free of the chains threatening to bind her to a man she could never love.

"Enough!" he roared. "I think the time has come for you to return to this Rancho de los Robles of yours."

After the words left him, Michael had second thoughts. He turned to Mano and spoke in English, his native tongue and one of the five languages in which he easily conversed. His main purpose for now was to keep such a brazen wench in the dark.

"I believe she's offering me a gift I find exceedingly difficult to decline," he said in a deep voice brimming with desires of his own. "The least I can do is see to her foot. And who knows, she may even enjoy a personally guided tour of the ship before I send her along her way."

The Indian, who had lived with the captain long

and traveled to many lands with the man, answered him in English. "The ways of man are not always predictable. But do you think it wise to let this mere twig of a girl pierce beneath your skin? Such a response to a female I have never witnessed in you before, my brother. You may be wise to reconsider."

"She has not pricked my skin. She's merely a young wench in need of medical attention. We certainly cannot leave her out here to fall victim to some unfortunate fate, now can we?" But even while he spoke the words, doubts lingered in the back of his mind.

Mano knew his captain. Regardless of what Michael Domino might be feeling inside, there was no swaying him from his course once his mind was set to something. Mano shrugged his shoulders in silence.

Antonia was well tutored in several languages herself. Secretly she smiled at the words she had just heard uttered. She was strangely pleased such a rash plan was proving so easily successful. Yet caution suddenly reared its level head, warning her she might not be able to control the situation if not handled skillfully.

Reason was not to prevail.

With the thought of abandoning her hasty decision to go with the man overshadowed by the thought of her engagement, she tucked the rashness of her venture deep within her mind. She broadened her smile and leaned meekly against his supporting arm. She visualized him as a rescuing vaquero who would help her escape a fate worse than death, and did not further reconsider an earlier fleeting thought that she could get burned by the spark which already had been ignited between them.

As she gazed winsomely up at the handsome stranger, amber-green met blue once again sending a similar warming sensation flooding through them both.

Michael was further made aware that the soft, rounded swell of breasts molded against his body was not the form of a child. "Damn me, that mouth is too desirable to resist," he moaned.

Spurred on by the unchecked, gnawing tension between them, he took possession of her lips in a searing kiss. He hungrily dipped his tongue into every corner of her moist inner recesses, exploring and demanding she respond, his breath titillating and ragged as the girl willingly answered him with her own tongue.

A thirst for the newly kindled sparks flickering within her, Antonia's lips parted with a mind of their own in answer to his quest. She was rarely, if ever, at a loss for words, but he had managed to momentarily stun her with the raw display of passion. She had never experienced such a kiss before. Instead of being frightened or indignant, as expected of any respectable Spanish lady, she laced her fingers tighter around his neck and pressed her lips to his with a heightening forcefulness of her own.

"Come, my princess," Michael murmured, breaking the kiss. He felt helplessly mesmerized by the enchanting young girl who was so honest with her own emotions.

A strong arm curling around her slender waist, he held her tightly against him. He supported her weight and strode over to his horse, easily swinging her up into the saddle. Positioning himself directly behind her, he nudged at the animal's flanks.

"Where are we going?" Antonia asked, the slightest apprehension tugging at her as she forced herself to hold to the picture of him as her protector. Hardly realistic for one so determined to control her own future, but a childhood fantasy which refused to surrender to the advent of adulthood!

"Maybe we should meet later after I've seen to my

mishap and could be considered presentable," she offered in Spanish. She did not wish to let on that she understood every word he had spoken earlier.

Michael turned to Mano. "Do you hear that, my friend? My señorita desires to make herself beautiful for me. No need, princess." He chuckled, swallowing the urgings from a small voice within him to set her free.

Michael rested his chin on Antonia's shoulder, his warm, moist breath stroking the sensitive skin on her neck. "You are beautiful to me just the way you are," he said and another kick to the soft flesh of the mighty animal hastened its pace toward the sea.

Antonia swallowed hard but quickly resigned herself to her chosen course. She nestled back against him. While her body remained quietly resting, her mind reeled with a myriad of thoughts and newly awakened emotions as he carried her along the welltroddened path leading away from the home and security she had always known.

Chapter Four

Doña Maria parted the shutters in Antonia's room, squinting aging eyes that reflected her fifty years of suffering. She gazed out the large window wringing her puffy fingers as she waited for Pedro Montoya to return from his chartered mission with her willful niece aptly in tow.

Unable to remain passively biding her time any longer, she hurried to the study.

Bursting into the room, she grumbled to Don Diego. "Where is Antonia? That daughter of yours has not been easy to rear. You have always doted on that girl, never refusing her anything. Lucky for you I saw my duty after Rafaela's death and returned from Spain to care for Antonia. Otherwise she never would have received any training on becoming a proper lady. Heaven only knows how she would have turned out if I had not taken total charge of that headstrong girl."

"Don't you mean total charge of the entire household, which I allowed you to run with iron-handed efficiency?" retorted Don Diego, tired of her complaining tongue.

"Your worthless household staff quickly learned that my word was law — all that is except Antonia," she said in exasperation. "That girl is capricious and obstinate and in dire need of discipline."

"A minute ago you were bragging about taking charge of Antonia."

Affronted, Doña Maria gasped. "I have done my best by that child." But Doña Maria could not help but feel that somewhere she had failed. The harder she'd tried to teach Antonia the proper behaviors for her station in life, even personally serving as her *dueña,* the more stubborn Antonia had become.

She narrowed her eyes once more and then jostled her heavy frame over to Don Diego's desk.

"Díos mío, I have failed my poor departed sister." Doña Maria sighed sorrowfully. "Why, just last night I specifically told that girl not to leave the hacienda, for today her *novio* would visit her."

Don Diego's graying blond head snapped back up from his papers when the shrill voice continued to assault his ears. For fifteen years he had neglected Antonia, submerging himself in the pursuit of wealth in order to put from his mind the haunting image of a young widowed father with a five-year-old daughter standing at the cold, damp graveside of the only woman he had ever loved.

Unlike many of his contemporaries, who had married "California ladies" in order to gain large Spanish land grants, Don Diego truly had loved and cherished his beautiful young wife. Married too few years, she died shortly after her parents from the dreaded strangling of *el garrotillo* — a sight branded in his memory to forever torment the very depths of his soul. At the time many Indians were dying of diphtheria and his Rafaela had tried to nurse them, only to be lost to it herself. Dragging his thoughts from the nightmarish memories, he forced his attention back to Doña Maria.

"What is it, woman?" he snorted, although he, too,

had been anxiously waiting for his daughter's return.

"Oh, I knew Antonia would be upset by the betrothal," she huffed and plunked down on the overstuffed settee near the desk. "All I want is what's best for her. A union to such an important man should have made her very happy. Instead, she threw a childish temper tantrum. And to make matters worse, you just seemed to crumble in front of her."

"That is not exactly true," Don Diego said, closing his account book in an attempt to be patient with the woman.

"Not true?" Her voice raised an octave. "If I had not stood firm and demanded Antonia honor the agreement, she would be well on her way to becoming an old maid. Later I even tried to explain all the benefits of such a marriage. But she kept shaking her head and mumbling some nonsense about love. She just cannot seem to understand that love is not important to a successful union and in time she will grow to care for her husband."

"I suppose I must admit I have had doubts." He sighed and ran his hand through his hair. If only his Rafaela were here, she would know how to handle Antonia. Or would she give the girl her blessing? Without turning Doña Maria's attention to the revered likeness of his beloved, he glanced at the treasured piece he had placed in front of him earlier and then silently slipped it into its resting place in the drawer of his desk.

Many doubts still lurked in his mind. Memories of his own youth, his desperate love, and Rafaela's jilted betrothed . . . He wondered what the man left standing at the altar had been like, since he had left for Europe immediately after being rejected. Doña Maria had convinced him of the importance of protecting Antonia's future after he was gone. He clenched his fists beneath his desk in an effort to reassure himself that he was doing what was best for Antonia and not merely seeking to unite two empires.

Doña Maria rolled her eyes, bemoaning her efforts, and chose to ignore the delicate subject of the *ranchero*'s doubts. "Ah, youth! What is this world coming to? In my day young ladies did not act in such a shameless way. They accepted their parents' choices."

She had long ago forgotten her sister, who had shared a similar circumstance. Other than a harmless flirtation with a matador long ago, Doña Maria had been robbed of ever knowing love so she simply could not understand Antonia's aversion to such an important merger.

Thunderous sounds signaling an approaching horse interrupted their strained conversation. Doña Maria lumbered to the window. "Montoya, at last," she cried and hurried outside to await their trusted vaquero.

Don Diego rose, straightened the fringed *bolero* around his trim waistline, and rushed to the front of the hacienda. In his haste he left the large flat-brimmed sombrero in the study. Shading his blue eyes from the glare of the hot sun, he watched the wiry figure of a man advance rapidly toward them. Impatiently he waited until the vaquero reached them.

"Where is my daughter?" Don Diego questioned Montoya. He leaned forward, hopeful, as he raked his fingers through his hair. A smile came to his lips when he thought about the flesh of his blood.

As a young Englishman he had possessed that same stubborn streak of one who refused to follow in his father's footsteps. He had gone to sea to seek his own fortune. Then there was the trouble with Rafaela's *padre,* who, like himself, had arranged for his daughter's betrothal. Rafaela had been such a fragile young woman, but she, too, refused her *padre*'s dictates.

Antonia had inherited her *madre*'s fiery temper and his stubborn streak. In appearance she resembled his mother with her golden locks and amber-green eyes. Sometimes he wondered whether Antonia had received the best or worst characteristics from his union with Rafaela. Antonia was a fiery, stubborn and independent beauty. Quite a combination, he thought.

"Señor Winston." Montoya dismounted with hat in hands. "I am terribly sorry to be the bearer of such news . . ."

The vaquero related the encounter which had taken place with Antonia. He described the peasant dress she had used as a disguise to leave the rancho unnoticed. Being a tactful man, he deliberately neglected to tell them of Antonia's rather uncomplimentary reference to her *novio*. He had learned long ago that discretion was often well paid. His sagacity had served him well over the years and had brought many rewards from an appreciative don.

Doña Maria, rarely one to give way to fitful hysterics, could not bear to hear more. She swung the back of her hand to her forehead and screeched, "No! That girl has gone too far this time. What will El . . . He will be so upset after all I . . . ah . . . we have done for that ungrateful girl."

She raised the other hand, which held a tiny lace handkerchief, to her nose and sniffled. "Don Diego, you must make her see the error of her ways before it is too late. Oh —"

"No more! Antonia is a Winston and knows her duty. She is just young and high-spirited. Go inside and see to the refreshments. Our guest will be arriving shortly and will be in need of something to quench his thirst from the long journey."

Even while he spoke to Antonia's distraught *tía,* he was not certain himself what action Antonia might resort to in order to gain her way.

After Doña Maria left the two men in front of the hacienda, Montoya stepped closer to Don Diego. Making certain no one could hear their conversation, he spoke in a low voice. "You will forgive me, Señor Winston, but I am afraid there is more which I dared not speak of in front of the doña."

Don Diego's brows drew together in frustration. What else could there be? he wondered as Montoya began the tale of his conversation with Antonia.

The vaquero hung his head while Don Diego patted him on the shoulder. *"Gracias,* Pedro. You have served my family well." Pedro's bowed head concealed a wry smile. Pedro Montoya was well versed in twisting his words to serve his advantage. He had no doubt Antonia would return to the hacienda, but he planned to reap a double reward for his services, anticipating what Don Diego would propose next.

"Antonia will return." Don Diego spoke with bolstered confidence. "But to speed her journey, I ask you to select two trusted riders to accompany you and escort her back personally. Her prompt arrival will not go unrewarded."

Antonia had carried her protest too far this time. For years the vaquero had watched the mulish girl wrap her *padre* around her finger. Such willfulness should have been served with the strap. If she belonged to him, he would have known how to handle her! His lecherous thoughts of possessing Antonia had plagued him from the time years ago when she had gored his left cheek with her riding whip after she caught him spying on her at the lake.

The memory of that day was ingrained vividly in his mind. She was a wild hellion and needed a man who would know how to tame her. Her *padre*'s order for a personal escort could provide him with an opportunity both to possess her and get revenge for what she'd done to his face.

Montoya swung his leg up into the stirrup. "Do not worry, Señor Winston, I shall bring back the señorita."

With a nod he left Don Diego in his dust. As Montoya and the two men he'd summoned drew near the stream where Montoya had left his prey earlier, little did he know that Antonia had already been delivered a twist of fate.

Chapter Five

The party of three passed only two Indians on the long, hot journey past the sleepy pueblo of San Diego, reinforcing Antonia's hopes that word of her flight would not reach her padre. At dusk they neared the soaring bluffs overlooking the gently rolling sea. The sky glowed in magnificent shades of deepening red-orange interspersed with puffy white clouds tinged pink around the edges.

"I shall leave you here, my brother, and see to the arrangements for your comfort on board ship," Mano said, taking his leave.

Antonia watched the Indian make his way to the beach, then she nestled closer against Michael to enjoy a moment's reverie.

Pressed to Michael's chest like an enticing invitation, Antonia's body was soft and warm. It caused his heart to race, and he tightened his fingers around her waist.

"There is something very peaceful about the sea, watching the waves crash against the shore," Michael observed.

It seemed natural to enjoy the moment with this young señorita. He discovered himself wanting to learn more about her, considering her not merely another woman he found physically attractive and wanted to bed.

Antonia was also lost to the serene beauty of the sea. She leaned her head back, feeling secure and content seated before this man she had only just met.

"*Sí*, it is magnificent," she breathed.

Although she had spent many hours at the seashore, she felt as if she were seeing it for the first time. It was unsettling that it had taken such an occasion for her to actually appreciate the downy green splendor that spread before her. Or was the feeling because of whom she was with? That consideration disturbed her even more.

She arched her chin to gaze up at him. Her face held the expression of a child awakening to the joys of discovery. Her heart fluttered. She did not even know his last name and had spent only a few hours with him. But he was not a stranger. By sharing a kiss they had immediately dispensed with the stiff formalities which were the custom among members of the *gente de razón*.

A warm feeling began to swell deep within her as his fingers gently curved over her hands and he rubbed his thumbs along her sensitive flesh. She responded by entwining her fingers through his.

Michael was pleasantly surprised by her natural response to his gesture, and he began to have second thoughts about taking her out on his ship. She was different from the women he had spent his time with in the past and it greatly disquieted him.

"Are you certain you wish to visit the ship?" he asked, wanting yet not wanting to take the young girl back with him.

"Of course, señor, unless your *capitán* would disapprove," she answered, taking a deep breath.

Antonia, too, was having second thoughts. It had

seemed like a good plan at the time, but she had not counted on the strange feelings she was experiencing. And she did not want to return to the rancho yet.

"I'm sure the captain would approve any decision I make." He grinned wickedly. "Shall we walk down to the beach?"

Antonia nodded her acceptance.

He helped her down from the horse. She was painfully reminded of her situation as a sharp pain shot through her blood-encrusted foot. She clutched at his neck in order to stop herself from falling.

"Oh," she whimpered and gritted her teeth.

"My poor princess, how neglectful of your injury I have been," he said. He tenderly lifted her high into his arms.

"Maybe I should seek aid for my wound before I visit the ship," Antonia stammered as she fought the feelings he'd aroused by holding her so closely. "If you will release me—"

"Who is holding whom, Princess? With your arms wound so tightly around my neck how could I ever dream of releasing you?" he said with smiling eyes. What he did not say was that for some reason he could not bear to let her go for fear he would never see her again.

A wave of inbred reserve streaked through Antonia and she abruptly let go of him. She started to panic. No! A Winston did not do such things.

She quickly regained her composure.

"I should seek medical aid for my foot," she repeated.

"Don't worry, there's medical assistance on board the ship. My friend is seeing to it now. Your foot will be properly attended, and until it is, I could not possibly rest."

Antonia could not help but giggle at such a display

of gallantry. She was not totally naive and was fully aware of the tension between them. She had watched women from the town with sailors before. She shut her eyes tight, took a deep gulp of air, and allowed him to lift her into the gig bobbing in the waves off shore.

Positioning her snugly near him, Michael rowed to the ship anchored a cable's distance from the smooth, hard beach.

Once on board the merchant brig, Antonia realized there was no turning back. She had made a choice and she would see it through. She was lifted from her aching foot with little pomp and carried directly toward the cabins on the quarter deck amidst stares and whispers of the crew.

The captain had made it a practice to take his pleasures away from the one place he considered his sanctuary. The sight of him crossing the deck with a wench in his arms caused much speculation.

"Me thinks the cap'n 'as got himself a fine little bit, me does," one of the crew chuckled.

"Can't reckon I has laid me eyes on the cap'n totin' such a piece of baggage on board before. An' me bein' with 'im long enough, too," another rasped, gnawing on a plug of tobacco before turning to send it flying overboard.

One of the sailors looked over his shoulder to catch a disapproving stare from coal-black eyes. After exchanging glances, the seamen moved off.

"We best be more careful in the future, mate. That Indian frowns upon loose tongues."

"Aye, but he knows we be loyal to the cap'n."

"That he does. But he guards Cap'n Domino much as a cur does a bone."

The hands, dressed in baggy duck trousers, checked shirts and black tarpaulin hats, returned to their watch duties. Many of the crew had been on shore leave and would be returning shortly to begin loading the cured hides, adding them to those they had already obtained.

"This is a merchant ship, is it not?" Antonia asked, remembering her dream of only a few short hours ago about sailing away on such a vessel.

"That it is," Michael said absently.

"Then you are here in San Diego trading for hides?"

"Yes. We have most of them pickled, dried, and cleaned already. They're stored in a hidehouse now awaiting their removal to the ship."

"Is it really necessary to cure them before bringing them on board?"

"They would spoil during the long voyage around Cape Horn in the warn climes if they were not preserved."

"How long have you been out?" Antonia asked, fascinated by the workings of the ship.

"The *Áureo Princesa* has been plying the waters along the coast of California, trading for nearly two years."

The *Áureo Princesa*—the *Golden Princess*—brought to mind the girl before him and the strange way he had come to name his ship.

He had been on his way to a gaming house in London when an old woman dressed in a multitude of brightly colored scarves and beads stopped him in the street and offered to tell his fortune. Michael turned her down, but his companions paid her handsomely and soon goaded him into humoring the persistent Gypsy.

The strangely dressed woman had appeared from a dark alley that cold, fog-shrouded night, and it had been Michael's fortune she had insisted on telling. Michael had thought it unusual at the time that although

45

his companions were willing to pay for her services, she would read only his palm. He had forgotten the incident—until now.

The Gypsy had foretold of a voyage to a faraway land and of a beautiful woman with hair the color of sunlight who would change his life forever. He had scoffed at the woman, but when he won the ship, the woman's words had caused him to rename the vessel the *Áureo Princesa*.

He stared at the golden-haired girl before him. It was a strange coincidence. That was all, nothing more, he decided and let the remembrance slide into the back of his mind as the girl's voice jerked him back to the present.

"I beg your pardon, señorita. What were you saying?"

"I said, then you must nearly be ready to leave California," Antonia repeated.

"Another two fortnights should see the vessel stowed to capacity with forty thousand hides. Once loading is completed, the brig sails for Boston. We'll deposit our cargo there and then return home to England. The crew hasn't seen their families for several years."

"And you, señor? Do you also have a family in England?" Antonia asked, fearing the answer.

"Mano, the Indian with me when we met, is my only family," Michael said stiffly, remembering his dead mother.

"The *indio*," Antonia repeated with a sigh of relief. Then strangely needing reassurance, she asked, "Will you return to California?"

"The captain just made a deal with one of the *rancheros*, which will lessen the length of the voyage in the future. We'll no longer have to sail along the coast in search of trade. Next voyage there will be forty thousand dried skins and tallow waiting for us in a special hidehouse. So I would say I shall be returning."

Antonia brightened. "This business transaction, señor, it would not be with the Rancho de los Robles, would it?"

Michael sent her a hard, questioning look. For a young peasant girl, she was awfully curious. "No," he stated flatly.

Noticing the strange glimmer in his eyes, Antonia quickly explained. "I ask only because it would have brought much work to my people, which would have meant more food in their bellies. You see, señor, curing a hide entails a lengthy process and offers much work, beginning with removing the hide from the animal, then staking it out to dry in the sun. It is a complicated process involving many tasks, so you see, this deal you speak of would have been looked upon favorably by many of us at the Rancho de los Robles," she added in an attempt to disarm his look of distrust.

"You know an awful lot for a young girl who just asked if it was necessary to cure the hides before bringing them on board."

"I know the process, having worked at the rancho many years. I simply never understood why one had to cure the hides before loading, señor."

Michael relaxed, accepting her explanation.

Once inside his cabin, Michael hooked the back of his boot around the edge of the door and nudged it shut. He strode over to the bunk and gently lowered Antonia to the soft feather mattress. Antonia was startled as she sank into the thick bed. She held her breath while she quietly studied her new surroundings.

47

Chapter Six

Michael watched the young girl take close note of his cabin. She probably had never enjoyed surroundings quite as plush before—had never seen anything like them except, of course, while cleaning the rooms at the hacienda at which she worked.

"Ah yes, my princess, it's good for you to become familiar with your new abode," Michael said, and turned to leave the room.

"But, señor," Antonia gasped, "this looks like the *capitán*'s cabin; it has so many charts and so much equipment. Surely he will be angry to find one of his crew has taken such advantage of his accommodations."

"Oh, I think not. You see, the captain and I have always been very close. One might even venture to say we share so much in common that we are inseparable."

Antonia's eyes grew wide with fear that more might come of this than she had intended when she so rashly agreed to accompany him. "You do not mean that you plan to—"

"Do not concern yourself. Although one might say we share everything, I've no intention of allowing anyone else near you. You look as if you could use some rest. I shall see you in the morning."

"But my foot—"

Without touching her, Michael made a quick examination of her tiny foot. "If you wash that nasty cut and stay off it for the night, it should be all right in the morning. There is water next to the desk. If it still troubles you after you are rested I'll have someone take a look at it."

Michael did not wait for her to seek additional information. Despite his desire to remain, he turned on his heel and left her alone to contemplate his decision to bring her on board.

Antonia's eyes were heavy from the exhausting day and, despite her trepidation, she laid her head back on the plump pillow and fell asleep.

Lost within sleep's netherworld of dreams and fantasies, Antonia found herself caught in the encircling arms of a man resembling Michael. With wild abandon they tumbled to the ground to explore the treasures offered a man and woman.

Antonia felt herself moan with delight at his intimate touch. Her fingers curled through his thick thatch of hair. This was truly heaven, bliss, passion . . . But just as they stood on the edge of a spiraling precipice, Antonia jolted. She fluttered her eyes open and bolted upright.

"It was a dream," she panted, her heart pounding.

She glanced down to observe the fringe edging the heavy quilt clutched between her fingers. She sighed and collapsed back against the pillows, hugging the much-patched blanket up around her throat. The dream further unnerved her already reeling senses.

"Oh, dear God, what is happening to me? I am behaving so irrationally. Do I no longer control my mind or body?" she asked herself, trembling at the frightening change in her.

After a long time she closed her troubled eyes and, tossing and turning, finally managed to fall into a deep sleep.

The early morning sun streamed through the porthole. Antonia opened her eyes and looked around. *It is true, I really am on a ship. It was not all just a dream after all.*

She sprang from the bunk and hobbled about the luxurious cabin, seeking clues which would tell her more about the intriguing sailor. Stopping at the window, she gazed out at the harbor. The shore looked so distant. For a moment she imagined herself aboard one of the ships her *padre* had told her about. She was a grand lady sailing to Spain . . . Her fantasy only lasted an instant, for a knock at the door sent her scurrying back to the bunk.

The door squeaked slowly open and Mano entered, carrying buckets of hot, steaming water. Antonia was momentarily taken aback at the Indian's severe appearance and drew herself up into a tight ball.

"The captain ordered water for your pleasure," he brusquely explained, his stoic face silently disapproving her presence as he poured the last of the contents of the pails into the copper tub. The tub was one luxury his captain had allowed himself. He often soaked in the soothing waters in order to help relieve his tensions. Mano set the empty containers down and turned to Antonia.

"Do not bathe until I return with your gown."

As Mano left to fetch the garment, he wondered at the captain's reason for bringing the young girl on board the ship, and pondered the wisdom of it. He would never question the captain's authority aloud, but only hoped the captain had not met his match in the form of the young señorita.

Antonia had no intention of disrobing in a strange man's cabin either before or after the Indian delivered clean attire. She made up her mind to refuse his hospitality, although the thought of a hot bath was terribly inviting.

The Indian returned with the gown and placed it on the chair at Michael's desk. "Prepare yourself. The captain will be here shortly," he said as matter-of-factly and turned to leave the puzzled young woman.

"No . . . not the *capitán*," she choked. But the Indian ignored her and left before she could insist her original companion return.

A short while later the door handle turned. As Michael stepped inside his blue eyes hardened when they fell on the bedraggled señorita cringing like a scared kitten on his bunk.

"I see you have not availed yourself of the gracious hospitality." He grinned. "Could it be that you were waiting for assistance with your bath? Yes, that must be it. You see, my little princess, since there's no one else available, you will have to content yourself with my services. It is the least, I, your devoted servant, can offer." He was across the room in three strides, standing before her.

Michael waited patiently for a moment to give her the opportunity to respond.

Antonia gave only passing thought to such an outrageous notion. The very outlandishness of the man—and the erratic thudding of her heart between her ears—caused her to remain still, studying those muscular thighs. Her questioning gaze shifted to his outstretched hand—and such a large, strong hand it was. A newly familiar sensation crept over her, and her cheeks flushed hot. Her eyes trailed up his chest to his eyes, where all doubts melted in the warmth of his gaze.

Without further thought to the consequences of her next step, Antonia placed her hand in his. Michael drew her from the bunk, never once taking his eyes from hers and bent over to gently caress her lips.

Antonia sighed and closed her eyes as she lifted her head. What had started as a way to rid herself of a hated *novio* had turned into an answer to a long-ago abandoned prayer—that someday, when she was ready, she would meet the man of her dreams and give herself to him freely. What did it matter that he was a lowly sailor and they had just met under less than proper circumstances? Even though she was a lady of breeding, she was following her heart's awakening desire. And follow it she would—to the very ends of the earth.

Michael had originally planned to give the young woman a good scare about what could happen to one so foolish as to take up with strangers. He had expected her to run from him after his first suggestive offer. She had not. She had at first tried to bait him and then came with him so willingly, so innocently. She had allowed herself to be taken aboard a vessel on which any number of horrible fates could have befallen her. And in face of the prospect of being shared with another, she still held out her hand to him. But what bothered him most of all was he had kissed her with a tenderness before unknown to him. It had been an unsettling kiss—a kiss which set alarms flashing before him and warned him to keep his distance.

"Damn!" he stormed, breaking the spell. "This isn't happening the way I had intended."

Antonia stepped back with a puzzled look on her face. She had been about to respond to him in a way no other man had known her.

"I . . . I do not understand," she mumbled, confusion still clouding her thinking.

"That is just it. You really don't understand. You are more innocent and naive than I at first realized," he said.

"I am not naive! I knew my fate before I boarded this ship. I just thought—"

"No. You didn't think! Don't you realize I could have been a less than reputable sailor off any lowly ship. And you could have exposed yourself to any number of ill-fated ventures!" His voice boomed with rising anger.

"Quit shouting!" she retorted, unused to being spoken to in such a rough manner.

"I am not shouting!"

"Yes, you are. And you are being rude, too." She raised her voice in symphony with his.

"Rude is it now? The wench accuses me of being *rude!*" He threw up his hands in exasperation. "I try to save you from yourself and I am considered rude!"

"Save me from myself? How dare you! Why, I will have you know I do not require saving." Antonia's rage was rising, she no longer desired to maintain control of her words or deeds. "Furthermore, Señor—"

"Captain Michael Domino if you're addressing me, señorita," he spat.

Hearing the captain's name, Antonia momentarily thought it odd. "But no, it is just a strange coincidence," she mumbled and dismissed the similarity of the captain's name with her *novios* from her thoughts. "Oh, *capitán,* is it?" she venomously added. "Well, *Capitán* Domino, if you are addressing me, you may as well use my rightful name—Señorita Antonia Rafaela Winston y Ortega," she said through tightly gritted teeth, her chin jutted out in defiance, her hands resting plaintifly on her hips. "No wonder you and the *capitán share* such an intimate relationship. And to

53

set the record straight, Señor *Capitán,* you felt something for me, as I did for you. You cannot deny it!" she added.

For a moment their eyes locked in silent fury.

"My God but you are a feisty young wench," Michael suddenly said, breaking the tension. With a swift move he grabbed her upper arms and stood glaring at her, his temper threatening to flare again as he silently fumed.

"My goodness, if I did not know better, I would expect to see black smoke escape your collar," Antonia said, unable to contain herself.

Instead of answering her jibe, Michael dropped his hands and turned toward the door.

"Wait just a moment, Capitán Domino!" Antonia commanded. She began to hobble toward him but misjudged her injury and lost her footing in her haste.

Michael swung around and reached her just in time to still her fall.

His touch prompted her to throw all caution and decorum out the porthole. She threw her arms around his neck and drew his head down to hers into a burning kiss born out of the preceding tempestuous moments.

Their kiss deepened. Antonia's lips parted as Michael's tongue sought entry into her warm moist cavern to explore the sweet, honeyed entrance.

Antonia had never dreamed a kiss could be so sweet, so mind-shattering. Although she barely knew more than his name, she found herself wanting to know more of him — much, much more.

Michael, too, was tasting more than just a kiss, and he drew Antonia even more tightly against him, suddenly wanting to possess her with his entire being.

A timid knock at the door brought an abrupt halt to their kiss.

"Cap'n sir, 'tis sorry I be to disturb ye this way. Ye be needed topside, and I be sent t' fetch ye." The humble voice crackled in no more than a whisper.

Michael held Antonia away from him, grimaced, then turned toward the door.

"I'll be right there," Michael called out harshly, then softened his tone as he glanced at Antonia. "I'm afraid I must leave. I promise to return as soon as time allows," he said, gently pinching her chin between his index finger and thumb. "I'll send someone to look after that foot."

In an attempt to understand the nature of this man, Antonia bit her lip and remained still, watching the door close behind him.

Chapter Seven

Once the crewman serving as the ship's doctor left her, Antonia could no longer ignore the inviting waters of the tub. She stripped off her clothing, settled in neck-deep, and scrubbed herself vigorously.

After washing her long tresses, she stepped out of the tub and toweled dry with the soft cloth left for her use, then wrapped her hair in the cloth and stepped to the gown. Holding it up in front of her, she was stunned, for she had never seen anything like it.

The gown was of the softest red velvet with a billowing skirt, enormous puffed sleeves, embellished all over with flower garlands, ruffles and lace flounces. The neckline was cut into an extremely revealing décolletage, causing Antonia to worry whether it would adequately cover her.

It appeared the captain had seen to everything, for next to the gown were all the undergarments she would require. Several pettiskirts trimmed with deep ruffles lay next to a delicate chemise and white silk stockings adorned with rosebuds. On the floor underneath the apparel were a dainty pair of low-cut *escarpin* pumps with slender toes and a slight heel. Knitted garters laced with scarlet ribbons peeked out of the slippers.

While Antonia was most familiar with European designs and fabrics, she was used to the short-sleeved gowns worn loosely about the waist, but she quickly slipped into the garments.

Oh, my dear tía, if you could see me now, dressing to please a man, she reflected. *How we used to argue and I would vow never to do such a thing.* Antonia smiled at her change of heart. Doña Maria had often tried to instruct her in the ways of a lady. And how she had laughed and pulled her very plainest gown from the wardrobe, stating firmly she would never resort to such nonsense for any man. *But no,* she mused, sighing. *The capitán is not just any man.*

Even now, still not totally understanding such willingness to dress just to please a man, Antonia completed her toilette by coiffing her long golden tresses and adorning them with the red velvet ribbons left for that very purpose.

Standing in front of the small mirror the captain had provided, she gazed at the figure in the glass. The young señorita who stared back at her looked like a member of a king's court—not the daughter of a *ranchero*. The figure in the mirror was exquisite. Antonia had known she was attractive and on occasion used it to her advantage, but now her appearance surprised her.

She perused her reflection as if seeing herself for the first time. She was so involved in the study that Michael unlocked the door and entered the cabin unnoticed. For a moment he stood staring at Antonia in amazement. She stood before him like a work of art. She was a man's fantasy, with no words to adequately describe her.

"I had no idea when I hoisted you upon my horse that I had chosen a princess of such ripe perfection."

"This gown, Señor Capitán, is hardly a garment

one would expect to find on a vessel such as this," Antonia blurted out, startled to see him standing inside the door.

"A vessel such as this? And exactly what's wrong with my ship?" he asked in a pointed voice.

"I suppose I could make a thorough inspection and let you know."

"My dearest princess" — Michael smiled while his eyes openly admired her — "you have a sharp wit." How different this one was than the vast number of mindless feminine bodies he was used to. "I must remember to be on guard, lest you wound me with it."

"Somehow, Capitán Domino, I cannot imagine you allowing anyone to catch you off guard."

"I fear you already have."

The blush of innocent modesty flickered across her face before she changed her stance and then boldly swayed over to him. Holding the skirt out, Antonia slowly circled in front him. "Your eyes, Señor Capitán, tell a woman all she needs to know," she said wickedly, suddenly feeling coquettish.

"Do not try to tell me you are a lady of vast experience," Michael said, skeptically arching a brow.

"It does not take a woman of vast experience to read a look such as yours in a man's eyes."

"Don't you mean *no experience?*" he taunted with a questioning chuckle.

Antonia's lips thinned into a cool line. He was laughing at her!

Men only want women of many experiences for one thing. Had Doña Maria not drummed that into her head? She was not going to allow any man to upset her. Not even this one, who had so easily sparked her interest and awakened an untamed need, an uncontrollable hunger in her.

"Experience or not, señor, a woman knows such

things."

"A woman?"

"Does my appearance not tell you that I am a woman?" she returned rashly.

"Yes, so it appears," he mumbled, his eyes burning over the length of her.

She cocked her head in question, quietly pleased she was affecting the man. *"Capitán?* Is there something which bothers you?"

"Nothing," he grumbled, and turned his gaze to her foot. "It appears your injury was not too serious to keep you from donning the slippers I provided."

"Ah . . . no . . . no, it was merely a nasty bruise. I am fine now."

"You recovered quite rapidly," he noted, smiling broadly.

"In a world so often void of life's pleasures, is it not the wisest course of action, to put one's minor infirmities out of mind and not allow them to control one's life?" Antonia said, reflecting on her *padre's* plans for her.

"If you are who you say you are, life cannot have been so difficult," he said, vaguely recalling the mention of Antonia's background in an earlier conversation.

"I have had a good life," Antonia stated flatly. It was true. Life had generally smiled on her. Did her *tía* not remind her of that fact often enough? Was she not truly fortunate to have been born a member of the *gente de razón,* instead one of those soulless savages, Doña Maria had repeatedly harped. She wondered if she would have been allowed to take part in the selection of a mate had she been of low birth.

"You look as one whose thoughts are faraway. Is there something troubling you?"

"No, of course not, should there be?" Antonia answered a little too quickly. She could not unload her burdens on this man, no matter how heavy. She was a proud California lady and she would resolve her own problems.

Mano's arrival with the midday fare ended what was becoming an increasingly dangerous conversation. The Indian spread the meal out upon a small table in the corner of the paneled cabin with little more than a polite acknowledgment of Antonia's presence.

His mission accomplished, Mano left the couple to their meal. It was obvious she was no ordinary peasant wench. She was so unlike the women his brother usually took his pleasure with then discarded. There was something unusual about her and he worried for his brother.

When Mano reached the forecastle, a brave sailor turned to him in question. "Ahoy me matey, what bein' it that troublin' yer soul? 'Tis the cap'n, ain't it? Not like Cap'n Mick t' bring a blimy wench on board. Me thinks he's got 'isself trouble this time, me does."

The Indian merely looked at the man and shrugged. But he, too, was troubled for his captain.

Antonia had voraciously eaten and drunk enough spirits to make her feel light-headed; her over-indulgence an effort to buoy her sagging nerves.

Mano returned with another bottle and began to clear away the remnants of the repast. Turning to his captain and speaking in English so the señorita would not understand his words, he said. "It is not the way of my people to interfere in the affairs of another, but do you think your actions wise, my brother? The young señorita is not of common birth. I worry for you."

Answering in English, Michael attempted to alleviate his companion's concern, though the señorita troubled him as well. "I know you speak out of concern, my friend. But there are times in life when one must play out the hand dealt him." Michael had always been a gambler, and although decidedly this was no ordinary wench, he had felt something and could not bear to let her go yet. "Don't worry, I'll not allow the lady to keep me from our mission. Now be gone and leave us our time together."

The Indian left without another word.

Michael stepped to the door and turned the lock, placing the key on the table. He seated himself in a chair across from Antonia and poured another glass of spirits. "As you can see, I have set the key in a visible location. If at any time you feel so inclined, it is at your disposal."

Antonia was not quite certain what to make of his actions but chose to enlighten him in one respect at least. She leaned forward in her chair, and in perfect English said, "I must tell you, I speak your foreign tongue."

"So you toy with me?"

"I did not intend it to be a game. But what is this *mission* you speak of? Possibly I may be of assistance," she quickly added, changing the subject from more dangerous ground.

"It's of no consequence. Do not concern yourself with it."

Michael was surprised to hear his native tongue spoken so articulately by the señorita, but he was not daunted. He proceeded to finish the bottle in silence, studying the beautiful young woman.

Antonia had no intention of letting the matter drop and proceeded to insist that he allow her to help. After all, who better than someone who was familiar with the area and knew the people?

Michael, feeling the effects of the spirits, rose awkwardly, knocking the chair over behind him.

"Enough! I can't stand anymore. Be silent! Your tongue would strip a man of his pride, and your beauty and intelligence would rob him of his very soul."

Antonia was shocked by his sudden outburst. "If you prefer, *capitán*, I will return to my own garments, smudge my nose, and pretend ignorance," she offered.

Again she was drawing a similarity between seemingly incongruous things, shaking the foundation of detachment he had carefully erected many years ago. Michael stepped closer to her. "You drive me to complete, utter distraction!"

The spirits had served her well, for Antonia managed to stand her ground. "Oh? And just how distracted are you?"

Michael roughly pulled her to him, staring into the enticing amber-green eyes. He silently ran his thumb along the delicate outline of her slightly parted lips. Her chest heaved against him as she swallowed hard, aching to put an end to the heightening tension surrounding them. Michael raised her chin between his fingers, and moistening his lips with his tongue, lowered his hungry lips to hers.

A kiss with such undiluted force should have warned her to flee. But assisted by the wine and burning desire to know more of him, Antonia returned his kiss with a compulsion of her own.

Breathing heavily with passion, Michael held her from him. "I warn you, if you don't leave this cabin immediately, I'll not be responsible for my actions. You are more than one man can resist."

Antonia's chest was also rising and falling at an

alarming pace, and the heat of desire held her tightly within its grip. She was locked in the binding spell of the moment, and as she gazed into his questioning eyes with unbridled longing, she had no other thought than satisfying her need for him.

"I do not want you to resist," she whispered.

Without waiting any longer, he lifted her into his arms and carried her to his bed. Setting her gently on the bunk, he tenderly kissed the indent of each shoulder as he slid the gown down over her arms. His kisses were like fire, engulfing her within their burning flames. She felt herself lose all sense of time.

Continuing his caresses, Michael's lips blazed a trail to her bosom. He freed one delicious, full breast, teasing it into a taut rosy peak. Not ignoring the other straining delicacy, he circled the darkening center with his hot tongue. Antonia moaned and sat up to slip from her garments as if in a trance.

At the sight of her curvaceous body, Michael stopped to devour the vision before him while he, too, shed his clothing. A smile came to his lips.

"You're the most beautiful woman I've ever seen. This time we have together shall be truly memorable."

"Of that, *mi capitán,* there is no doubt," she breathed, her lips inviting him to quench his thirsts.

He stroked her cheek, wanting to whisper the words a woman longed to hear, but they stuck to his tongue. He had a mission to attend to first before he could think of involving himself with any woman. So with silent longing, his hands slowly began their descent down her graceful neck, over her soft smooth shoulders, to rest upon her creamy breasts once again.

Ever so slowly he caressed and kissed her waist and hip bones. His fingers then sensuously curved over her belly, and his rough tongue, wanting to savor every delicious inch of her, traced circles and figure eights around her navel to drop into the hollow.

Antonia let nature guide her as she massaged his lowering head. When his probing fingers brushed against the silky smooth, tender flesh on the inside of her thighs she automatically opened to him.

"I know I should tell you to stop before it is too late, but I cannot," she murmured, rapturous sensations scoring her burning flesh.

"No, my princess, *we* cannot," he corrected as he positioned himself in between her thighs and thrust his throbbing manhood into her dark, secret sweetness.

As the tension thickened, and after those first moments to accustom her to a woman's experience, their bodies moved with an increasing rhythm until they were gloriously spent.

Afterward Michael stood looking at the exhausted beauty before him. He then gazed at the sheet beneath her and the blood staining it and her thighs. A scowl overpowered his features.

"You really were a maiden," he pronounced. He was furious with himself, for it had not been his way to initiate young virgins into the secrets of the sensual world. He stood with his hands on his hips glowering as if he gazed upon a hated foe.

Noting the darkening of his countenance, Antonia innocently asked, "What is wrong? Was it not good for you?"

"Good? Good!"

"I thought—"

"Oh, you were good!" he raged. "As a matter of fact, you're one of the best little performers around."

"Performers?" she repeated, still not understanding the gravity of his anger.

"Why, yes, Princess. You teased me into believing you were already versed in the ways of pleasing a man with that coy act of yours."

"Coy act?"

"You pretended innocence while you enticed and led me on."

"Why, I never did any such thing!" Antonia said, a tinge of indignation starting to overtake her.

"Oh, no? You ask me if I really think you a child, and then play the enchantress until I can no longer resist. Well, *Princess,* if you think you have trapped some fool, you are sorely mistaken!" he snarled.

"It appears I *was sorely mistaken* about a number of things," Antonia snapped back. Her wounded pride was piqued after the initial shock wore off that she had allowed herself such passionate feelings for this blackheart.

She swung away from him and stifled a sob, covering her shame with trembling rage. She had never been one to give way easily to tears and she had no intention of starting now, although her every ounce of courage went into staying the tidal wave threatening to sweep her into its drowning grasp. She was so totally drained, and her head pounded so loudly between her ears that she barely heard him stomp from the cabin.

Chapter Eight

Antonia opened her eyes and found herself alone in the cabin. For a moment she thought she was dreaming again, but her aching body reminded her that she no longer was a maiden and had not imagined her initiation into the ways of the world. Sitting up, she wrapped the rough coverlet protectively around her.

She grimaced at the scratchy fabric. *Of course, sailors would use such blankets,* she scoffed to herself.

With remembrances of the previous night vividly before her eyes, she knew she had to leave before the captain returned. Frantically she searched the room for her skirt and blouse, but they were nowhere to be found, nor was the creation she had so proudly modeled for him.

Instead, neatly draped over the sea chest near the foot of the bunk was a *tunic à la greque* gown. It was of the palest pink with a daringly low ruffle-trimmed neckline spreading out to puffed sleeves laced about the arms and three slender golden belts hanging about the waist. She picked up the gown and sought the undergarments which must accompany such a flimsy fashion. In exasperation she tossed the gown to the floor.

"How can he expect me to wear such a transparent

piece without undergarments? Only a wanton beast would provide such immodest attire. And he accused *me* of attempting to trap *him!*" she sputtered angrily, not considering her own actions as a contributing factor.

Antonia ran to the door and tugged at the knob, but to no avail. Hearing a click and seeing the knob begin to turn, she rushed back to the bunk and huddled in the corner, pulling the coverlet over her.

Michael opened the door and entered, carrying a tray of eggs, biscuits and steaming coffee.

"You may leave the tray over there," she said haughtily and pointed toward the table. The pulse in her neck drummed, but she had no intention of letting him know how his presence affected her.

"Ah . . . but my princess, I haven't the least intention of being so rude as to deny you the pleasure of my company. What would the crew say of such treatment given to such an honored seductress?"

Attempting to maintain an air of hauteur and show him that she was above such banter, Antonia lifted her small turned-up nose high in the air as she replied, "Señor Capitán, I am certain the people of whom you speak would say naught. And as for myself, I would be quite pleased to enjoy my meal alone. Oh, and if you would be so kind as to return my garments I would dress."

"I'm sorry to be the one to inform you, but your original clothing did not withstand the washing meted out by my crew." A wicked smile twisted his lips. "I fear you'll be forced to make do with the articles that I, your humble host, am able to provide."

Antonia could not believe such a brazen answer. Trying to retain her dignity, she made another attempt to reason with the man.

"Surely you cannot be totally . . ." She sucked in a

breath trying to select her words carefully. "Ah . . . lost to virtue. You have left me without my maidenhood. But must you now leave me without proper covering as well?"

Michael had been enjoying their verbal sparring. Mention of her lost virginity sobered him. A wave of intense displeasure and pain at being reminded of what he had done washed over him. He had never taken a maiden, always selecting with care the women with whom he took his pleasure. More than being angry with her, he was furious with himself.

Many years before, Michael had promised himself he would never be the cause of some poor, innocent girl being initiated into the ways of the world, for his own mother had suffered such a fate. Until this señorita, he had been fiercely true to that oath. Thoughts of his mother and his childhood flooded his mind.

His mother had been a proper young English girl in her fifteenth year when a young man barely in his twentieth summer had taken her. He had been a visitor to the country and promised the young dishonored girl vows to ease her conscience. But from the first night after he had taken her forcibly while in a drunken state, he had never meant to be true to his word.

The young girl had been on her way home from a late visit to an ailing relative when a landau pulled alongside her and two men jumped out and abducted her. Too embarrassed at first, and shortly thereafter too smitten and blind with promises, she had remained with the man who had taken her.

All his words of honor proved but empty falsehoods when he discovered she was with child. That night he had beaten her senseless with a riding whip he had purchased that very day. Michael recalled his mother explaining that it was an unusual quirt, with

68

heavy silver threads laced through the short, braided handle. The man even had had the shopkeeper burnish his initial in the rawhide lashes.

He had left her without so much as a farewell. Although her back had been flailed, laid open and raw, she had managed to protect the child growing within her from the cruel blows.

Michael was the issue of that unfortunate union. His mother, too proud to beg for mercy from her wealthy, titled family, had assumed the last name "Domino" and reared him as best she could. His childhood had been the sorry one of many poor urchins on the streets of London. Child though he was, he did whatever necessary to help with his support.

Once, while caring for his ill mother, he had the sad occasion to view the lash marks which had scarred her back. She had run a high fever requiring her to sit in a cold tub of water. The fiercely proud boy of nine refused assistance from the other women in the inn where they lived and worked. He had carried the buckets of cold water from the well to the tiny attic room. Without help, he lifted his frail mother into the tub.

As he stood behind her, the thin gown she wore became transparent revealing the ugly scars. He had persisted in his questioning until his mother finally told him the cause of the unsightly scars. Before she refused to say another word about his father he had managed to learn that the man owned a ranch in California, north of a town called San Diego. He swore the man who had done such a vicious deed would pay for it with his life one day.

Michael's youth had been filled with a hatred of a father he had never known and an obsession both to earn his fortune to ease his mother's plight and seek revenge on the man whose identity he vowed to learn someday in spite of his mother's refusal to name him. Even as a reckless young man he had kept his vow never to touch a maiden. He had sworn he would never cause an innocent to suffer the wretched life he and his mother had known.

"Well, are you or are you not going to provide me with proper clothing?" Antonia repeated.

He shook his head, his thoughts returning to the present, hating himself for breaking his oath. For a long moment he stared at the fuming señorita. She was everything he had always found distasteful in a woman — scheming and sharp-tongued. Yet a glimmer of light continued to glow in the dark inner recesses of his brain, refusing to relinquish entirely the image of the young señorita beneath him, giving herself willingly with wild, abandon.

"You see before you all I have to offer at the moment."

Antonia pinched her lips, unconvinced. "If you do not provide me with something decent to wear, you will come to regret it," she snapped.

"You are a sorceress then? Maybe I should seek a talisman with which to protect myself from you," he grunted.

"If I were a true witch, I can only assure you that I would not find myself in such a predicament. And you, Señor Capitán, right now most assuredly would be wishing our paths had not crossed," Antonia hissed. "Now, will you not reconsider my need for proper clothing?"

"I shall only think of such a request after an acceptable reason is offered," he said, thinking how beautiful she would look in the flimsy gown.

"Then you do have other clothing available," she spat.

"As I said, not at the moment."

"Must I be forced to remain clad only in this blanket?" She glanced down at the rough coverlet and gestured at the state of her sorry attire.

"Only if you refuse the garments I have offered. I have to admit, though, my blanket never looked better."

"Why, you insufferable—"

"I warn you, you would be wise to hold your sharp tongue."

Antonia made no further argument. Tucking the coverlet securely about her, she glared at him, knowing the gold flecks in her eyes flared like angry green fires. He dared to seduce her and then attempted to claim he was the injured party! She swore she would personally see to an appropriate payment for his deeds.

"I must soon oversee the loading of the hides, so I suggest you prepare yourself, for when I return I shall take you ashore."

"No!" Antonia exclaimed, startled. While she wanted to be gone from him, she did not want to return to the rancho and a fate too terrible to contemplate—and assuredly not dressed like this!

"What? Do I hear correctly? Have you changed your mind and now desire to remain with me?" He chuckled, an undefinable tone coloring his voice.

"No! I . . . I mean yes," she gulped, the haughty air gone from her voice.

"I see," he responded, arching a brow.

"No. You do not see at all."

"Then by all means, enlighten your humble host."

Antonia pressed her lips into a tight line and made no attempt to explain. How could she? She certainly could not tell him she had gone with him originally to escape a disdained betrothed and that she knew she was a willing participant in what had happened be-

71

tween them. No. She would not compromise her pride for a man who had turned out to be little better then her dreaded *novio* and who had forever altered her life.

"There . . . there is nothing which concerns you," she hesitantly offered, uncertain of his response.

"I rarely accept an explanation void of any content such as you offer. But I'll be generous this time. I may just find a need for your services after I return," he glibly set forth. Even while he spoke he was surprised at himself. He meant not to touch her again and here he was implying — no, stating — that he planned to have her.

Antonia bit her lip to keep from replying. Instead, she sought to learn how long he would be ashore. "I am surprised to hear that the *capitán* of such a vessel finds it necessary to attend to the labors of his crew personally," she goaded.

"I plead your forgiveness, for life's circumstances have not dealt me the fate of gentle birth. I must attend to the tasks of earning coin," he said on a sarcastic note. "The hides of your country are worth twelve coins per pound — a tidy sum. But for the time being I pray you will enjoy my humble hospitality. And be sure that you slip into the gown I provided," he said, grudgingly acknowledging to himself that the young woman had penetrated that previously invincible shield he had erected long ago.

Chapter Nine

After Michael left Antonia safely ensconced in his cabin he hailed Mano and directed him to keep a watchful eye on his guest during his absence. On shore he busied himself to blank thoughts of Antonia from his mind by keeping a close eye on the crew while four men tossed hides down from the top of the steep bluffs to three men waiting below to collect and load them into the boats.

Satisfied with the progress, Michael made his way up the precipitous path. At the top he mounted a tethered horse and rode swiftly toward the presidio to see to the formalities required to secure a license for his vessel. Horses were plentiful in California and a sufficient number had been provided by El Señor Dominguez for the captain's use while in San Diego. When he had no further need of the animals, he had been instructed to release them and allow them to find their own way home. That was the way of the Californios.

"Why don't we get out of this hot sun and enjoy something refreshing while we conclude our business?" offered Commandant Juan Velasco, thrusting open the door to his austere quarters, which were nestled amongst a row of rudimentary wood plank buildings.

"After you, Commandant," Michael said, nodding his agreement.

Velasco motioned for Michael to sit across from him at the roughly hewn table. Although seven years Michael's senior and only of medium height and build, the commandant cut a dashing figure impeccably dressed as he was in a black, broad-brimmed sombrero, short silk jacket, and pantaloons laced with stripes of gold velvet. A red silk *bolero,* fringed at both ends, completed the impressive wear.

"You are an interesting man, Señor capitán." Velasco grinned, and leaned over to grab a bottle from a nearby shelf. "There are not many men who have called El Señor Dominguez 'partner'." He gave a short laugh. "And even fewer fortunate enough to escape the necessity of donating a bottle or two for the privilege of anchoring in my harbor. You have here," he lifted his mug and studied it for a moment, "the fine spirits from a French frigate visiting these shores not long ago."

"I shall consider myself indeed fortunate." Michael had to smile over the game they played.

"*Sí,* Señor Capitán, you are fortunate to travel the world. I envy you. As a young man it had been my desire to see the world, but alas you see before you my fate. Ah, but to own a ship such as yours." He poured more spirits, nodded a salutation, and lifted the mug to his lips. "Of course, at my age, even a comfortable life in Mexico City would suit me well."

"I well understand. The sea has been my mistress for many years. After a time one longs to make other conquests. I, too, have had thoughts of another life. But I fear my heart shall always return to my first

74

love." Michael's eyes shone as he spoke of his life at sea.

"I can see you and I have much in common, Señor Capitán. We both have our longings. El Señor Dominguez is a very rich man and can provide the wise man with many coins. But you have chosen a difficult trail." Velasco raised his brows, casting Michael a knowing smirk. "You do realize, *mi amigo,* that should you stumble from the trail, you will struggle alone." He hesitated to meet Michael's eye. "Men as adept as yourself have fallen. Since you are a man after my own heart, let it be known that you are aware of the path you walk."

"I shall consider myself forewarned." Michael nodded with the nonchalance due a most recent acquaintance. He then hoisted his mug, his cold, determined eyes closely observing the commandant from behind the rim while he drank.

Taking a swig of the fiery liquid, the commandant returned to the small talk of life at the presidio.

Commandant Velasco had learned long ago that to survive he must close his eyes to certain matters. Yet for years he had silently watched Dominguez with a patience known only to men with unsettled accounts long overdue.

Antonia was furious that the captain could even dare to assume she would make herself available to his whims. She angrily paced back and forth, still adorned only in the rough coverlet. She was not about to wear such a flimsy gown! Captain Michael Domino was strong enough to force the coverlet from her, but he could not force her into *that* gown! Her pride would never allow it.

A knock at the door sent her scampering back to

the bunk, although this time she sat rigidly upright, her arms folded squarely across her chest. She deliberately set her countenance with a glitter of indignation. When the door opened to reveal the tall, dark, silhouette of a man, Antonia's expression changed to annoyance, and a flicker of disappointment settled on her shoulders. It was not Captain Michael Domino as she had expected, but the Indian.

"Buenas días, señorita," Mano greeted her, his lips carved in a line of stone. "I have brought word from Captain Domino."

"Is that so? And where, pray tell, is your illustrious *capitán?"*

He ignored her sarcasm. "He requested it be made known he has been detained but shall join you as soon as time allows."

"How nice," she said sarcastically again.

Antonia then changed her pose. Thinking she might be able to charm him into setting her ashore, she smiled sweetly.

"It really was kind of you to bring the *capitán's* message. Since he has been delayed I should return to the rancho. If you would be kind enough to request a boat to take me ashore, señor . . ."

When she did not receive an immediate reply, she became impatient. "Of course, Capitán Domino told you of your task to see me safely ashore," she continued, watching him closely from beneath her lashes. "I will not dally. So if you would be kind enough to fetch me more appropriate clothing in which to travel that Capitán Domino said would be provided, I shall ready myself."

Antonia was certain her ruse would gain her way, and decided to add what she felt would be the finishing touch.

"And I do want to say *gracias* for the hospitality I

have received. I want you and the *capitán* to be assured, given the opportunity, I would delight in repaying, in kind and more, the generosity shown me while aboard such a celebrated vessel."

The expression on Mano's face did not change. "No doubt Captain Domino will be most pleased to hear such words of praise," he said, choosing to ignore the barbed compliment.

"I always attempt to please," Antonia answered.

Mano had listened to Antonia without giving her cause to hope. It had been the girl who had hoped for that which would not be. He had his orders. Mano knew his captain too well to be deceived by such measures. She had a way with words that left him questioning her true intent. And he found himself viewing the small señorita with a growing, if not puzzling, respect.

Turning to withdraw from the cabin without responding to Antonia's clever circumvention of the truth, Mano pondered the question of aiding her departure. He wondered if it would be better to incur his captain's wrath, or, if she remained, would he send her ashore without a second thought before they sailed. Mano was troubled by his thoughts.

"You will not be long, will you? I must be returning before I am missed or I will be severely punished," she said for good measure.

"No, señorita, I will not be long." As he shut the door the only decision he had made regarding the young señorita was to see to her need for appropriate garments. That much he would do. He headed toward the hold to retrieve the requested clothing from the captain's large sea chest.

Closing the chest, he picked up the clothing and began the trek back to the captain's cabin. Still troubling over the events of the last few days, he nearly ran headlong into a young member of the crew.

"Where are you off to in such a hurry?" Mano quizzed the lad.

"To take over from the forenoon watch, sir."

"Stop by the captain's cabin and deliver these garments to the señorita there," Mano instructed, intending to take the sailor from his duties but a few moments and not wanting to face the girl before he had time to give serious consideration to the tangled situation.

Once outside the captain's cabin the young sailor lightly rapped on the door.

Antonia bid him entrance. "Where is the *indio?* I thought he was seeing to my needs," she said, exasperated that her hasty plan had failed.

"I . . . ah . . . he told me to bring you these because he was called topside," he lied, not knowing what else to say. He held out his arms, an embarrassed blush creeping up his cheeks.

Not wasting any time, she snatched the simple gown from the young man. "Turn your back so I may change," she ordered. She wanted him to remain in the room for fear she would not have another chance to leave the ship before the captain returned.

His head bobbed. "Yes, miss."

She hurriedly donned the garments. "You may turn around now," she said when properly attired.

The young sailor shifted from foot to foot and fidgeted with strands of his dark blond hair in an attempt to offer a compliment worthy of her beauty.

"Gosh, jeez, you're the prettiest girl I've . . . ah . . . ever seen."

Noting that the impression she had made could be used to her advantage, she wasted no time responding. *"Gracias.* I am so pleased that you, sir, have been selected to escort me ashore. I shall feel entirely protected with you by my side. Shall we?" Antonia wound her arm around the boy's and without benefit of shoes left the cabin, padding alongside him.

The young man was in such a state that he blindly followed Antonia's lead. Once on deck Antonia hurried the sailor into readying one of the quarterboats. He had been somewhat hesitant. "I should check with the chief mate or at least make sure someone has taken my place on watch."

Antonia clung to his arm and adeptly changed topics, flattering and convincing him that he had been specifically chosen to escort her.

When no one made an attempt to question the girl's appearance on deck, he assumed she was telling the truth. He finally ceased insisting on the necessity of checking with an authority before going ashore and helped Antonia into the boat.

Antonia sat back demurely and lowered her head, expelling a sigh of relief as the quarterboat slowly inched its way to shore. Beneath her long, feathered lashes she attempted to scan the approaching rise of bluffs. She prayed she would not run into Captain Michael Domino. She felt pity for the young sailor she was forced to deceive, but thought him a fool for sailing with such a heartless man. She studied the lad's youthful face and hoped his punishment would not be too harsh when Captain Michael Domino discovered she had outwitted him.

Chapter Ten

At shore the young lad lifted Antonia from the boat over the licking waves and set her on the dry beach.

"If it pl-pleases you, señorita, I shall be honored to s-see you home," the young man stuttered, shuffling the fine grains of sand around with the toe of his shoe.

"You are very kind, but I know you must have many responsibilities on board ship. I shall be fine." Antonia reached out and gently squeezed his arm in thanks, then accepted the offer of one of the steeds tethered at the top of the bluffs. Stumbling her way up the steep path she stepped on several jagged pebbles, causing her to flinch in pain. Ignoring her foot, she reached the horses and, not worrying about modesty, mounted a steed to sit astride the crude saddle constructed of skeleton trees covered with rawhide. It was held together with thongs of leather and tied to the animal by a bellyband circling the middle of the seat, which sported stirrups fashioned from wooden blocks.

Antonia knotted her hands in the reins. She yanked the horse toward the presidio and slapped her stockinged feet against the animal's sides. Once she was out of the watchful sight of the ship's crewman, she slowed her pace and mindfully scanned the trail for riders. She did not want to run into Captain Michael Domino returning to his ship. Once had been enough!

Members of the *gente de razón* had always been very protective of their ladies' honor, guarding them with a deadly fierceness. Antonia knew if she explained her absence to her *padre* that Captain Michael Domino would be severely dealt with. But deep inside she did not want harm to come to him.

As she left the bobbing ship and coast farther in the distance, she began to relax. She breathed deeply and noticed the thick, fragrant chaparral adorning the trail. The sky was a pearlized blue providing a stunning contrast to the golden rolling hills. The swaying grass-covered hillocks were dotted with jagged granite outcroppings, and to her right was a gently trickling brook sprinkled with sycamore and scrub oak trees. She loved her home. She would always love this rich land.

A dark storm cloud shadowed her mind when thoughts of her *novio* suddenly sprang from nowhere, causing her serene expression to dramatically change into a scowl. Her brows drew together and her nose wrinkled at the very thought of him. All of a sudden an impish grin replaced the sullen look and a twinkle lit up her amber-green eyes.

"Perhaps, just perhaps," she brightened, "my misadventure may have saved me from a fate worse than death."

Not considering the possible consequences, Antonia decided she would confess all but the most intimate details of her adventure. Of course, she would add a few harmless details—just to lend a little more color to her tale. She was certain her *novio* would not want her after she finished her story. She would dramatize the events and plead with her *padre* to release the man from his offer of marriage. She could even tell them she could be carrying a child. No, she must not overdo it. She did not want to find herself with more woes than she already had. But if handled properly, it could still be her salvation.

Continuing along the trail, a sudden strange tingling sensation overtook her—one so recently awakened. She shook her head and tried to regain conscious control of her thoughts, but her efforts to dismiss Captain Michael Domino from her mind proved futile; she could feel his tender hands on her body, touching and caressing her responsive flesh in that most sensitive of hidden places. His questing lips were moist and warm and tender. His darkened eyes were so blue, so searching.

"No!" she exclaimed and attempted once again to force her attention to the task at hand.

Ahead of her, atop a looming hill, was the presidio, the first such fort built in California. It was an impressive assortment of structures, with walls of thick stone and adobe. It had one shore battery at a high point on the far corner, which allowed it to fire on ships in the harbor if needed.

The presidio at San Diego had been especially important to help Christianize the Indians. The armed soldiers aided the friars with their efforts when it was required. Antonia thought of the freedom the Indians had lost since the Spanish saw their duty to save them from themselves. And she wondered what it must have been like to live their simple life. They had been a simple people before the white man. She sighed wistfully, wishing she, too, could return to a less complex life. But life moved forward, and Antonia knew she could only learn from the past and use that knowledge to help better the future.

As Michael rode back toward his ship, visions of Antonia crowded their way into his mind. He could see her face as she had looked up at him with those fiery, amber-green eyes. Her golden curls were spread out, framing her countenance while she rested on his bunk. Her creamy white body was like molten silk, velvety smooth to the touch. He imagined her well-rounded bosom, the rosy nipples which responded so willingly to his tongue.

He grew hard with desire when he thought of holding the lovely sorceress again. He would retrieve a few trinkets from his sea chest and present them to her. Perhaps the costly brooch would soften her toward him. He dug his boots into the horse's flanks to speed his journey.

Not far outside the presidio he sighted a horse and rider coming toward him. There was something all too familiar about the rider, but it was not until the mounted figure abruptly left the trail that Michael realized it was Antonia.

* * *

After arriving at the Rancho de los Robles for the second time in a week, the enormous figure of a man with silvering black hair beneath a broad-brimmed sombrero, lumbered from his coach. His huge belly protruded from the top of short breeches like an overfed fowl ready for market.

"Mi amigo, how good to see you so well." Don Diego offered his hand to the dark, overpowering man irritably swabbing his brow with a linen handkerchief.

Doña Maria came scurrying to greet the recently arrived *novio.* Hands clasped together and face ashen with a worried frown, she opened her mouth to explain the continued absence of her charge. "Oh—"

"Doña Maria!" Don Diego intruded. "See to the refreshments. Our guest has traveled far on such a warm day and is in need of something to quench his thirst. We shall be in the study. Now go, woman."

Doña Maria threw Don Diego an unsettled grimace and hurried off to see to the drinks.

"You must forgive Doña Maria, she does not appear to be herself these days," Don Diego explained as the two men entered the book-filled room.

"Do not let it concern yourself, *mi amigo,* it is not for Doña Maria I come. But where is my delicate flower?" the hopeful *novio* asked, impatiently tapping his foot. "Since she was so suddenly called away from the rancho just before my last visit," he looked doubtful, "and I did not have the pleasure of my beloved's company, you understand that I am most impatient."

Doña Maria reappeared, her face pinched with

tension. "Excuse me, Diego, but your presence is required outside." After Don Diego left, she began to crumble before the imposing figure of a man awaiting his betrothed's return.

"Oh, that impossible girl! I tried to warn you she would not be an easy conquest. We must continue to reassure Don Diego that you are the best choice for Antonia. She is a willful young girl, not one to have choices made for her. You realize it was not an errand she left the rancho to attend a couple of days ago but to demonstrate her objections to this match. Oh, *Diós mío* . . . perhaps I should not have become involved. I only wanted to secure the girl's future . . . And now she has left again—"

"Doña Maria," the perturbed *novio* broke in, "remember it is *your* future as well. Be reminded I can give Antonia all the luxuries she is accustomed to and more, assure Don Diego continuing prosperity, and grant you enough coins to allow your return to Spain as an independent woman. No one will suffer, I promise you. Now do not forget our bargain and there will be no need for any unpleasantness."

"But, I must tell you—"

His face darkened. "No more! Silence now. And remember our agreement."

After being informed of Antonia's doubtful return due to her probable abduction by a group of *bandidos* the enraged *novio* had returned to his rancho and summoned one of his henchmen.

He was furious his spies had failed to keep him abreast of these latest developments and swore vengeance as he restlessly paced the length of his lavish living room. He paused to grab a small *latígo* from the mantel and repeatedly thrust it into his open palm.

His blood boiled in his veins, and his very soul filled with poison over Antonia's disappearance as he thought of the loved one he had long ago lost. Since that time he had become engaged to the Winston girl, but no one had meant anything to him. He was not going to allow the loss of another. No one was going to take her from him—no one!

He had just begun to devise the perfect form of "justice" for those who would dare to place a hand upon his *novia* when Luis Sanchez entered the room.

Sanchez was a squat mass of a man. Dressed in black from head to toe, he resembled an evil bat. The two gun belts crossed at his chest compensated for his lack of stature. The thick black bushy mustache contributed to his unsavory appearance.

"To what do I owe your most gracious invitation?" Sanchez asked sarcastically. It could not be said that Luis Sanchez dreaded his partner. Like most men engaged in rather dubious pursuits, he had learned not to put his trust in others. This was at best an uneasy partnership built and sustained on the knowledge of the past.

"Either someone very foolish has forgotten a bargain, or someone ignorantly unaware of the mistake made by taking something of mine has kidnapped my *novia,*" the raging Dominguez snarled, not wasting time with preliminaries.

"No offense, but are you certain it was not the señorita who took herself away? The Winston hacienda has many ears, and it is spoken that the lady in question was, shall we say, not the most eager future bride."

"My dear Sanchez, señoritas of a such tender age often do not know their own feelings and must be guided to make the proper choices in life," he lashed out.

Sanchez had not survived so long without knowing when to hold his tongue. He could see the dark fires flare in the black eyes and knew he would be wise to still his lips. Right now he continued to need the man, but soon there would come a time . . .

Sanchez, like many others, had been captivated by Antonia. He felt her beauty would be wasted on the likes of his partner, and if everything went according to his plans, he not only would own the rancho he now visited but take the delicious morsel for his bride.

He would keep Carmen on the side, of course, his woman of long-standing who had delivered him a daughter. But Antonia—not only would she add to his respectability, but there was not another woman in all of California who could compare in beauty.

Noting the disgruntled *novio*'s bulging eyes spark with the slightest hint of madness, Sanchez sensed the discovery of a long-sought weakness. As the wheels turned in his mind, devising a plan to maintain the upper hand he felt within his grasp, he quickly concluded his audience with Dominguez's assurances of assistance and left the rancho.

Riding toward his camp in the hills, he laughed. "This could not be better if I planned it myself. Just like the Garden of Eden, woman led man to his downfall. Hah! How fitting."

The closer Sanchez came to his encampment, the more certain he was that he would soon be in control of the entire empire belonging to his partner, and, at long last, possess the Winston girl.

Chapter Eleven

"What the hell?" Michael cursed, and headed in pursuit of the retreating señorita.

Antonia sighted him seconds before he saw her. Her heart began to beat wildly and fear overtook her entire being. At first she looked around frantically for someone to aid her. When she realized there would be no one to render assistance, she panicked. She had always been known to keep her head in difficult situations, but the thought of a confrontation at this time with Michael Domino unnerved her and sent an icy chill down her spine. Pushing the animal to its limits, she hoped to escape into the dry brush.

Fortune did not smile on Antonia.

Michael's horse caught up to her animal just as she reached the other side of the stream and was about to ride into a massive thicket of sage, sumac, horehound, and poison oak. As Michael reached over to snatch her from her horse, his animal suddenly turned, sending them both tumbling to the ground. Somewhat shaken but not hurt, Antonia attempted to scramble into the brush. Michael grabbed for her thigh and dragged her back toward him. Enraged, she whipped around and faced him squarely.

"Why, my mysterious sorceress," he grinned, "couldn't you wait for me to return to the ship to be with me? Are you so anxious for me that you follow me and lead me here underneath this inviting umbrella of a tree beside a quiet stream?" While his words mocked her, his eyes held a warm, though troubled light.

"You, you . . . bast—"

"Por favor, such language does not become you, señorita," he warned. "Your choice of beauty aids does not do you justice, either." Pinning her beneath him, he untied the kerchief from his neck and wiped the smudges from her nose and chin.

"Let me go!" Antonia screamed at him, struggling to no avail. She was terrified, as much of herself and her heightening excitement as well as the man who held her fast.

"But Princess, if I release you, you probably would do yourself more harm. I could not tolerate your unnecessary discomfort." He looked up and pointed toward the bright red and orange leaves clustered in groups of three, signifying poison oak. "It would be a pity to have to stand helplessly by while your creamy flesh turned to large red rashes. Such would increase an already ill temper."

"If that is your only cause for so abruptly interrupting my ride, then I can promise you I shall take great pains to avoid the troublesome plant. So if you will be so kind as to release me, I shall be on my way." Antonia's eyes burned with the intensity of a stormy night and her chest heaved with denied desire.

"I couldn't conceive of allowing such a fragile señorita such as yourself to travel unprotected. Why, who knows what dangers lurk about. I wouldn't want such a luscious body marred."

"I fear the only danger here is from you. Now, if you will kindly remove yourself from my person . . ."

"Are you so sure that it is not you, Antonia, whom you fear?"

"I do not know what you are talking about," she lamely protested.

"Don't you?"

Antonia's pulse was rising to new heights as she gazed up into his smiling eyes. She *was* afraid of herself but would never admit it.

Grasping Antonia by the wrist, he pulled her to her feet. Her gown was soiled with unsightly brown patches and leaves were entangled all through her hair. Michael had not fared much better. His white linen shirt was covered with grimy dirt as were his fawn-colored trousers.

"Heaven be damned, I can't seem to control myself around you," he muttered under his breath just before he lowered his head.

As their lips met, Antonia considered continuing her struggle but instead relaxed against him. He was arrogant, so sure of himself—and her. Why was she not fighting him? Because she did not want to; it was that simple. Her body longed for him, and she moved closer into his arms, melting into his intoxicating embrace.

After he finally released her, she stood before him with her arms dangling at her sides, strangely quiet. Her eyes searched his face as her fingers snaked up to trace the outline of his lips. What was happening to her? She felt weak and light-headed.

What had begun as a simple plan had suddenly backfired and she found herself embroiled in two battles: one against a marriage she could never accept and the other against her own body. Confused feelings tugged at her, and she had to bite down on her lower lip to keep it from trembling.

"Ca-capitán—" she stammered.

"Michael," he corrected, raising her chin with his finger to study her face.

"I must return home. I will be missed."

"Stay for just a while," he whispered.

"No. I must not."

"Tonia—"

Antonia's brows flew upward and a puzzled frown pursed the corners of her lips. She had not been called Tonia since her early childhood, and then only by her *padre* prior to her *madre*'s death. Since that time she had not allowed anyone to call her by that name. But she only offered the slimmest of protests when Michael said the name long left in the past, as now was her childhood.

"My name is Antonia. Please remember that," she reminded him weakly.

"It would be difficult to forget," he murmured in a husky voice. "But I rather like the sound of Tonia. So much like an inviting whisper, don't you agree?"

"Certainly not!"

"Pity. To me, you'll always be Tonia."

"If you must," she ground out, conceding defeat. "I am sorry, but I must leave now," she said and

92

turned from him to retreat. She wanted to run—from herself. To escape. But where? Where would she go? She was the daughter of one of the most powerful *rancheros* in California. There was nowhere to hide.

"Not yet." He took hold of her shoulders to stop her. "I won't harm you. I won't even touch you again if that's what you're afraid of, Tonia."

"I am not afraid," she snapped, feeling fear overtake her.

"Then stay, or return to the ship with me. I want to get to really know you."

Desperation gripped her. She dared not remain with him or she would not be able to control herself.

"What makes you think I desire to know some common *capitán,*" she forced herself to say.

Michael dropped his hands. His eyes hardened to glacial chips. Then a mocking grin twisted his lips.

"Now I understand. The fine lady merely was in search of amusement from a lowly sea captain to entertain her whims," he snarled like a wounded boar.

"No," she sputtered.

"No? I think we played this scene already, *Princess*. Well, if it's a diversion you were seeking, I don't want to send you away disappointed."

Michael swooped down upon her. She felt like a small animal caught within the mighty talons of a deadly predator.

"*Por favor,*" she cried as he tumbled her back to the ground as if she had been bought and paid for.

Ignoring her pleas, Michael pinned her shoulders against a bed of fallen leaves. He kissed her fiercely, passionately. His tongue forced her lips

93

apart, ravaging her mouth. Then he was kissing her neck and chest, dipping his head lower.

Antonia dug her nails into his back. She was frantic and excited at the same time as surging waves of desire swept over her. She tried to squirm from beneath him but only sank deeper into a turbulent sea. He grabbed her wrists and pinioned them over her head as he lay over the length of her.

"Your body tells me you want me as much I want you," he said.

"No! Don't touch me!" she beseeched, uncontrollably shaking her head from side to side.

"God, woman, you would try the soul of a saint. You desire me, I know it. I see it in your eyes; I feel it in your body; I hear it in your voice. But you deny me. Damn you! I shall someday burn in hell over you!" he roared and then rolled from her to sit up.

Antonia was stunned. She had half expected him to take her right there. She had felt his passion pressing hard against her loins, his rapid heartbeat against her chest. She was relieved, yet a strange longing ache of unquenched feelings lay heavy on her mind.

Nice young ladies did not have those feelings. Had not her *tía* drilled that into her head often enough? They remained pure until their marriage bed and only than did they suffer the wills of their husbands, and only because it was a wife's duty. But no, she was different. More like the women who lived in town. The ones she had sometimes heard talking about the soldiers and vaqueros when she had visited the store with her *tía*. Doña Maria had always raised her brows in disgust and looked down her nose at them before she hurried her niece from the shop. But Antonia had heard how they spoke of the pleasures of men while they fondled the bolts of fabric they would buy to fashion clothing to please their lovers.

In silence Antonia straightened her soiled gown and rose to her feet to brush off the clinging twigs. She stood with her back toward Michael, her arms folded and her head tilted back waiting for him to make the next move. She tensed when she heard the sound of a branch snapping under his boot.

Michael stood right behind her, his fists clenched into hard leaden balls at his sides. Damn, he wanted her as he had never before desired a woman. He found himself wanting more than just her body. He had been the first man to possess her and he wanted to protect her from others who might take advantage of her loss of innocence. But it was more than that. He did not want another man to touch her. He had been the first, and not understanding why, he wanted to be the last.

"Tonia, turn around and look at me," he said quietly.

Antonia took a deep breath. There was no escaping; she would have to face him. Slowly she pivoted, her lips drawn into a tight line, crimson flushing her cheeks.

"Tonia . . ." He reached out his hand. "It wasn't my intention to frighten or harm you. Now come, we shall return to the ship and get to know each other better."

Antonia gazed down at the hand suspended in midair. What was he offering? What did he really want? He was exciting and forceful, yet there was also a glimmer of warmth beneath the hard veneer.

She tried to swallow, but a dry lump stuck in her throat like caked sand. She was being foolish. Her thoughts were but childish dreams, but she was no longer a child; he had changed that.

Michael shifted his stance from foot to foot. Impatience simmered within him. For the first time in his life he felt something for a woman, and she just stood there.

"Come along, it's getting late. It'll be dark soon and since the horses seem to have wandered away, we have a long walk ahead of us."

"No. I am not going with you," she stated firmly.

"What do you mean, you're not going with me?" His eyes flashed with anger.

"I am not going."

"Yes, you are. It's not safe out here alone." He reached for her arm. "I can't just leave you here."

Antonia flung her arm out of his grasp and said with unmovable resolve, "What makes you, a filthy sea *capitán,* think I would want to get to know you?" Even as she spat the cruel words, deep down she hoped he would convince her to change her mind.

A sharp pain jolted through his heart like a merciless cannon striking its target, and his temper boiled over to the surface.

"Filthy sea captain am I? Last night you didn't seem to think so. But of course that was before I accepted what you offered. Well, you needn't worry, señorita." He ground his teeth. "I wouldn't touch you again if you threw yourself at my feet."

"You really are nothing better than one of those soldiers at the presidio," she cried. His words had wounded her with as much force as the blade of a

96

sword.

"You may be wise to hold that sharp tongue of yours before I act like one of your soldiers," he shot back.

Antonia's chest was heaving with anger. Furious, she whirled around and started for the presidio. Michael was right behind her. He grabbed her shoulders and swung her to face him. His fingers closed around her hair and yanked her head back as his other arm encircled her waist.

Rage blazed in his eyes. "Here's something to help you remember your little adventure," he said.

He forced her lips to his and brutally ravaged her mouth. Antonia struggled, but she was no match for his strength. His lips pried hers apart and his tongue invaded her, plundering until she was breathless. Just as Antonia, unable to help herself, surrendered to the intense passion rising between them, he abruptly let her go.

"You're no different than any other seductress," he said coldly, and turned to leave her speechless.

A frenzied turbulence overtook Antonia. She dropped to the ground like a rock thrown into the center of a swirling maelstrom. Angry tears threatened to spill from her eyes and she cursed his retreating back.

Chapter Twelve

Antonia scrambled to her feet. Half running, half stumbling along the trail, she began to sob. Furious with herself for being so foolish, she made no attempt to stem the flow of tears which trickled down her cheeks.

Overcome with frustration, she ceased her journey and perched upon a boulder, burying her head in her hands. She was so upset she failed to note the position of the sun as it rapidly disappeared into a darkening ocean, turning the sky from an iridescent blue to glimmering black.

Alone when night replaced day, another concern was added to the heavy burden she already carried. She slid to the base of the mighty boulder, pulled her knees up into her chest, and sighed mournfully. Coyotes howled in the distance, crickets chirped nearby, and other eerie sounds of the night sang their haunting songs. She huddled into a tighter ball and listened to the symphony of nature until she fell into a troubled slumber.

Hours later, close to midnight, the sounds of familiar voices woke her, and she sat up and listened.

"Tonia! Tonia!" Michael called out, thrashing through the brush off in the distance.

Antonia started to rise, but sank back to the ground. Her stubborn pride would not allow her to go to him—not after the way they had parted. She needed time to sort out all the new feelings invading her body, feelings he had stirred within her.

"Tonia!" Michael shouted. He was frantic with worry, and berated himself for being so foolish as to leave her in a moment of anger. After he had returned to the ship, he realized he should have stayed and forced her to listen to him. He never wanted a woman so much in his life.

"My brother, it is hopeless in the dark. Come, we shall return in the morning." The Indian's voice drifted through the cool night air.

"Damn sorceress," Michael muttered.

Antonia perked up her ears. There was a rustle of brush for a few more moments and then the sound of thundering hooves before the stillness of the night returned. Antonia sighed, wondering why he had bothered to return to look for her; a hint of a smile curled her lips at the thought before she fell back to sleep.

At dawn's first light Antonia awoke. A chill rippled through her, and she rubbed her arms vigorously. Rising from the cold, damp earth, she brushed her bedraggled gown and sighed at her condition. Her hair was tangled with twigs and leaves. She bore a number of scrapes and was in dire need of a bath. Realizing she could no longer forestall her return, she climbed up to the trail and began the trek to the presidio.

She had not traveled far when Commandant Velasco and his men caught up with her.

"Well now, what do we have here?" chuckled the commandant. When he realized that the unkempt waif of a girl was Señorita Antonia Rafaela Winston y Ortega Velasco's demeanor immediately became stiffly formal. He knew the importance of the young girl's *padre,* as well as the power of her *novio.*

"You. Soldier," he ordered one of his men. "Dismount and wrap Señorita Winston in this." He took off his broadcloth cloak and passed it to the man. "Then give her your horse."

"Gracias, Comandante Velasco," Antonia said, feeling defeated. There would be no escaping the soldiers.

She was going home.

The soldier complied and then joined another man upon his animal. Before beginning the return ride to the presidio, Velasco sent messengers to inform Antonia's *padre* and *novio* that she had been found unharmed.

Arriving at the presidio, the commandant escorted Antonia into his office and offered her the best morning's fare available at such short notice. Antonia was ravenous and devoured the huge breakfast of tortillas and eggs set before her. She was thirsty, too, and the hot black coffee tasted especially good, warming her chilled body. Even when days were quite warm, the nights were cool and often damp.

Once satisfied, Antonia leaned back in the hard wooden chair and closed her eyes, but Velasco's voice intruded into her moment of quietude.

"Forgive me, Señorita Winston, but as *coman-*

dante of this presidio I am forced to seek your assistance to bring this most unfortunate incident to a proper conclusion. If you will be kind enough to describe your abductors I shall see that the men responsible are duly punished."

Antonia opened her eyes and stared past the commandant seated in front of her. As he spoke, her thoughts returned to the last forty-eight hours. She vividly recalled the heated argument with Doña Maria, her flight from the rancho, and every detail of the time spent with Captain Michael Domino.

"I beg your pardon, Señorita Winston. Are you ill? Shall I summon a physician to look after you until your *padre* arrives?" Velasco closely scrutinized Antonia, concerned that she might be suffering from shock caused by her ordeal.

"What? What did you say?" Antonia was startled back into the reality of her circumstance by the mere mention of her *padre*.

Velasco repeated his request for a description of the abductors, whom two old Indians had reported seeing her with—and which information they had relayed two days ago to Montoya. When she remained silent, Velasco vowed to see the men properly punished.

That was not part of her plan. Her dream of escaping a dreaded marriage was turning into a nightmare. If they caught Michael she would watch him swing from the end of a rope. A vision of him being marched to a scaffold between two husky soldiers and her *novio* personally binding his hands flashed before her eyes. She saw him refuse a blindfold and proudly climb the steps toward the noose, his head held proud. The unsettling thought held her, causing her to shift her glance out the window over the commandant's shoulder.

All her hesitancy was quickly dissolved in a fit of jealous anger when she recognized the figure of a man staggering along the dusty street outside the commandant's office, two *putas* within the circle of his arms.

Rubbing her amber-green eyes, Antonia leaped from the chair and ran to the window. It was Michael. He had become everything she had accused him of being last night! Her rescuing vaquero suddenly turned into a thief who had stolen her maidenhood. He had not wasted any time after leaving her to seek out another to satisfy him. No, two others. He was little better than her *novio*. Pointing an accusing finger toward the three people in the street, she began to tremble.

"That's him. That's him . . . the one over there. The one with his arms around those two . . . two women."

Her lips pressed hard together, she turned from the window unable to view the spectacle of Michael embracing two *putas,* remembering those same strong arms holding her, setting her senses afire, tantalizing her with the motion of his hips against hers, his searching, probing fingers; the male core of him filling her so completely that she thought she would die with the ecstasy of it. She blinked her eyes to force her thoughts back to the present — and the reality that she had been just another one of his conquests.

Velasco, who had come to stand behind her at the window, consoled her within his embrace as long as he dared. Then he led Antonia back to her seat and summoned two of his guards.

"Sí, comandante," saluted the short, dark ser-

geant.

"Sir," the other chimed in.

"You see the man out there with his arms around Martina and Lolita?"

"*Sí*," they said in unison.

"Arrest him for the abduction of Señorita Winston."

The two stocky men grinned at each other, saluted, and turned to carry out the order. They were most happy to dispose of the man who had taken not one but two of the women who regularly saw to the soldiers' needs.

True to the custom of chivalry, Commandant Velasco offered Antonia his handkerchief. Antonia accepted it and blew her nose, clutching the small bit of fabric. Although very early in the day, Velasco poured both of them a glass of his most carefully guarded spirits. While he wished that she were sharing his private stock under different conditions, he was a wise man and knew this unfortunate incident could be used to his advantage if he proceeded cautiously. He took a sip and let his eyes trail out the window.

"Halt!" One of the soldiers commanded, raising his rifle. "You are under arrest."

"What the devil?" Michael looked up, still in a fog from the spirits he had guzzled in town after his fruitless search for Antonia the night before. Through red eyes he glanced at the two women. He barely remembered the pair offering to console him last night before he'd passed out.

One of the soldiers shoved the women out of the way and grabbed his arm. "Maybe you touch the wrong woman this time, eh, *capitán?*" he sneered.

103

Michael swung out of their grasp, but before he could seek clarification of the charges, the butt of a rifle crashed into his head and he slumped to the ground.

Chapter Thirteen

It was a hot, dusty ride to the presidio, especially inside the rocking coach. By the time Don Diego and Doña Maria had received the commandant's note and reached the presidio, it was late afternoon. Entering the commandant's office, they found an angry, disheveled Antonia standing in front of a dismayed commandant. Doña Maria brushed past the two men and threw her arms around her dead sister's child.

"My child," she cried, "are you all right? *Dios mío,* look at you!"

Antonia struggled free and stood stiffly, glaring at the commandant.

"Antonia, Comandante Velasco," Don Diego summoned, looking from the nettled girl to the shaken man. "What is the meaning of this?"

Antonia turned and flew to her *padre.* She hesitated for a moment and then threw herself into his arms, sobbing, "Oh, *padre,* I am so glad you are here." Tears of joy flowed down her cheeks.

"It's all right now, child. You needn't be frightened any longer. No further harm will come to you, I'll see to that," Don Diego said with tender authority.

It had been a long time since Don Diego had embraced his only daughter. Her ordeal and pleading eyes caused him to tighten his hold on the trembling young girl. Tears long unspent welled in his eyes as he held her.

"What is this all about, *comandante?* I demand an explanation," Don Diego said harshly, stroking Antonia's tangled tresses.

"Señor Winston, I assure you it was not my intention to add to the señorita's distress. We have the accused behind bars and I was merely attempting to make Señorita Winston understand the necessity of accompanying me so she can make a positive identification of the prisoner."

Don Diego lifted Antonia's chin. His expression softened as he gazed into her silently pleading amber-green eyes. "I know this is difficult for you, Daughter. But Comandante Velasco is right. If the man is to be brought to justice it is necessary for you to identify him."

"But, *padre,* I cannot stand to be in the same room as that . . . that man. Oh *por favor,* please, not after what has happened." Antonia beseeched her *padre* not to force her to see the captain again.

"Oh, my poor child, what has that dreadful man done to you?" Concern filled Doña Maria's voice as she stepped near Antonia and placed a hand on her trembling shoulder.

"Hush, woman!" Don Diego commanded the distraught *tía.* "There will be time later for details. Now we must dispense with the unpleasantries and then take Antonia home where she belongs." He

106

gave his daughter's hand a squeeze of reassurance. "Come, Antonia, we shall face this man together."

"No! Oh, *padre, por favor,* if I must face him, *por favor* wait here."

"But wouldn't it be easier if I accompany you?"

"No! If I must face him I shall like to show him I am not afraid. After all, am I not a Winston?" Antonia quickly added. She watched her *padre* closely as she spoke, hoping her reasons would satisfy him. She could not allow him to speak to Michael. What if he told her *padre* how she had gone willingly with him? But worse, what if her *padre* believed him? Nothing was working out the way she had planned, and now she felt herself caught in the intricately entangled web of her own dream's desire.

"If you insist, but—"

"*Sí,* I do, *padre,*" Antonia interrupted.

"You are a Winston," Don Diego said hesitantly, yet with pride. He turned to Velasco. "You will not let that man any closer to my daughter than is absolutely necessary to identify him."

"He is behind bars, señor," Velasco reassured. "He will not be able to come anywhere near Señorita Winston. You have my guarantee."

"Then go with the *comandante,* Antonia. But do not tarry. We have a long journey ahead of us."

"*Gracias, padre.*" Antonia reached up on her tiptoes and placed a peck on his cheek.

Don Diego, unaccustomed to any public display of affection, uneasily cleared his throat and moved to the door.

Antonia took the commandant's arm and with a deep breath raised her chin and walked toward the jail.

* * *

Michael had spent the day in troubled thought after the commandant had laid forth the accusations against him. The señorita meant nothing to him, he had assured himself. Hadn't he attempted to prove that with the two whores last night after he could not locate the troublesome wench? Antonia was just another young woman. But she had not been a woman until he had taken her. He tried to rationalize his feelings—distant dreams which had haunted him since he first encountered her. She must have been a tease who had not met a determined man before.

"Damn the sorceress! Damn her. And damn that Gypsy and her predictions," he growled like the caged lion he was.

He squinted at the light as the door creaked open. Seeing Antonia, his eyes turned hard as steel. Anger flared in his heart. He rose to his feet and casually leaned against the bars, crossing his arms over his chest. His eyes slowly traveled the length of her body and a devilish grin rose from his lips to dance about his face.

"To what do I owe the pleasure of your visit?"

Antonia stood rigidly still, horrified by the squalor surrounding him.

"I knew you could not tolerate our separation for long, but I never expected you so soon, Princess."

"Is this the man, Señorita Winston?" Velasco questioned, stepping inside behind Antonia.

Antonia hesitantly inched closer to the bars and stared at Michael. Her heart was thudding against her chest. Then she remembered the two women and how easily he had discarded her and shifted his attentions to two—not one but two—*putas*.

"*Sí, comandante,*" she said, staring at the prisoner, unable to remove her gaze, "he is the man."

Velasco arched a brow. It was a wise man who knew when to refrain from intruding into the business of others. The air was charged with the fire between the pair. He had no intention of getting himself involved in what could become a dangerous situation.

"*Gracias,* you may return to your *padre* now," Velasco said.

Pivoting to leave, Antonia wavered at the door and swung around. *"Comandante,* may I have a moment alone with the prisoner?"

Velasco's glance flitted from Captain Domino to Antonia. He frowned briefly in confusion, then nodded his consent. *"Sí,* of course, Señorita Winston. Do not be long. Your *padre* will begin to wonder." Reluctantly, he left them alone.

The instant they were alone, Antonia spun around to boldly face Michael. The gold flecks in her amber-green eyes glinted in anger. She stood with her arms crossed and slowly let her eyes travel the length of his body in a gesture of defiance for a similar assessment he had given her moments earlier.

"I never thought to see you at the presidio," she choked out.

"And I never thought you would accuse me of abducting you. Or should I remind you of the circumstances surrounding our meeting, Señorita Winston?" he shot back coldly.

"No!" she snapped. "But it was you who—"

"Who *seduced* you? I seem to recall the events somewhat differently." He arched a bitter brow in amusement.

"It was not my intention to . . . to . . ." she faltered.

109

A skeptical expression now lined his face. "Oh, really?"

"Stop! Just stop it!" she cried.

"Princess, you can't deny the beauty of our encounter. But it really is such a pity . . ." Michael was not about to allow Antonia to see her presence had stirred him so, and moved to lure her from such a delicate topic.

"What is a pity?" Antonia demanded, swallowing the bait. Her amber-green eyes flared with a myriad of emotions.

"Since you are my captor, your slightest wish is my command," he mocked, bowing. "It's a pity that such a beauty be wasted on the likes of El Señor Dominguez. But then perhaps you two deserve each other."

"Like you and those two women?"

"I only came to be with those two after I couldn't find you last night. And then only just before I passed out. And for your information, they sought *me* out. If you hadn't hidden from me, I never would have gotten drunk in the first place."

Michael returned to his cot as if to dismiss her.

"Wait, you are not going to blame me for your late-night adventures." Her tone held anger, but inside she was glad for his confession.

Guilt over Michael's predicament due to her jealousy began to pour over her. Then what he had said about El Señor Dominguez hit her. "How did you find out about El Señor. . . ?"

Antonia's face reddened and the cell seemed to close in around her. How dare he say she deserved her *novio*, and how did he know? She whirled around and rushed out of the filthy jail and past the commandant, unable to quiet the panic threatening to engulf her, all the while hot, angry tears cascaded down her cheeks.

Velasco stepped inside the hut. *"Capitán,* it appears that you are even a bigger fool than I had originally thought during our earlier conversation. I warned you, señor." He slyly winked at Michael and left to follow Antonia back to his office.

Before Velasco reached his office, he was met outside by Antonia and Don Diego.

"Please be kind enough to convey our apologies to the man in your cell. It appears that my daughter was mistaken earlier when she identified the poor wretch. *Por favor,* release him at once. Now, I must take my daughter home."

Velasco's eyes widened in surprise and darted from Don Diego to Antonia when he heard the *ranchero*'s words. He knew there was an unmistakable look of shock on his face, but he remained mute. Don Diego thanked him again and pledged a generous reward for the arrest of his daughter's abductors.

Don Diego helped his daughter into the carriage. Antonia, still attired in the tattered gown, positioned herself across from Doña Maria. After Don Diego gave orders to the driver he climbed in beside his daughter. Montoya glanced at the commandant with a questioning expression on his face, then snapped the whip over the heads of the spirited roans.

Commandant Velasco, shaking his head in bewilderment, returned to the jail and picked up the keys to the cell.

"Well, Señor Capitán, it looks as if I will have to reserve judgment as to whether or not you are foolish. It appears Señorita Winston was mistaken in her identification of you. Or at least that is what she told her *padre*." Velasco's eyes narrowed, and

111

he closely scrutinized the captain's reaction to his words. "After a closer look, the lady realized you were not her abductor after all. You are a free man."

As Michael was about to leave the cell, Velasco halted him. "You are a very fortunate man. Perhaps after checking your cargo you will find you have enough hides and wisely decide it is time to leave San Diego. Heed my words, Señor Capitán, do not push your luck too far."

Michael shrugged nonchalantly, turned, and stepped into the street. He was quickly joined by Mano, who had kept watch from behind a building across the dusty street.

"I thought I would have to wait until after dark to free you, my brother. What happened to cause the commandant to release you?"

"After accusing me of being her abductor, the lady suddenly changed her story and said she was mistaken." Michael stroked his chin. "And I intend to find out why."

Chapter Fourteen

Antonia steadfastly refused to discuss her abduction during the long ride back to the hacienda. She sat quietly, hunched in the corner of the carriage, staring blankly out the window.

"Antonia, Daughter . . ." Don Diego began, "you will feel better if you let your *tía* and me share your burden."

"I cannot speak of it," she returned for the fourth time.

"Do not be foolish, of course you can," Doña Maria insisted.

"No. I cannot," she said with deliberation, then huddled even deeper into the corner of the rumbling coach with her head turned away.

Silent tears of frustration streamed down her flushed cheeks as she thought of her stupidity in believing, even for a moment, that Michael Domino was special. She had been a fool, and now she would pay. The realization made her wonder how many other women had given themselves to men only to experience the crushing loss which accompanies rejection. Her heart ached for those nameless trusting ones. She quietly questioned whether she would have behaved differently if given a second chance. In the back of her heart she knew she would still have gone to Michael Domino willingly.

Once back at the hacienda Antonia rushed to her room and locked the door.

Doña Maria started after her.

"Doña Maria, where are you going?" Don Diego's voice halted her.

"To see after the girl. She needs a woman to look in on her."

"Right now, what she needs is to be left alone. For your sake, I hope we understand each other."

"If that is what you wish," she huffed. "I shall retire to my room." Doña Maria was not used to anyone interfering with her methods of running the household or dealing with Antonia and promptly drew herself up to her full height to leave Don Diego while she still had her dignity intact. "If you have a change of heart, you know where I shall be."

She expected the *ranchero* to relent to her wishes. She waited, seated at her secretary, which had been shipped from Baltimore, and was finished in Sheraton style and adorned with handpainted glass panels of *Temperance and Hope*. The matching mahogany chair was carved at the top of the center splat with five feathers and bellflowers below. At the base of the splats were festoons of drapery and acathus leaves.

When Doña Maria had seen the elaborately constructed set in town, she immediately had it sent out to the rancho. It had reminded her of a time in her youth, of a public room in Spain where she once enjoyed a brief flirtation with a dashing matador. She had spurned his advances, of course and shortly thereafter returned to care for Antonia. The pieces had become symbols of her own lost life, and she kept them as a harsh reminder of her sacrifices.

When Don Diego did not come to her room, Doña Maria opened the rolltop desk and scratched a note to Dominguez. She outlined her concerns that Antonia's ordeal would interfere with the plans they had made for the girl. She fretted all the while she scribbled the words of warning.

She wanted Antonia to marry a man who could provide well for her. Don Diego had never questioned her judgment in handling the girl before. But he seemed to change during the time Antonia was missing. After Antonia had thrown herself into his arms, his manner toward the young girl softened all the more. It had taken a lot of masterful planning to manipulate Don Diego into thinking the betrothal was his idea. Now Doña Maria could not afford to have her plans thwarted.

Relieved Doña Maria had not put up more of a fight before withdrawing, Don Diego ordered hot water sent to Antonia's room. He allowed her sufficient time to bathe and complete her toilette before he walked down the hall toward her room. He lightly rapped at the door.

Antonia, dressed in slippers and a wrapper, slowly opened it expecting Doña Maria to be standing there like a stern *dueña*. Grateful when it was not the foreboding figure of her *tía,* Antonia stepped aside and allowed her *padre* entrance.

"My child, I realize I have done you a great injustice ignoring you all these years. Can you ever forgive me?"

When Antonia heard her *padre*'s confession, it was if a floodgate of emotions was opened, releas-

115

ing years of pent-up tears and sobs. She rushed into his open arms and buried her face against his chest.

Don Diego stroked her golden curls and spoke softly to his only child in an effort to comfort her.

He waited a reasonable length of time, then held her from him to gaze into her red-rimmed eyes. "My dear," he said, reassuringly, "I know you have been through much and would like nothing more than to forget the entire unfortunate ordeal, but there is certain information we must have . . ."

"Oh, *padre,* not now, *por favor,*" Antonia pleaded through glistening eyes.

Don Diego was a shrewd man. He had spent years building an empire and had learned to read people well. He had noticed the expression on the commandant's face when the man told him of the mistaken identification and he had wondered what caused the commandant's surprise. He was concerned for his daughter. She was obviously hiding something, and Don Diego was not a man to allow his questions to go unanswered.

"Antonia, I realize you are still quite upset, but it is imperative this matter be settled. Even El Señor Dominguez has written of his concern."

"El Señor Dominguez!" Antonia spat the name. "What does he have to do with this? Oh, why does not he leave me be?" she groaned.

"I'm afraid, Daughter, that as your *novio* he has every right to be concerned about your welfare and your reputation."

"My reputation?" Antonia questioned, incredulous. "What about *his* reputation? I know as well as you do what his reputation is. He has tasted the favors of every *puta* in town."

"Watch your mouth, young lady," Don Diego

116

warned.

"Well, he has." She stood by her blunt statement.

"It's not El Señor Dominguez's reputation that is in question here. It's yours we must safeguard. You know perfectly well men have always enjoyed the pleasures of willing women. They just do not marry them. El Señor Dominguez is no different from any other man. He wants his bride to be a virgin on his wedding night. He has a right to expect nothing less."

"Then, if you must know, I . . ." Antonia began with the ferocity of a violent storm about to be unleashed, "I can never marry anyone now."

"You're talking nonsense; of course you can," Don Diego returned, holding his evaporating patience in tight rein.

"No, I cannot," she insisted, thinking how unfair society was toward women.

"And just why not?"

"Because I am no longer pure," she blurted out before she realized she had even said the words.

Chapter Fifteen

Don Diego stiffened when he heard Antonia's confession. He grabbed her shoulders and shook her. "I will have the man hung for this!"

"No," she protested.

Ignoring her, he demanded, "And now you will give me the information we need to capture the man, do you hear me?" he raged.

"I hear you."

The tenderness Don Diego had shown his only child drained from him. He turned ashen. "I saw the exchange between you and Comandante Velasco at the presidio. What is it you are trying to hide? I order you to tell me. Now!"

Antonia bit her lip and lowered her eyes. Her memories of the time she had spent with Michael Domino were hers alone and would remain locked away in her heart, no matter how hard her *padre* tried to force them from her.

"Why was the *comandante* so surprised when I told him you had been mistaken? Why?"

Don Diego was furious. He had ceased shaking her but continued to grasp her shoulders angrily. He forced her chin up and looked directly into her stunned, amber-green eyes.

"*Padre, por favor,* I do not know what you mean." Antonia could not understand his behavior. He had never been one to lose control to emotion. Since her abduction he had changed. She had changed. She was a woman now, and she was covering up for the very man who had brought about the transformation.

"I shall get to the bottom of this!" Don Diego raged on. "Consider yourself fortunate. I received a message from El Señor upon our return this evening. With luck he will still want to marry you; the sooner the better in order to put a stop to any rumors which might cause him to change his mind."

"No! No! He cannot. It was not supposed to happen this way. No!"

Antonia was near to hysteria and struggled to free herself from her *padre*.

Don Diego could not believe his ears. "You planned this?"

"No. I only thought afterward . . . afterward I would no longer be forced to marry that swine. No! No! No!"

Antonia's frenzied state grew until she was half laughing, half crying. She shook her head and kept sobbing the word "no" until Don Diego was forced to strike her in order to make her stop.

Antonia rubbed her cheek in complete, utter horror. Her *padre* had never laid a hand on her in anger before.

Don Diego was stunned at himself. His arms

119

dropped limply to his sides. "Antonia, I . . ."

The indignity of the affront returned Antonia to her senses. Regaining the composure she had lost, she coolly looked her *padre* in the eyes. She masked her expression until she knew she no longer displayed the slightest glimmer of emotion.

"*Padre*, it has been a very trying day for both of us. Now, if you will please leave, I would like to get some rest," she said blandly, then she turned away. Walking to her canopy bed, she stood at the edge with her back to him.

Dismayed, Don Diego started toward the door. Before he left, he said quietly, "We shall continue this discussion in the morning, when we both have had a chance to calm down. In the meantime I'll send word to El Señor Dominguez that you are looking forward to seeing him."

Antonia remained stoically silent, her heart splintering into a multitude of pieces.

Dominguez's visit the next day did not go well for Antonia. He was too understanding.

Moving to her side in the spacious study, he took her hands in his. "It is now more important than ever to set our wedding date."

"You are truly a generous man under the circumstances, El Señor," Don Diego said.

"*Sí*," Doña Maria seconded. "A prompt marriage would be just the thing to dispel any rumors."

"No!" Antonia blurted out, grabbing back her hands. "I can no longer marry you, El Señor." She dropped her eyes. "I am no longer innocent."

Dominguez lifted her chin. Inside he fumed, but he gave nothing away. "You were the innocent victim in this unfortunate affair. I have no intention of letting such a misfortune come between us. The loss of your maidenhood has not changed my feelings toward you."

"But I may be with child."

"If that is the case, the sooner we are married the better. There would be less cause for speculation. But regardless . . . any issue, my flower, I shall consider to be my own."

"The saints be blessed," Doña Maria said, clasping her hands.

"You are a rare man, El Señor," added Don Diego, relaxing his tense stance. "My daughter is most fortunate to have such an understanding *novio*."

Antonia wanted to fight back at their serene acceptance. She wanted to make them understand that she needed to love the man she married. She wanted to feel, to experience, to revel in life's joys with that one special man. She could never share those feelings with the likes of El Señor Dominguez. She wanted to remind her *padre* of his own youth and the love he had shared with her *madre*.

But Antonia remained silent after her first attempts to dissuade them had failed. She felt outnumbered, drained, and defeated after her *padre* had struck her the night before.

"Since this nasty business of the abduction is settled, and my flower and I shall not be kept apart, might I suggest a dual cause for the upcoming fiesta next week?"

"Of course, El Señor," Doña Maria urged.

"Not only can a business success be celebrated, but the date for our nuptials can also be formally announced and the marriage can take place within two weeks."

"*Sí*, an excellent idea," Don Diego agreed.

Dominguez stood next to Antonia. He was pleased that his way had prevailed so easily. His sources within the Winston hacienda had informed him of the wisdom of refraining from such a tender subject as demanding to know more of his flower's abductors. Several of the members of the household had conveniently overheard the argument between Antonia and her *padre* the night before and reported the incident for a pocketful of coins.

As Dominguez, Don Diego, and Doña Maria huddled over the guest list for the private entertainment inside the hacienda and finalized the wedding plans, Antonia sank into a despair as deep and cold as a glacial lake. She could not believe that her fate had not been changed in the last few days. Everything was proceeding as if nothing had happened to her. Unable to endure the preparations any longer, she excused herself and returned to her room.

It had been decided, her fate sealed. She would become the wife of a man she detested. To her total horror and disbelief, the marriage would take place within a fortnight.

Chapter Sixteen

Michael awoke after noon and summoned the cabin boy to fetch a tray of food and a pitcher of fresh water with which to wash. After a hearty fare of meat, fruits, and cheeses he forced himself to sit at his desk and go over the ship's accounts. Glancing over at his bunk from time to time, his thoughts strayed to Tonia; to him she had become his Tonia. Attempting to force her from his mind, he bent closer over the books. After entering three figures into the wrong column, Michael leaned back in his chair. In frustration he snapped his eyes shut.

"Damn you, Tonia. Damn you to hell. You, with those golder curls, eyes of the sea, and that silken body. You, so capable of reaching into the very depths of passion and inciting a man to behave against his very will. Damn you!"

Thoughts of Antonia continued to plague his mind. Finally, in total exasperation he slammed the ledgers shut. Rising from the desk, he crossed to the door in two strides and swung it open with a bang.

"You! Boy!" he barked at a passing lad. "Fetch Mano and have a gig readied to take us ashore."

Michael was too restless to continue his attempts at ordering the ledgers. He needed to be settled of a score, and he had to erase Antonia from his mind. Until he accomplished those two tasks, he knew he could never leave California's shores.

Mano entered Michael's cabin to find him donning some of his most elegant attire. He cut a handsome figure in his claw hammer coat, tucked shirt with foulard silk cravat, and long cream-colored trousers of nankeen.

As Michael slipped his arms through the sleeves of the double-breasted coat he noticed his companion.

Mano did not speak but bore a questioning look on his countenance. His expression prompted Michael to explain. "I'm glad you're here. I think it's time we paid a visit to the mission. I want to show that friar that we did not meet the sorry end he had predicted for us."

Michael's words brought to mind how the friar had nursed their battered bodies all those years ago. "I will clean up and change."

The Indian left only to return to Michael's cabin after a few short moments dressed in trousers of brown corduroy and a linen shirt topped by a sleeveless waistcoat. Michael grinned at his friend's fancy dress, since it was not Mano's custom to don such finery.

"You smile, my brother, but I, too, have reason to demonstrate to Father Manuel that I am not the savage he feared."

"The good friar meant well. He merely was influenced by his predecessors, who thought that any people who did not adhere to their way of life were uncivilized. He was sure I'd meet my end before I could be saved.

"Well, we will just let him see we're no longer the same penniless men who had to hire out our services for six months to earn passage on the first available ship sailing for England and prove I was not a deserter before I won the *Áureo Princesa*. This time no one is going to beat either one of us within an inch of our lives, or barbecue your hand over a fire."

"We have come far."

"Then shall we go?" Michael opened the door and swung out his arm.

The two finely dressed men went out on deck. After leaving instructions with Thadius, a crusty old sea dog of a chief mate with bushy red hair and mustache, they boarded the gig and were rowed ashore.

Selecting two of the finest animals, they mounted and began a leisurely ride to the Mission San Diego de Alcalá.

As they neared their destination, they could see the mission in the distance and hear the ringing of the five bells at its entrance.

"It is still an impressive sight," remarked Michael.

"That it is."

"The friars were wise to build it high atop a hill above the river valley."

"You know the mission was originally founded nearer the presidio by Fray Junipero Serra, but due to the varying conflicts with the soldiers over their conduct, the site was moved five miles upriver of the fort."

"How well I remember Father Manuel's lessons." Michael grinned. "Let me see . . . the mission system consisted of three parts planned by the Spanish to settle California. Missions were to provide religion for the Indians and teach them useful skills. The other two-thirds of the plan utilized presidios for defense and pueblos to attract colonists."

"Please, my brother. Enough is enough."

The two men laughed.

Drawing closer to their journey's end, they discussed their plans for the upcoming days.

"Do you think it wise to attend the fiesta given by Dominguez—especially after your encounter with the man's betrothed?" Mano questioned. "She could identify you, if she has not already."

Michael's mood darkened at the mention of Antonia in the same breath with Dominguez. "She was responsible for my release from jail. I do not believe she will speak of our time together with Dominguez; besides, I am expected."

"You may be inviting unnecessary danger. Women have been known to have a change of heart, my brother," Mano argued.

"I know. It may be foolhardy to risk so much when it is not required in order to make our plan a success. But it is something I must do. And I don't want to arouse suspicions on the part of Dominguez by not attending the festivities given in my honor."

The second reason Michael could not discuss even with his closest companion: He had to find out more about Señorita Antonia Rafaela Winston y Ortega. He knew he could never rest until he learned the truth about the beautiful señorita. No woman had ever made such an impression on him, and he had to find out why.

126

As Michael's silence stretched, his blue eyes reflected his thoughts and deepened to a husky violet. Mano, not one to miss even the slightest change in his captain, remarked on Michael's countenance.

"Could it be, my brother, that there is more than one reason which draws you to the rancho of Él Señor Dominguez?"

Michael shot Mano a cold, foreboding look before turning back to watch the trail ahead of them.

"And just what do you mean?" The question was asked with a warning tone.

"Perhaps you forget we have been as brothers for many years. There is little that troubles you that I do not feel as well."

Mano's answer took Michael by surprise. He had not considered that Mano knew of his feelings, for he was just beginning to admit the depth of them to himself.

"You are most observant," Michael brooded, "but now is not the time to discuss such matters."

Mano merely nodded. He knew better than to question his captain when he was in such a mood.

The two men completed the remainder of the journey to the mission in thought-filled silence.

The balding friar stood in the warming sun in front of the mission, his hand shielding eyes from the glare. Summer was a time he always enjoyed, for it seemed to bring more of his flock, as well as visitors, to the mission church. As the strangers approached, Father Manuel closed the distance between them.

"My sons, what brings two of our seafarers to my humble church?"

127

"Have we changed so much that you no longer remember two of your lost souls?" Michael questioned, dismounting.

The friar strained his eyes. "You are older, my son, but I remember. And the *indio,* too. What brings you back to our shores? I pray it is not to carry out the revenge you two swore so long ago. But come, let us go inside where we can speak."

He motioned for Michael and Mano to follow him.

"I see there have been many changes," Michael said, noticing the state of disrepair of the mission.

"There have been many changes, indeed. The missions were once a powerful center of life, but after secularization all functions of the mission except as a parish church were taken from us." He sighed, forlorn with the remembrance of the lost status. "Many of my children have drifted so far away from the teachings of the Church. And many of the mission *indios* left to work for the large ranchos and others who were given lands confiscated from the Church."

"El Señor Dominguez," Michael mumbled, clenching his fists into hard balls.

"The man has benefited greatly, and his fortunes have grown immense."

"Not for long," Michael said more to himself than in response to the friar.

A worried look fell over the friar's weary face. "I had hoped that time would have healed your wounds and mellowed your hearts."

"There are some things that time cannot heal," Michael said with an edge to his voice.

"I see. But tell me of all these years of travelling since you left the mission."

As Michael and Mano followed the friar inside

and settled themselves on the crude wooden chairs provided by the aging priest, Michael told of working their way to England, winning his ship, and of the path their lives had taken.

After a few more moments of lament about the Church's fate, Father Manuel tented his fingers. "I fear I must be boring you with my sorrowful tales. And I have not even offered you some refreshment to quench your thirsts. It is a warm day and you have journeyed far." The friar rose.

"Gracias, but we have not come for refreshments and idle chatter."

"Wasn't having your hand held over a fire," his gaze shifted to Mano's gloved fingers and back to Michael, "and the vicious beating you took at the command of El Señor Dominguez enough? He is even more powerful today than at the time of your last encounter. Now, except for the Rancho de los Robles, Dominguez controls most the lands surrounding San Diego. Stay away from him, my sons. You have more to lose than to gain from this vendetta . . ."

Michael and Mano remained stoical while the friar urged the pair to board the ship and leave before more grief was brought down upon them.

Michael glanced at the sundial standing in the rose garden just outside the window. "The hour grows late and we must return to the ship. But if you don't mind, perhaps we shall again return before we sail," Michael said.

"My sons, of course you are always welcome in this humble house of God." Father Manuel laced his arms with Michael and Mano's, and escorted them to their horses. Before the pair mounted, Michael gave the man an offering to repay his past kindnesses toward them. *"Gracias* for your generosity," the friar said with gratitude. *"Vaya con Dios."*

Absorbed in their own thoughts they rode from the mission. They had not ridden far when six rough-looking riders, pushing their animals hard, galloped past them toward the mission. Michael twisted in the saddle to watch them.

Michael furrowed his brows. "Strange."

Mano crossed his wrists on the saddle horn and followed Michael's line of vision. "What is, my brother?"

"Those men. They don't appear the type who would be in a hurry to seek the blessings of the Church on such a warm day." He watched a moment longer while the friar greeted them with open arms, then shrugged and returned his attention to the path leading to the sea. All the while he continued to wonder why those men had been in such an all-fired rush.

Chapter Seventeen

Antonia's days blurred into one constant state of shock. She moved through her daily routine as if in a trance. Even when Doña Maria summoned the seamstress to fit her for the special gown she was to wear to the fiesta, Antonia put up none of her usual resistance.

Worry creased Doña Maria's face as she hurried down the long hall. Craning her neck through the doorway to Don Diego's study, she asked, "May I speak with you, Diego?"

"Of course. Come in," he said and laid his pen down.

"I know you are a busy man, but heavens knows I try." She groaned. "Antonia has not been herself lately. I wonder if we should send for a doctor?"

"You worry too much about Antonia. She will be fine. She has been through a lot lately, that's all," he said. He also had been worried over the girl's strange behavior of late, but he gave further reassurances of Antonia's actions and dismissed Doña Maria.

Don Diego slumped in his chair and rested his head on his hands. Antonia *had* changed. She was not the bright, carefree young girl she had been. "I know what will perk her up," he said to himself, a glimmer of light flickering into his eyes. "Josephina! Josephina! Come in here," he called to the aging servant, who had been with the family since the death of Antonia's maternal grandfather.

"Sí, señor?" Hands lined with age smoothed a silver bun on the back of her head as the old woman entered the study.

"Have my prize stallion readied for Antonia."

"Sí, señor." She nodded dutifully and hurried off to carry out his wishes.

It had been no easy task to have the magnificent Andalusian gray steed shipped from Spain several years ago, considering Mexico's relations with its former mother country. From the first moment Antonia had seen the animal she had wanted to possess it. Don Diego had not even allowed her to ride it, steadfastly insisting the animal was too much for her. Now worried about the girl, he hoped this change of heart would bring back the rosy color to her ashen cheeks.

Antonia, pleased for the opportunity to be away from Doña Maria's watchful eyes, readily accepted the offer. Not bothering to change her attire, she mounted the waiting stallion. Without a word or backward glance, she dug her bare heels into the animal's flanks and rode from the rancho with golden curls flying loose of the kerchief tied around her head.

She felt free atop the mighty stallion, riding as if she had wings. It was a clear, hot day; the sun's heat reflected off the jagged boulders when she left the trail and flew over the golden, rolling hills. She

132

traveled toward the beach, watching a hawk soar overhead and thought of its freedom. It reminded her of Michael — so strong, not bowing to anyone, and capable of crushing its prey within its unyielding talons.

She drove the animal into the surging surf while waves crashed against the shore and receded to return again.

"Oh, how I wish you and I, my fine Lobo," Antonia patted the horse on the neck, "could continue riding until we were far away from here." She sighed thoughtfully and stroked the animal's mane.

Leaving the churning water, she secured the stallion to a nearby shrub and scanned the beach. Not seeing anyone, she stripped off her wet garments and splashed into the cool, briny ocean. The pulsating waves soothed her tense body, and she swam far out, her strokes barely cutting a wake in the emerald green sea.

Exhausted, she returned and collapsed on the warm sand. Staring up at the sky, she spread her arms and allowed the sun to leave its blushing kiss upon her skin.

After a while she closed her eyes, and as the golden warmth seeped into her body, she envisioned Michael Domino kneeling beside her. A gentle breeze caressed her lips, sending reminders of his touch whispering across her flesh. She drew her fingers to her lips and kissed them softly, remembering his inflaming touch so vividly that she bolted upright and hugged her upper arms to lessen a flash of goosebumps.

With a sigh she sank back against the sand and returned to her private thoughts. She was so involved that she did not hear the approaching, gravelly footfalls sink in the sand.

"I must say, you're a tempting sight," Michael said, standing over her with his arms crossed at his chest.

"What are you doing here?" Antonia gasped, and grabbed at her nearby garments in order to cover herself from his burning gaze.

"Is an apology due? I wasn't aware this was a private beach."

"The only apology which needs be delivered is for sneaking up on me. If you were the gentlemen you once professed, you would have considered my state and given me fair warning."

"Oh, but I did consider your state. And as you so aptly put it, I'm no gentleman but merely a lowly sailor." He smiled at her, all the while thanking his lucky stars for Thadius's insistence that he take a walk along the beach to calm his ill temper. She was so divinely beautiful in her efforts to cover her nakedness that he did not know how long he could stand there without touching her.

"Why you . . . you—"

"Princess, please, such venom, tch, tch, tch."

"Will you just leave?" Antonia sighed in exasperation. Her nipples were peaking against her forearms and she could feel a tingling moistness in her loins just being near the man. Why did he have to affect her so? In an attempt to keep him from seeing her discomfort, she swung her back to him. His manly scent surrounded her.

"Such a beautiful back to be shrouded with sand," he observed in a husky voice and began to brush the fine grains from her creamy flesh.

His fingers were electrifying and sent shock waves through her entire being. Antonia tilted her head back and squeezed her eyes shut in an effort to gain control of her emotions before she forgot their last encounter and let nature take its course. Michael's fingers glided to her shoulders and he pulled her back against him until she could feel the rapid thudding of his heart and his growing desire for her.

"Por favor," she groaned, barely able to force the words from her lips.

"Your desire is my command," he murmured, his warm, moist breath caressing the back of her ear.

As Antonia opened her mouth while she still could to plead he leave her, he ended her feeble efforts with his hot, wet lips and tongue. He turned her in his arms, and the blouse she held fell away. With expert fingers he traced a searing path around her bare waist. Her heaving, full breasts pressed against his chest and he held her to him. His need throbbed hard at her belly. Without taking his lips from hers, Michael held her with one hand while the other traced a trail of fire to her thighs. Just as he brushed her most intimate parts with his fingers and moved to caress her inner thigh, Antonia shoved against his chest.

He held fast.

"No," she said into his mouth.

He moved but inches from her. "You want me, my princess. I can feel your body responding, burning for my touch."

"No," she whispered halfheartedly, for what he said was true.

"Yes." He left no room for further debate as he fastened their lips in a grinding, molten kiss.

Her entire body drowned in the sense of him. Every nerve cried out to be satiated. Her own hands deserted her and began a quest of their own. Nimble fingers deftly loosened each button on his shirt. Once he shed his shirt, she snaked them up his chest to curl in the dark hairs.

With precise movements, Michael spread his shirt and settled Antonia back against it. She watched, mesmerized, as he freed himself from his breeches. He was a magnificent sight. Tentatively, she reached out and touched him.

"Oh, yes, Princess. Feel me, too," he groaned, and remained kneeling until he thought he was going to explode.

He positioned himself astride her and leaned over to take a sensitive nipple between his lips. Around and around his tongue flicked while his hands were all over her, squeezing, delving, memorizing every inch of her.

"Tell me you want me, Tonia."

She remained silent, but inside she screamed Yes.

"Tell me," he demanded and caressed her breasts, dropping fiery kisses along her neck.

Totally pliant now, the words slipped out as part of a natural response. "I want you. I do."

Michael's eyes were aflame and he mumbled something she could not fathom against her lips before plunging himself into her.

The thrusting sensations were nearly unbearable, and she met his strokes with an urgency of her own. The liquid heat from the friction of their movements grew, building animal desire between them. The raw pleasure climbed, spiraled, soared, and then shattered into an exquisite, tumultuous ecstasy.

Spent, he collapsed on her, remaining still, continuing to sheath himself inside her. Then he began to nuzzle her neck and toy with her drenched hair.

Regaining control of her senses, Antonia was mortified by how easily he was able to seduce her, aghast at her own craving wantonness. "No more!"

she cried. "You really are nothing but a beast." She pushed him back, toppling him against the sand while she grabbed her clothes and frantically scrambled toward her horse.

"Tonia, wait," Michael called after her, slamming his fist into the sand. "Dammit!" He angrily beat his knuckles against his side, furious at himself for not having better control.

When he had seen it was Antonia on the beach before him all he had meant to do was talk. He had wanted to know why she had changed the story she told the commandant. But just being near her had melted his will like tallow. Why could he not have walked the other way when he discovered it was Antonia, he thought with remorse, watching her mighty steed disappear in the distance.

"Look at you! Where have you been? I sent riders out to fetch you hours ago. If your gown is to be finished before the fiesta, you must make yourself available," Doña Maria scolded, wringing her hands as she shooed Antonia toward her room.

"*Por favor,* leave me be," Antonia beseeched, too exhausted and upset to protest further.

"You will have a hot bath, then you will be ready to be fitted," Doña Maria snapped. "And get out of those filthy clothes," she ordered as she walked to the door. "You look like a peasant."

Later, reclining in the tub, Antonia reluctantly began to lather her body. With the lavender-scented soap, she stretched her shapely leg high in the air. Beginning with her toes, she stroked the bar over her ankle and followed the lines of her calf and up the inside of her thigh.

An uninvited image of Michael Domino's strong hands tenderly caressing her eager body invaded her mind. Just thinking about his muscular body possessing her so completely—physically and emotionally—made her tingle, and she shivered with the remembrance of their passionate encounter. No matter how hard she tried to chase him from her thoughts her body would not allow it.

"Más agua, señorita?" the servant girl asked.

The young girl's voice startled Antonia back to reality. She had forgotten she was not alone.

"No . . . no more water," she said, lowering her leg.

Stepping out of the wooden tub, the servant girl wrapped the large cloth around her and bundled her over to the dressing table.

"I brush now, *sí?*"

"Sí, gracias," Antonia said with a sigh.

After knotting Antonia's hair back from her face, the servant picked up her undergarments.

"You dress now."

Antonia bit her lip to keep from saying anything. It was not the servant's fault she was in her present predicament. She stepped into the lace-fringed pantalettes, similar to the ones she had first seen aboard Michael's ship. Not giving the slightest thought as to where Doña Maria had secured them, her mind drifted back to Michael, and once again she relived the shared moments of rapture which plagued her mind.

"You ready to try dress now?"

"I suppose if I must. Go announce that I am prepared for the fitting," she said glumly.

The girl hurried from the room to inform Doña Maria that Antonia was waiting. Doña Maria immediately picked up part of the seamstress's load.

With authority to her heavy steps, she walked toward Antonia's room, the seamstress trailing behind her.

"Por favor señorita, you stand." The woman set a stool down in the middle of the room and motioned for Antonia to step up onto it.

Antonia slipped into the gown and climbed onto the stool. Nimble fingers took tucks here, let the gown out there, placed additional pins in the bodice, and trimmed the hemline. Antonia was poked, pinched, and turned until she felt like a fowl on a spit and wanted to scream.

"Must it be so snug?" Antonia groaned, barely able to breathe. "And why all this fuss?"

"Hush, girl," Doña Maria commanded. "You must look your best, that is all."

Antonia shrugged, conceding defeat, and did as she was bid. It seemed like an eternity as the two women continued to twist and tug at her. When at last she was allowed to step down, she caught sight of herself in the full-length looking glass. Her lips parted in utter amazement. She was dressed in the most exquisite gown she had ever seen. The heavy white silk overblouse was ruffled with lace around the plunging neckline. Tiny pink embroidered rosettes adorned the edges of the ruffles. She whirled around, sending the billowing skirt swirling about her. The tiny velvet ribbons and matching embroidered rosettes clung to the swinging overskirt of lace.

"Here, dear," Doña Maria said, and gave Antonia a hand mirror. "Turn around and look at those rosettes cascading down the back of the gown. Of course, the night of the fiesta you will wear three slips to increase the fullness of the skirt." Doña Maria stepped back and surveyed her creation.

139

"Without a doubt, you will be the most beautiful girl there. You will dazzle all the men and make them green with envy to be in El Señor's shoes," she said proudly.

Antonia took the pearl-handled mirror and gazed at her reflection. The three rows of pink rosettes beginning at her waist grew in size as they dropped to the floor.

"If only I were wearing this for someone special," Antonia said with a twinge of regret, unable to restrain herself.

"You are! Now, do not be foolish. You are to marry one of the most important men in California," Doña Maria reminded curtly.

"I know." Antonia forced a smile.

"No more of this foolishness. Just remember how lucky you are that El Señor still wants you."

"I shall try," Antonia said, less than convinced.

"You will do more than try! Now, get out of that gown so it can be altered."

Antonia stepped out of the creation and swung around to grab an old doll from her dresser. Clutching the worn figure, she cradled it in her arms and rocked back and forth.

"Why can't you and *padre* understand . . . ?" she began, her voice cracking. "I do not want to make any impression on that man, and I do not consider myself lucky. I can't marry him; I simply do not love him."

Doña Maria, attempting to keep the situation under control, spoke in a soft but deadly determined voice. "We have been over this time and time again. You know the matter is settled. You must stop acting so childish. Put something on and join your *padre* in his study. He wants to discuss the arrangements for the fiesta with you."

Doña Maria would hear no more. Shaking her head, she left Antonia clutching the doll to her breast.

Hot, angry tears streamed down Antonia's cheeks, falling upon the tattered old doll. She threw herself on the large canopy bed and stared, unseeing, into the empty space of youth's shattered dreams.

Chapter Eighteen

Young and old alike arrived for the fiesta in steady streams. They tied their horses to strategically placed hitching posts. Unlike many Californios who displayed little regard for their horses, Dominguez knew Antonia and her *padre* held their animals in high regard. Thus he had stationed a young boy to stand in attendance and provide food and water for the animals while the owners took their pleasure during the three-day fiesta.

Soon the giant *carpa,* a tent Dominguez specially had erected in front of the hacienda, would be filled with palate-tickling morsels. He planned the usual dancing, drinking, and games. Three large, colorful *piñatas* had been constructed by the older children who lived at the rancho, and each evening of the fiesta one hollowed animal form filled with sweets and other prizes would be hung on a hook provided. Children would be blindfolded and take turns striking at the brightly decorated animal shape with a stick until the contents spilled forth and the children scrambled for the prizes.

The first night of the fiesta Dominguez made a brief appearance in the giant tent.

"El Señor!" went up the cries of jubilation from the crowd.

Dominguez held up a silencing hand. "I hope you all are enjoying yourselves."

"Sí, sí, El Señor," the crowd roared.

The enormous man wore a mask of benevolence on his countenance, but underneath his smile was the desire to remove himself from such common peasants. The people who celebrated in the *carpa* were of little use to the man—except for an occasional *puta* or hopeful young señorita. He made his way through the crowd of merrymakers as rapidly as was possible without being obvious.

He turned one last time and waved before entering the hacienda. *"Bastardos,"* he muttered under his breath as he smiled at the crowd.

Once inside the hacienda, his manservant hurried to his side with warmed, damp cloths.

"What took you so long?" Dominguez demanded, anxious to wipe the touch of the peasants from his fat hands.

He smoothed his kinky, gray-streaked hair and straightened his collar. "That should keep the filthy peasants happy." He wiped his hands again, tossed the cloth at the servant, and headed toward the private party underway on the patio.

On the courtyard he stopped to survey the scene before him. Musicians strummed their guitars softly. The hanging lanterns swayed gently in the breeze and cast the muted glow of a rainbow on the flowered walls. The honored guests clustered in small groups discussing politics and life in California. The fine ladies dressed in the latest fashions from Europe were seated on stone benches positioned throughout the spacious courtyard fanning themselves. Swaying, multicolored fans kept time with the music and dotted the enclosure, and sounds of clinking glasses mingled with the merry chords of voices enjoying El Señor Dominguez's hospitality.

Antonia's carriage jolted to a halt in front of the grand hacienda.

"Oh, the inconvenience of travel," Don Diego muttered as he climbed down from the coach and helped the two ladies to alight.

"We shall make quite an entrance." He beamed. "I am escorting the two most beautiful señoritas in all of California," he said, gazing into the eyes of his daughter.

Turning to the older woman, he said, "Doña Maria, you go on ahead. I wish to speak to my child alone for a moment."

Doña Maria cast an annoyed glance at Antonia but did as told.

"Antonia, my child . . ." Don Diego began, looking down at Antonia, "I know how you feel. But what has been done is for your own good. Someday you will thank me. Now remember—you are a Winston. And the Winstons hold their heads high."

"*Sí, padre.*" Antonia forced a smile, wanting to say more but remaining silent as she took his arm and entered the hacienda.

When the pair walked through the double doors and out onto the courtyard, all conversation ceased. Eyes turned to her.

"She is a vision to behold," remarked one Californio, who could not take his eyes from her. "There is not another señorita present who can come near the beauty of Antonia Rafaela Winston y Ortega."

Catching sight of her and pleased with his guests' awe of his lovely flower, Dominguez immediately left his guests to join his *novia*.

He took her slender hand and caressed it lightly with his lips.

"My precious flower, your beauty is truly unequaled." Dominguez tore his eyes from Antonia to greet her *padre*. "Don Diego, you must be most proud this night. Your daughter is without equal."

"*Sí*, Antonia has and will continue to make her *padre* proud of the Winston heritage," Don Diego said. "Now, if you will excuse me, I shall see that Doña Maria hears her efforts with Antonia have met with your praise."

Dominguez nodded. The old fool had no idea how much was due Doña Maria for her help with Antonia! He waited until Don Diego was a respectable distance away, then tightened his fingers around Antonia's arm.

"Come, I want you by my side so I can display you properly."

Antonia bit her lower lip as he led her toward a group of men. He made her feel as if she were a possession, and she had to force herself to remember her *padre*'s advice. Trying to keep in mind that she was a Winston and would make her *padre* proud, Antonia raised her head high and took a deep breath. She stopped to buoy her resolve just before they reached the nearest group.

Dominguez turned to her and whispered in her

ear. "My dear, these are our most honored guests. I want you to meet them first."

"*Our* guests?" she asked, feeling her skin crawl from his heavy, booze-scented breath on her neck.

"Why, my flower, he explained as he leaned over to kiss her on the forehead, "very soon this will be your home, too. I want you to begin feeling as if you are the señora of this humble house. Now smile."

He led her to his guests.

"Governor Figueroa, you remember Señorita Antonia Rafaela Winston y Ortega?"

"Of course," the governor replied, taking Antonia's hand and dropping a kiss upon it. "I could never forget the daughter of my dear *amigo*. You are so very lovely, my dear. By the way, where is that *padre* of yours?"

"You are very kind, Governor—"

"You will find Don Diego is enjoying my hospitality, Governor Figueroa," put in Dominguez.

"I think I shall join him and do likewise. Antonia, I hope you will save a dance for me later."

"Of course. The people of California are most fortunate, indeed, to have a man such as yourself in the position of leadership." She lowered her head when she finished speaking but watched from beneath her thick, ebony lashes.

"You are wise beyond your years, my dear." He narrowed his eyes. "I understand congratulations are in order."

"I am a lucky man."

"*Sí*, you are. Well, until later . . ." He gave a nod and sauntered off to join the others.

Dominguez stared after the governor until a matron of ample proportions furiously fanning herself took Dominguez by the arm. "I hear you have an important announcement to make this evening. Such a pity my Rosa was abroad for several years," Señora Pica said, glaring at Antonia as if she were a vile snake.

"*Sí*, it is." Antonia smiled sweetly. She wanted to say the woman's daughter could have her *novio* gladly. Over the years Señora Pica had tried hard enough to secure an important match for Rosa.

As Dominguez introduced Antonia to the remainder of the group, the woman maintained her clutching grasp.

"If you will all please excuse us, the music beckons and I am most anxious to dance with my precious flower."

"Oh, El Señor, I must have you greet my Rosa. She has grown much and blossomed during the last three years. She dances with the grace of a bird in flight. Now, where is that girl?" The woman hung on, anxiously scanning the courtyard.

"Señora Pica, I shall be honored, but now if you will excuse us . . ." Dominguez pried her grip from his arm, restraining himself from breaking the old hag's fingers.

When Antonia was ushered out to the dance floor, the music stopped and a special waltz began. All eyes turned to watch the two for a moment before other couples joined in and the courtyard came alive with flowing skirts gliding about the floor.

Dominguez glanced at the other couples about them. The waltz was a true sign of gentility. Only the *gente de razón* danced the waltz. Outside the hacienda within the giant *carpa,* the music and dancers were more lively.

147

* * *

Rosa loosened the pins from her thick black hair. She swung her hips and clapped her hands, sending her ebony tresses tumbling freely down her back. She dangled the mass of curls over her face and back again, throwing her head to the spirited rhythm. Men joined in the dancing around her. The dark beauty knew she could have her pick of men this night. But she had her black eyes set on the tall, handsome sea captain watching her from the end of the refreshment table.

The dark Rosa moved her body invitingly over to the man. Her eyes seductively traveled over the length of his lean body.

Michael had slipped out of the staid celebration inside the hacienda to join his crew shortly after making an appearance earlier to satisfy his host and now smiled at the señorita. He raised his glass in her direction.

Rosa stopped dancing, raised her brows, and held out a brown hand to the tall sea captain. "Señor, would you offer a lady with much thirst a drink?"

"The name is Captain Michael Domino, señorita," Michael said, taking a glass of spirits off the table and handing it to the pouting señorita.

"And I am Rosa." She raised the glass to her ruby red lips. As she sipped the drink, her eyes never once left him. "Capitán, it is so warm in here, would you mind escorting a lady out into the cooling air?"

Michael offered his arm. As they disappeared into the night, he winked at Mano.

For over an hour Antonia had been charming to all the guests. She had flattered the envious women; she had blushed at all the compliments and attentions of the men; she had spent a considerable amount of time dodging awkward steps on the dance floor with partners anxious to demonstrate their knowledge of the waltz. Pleading the need to rest for a moment, Antonia escaped to a table to join her *padre*, a number of other prominent Californios, and, to her dismay, her *novio* and the matronly Señora Pica.

Over the other voices at the table, the señora's voice boomed forth impatiently. "At last. Rosa, come over here."

A slightly disheveled Rosa hooked her arm with her handsome companion's and complied with her *madre*'s directive.

"El Señor, this is my Rosa," the señora said proudly.

The gentlemen rose from their seats and the greetings began. Antonia glanced up in anticipation of concluding yet another introduction, and was surprised to see the tall, dark beauty dressed in crimson silk standing before her; her memory of Rosa was of a gangly girl. But Antonia's surprise was unequaled when she caught sight of Michael standing with his arm casually around Rosa's waist.

Antonia started. Attempting to recover from her shock at seeing Michael, she rose from her seat, spilling the drink which had just been set in front of her. She bent to mop up the spill.

"My flower, the servants will clean that up." Dominguez cast her a look of disapproval, slipped his heavy arm around her, and pulled her tightly against him. "I want you to meet one of my new business associates.

"Capitán Michael Domino, may I introduce to you a very special lady, Señorita Antonia Rafaela Winston y Ortega—my bride-to-be."

Michael acted as if he were meeting Antonia for the first time. He took her trembling hand in his and squeezed her slender fingers together tightly, raising her hand to meet his lips. While his lips caressed her hand, his piercing blue eyes never left her silently pleading amber-green ones.

"Señorita Winston, I am honored. I've heard much about you from your *novio*." His eyes mocked her as he spoke.

"Capitán Domino, is it? You are too kind." Antonia, attempting nonchalance, freed her aching hand from his grasp.

For a fleeting moment Dominguez thought he detected something unusual about the introduction. He put the thought from his mind when Rosa stepped closer to the captain and pressed her ample bosom against his arm. The sight caused Dominguez to picture the dark señorita unclothed, squirming against his riding whip. He made a mental note to invite the young woman and her *madre* to be his houseguests.

A servant entered the courtyard and announced the evening's formal fare was being served in the large dining room. Specially selected thick slices of beef cut from the hindquarter and cooked to perfection on a grill just outside the kitchen lay on each plate next to large tender shellfish caught off the coast in traps. Rice, fresh vegetables, and tortillas awaited service, as well as a vintage wine imported from France. After the meal, a sweet, coffee-flavored liqueur had been readied to be served in small crystal-stemmed goblets.

As the guests strolled toward the massive dining room, a pouting Rosa tugged on Michael's arm. "I have other things on my mind than food," she whispered. "Let us be done with the meal without delay."

Lagging behind the others were Dominguez and Antonia.

"You appear a little pale. Are you feeling ill, my flower?" Dominguez asked in a huff that she would dare to be anything but the perfect hostess.

"I am fine. It is merely all the excitement; I have not eaten all day," she answered too quickly.

"Then your color should return after taking a little nourishment."

She forced a smile. *"Sí."*

"Shall we then join the others?"

A little nourishment was all Antonia did take. Seated across from Michael during dinner, she was unable to force down more than a bite or two. Antonia was grateful that Dominguez was too busily engaged in conversation with the governor to notice the silent exchange taking place between his *novia* and the man she had just learned was Dominguez's business associate.

"Señorita Winston, you appear so young to become the matron of such a vast and powerful rancho such as this." The piercing look of disgust Michael shot her as they spoke did not waver.

Antonia attempted to ignore his gaze, but her heart was pounding so loud she feared her *padre*, seated next to her, could hear. She could feel the friction sparking across the table. Although their conversation was that of polite strangers, she noted an underlying sarcasm in his voice. Who was he to behave in such a way? She was the injured party; the one foolish enough to give herself to him — eagerly, no less.

"*Sí*, Capitán Domino, I do appear to be young. But you, I am certain, know that appearances can be deceiving."

He ignored her remark and said, "I confess, I must congratulate El Señor Dominguez on his eye for beauty. You will make a most desirable bride."

"*Gracias*," she responded demurely, although she wanted to strangle him.

Michael nodded and lifted his glass. "Oh, it is I who should have thanked you."

He narrowed his eyes ever so slightly over the rim of his goblet. Inside he was seething. It continued to gnaw at him when he pictured her with Dominguez. As he watched her, he kept trying to convince himself that she meant nothing to him, but his anger did not abate.

"*Cara mía*." Rosa pouted. She placed her brown fingers on Michael's thigh and leaned close to him to whisper in his ear. "Why do not we leave this stuffy place and take another stroll in the moonlight?"

Rosa had been watching the exchange with growing disdain and questions about the captain and Antonia. Two strangers did not act as they were; somehow they had to have known each other before tonight. The captain was easily the most handsome man at the fiesta, and she was determined to have him for herself — at least while he was in San Diego. Her brow quirked at the thought of learning more of him and Antonia. The information could be of use if she, instead of the Winston bitch, were to become the señora of the vast rancho. Her lips twisted into a calculating grin.

"Rosa, as one of the honored guests, it would be impolite to leave the table before the others. What would our gracious hostess think?" Michael cast Antonia a mocking smirk as he spoke.

"Por favor, Capitán Domino . . ." Antonia, using her most innocent smile, spoke sweetly. "Do not think you must remain on my account. I am certain your host understands that a man such as yourself is not accustomed to our way of life."

Although anyone else overhearing the conversation would consider Antonia's response most generous, Michael knew differently. She had implied, quite adroitly, that he was no gentleman. He had all he could do to restrain himself. He wanted to leap across the table and demonstrate with a kiss to her sensuously full mouth what being less than a gentleman meant. Instead, he maintained an indifferent facade.

"You're most gracious, Señorita Winston. Since you don't mind, we'll take our leave. I hope we shall have the pleasure of seeing you later during the fiesta."

After stopping to speak for a brief moment to Dominguez, Michael casually strolled from the dining table with Rosa on his arm.

Don Diego turned to his daughter. "Antonia, you are rapidly becoming quite a gracious hostess. As an old sea dog myself, I'm certain the captain appreciated the opportunity to be alone with such a lovely Spanish señorita. And one so willing, too," he observed in a low voice.

Antonia reddened. Her *padre* had noticed how Rosa had hung all over Michael. What made matters worse was the way Michael blatantly flaunted Rosa in front of her. Antonia felt a stab of jealousy flare in her heart and wondered whether her *tía* was not right after all when she had counseled her on the unimportance of love.

Noticing his daughter's expression, Don Diego said, "Do not let my words embarrass you, child, but be aware that many women as well as men lust for the taste of the flesh. A man as handsome and virile as Captain Domino undoubtedly read the desires of such an eager señorita. Do not judge him too harshly. After all, he is human."

"I wonder," she mumbled under her breath, and turned her attention back to pushing her dinner around her plate.

Michael was furious with Antonia. He was certain she didn't care for Dominguez, and she had every right to be angry at him for how he had accused her of trying to trick him. But to play the part of a society bitch pricked him deeply. He wanted to go back inside and yank her off her silver pedestal. But he had an important mission to accomplish tonight, and Rosa would provide the perfect cover.

His plans were proceeding even more smoothly than he had anticipated. He escorted Rosa out of the enclosed courtyard and around the giant tent. As they strolled past the Indian, Michael arched his brow; Mano returned a knowing smile.

The Indian would allow his captain an hour, then head for his room.

Chapter Nineteen

Once inside the spacious guest room at the far end of the hacienda, Rosa slipped out of her shoes. Pulling her skirts up, she plopped down on Michael's bed, giving him a clear view of the dark mound at the top of her thighs.

"Do you see anything of interest to you, Señor Capitán?" she purred, and let her long-nailed fingers slide up her legs and caress her flesh. "You like, *sí?*"

Michael stood by a table and watched her. She was so obvious it nearly bored him to tears, but she provided the perfect cover; he would amuse himself with her little game.

"You're a woman in a class by yourself."

Michael sighed to himself. Rosa held absolutely no interest for him except perhaps to try to erase the persistent memories of the time he had spent with Antonia. There was no comparison between the two women. Antonia had been an innocent whose passion had been spontaneous and giving.

Rosa could hardly be considered more than a scheming, common *puta*.

"Fix a lady a drink, then come"—she patted the bed—"and join Rosa."

He poured two generous glasses of spirits, slipping a sleeping potion into Rosa's glass. He moved to her side and handed her the drugged wine.

"To thirsts quenched."

"Rosa has many thirsts, Señor Capitán." She drank greedily, then licked her lips.

Michael cocked a brow. "As do we all."

"Do you not want to kiss Rosa?" she asked in a throaty voice. She had barely finished her words when the glass slipped from her fingers, and she slid into a silent heap.

Michael looked at the sleeping señorita and pulled the coverlet up over her.

"Are you ready, my brother?" Mano asked, climbing in through the window.

"As soon as I change. I don't dare ride out to the range and affix false brands to Dominguez's cattle in this finery.

"Think of it! Our work tonight should put an end to Dominguez's thievery against his neighbors as well as serve our purpose."

"It is the perfect plan to repay a debt long overdue," Michael added.

"And help the surrounding *rancheros* at the same time."

"Your interests have broadened, my brother. It would not have anything to do with the beautiful señorita, would it?"

"You know me too well," Michael returned. "Let's hurry."

Michael gave one last glance at Rosa. Not more

156

than two fortnights before, he would not have passed up the opportunity to take such a sensual woman. He frowned. He was interested in only one woman now, and he had turned her away. "Damned witch!" he muttered and silently left the hacienda.

Once back in his room, Michael carefully stored the irons they had procured from Dominguez's private rooms, while Mano went to check on the dark beauty. The Indian removed the coverlet from the sleeping Rosa. She had turned over on her stomach and rested peacefully, her head on her arm. Her mane of black curls spread around her head and down over her back like a cascading waterfall.

"She continues to slumber peacefully." Mano leaned over the bed and stroked Rosa's soft back and along the sides of her full breasts. She did not stir. He turned to his captain, a telling smile adorning his lips. "I shall see to the señorita while you rejoin the other guests."

On his way out, Michael cast a knowing nod over his shoulder. "No doubt she will no longer thirst by the time I return."

Returning to the fiesta under the guise of replenishing his empty bottle, Michael engaged Dominguez in conversation. "El Señor . . . hic . . . this is quite a celebration . . . hic."

Antonia made an inaudible but apparently disgruntled remark and cast him a disapproving glance, which he returned with a mocking, lopsided smile.

Michael's obviously intoxicated state flustered Antonia, and made her want to escape his presence

157

for fear he would slip and mention their relationship.

"If you gentleman will excuse me, I should see if the guests have everything they need," she said, unable to endure another moment of his awkward antics.

She hurried off away from Michael to join another group at the farthest corner.

"One would think, if my *novia* knew you better, she was angry with you, Capitán Domino." Dominguez looked Michael penetratingly straight into his eyes while he chuckled.

Sensing the man's thoughts, Michael sought to dispel them by swaying on his feet and pretending to focus spirit-blurred vision. "I'm afraid your Señorita Winston doesn't approve of my lifestyle . . . hic."

Michael was careful to avoid Antonia for the remainder of the time he spent in the courtyard. His plan was progressing too well to jeopardize it by provoking the young señorita into a careless act.

Antonia, too, knew that putting distance between herself and the captain was the wisest course to take, but noticing that he was purposely avoiding her only served to heighten her annoyance.

Michael glanced at the clock next to him. He had been at the fiesta for an hour and a half playing the drunken fool. He decided to make a grand exit. It would serve to further dispel any question Dominguez might have and help with his plans for the next evening.

Michael clumsily gained his feet and promptly spilled his drink. He then grabbed a passing servant's arm and removed a bottle of spirits from the man's hand. The watching guests attempted to sup-

158

press their laughter. But when Michael stepped on Doña Maria's skirt, causing a loud ripping noise to reverberate about the room, sounds of laughter and raised brows filled the air.

Antonia smiled behind her fan when Doña Maria turned to gasp her apparent horror at the newly altered gown. "Clumsy, drunken oaf!"

"Forgive me, señora . . . hic . . . hic. Here, let me assist you," Michael apologized profusely and grabbed at the hem of her skirt.

She slapped his hands away from her torn gown. "Get away from me, you disgusting drunk. And it is 'señorita' not 'señora.' "

Antonia could not help herself. A girlish giggle erupted from her lips, and she looked to each side of her, fearing she had been caught in such an unladylike display.

Michael bowed to the furious Doña Maria and stumbled up the stairs, leaving a house filled with amused guests.

When he was out of sight he dropped the guise and returned to his room to find Mano sitting on the edge of the bed buttoning his shirt. Rosa continued to slumber soundly. Mano lifted the coverlet and displayed a lover's mark high on the dark señorita's right bosom.

"I'm afraid Rosa will have to wear a gown with a high neckline tomorrow night or she'll have some explaining to do to that witch of a mother," Michael said, chuckling.

"It is so," Mano said dryly. "Although she will not be able to recall how she has just spent the night, the mark will leave no doubt in her mind that she had a most pleasurable evening."

After the Indian was gone, Michael poured himself a glass of spirits. He enjoyed the burgundy-colored liquid, then removed his clothes and joined the sleeping señorita on the bed.

Chapter Twenty

By the time Rosa awoke the next morning, the captain was gone. She sat up and rubbed the sleep from her eyes. Her head throbbed and her entire body ached. She could not remember a thing that had happened after she finished the drink the captain had given her. Standing in front of the mirror gave her some idea. A large violet love bite adorned her right bosom. Angrily she ran her brown fingers over the oblong mark.

"Damn him, how will I ever explain this?" she spat at her reflection, furious that she would be unable to wear the low-cut gown planned for the evening.

After she read the note the captain had left, she was livid over its implication. Neatly concealed within the folded paper, four coins tumbled to the floor when she'd opened it. He had thanked her for a memorable evening and suggested that they meet again some time when his need arose.

"You will be sorry you ever met me, Capitán

Domino," she swore to herself.

She threw her gown on, straightened her snarled tresses, and stormed toward the door. Flinging open the door, she paused, slowly turned, and greedily retrieved the coins. She held them tightly within her hand and raised her chin high to stalk from the room.

The Winstons and Doña Maria had remained at the rancho at Dominguez's insistence; he had even sent a messenger to Antonia's home and had her clothes packed and delivered to her. Antonia had just left her room and was making her way down the long, winding hallway when Doña Maria's shrill voice sounded from the library. The woman was obviously upset about something. She kept referring to last night's fiesta and a special gown. Antonia could not understand the entire conversation but decided her *tía* must be upset over her own torn garment.

She hesitated but then joined Dominguez and Doña Maria. When she entered the book-filled room, an awkward silence descended over its occupants like a heavy, dampened shroud. The uneasy stillness was not broken until Don Diego strolled in with the governor. The conversation quickly turned to the ongoing fiesta.

Don Diego walked over to Antonia and kissed her on the cheek. "My child, I trust you rested well. Have you partaken of the delicious buffet in the courtyard yet?"

Antonia smiled tenderly at her *padre*. "I was just about to join the others on the patio. Will anyone else be joining me?" She glanced around the room.

When Antonia received a negative response, she

excused herself and strolled out onto the sunny courtyard.

"Your daughter is truly the most lovely young señorita in all of California." The governor patted the proud *padre* on the back.

"*Sí*, she reminds me very much of her *madre*," Don Diego wistfully replied.

"Rafaela would have been proud of her, as I know you are. She has the fire of an Ortega," Governor Figueroa observed.

"She certainly has," grumbled Doña Maria.

"If you will excuse me, I must attempt to ready another gown for Antonia to wear tonight," Doña Maria stated fretfully, rubbing her hands.

"*Sí*, what happened last night?" Don Diego directed his question toward a sullen Dominguez. "I thought . . ." He stopped to clear his throat in mid-sentence, remembering himself.

"Señores and Doña Maria, I pray I am not intruding upon a private discussion," the governor queried, noting the uneasiness surrounding them all of a sudden.

"Of course not, Governor," Dominguez reassured him, then called toward a receding Doña Maria. "Doña Maria, summon the seamstresses and tell them your needs. The gown will be ready for the evening's entertainment," he said pointedly.

Doña Maria left the library and sent an urgent message to the head seamstress. The woman arrived and was given instructions. When the question of fabrics was broached, Doña Maria decided to accompany the woman to her workroom. In the room behind the kitchen were bolts of cloth stacked to the ceiling. Threads and needles were neatly organized, and every imaginable decoration and accessory filled row after row of the huge

163

room.

She surveyed the materials closely, and then ordered a gown sewn from white brocade with gold embroidery, and ribbons similar in design to the one Antonia had worn the previous evening.

The seamstress sighed as she watched the large woman add more decorations to the stack. Resigned to the task before her, she called in her entire staff of workers. The intricately detailed gown had to be finished by late afternoon.

Late in the afternoon a young friar of small stature who said he was visiting Father Manuel arrived at the hacienda. He was immediately ushered into the library.

"Excuse me, El Señor," the servant interrupted in a choked voice. "Your bath is ready." The servant quickly excused himself to await Dominguez in his private rooms.

"*Por favor,* remain, Friar, and enjoy the festivities. We shall speak later."

After bathing, Dominguez swore as he personally selected his attire for the evening. He had worn his most fashionable costume the night before. If he had been informed of the friar's illness earlier, he would have kept the clothing for the upcoming evening.

After failing to satisfy El Señor with his selections, the harried servant at last managed to assemble a suitable wardrobe. On Dominguez's bed lay a brown cutaway coat, fawn waistcoat, spotted fawn cravat, and white trousers with pink-striped stockings.

Dominguez removed the small box he had slipped into his pocket the night before. Opening the lid, an evil glint captured his eyes. "At last, my treasure, I shall be able to deliver you." He tucked it into his cutaway coat. Hurriedly, he smoothed his hair. There was not time to spend preening. He had important matters to discuss with the friar prior to the evening's merriment.

Doña Maria finished dressing. She felt comfortable in the loose cream gown with its open lacework overlay. Fashion had not been one of her concerns for over ten years.

The seamstress had delivered Antonia's gown for her inspection only moments before. She checked each stitch, then carried the creation to Antonia's room. "Here, I have brought your gown," Doña Maria announced.

"I do not understand. What is wrong with the gown I brought with me?" Antonia questioned.

"Nothing. We just want you to dazzle everyone again tonight," she said, dismissing Antonia's concern. "Now, put it on."

Still puzzled, Antonia relented and was helped into the flowing skirts.

"You are so lovely. It is almost as if it were made just for you," Doña Maria chirped, careful not to mention the special pains taken to design the gown for Antonia.

"But I do not understand. Where did this gown come from? And why—"

"El Señor wanted his future bride to be especially beautiful when he announces the date of your wedding this evening. Now, no more talk. Set yourself down and let me style those curls."

When the older woman was finished, Antonia's curls were adorned with pearl ropes and golden ribbons. Over her coiffure Doña Maria had placed a pearl comb and traditional white lace mantilla.

"You will dazzle them again tonight," Doña Maria pronounced. "Come, we must not keep El Señor waiting."

Michael had just left his room and was about to join the fiesta when Antonia appeared down the hallway. He ceased his steps and stood staring at the vision before him. A strange twinge stabbed at his heart.

"You're so beautiful," he grumbled as he watched her graceful movements, which caused her long golden curls to sway tantalizingly with each step.

Doña Maria continued to fuss with Antonia's gown as she glided along. Antonia felt overwhelmed and distraught at such unwanted attention and stepped up her pace, hoping to free herself from the doting *tía*. In her haste, she failed to notice Michael standing in front of her.

He opened his arms in anticipation.

"Oh!" Antonia was sorely surprised as his arms encircled her.

"We really must stop meeting like this." He chuckled at his fortune.

For a moment Antonia acquiesced, then, recovering, pushed herself from his embrace. Staring at him with fire in her eyes, she snapped, "Oh, if only I would have never met you I would not be in this miserable predicament now."

"I beg your pardon, Señorita Winston?"

"You . . . you . . . Oh, what is the use," Antonia said, exasperated and uneasy to be so near Michael. *"Por favor,* now just step aside and allow me to pass." Her voice cracked with hidden emotion and she felt goosebumps rise on her arms.

"Capitán Domino, if you will excuse us, we must hurry," Doña Maria interceded, protectively holding her skirts out of his way.

"I know my actions last night were inexcusable,

but I hope you will see your way clear to forgive me, dear lady. I'll replace your damaged gown, of course."

Doña Maria blushed like a schoolgirl and her attitude toward Michael softened. "I accept your apology, *capitán*. And I apologize for Antonia. She is nervous and still has much to learn before she takes her place as wife to such an important man as is El Señor."

Michael winked at Antonia. "So I have noticed."

Antonia bristled.

"Por favor, allow me." Michael held out both arms. "I shall be most honored if you would allow me to escort the two most lovely ladies in all of California to the fiesta."

"Of course, *capitán,*" Doña Maria said, falling victim to his charm. She took his proffered arm and cast an encouraging nod toward Antonia. Antonia hesitantly forced a smile and obliged her *tía.*

Electrifying bolts shot through Antonia when her fingers touched his arm, and her pulse raced. As they neared the library, a servant handed Doña Maria a message from El Señor. She excused herself and hurried off, leaving Michael and Antonia to proceed without her.

"We could forego the fiesta and run away together, Princess," Michael teased, masking the fire in his eyes.

Antonia was not amused. "I already tried that. I am afraid it does not work."

"Perhaps you didn't have the right companion along with you. What happened?"

"I met you."

"Touché, Princess." Michael kept his voice light, although he ached inside to sweep her up into his arms and spirit her away. "It's said we learn from our mistakes. Why not do it right this time?"

"If the thought ever enters my mind again, I can assure you, Capitán Domino, I shall not make the mistake of confiding in one of El Señor Dominguez's business associates."

"You wound me." He waited for a reply, but she remained silent, glaring at him. "Since you seem determined to ruin such a beautiful evening, shall we join the others?"

Entering the courtyard, whispers buzzed about the guests, for the captain and señorita made a most handsome couple. One señora was heard by Antonia to comment that they made the perfect pair, like two matching pieces of a puzzle.

"Por favor, capitán, I must join the others before there is more talk." Feeling awkwardly like a laboratory specimen, Antonia quickly disengaged herself and joined the milling guests.

Michael let her go without further protest, but his eyes followed her.

Chapter Twenty-one

Michael's plan was continuing to progress smoothly. The second night of the fiesta he mingled among the guests pretending to drink himself into the part he was to play later that night. If everyone thought he was drunk he'd never be suspected of taking Dominguez's irons and then replacing them where they would could conveniently be found thereby providing proof of Dominguez's guilt. Actually, a large potted plant near the double doors was the unfortunate recipient of the strong liquid. Michael acted the sotted buffoon with practiced precision. He spilled his drinks and spoke in a loud voice, slurring his words.

"Señorita Winston, here you are . . . hic . . . hic," Michael said, hiccupping for effect. "And Señorita Rosa, you look"—his gaze slid to the high neck of her gown and he grinned, thinking of the love bite she was forced to cover up—". . . hic, *refreshing* in that gown."

"Swine!" she hissed, and stomped off to wind

herself around Dominguez's arm.

"What did I say ... hic ... ?" he asked innocently, then slapped his fingers to his lips. "Excuse me. It must be something I ate."

"Or drank," snapped Antonia, uneasily fingering her glass. People had already begun to whisper when they saw Michael and her together, and now Antonia feared again that in his present state Michael might slip and divulge their involvement.

He gave her a crooked grin. "Are you saying that I have had too much to drink?" He tottered to an aging matron standing at the far end of the group with whom Antonia was mingling. "You don't think that, do you ... hic?"

"I never!" the woman returned, scandalized, and moved off.

"Maybe you should sometime," he retorted for Antonia's benefit.

"Perhaps you should sit down, *capitán*," Antonia suggested, her color heightening.

"You don't think I'm capable of remaining on my feet, do you? The lady probably doesn't think I could ... dance ... hic ... either ... hic ... hic," he said to the cluster of guests obviously enjoying his performance. "Therefore, the least I can do is dance with the lady and demonstrate that I'm perfectly sober ... hic ... hic," he announced.

"I do not think —" Antonia began.

"That's exactly what I have been telling you." In one swoop Michael gathered Antonia into his arms and whisked her out on the floor before she could decline to dance with him.

Unable to disengage herself politely without drawing undue attention, Antonia was subjected to a most torturous five minutes on the dance floor.

170

Michael was enjoying every moment, stumbling his way through a waltz with a terribly embarrassed and anxious Antonia.

Even as he took pleasure in taunting her for being promised to Dominguez, he longed to draw her into his embrace, hold her, and tell her all he was feeling—that she could not marry the likes of Dominguez; that he knew she felt something for him, and he in turn felt the twinges of deeper feelings for her.

He cared for her spirit, her pride, her determination, even her strong will and stubborn temper. With the realization finally hitting him with its full impact, Michael pulled her closer to him and gently stroked her back as they glided about the floor.

Antonia had been embarrassed and angered by his actions, but his sudden change of demeanor left her strangely puzzled. Her heart skipped a beat as his fingers caressed her back, and she found herself wishing they were in a less public position.

She had so many questions which needed answers, and a mixture of feelings she desperately wanted to explore and clarify with him. Most of all, she wanted to hold herself tightly to him and feel his body against hers; to wash away everything that had recently happened; to put Rosa and her *novio* in their past and only build for the future. It was just a dream—a silly dream left over from childhood—and she was merely imagining and translating her desires to him. She had to remember he was drunk and bent on making a spectacle of her. At the last thought Antonia stiffened.

At the music's end, feeling silent pangs of regret, Michael returned to his guise of drunkenness. He

awkwardly escorted her back to a watchful Dominguez and Rosa while the guests delighted in the
display, only adding to Antonia's dismay and his
own sorrow that he had subjected her to such un-
mitigated embarrassment.

"Thank you for the dance. You're a most gracious hostess . . . hic." His words slurred. "A most
gracious hostess, indeed. And if I might add . . ."
he began, forced to play out the game he had
started.

Antonia, fearing the worst, quickly interrupted.
"Capitán Domino, *gracias,* you have been kind
enough already."

"No, Señorita Winston, we know I'm anything
but kind." Michael forced a laugh, hating himself
for causing her to be so ill at ease.

"El Señor, if you will excuse me, I must make an
appearance outside . . . hic. Perhaps you'll join me
for the gaiety?"

The enormous man chuckled at what to him was
the captain's obvious lack of gentility. He also had
noted his *novia*'s apparent discomfort and distaste
for the captain, prompting his response. "Perhaps I
shall join you later. I see Governor Figueroa and
Don Diego together, and there are important matters I must discuss with them." Rosa pouted and
tugged on his arm. "Of course, I promised Señorita
Rosa a dance as well." He gave her hand a conde-
scending pat. "But if you would be so kind as to
escort Señorita Winston, capitán, I would be most
appreciative." He turned to Antonia. "I know you
have been wanting to visit the *carpa,* and I am
certain Capitán Domino would provide an ideal escort—other than myself of course. Now, go along
and enjoy yourselves."

"But—" Antonia started to protest.

"Now, no buts. I shall join you later, my flower," Dominguez ordered indulgently.

"I'll take good care of her," Michael said, fighting to maintain the semblance of an innocuous appearance.

"I do not need an escort to watch over me," Antonia protested.

"I must insist. You know how these peasants can get when they have no one to keep them in line. There will be no further discussion. The subject is closed," Dominguez insisted.

Dominguez placed Antonia's arm on Michael's. He patted the captain on the back and bid him to take good care of his *novia*. He then excused himself and lumbered toward the dance floor with a beaming Rosa, leaving Michael and Antonia standing alone together.

"Tonia . . ." Michael's blue eyes were suddenly cold sober and they seemed to pierce Antonia's very soul. "It appears we have your beloved's blessing to enjoy ourselves. And I must offer you my protection."

"I do not need your protection, *capitán*. Unless it is protection from you."

He did not smile. The idea of anyone else possessing her gnawed at him, and he continued to glare at her. "You do know how 'peasants' can get when there is no one to watch over them."

"Only to the extent of El Señor's remark," she retorted. "It is much more likely that a humble sea captain such as you have proved yourself to be is in need of a watchdog."

He ignored her reference to him as being of low birth and her accusation that he had taken advantage of her.

"I warn you, I am prepared to stand here at your side as long as it takes to convince you."

"*Por favor, capitán,* we are becoming even more of a spectacle standing here alone for so long," she beseeched, ignoring his intention to remain at her side.

"Then, by all means, allow me," he said, offering his lead.

Antonia did not take her eyes from him. She felt as if she wanted to run, but was forced to follow his lead.

Sensing the tension between them heighten under too many questioning eyes, Michael led her toward the double doors.

Antonia hesitated.

"Will you come with me, or do you want a scene in front of your guests?" he asked under his breath.

"No, of course not."

"Well then, smile and pretend you are enjoying my company."

Antonia smiled sweetly and whispered through clenched teeth. "Does this meet with your approval?"

"You're most beautiful even when you force a smile," he answered as if he were making polite conversation.

Leaving the hacienda, they met Commandant Velasco outfitted in full dress uniform.

"*Buenas noches,* Señorita Winston." He tipped his hat and showed no outward sign he was surprised by the couple. "Capitán Domino." The wink cast in Michael's direction was unmistakable.

"The entrance is over there." Antonia pointed in

the opposite direction from which they were walking. *"Por favor,* we must . . ." She tugged at his arm, fearing they might be observed by one of the guests.

Michael tightened his grasp and continued to stroll toward a large cluster of oak trees. "Tonia, I must speak with you."

After hearing him call her Tonia, she kept pace alongside him without another word of protest. Once out of view of the merrymakers and into the silvery shadows cast by the moonlight, he placed his hands around her waist and lifted her onto a flat boulder.

Sitting next to her, he took her trembling hand into his. With his other hand he slowly lifted her chin until their eyes locked in silent searching.

He stroked her cheek tenderly and whispered, "Tonia, you are even more lovely in the moonlight."

Her amber-green eyes locked with his blue ones through the darkness. Time stood still and they both became lost in the wondrous moments, the only sound they heard was the beating of their hearts, as all else faded into the distant night.

"What do you want to talk to me about?" Antonia asked, recovering.

"Why did you change your story and tell Commandant Velasco I was not the one who abducted you?"

Antonia dropped her eyes and studied her hands for a moment before she looked at Michael again. "Because you did not abduct me. Is there anything else you wanted to speak to me about?"

"This." Michael gently kissed Antonia's eyes, her ears, her nose. Then he held her away from him, once again gazing deeply into her face.

All the anger and hurt they had caused each other melted under the heat of the moment. The snap of twigs alerted Michael, and he broke his gaze from Antonia in time to sight the shadowy figure coming toward them.

"Capitán Domino, I see you have been most graciously entertaining my *novia* during my absence." The enormous man's bottom lip twitched and his foot tapped his impatience, causing Antonia to nervously smooth her disheveled tresses and straighten her gown.

Michael, noting the strange inflection in Dominguez's voice, measured his response. "Yes, El Señor, she was most kind in her efforts to sober one, whom I fear, overindulged himself. And she has been most kind in her attempts to dislodge a bit of foreign matter, which has found its way into my eye."

"*Capitán*, while we have hardly known one another long, I believe you know enough of me to realize I do not share my possessions — with any man," he said, a skeptical lilt to his brows.

"We are business partners," Michael said at this game of wits. "What is yours, is yours."

"*Sí*, and do not forget it," Dominguez warned.

"Why, El Señor," chided Antonia in an attempt to add credence to Michael's hastily concocted story, "as you can see" — she held out a crumpled handkerchief she had removed from her pocket — "I was indeed attempting to see to *our* guest's needs." Antonia cast a subtle smile at Michael at the slim success of their tale.

"Humph," Dominguez grumbled doubtfully. "Well, it is time to join the merriment. Come along, my flower." He lumbered over to Antonia

176

while Michael jumped down and aided her descent.

Antonia was escorted to the stage inside the tent as a blinded calf is led to slaughter and positioned directly to the right of her *padre*. Dominguez moved to the middle of the platform and raised his arms to silence the crowd. When the merrymakers had ceased all whispers he began.

"Are you all enjoying yourselves?" Cheers rose. "I have asked all my guests to come together under this roof at this time, not only to announce my engagement . . ." He held out a beefy hand toward Antonia. She blankly joined him but glanced back over her shoulder at Michael, who was smiling blandly. ". . . but my marriage this very evening to my lovely flower, Señorita Antonia Rafaela Winston y Ortega."

Applause caused him to pause for a moment. "And we are indeed blessed that while Father Manuel has been taken ill, Father Hernandez, who is visiting from Mexico City, has graciously offered to perform the ceremony."

The full impact of his announcement, and the reason for the special gown and Doña Maria's fuss over her earlier, slammed into Antonia, numbing her senses. Dominguez held her pressed steady against his bulk while the young friar solemnly mounted the stage and offered a prewedding prayer for the nuptial couple.

Don Diego weakly smiled at his only daughter, and took a seat near the platform, as did Michael.

Antonia silently beseeched Michael, frantic that after what they had just shared, he just sat there. How could he remain seated, benignly smiling at her?

Antonia could not believe this was really happening to her. The man whose arms she had just been locked in was sitting before her, allowing this wedding to take place. She had to be having a dreadful nightmare. Surely she would soon awake and find it was not true.

Such was not the case.

Realizing if she did not do something, and quick, she would be married to a man she detested, Antonia shook her head and opened her mouth to protest.

With the guests' heads bowed in prayer and their eyes closed to the quiet but dramatic battle ensuing on stage, Dominguez dug his nails into her arm and whispered, "If you cause me any embarrassment or do not cooperate, your *padre* will not live to see the next dawn."

"What are you saying?" she choked in disbelief, continuing to be stunned at the sudden turn of events.

"Simple. There are those who would not hesitate to carry out my instructions. If you do not comply, *my flower*"—he evilly grinned—"I shall make certain you will never see your *padre* again and then you will be left to my mercy anyway."

Antonia's mind spun. Michael just sat there. Could she refuse and risk her *padre*'s life? After all, he was allowing this to happen to her; he had arranged it. If she did stop the wedding, where would she go? A feeling of utter helplessness fell heavily over her like the chains of doom clamping shut around her heart. For a brief instant she thought of refusing before it was too late. She could make her own way if she had to, of that she was certain. But no, she could not be the cause of her *padre* losing his life.

She had no choice.

Antonia went through the motions of the ceremony in a total state of shock. When the friar pronounced them man and wife, she just stood still with her arms dangling.

Dominguez pulled her to him and kissed her. It was a rough, cold joining of lips. After enduring another round of cheers, Antonia allowed Dominguez to usher her from the stage.

Dominguez paused at the bottom of the steps. "Wait here for me, my flower. I have one final duty to attend to which will make our wedding complete."

Antonia stood, still stunned, and watched Dominguez rejoin the friar, take a small box from his pocket, and whisper something into the man's ear.

"Of course, El Señor, I will be glad to," Antonia heard the friar say.

Dominguez then led his bride through the congratulating crowds to a specially reserved place near the banquet table, on which sat a specially prepared cake. Guests bunched around and began forming a line to offer their best wishes to the newly wedded couple. Doña Maria took a place next to Antonia in the receiving line.

As the guests filed by, Antonia dutifully went through the motions required of a new bride. But out of the corner of her eyes she looked for her *padre*. She saw him across the room speaking to the friar. Hoping he would join her shortly, she returned her attention to the agonizing task of receiving all the well-wishers.

"Señor Winston, El Señor requested I present this gift to you as a very special token. He said

179

that would not require any explanation. He also said that it has been his constant prayer that the gift would be received in the same manner in which it was given," the visiting friar said and handed the box to Don Diego.

Don Diego looked puzzled but accepted the offering. "You are kind to deliver the gift, Friar," Don Diego said. He unwrapped the small box and slowly opened the lid. A shock wave reverberated through his bones. With trembling fingers he lifted the enclosed treasure from its resting place. A gasp tore from his lips. He fought for air, swayed, and then fell back into a nearby chair. For several moments he just sat staring at the object. He turned ghostly white and his lower lip quivered uncontrollably.

"Señor Winston, are you ill?" The young friar was startled by Don Diego's reaction, and placed his hand on the older man's shoulder. Michael rushed over to him.

Don Diego looked to have aged dramatically. He did not say a word. He just sat in the chair clutching the small object next to his heart. His eyes were glazed and hollow. Michael, unable to rouse Don Diego, summoned assistance to help him back to his room. Three men lifted the muttering, incoherent man to his feet and headed for the door.

Antonia noticed her *padre* had taken ill and hurriedly left the receiving line to rush across the room.

Dominguez, too, had been closely watching the events unfold from across the room. For the first time in years he felt truly gladdened by his circumstance. At last his dreams of revenge were coming true. He had waited so long for this moment. And in a few hours he would consummate his marriage to Rafaela's daughter. Then his revenge would be complete. He would possess the beautiful daughter of the only woman he had ever truly loved and desired. And at the same time he had destroyed the man who had taken his Rafaela from him at the altar so many years ago. He smiled broadly as he thought of his victory. Shaking the hand of a guest, he accepted the congratulations, offered his apologies, and followed after his bride.

"Padre, padre, what is it?" Antonia cried as the other rancheros began to crowd around. "What is wrong?"

Don Diego looked past his only child. He did not see her. He continued to mutter over and over again, "Rafaela, what have I done? What have I done?" Don Diego looked down at the small hand-painted cameo held tightly in his hand and continued to mumble.

"What is it?" Antonia pleaded.

Dominguez grabbed his bride's arm, clamping his fingers into her flesh to keep her from accompanying her *padre* back to the hacienda. Antonia struggled, but he spun her around to face him. Shaking her, his eyes burned into her.

"No one can help your *padre* now. He is beyond help. Now get ahold of yourself," he sneered.

"I . . . I do not understand. *Por favor,* my *padre . . ."*

"Your *padre* has just been repaid an old debt owed. You see, there comes a time in everyone's life when debts must be paid and all accounts settled . . . Now, come, we must rejoin our guests. This is now your home too, and as señora you will see to the needs of our guests first."

Antonia had withstood all the stress she could. Her *padre*'s sudden unexplained misfortune, in addition to the other events of the evening, was more than she could endure.

"No!" Antonia screamed.

Michael pushed his way back through the crowd to her side. She reached out for him. The room began to spin, and she brushed her fingertips with his before everything mercifully went black and she collapsed in his arms.

Chapter Twenty-two

Swallowing a desire to forget his vow of revenge and spirit Antonia away in all the confusion, Michael carried her to Dominguez's private rooms while Dominguez summoned a servant to provide cool compresses. To Michael's dismay, Dominguez and the servant joined them all too soon. At Dominguez's insistence the two men withdrew and left Antonia in the care of the servant girl.

Nearly an hour had passed before Antonia, drenched with perspiration, regained consciousness. Slowly blinking open her eyes, she raised her hand to her forehead. "Where am I? Where is my *padre?* Is he all right?" She stroked her throbbing temples.

"Señora, you are in El Señor's . . . ah . . . your private rooms. Does the señora want for anything?"

"Señora? Did you call me . . . señora?" Antonia asked, trying to clear the fog from her head.

"*Sí*, Señora Dominguez." The servant glanced at the clock on the bureau. "You have been the señora for over an hour now."

"Oh, no . . . no!" Suddenly she realized she was no longer wearing her gown but was dressed in only a thin nightgown. "Why am I dressed this way?" she demanded.

"Señora, El Señor, he tell me to help you prepare for bed. The wedding night. *Por favor señora,* you let me help you."

The thought of her husband exercising his husbandly rights—putting his hands on her body and touching her in the same intimate places where Michael had touched her so lovingly—caused her to cringe with revulsion.

The young servant wrung her hands. "The señora is just a new bride. I get you some wine. It will help you for later."

Before Antonia could protest, the girl rushed from the room. Not about to remain in Dominguez's private rooms and wait for his return, Antonia leaped from the bed. She frantically searched for her slippers and tugged them on. In a near panic she rummaged through his wardrobes; her clothes were gone. Grabbing his brown cape, she threw it over her shoulders.

She was in such a rush to get to the door she stumbled. Dominguez was not going to put his hands on her if she could help it! She fumbled with the knob. The door flew open and Antonia ran down the hallway.

For a moment Antonia feared she would be caught. Two men rounded a corner and headed down the hall toward her. She darted into a doorway and pressed herself against the carved wood frame. Fortunate for Antonia they were so engrossed in conversation that they passed by the frightened young woman without noticing her crouched near them.

Antonia waited after the men had disappeared into a room and her trembling had stopped to continue her flight. Looking back over her shoulder to make sure she was not being followed, she crashed right into El Señor Dominguez.

He grabbed her shoulders. "My flower, could you not wait to be with your new husband that you rush into my arms like this?"

"You! Let me go!" Antonia struggled, wishing some of the guests were nearby instead of outside where the music would drown out any cries for help. "What have you done to my *padre?* Let me go!"

Dominguez handed her over to two of his burly companions, and she found herself held tight between the pair.

"Escort the señora back to my rooms and see that no one enters or leaves. I have business to attend to before I join my bride." The enormous man let out a vicious rumble of laughter. "You make the anticipation of our wedding night almost unbearable," he said to Antonia, with a leer. "I have always enjoyed spitfires."

Dominguez cast Antonia a satanic grin and slowly devoured the length of her body with his cruel, hard eyes. Before he left to join his guests he bent over her heaving bosom.

"It would be rude of a new husband not to kiss his bride before he left her side, do you not think?"

He forced a kiss to her lips. Antonia continued to struggle. At last she managed to break away from his wet mouth.

"You disgust me!"

"I may disgust you now, but later, my passion flower, *you* will delight me."

Unable to restrain herself, she spit directly into his face.

He stepped back, and his eyes narrowed into slits. He took his handkerchief out and wiped the spittle from his face. "You best learn to become the adoring bride, at least in public, or I shall have my men tame you just as if you were a wild horse. It might even prove to be amusing to watch you being ridden by several of my vaqueros."

"You are a filthy animal!"

"You will soon find out how much of an animal you have married," he sneered. "Take her away."

Antonia was dragged, kicking and biting, back to Dominguez's private rooms. The men flung her inside and slammed the door. The lock turned, causing the rooms to become her private prison.

"No! You can't do this! Let me out!" She hammered against the door with her fists. "Let me out of here!"

Exhausted, she slid down along the massive carved door to the floor. She lay in a heap, cursing her new husband until she heard the men talking just outside.

"I would like to mount the beautiful señora. I can almost picture her slender body against mine, and feel that smooth white flesh, eh?"

"*Amigo,* she is a tempting one, for sure. And when El Señor touched her it was hard to restrain myself, but she belongs to him. He has killed men for less."

"He would not have to know. And who would believe her?"

"Your thinking interests me. But if he ever found out, our lives—"

"He will not find out if we are careful."

Antonia could not believe her ears. She quickly

186

rose to her feet and ran to the windows. To her dismay they were sealed from the outside. There was only one way from the room—past the guards. Finding that escape was not possible, she searched for something with which to arm herself. After tearing the room apart, the only item she found was an empty bottle of spirits. She struck it against the table, shattering it and leaving her with a jagged though formidable weapon. The element of surprise was the best way to gain the advantage, so she found what she considered a good hiding place and crouched down to wait.

Antonia did not have long to await their entry. One of the guards slipped into the room, and not seeing the young señora, he summoned his companion. The two men searched the room. They were about to leave, unsuccessful in their quest, when she accidentally caused a heavy leather waistband to fall. Its silver buckle crashed to the floor of the wardrobe. As the men immediately opened the wardrobe doors, Antonia lunged out waving the broken bottle in front of her.

The momentarily demoralized men looked at each other, taken by complete surprise that a lady could think of defending herself in such a way. They backed away from the frightened young woman.

As she was about to gain her freedom one of the men snapped his arm across hers and knocked the bottle from her hand. He grabbed her around the waist and flung her kicking and struggling onto the bed. Antonia fought as if her life depended on it, but she was no match for the two huge men. She tried to scream, but one of them ripped his kerchief from his throat and used it to silence her.

"That is right, señora, fight for all you are

worth. You make it all the more interesting, eh?"

One man held Antonia pinned to the bed while the other used four of Dominguez's *boleros* to bind her wrists and ankles to the posters. Antonia continued to writhe but she was bound, caught like a trapped animal. For a few minutes the men stood by the side of the bed panting, and arguing who had won the honor to take her first. When they could not reach an agreement, a coin was tossed. One man cursed and stomped from the room to guard the door. The other started unfastening his trousers and smiled, displaying a mouthful of decaying, broken teeth. "Señora, this is going to be a most pleasurable evening. By the time your husband arrives you will be well versed in the ways of a man."

Antonia's eyes were wide with terror. The tall, thick man bent over and grasped the décolletage of her gown. With one quick jerk he ripped open her bodice, leaving only her thin chemise to provide cover. Her breath came in heavy gasps from the struggle, which caused her full breasts to sway under the flimsy fabric.

"Oh, so nice, so full they are, eh?" He grinned and rubbed his eager, greedy fingers together in anticipation of enjoying his delectable conquest.

After a few minutes he stepped back and removed his thick member from his trousers. With lust in his eyes he stroked it. "Señora, one taste of your body causes mine to cry out for more of you. Look, my beautiful one. I am big enough to fill you."

Antonia squeezed her eyes shut, but he grabbed her chin and shook her. "Open your eyes," he demanded. Almost without warning he tore her skirts from her body until all that was left to afford her

188

any modesty were the lace pantelettes and sweat-dampened chemise. She was near exhaustion but continued to struggle at her bonds in desperation.

"Do not stop, my beautiful one. I like the wild ride."

Despite Antonia's efforts, the man's long, dirt-encrusted, brown fingers began to stroke along her sides. "Although you fight like the bear, I know you enjoy my lesson, eh? Too bad it must end so soon, but my body cannot wait and aches for the taste of yours."

With those words he moved to sit astride the anguished young woman when all of a sudden he slumped forward and then slid to the floor into a heap.

"It appears I can't leave you alone for even a few moments." Michael cast her a wicked grin and knelt by her side as he loosened her bonds.

"Oh, Michael, he was going to . . . to . . ." Antonia sobbed, unable to control herself.

He drew her into his embrace and cradled her against him. "It's all right, Tonia. I'm here now. No one is going to do anything to harm you," he soothed.

For long moments Antonia took in deep breaths to calm herself. It felt so good to be in his arms. So right. Then as the blow of truth hit her, she sat up straight, "How could you just sit there while I was forced to marry that swine?" she demanded.

"Is this the thanks I get for rescuing you from these men?" He held her back and motioned to the man lying by the side of the bed and the one he had relieved from his post outside the door and dragged into the room. "I must say I thought you had better taste."

She bristled. "How can you joke at a time like

this?"

"Oh, my precious Tonia." Again he pulled her into his embrace. "How could you ever think I would let anything happen to you?"

"But you watched while I was forced to marry that pig. How could you?" she asked, her voice shaking at the remembrance.

"It was simple."

She looked incredulous. "Simple!"

"Yes. Because you didn't marry him."

"You were there. You watched the friar perform the ceremony in front of the whole town," she cried.

"Didn't you notice something different about the good friar?"

"I did not know him. But El Señor . . . he said Father Manuel had been taken ill."

"Convenient, wasn't it?"

Antonia noticed the glimmer in his eyes, and suddenly it dawned on her. "You mean he was not really a—"

"That's right. Father Hernandez was none other than my trusted coxswain."

"But how? Why?" Antonia asked, confused and relieved at the same time. She felt as if a mighty storm cloud had been suddenly lifted from over her head.

"There's so much to explain but not enough time right now. But I will say I expected Dominguez might try to pull something like that after he made a special visit to my ship and requested that my cook whip up a special cake for tonight."

"A special cake?"

"Mr. Rogers, my cook, once worked in some of the best pastry shops in London before being impressed into the Royal Navy and then joining my crew. Dominguez had heard of his culinary expertise and requested the special confection for the fiesta. So I had a feeling he might be planning something. And while I was leaving the mission several riders passed me. They looked suspiciously like some of Dominguez's henchmen, so I merely revisited the mission and arranged for Father Manuel to be otherwise engaged this evening and replaced him with one of my crew."

"Father Manuel agreed?"

"It was not quite that simple. Although the man does not approve of Dominguez, he is a man of the cloth and found deception rather disagreeable. But since secularization of the missions and the loss of revenues and lands to the churches, a handful of gold coins donated to the mission eased his conscience. You know how scarce coin is here. The money I gave him will go far to ease the lot of many of his parishioners; a lot more than those California bank notes the *rancheros* use for coin. Hides make great wearing apparel but are a little bulky to carry around in one's pocket as money."

"Why didn't you tell me?" she said, ignoring his attempts at humor.

"I tried to earlier this evening but, if you will remember, we were interrupted by Dominguez before I had the chance. Come now, we must hurry. We've already spent too much time talking," he urged on a more serious note, "and I have to get back to the fiesta before I'm missed. I have an old score to settle and cannot leave until I do."

"No," Antonia stubbornly answered.

"Do I have to carry you? I will not allow Dominguez to touch you, and your presence here just complicates my plans."

"Then let me help; besides, I cannot leave

191

my *padre*. I have to find out what hold that swine has on him so I can help him," she said, steeling herself and raising her chin high in defiant determination.

"Damn, you're the most frustrating woman I've ever met!"

Michael furrowed his brows, contemplating her proposal. Studying the set to her lips, he realized if he didn't agree she might do something on her own and end up causing him more trouble.

"All right, you win. It might help if Dominguez is not alerted. But I'm going to have someone keeping an eye on you, and if things start to get too dangerous, you're leaving whether you want to or not. Do you understand?" Michael said firmly, holding that defiant chin in between his fingers to stare directly into those determined amber-green eyes.

"I understand perfectly. I am to continue as his wife—"

"In name only."

"You will get no argument from me on that point. Now, tell me what score it is you have to settle with Dominguez," Antonia asked with triumphant expectation, and settled back against the headboard to listen.

Michael glanced around at the two guards who continued to slumber and then begrudgingly began to enlighten Antonia.

"I was a curious young sailor on shore leave years ago when I made the mistake of riding across Dominguez's land. Three of his vaqueros caught me and chained me to a post. After summoning Dominguez, he laid my back open with his vicious blows with a bullwhip. But he wasn't satisfied with just a beating and kept striking me, waiting for me to plead for mercy. I woke up three days later at the mission barely alive."

Antonia's eyes grew wide in horror as she listened to his tale, and her heart went out to him.

"When I awoke there was another man beside me who had also encountered Dominguez's form of justice. Like many of his people, Mano preferred the taste of horseflesh to cattle. He made the mistake of smoking some of that wild Indian tobacco which grows on the hills, before he and a companion decided to relieve Dominguez of a couple of his animals. His companion died at Dominguez's hand. Mano, too, was savagely beaten. But Dominguez wasn't satisfied. He had Mano's hand held over a fire until it was charred beyond much use, leaving Mano's lot little better than the aged or very young. That's how Mano came by the Spanish name for hand and why he wears that black glove on his hand," he finished and stared off into space, his face clearly outlining the hatred he felt, but also silently speaking of an even deeper reason for his fierce hatred.

Antonia placed her hand on his shoulder. "How unspeakably terrible. You have to let me stay until the man is destroyed. We both have a debt to pay," she said to further reinforce her point.

"Only as long as it is not too dangerous. Now here . . ." He handed her one of the guard's pistols. "Do you know how to use this?"

"I am a *ranchero*'s daughter, am I not?" she said, examining the weapon with a glint in her eyes that told him that she would not hesitate to blow the guards' heads off if she had to.

"That you are." He rolled his eyes. "If either one of them comes anywhere near you, pull the trigger. In the meantime, I have to get back to the fiesta before I'm missed. But before I do I'll send someone to remove those two and keep an eye out for you."

"Michael, there is so much I want to say," Antonia said, searching his face.

"I, too, my princess. But not now." He squeezed her to him until Antonia felt the breath being hugged from her. He passionately kissed her, leaving her breathless. Moments later he was gone.

"Uhh," groaned the man on the floor, rubbing his aching head. "What happened?" He rose to his feet and took a step toward Antonia.

"You come one step closer and you will never have to worry about that aching head of yours again," she warned, pointing the pistol at him.

"All right, just stay calm, eh?" he said. "See, I am putting my hands in the air. Do not worry, señora. I have not the intention to bring more trouble. I do not know how you managed it, but neither one of us will try to touch you again," he whined, then walked over to his companion and hefted him to his feet. "We go back outside and watch the door, eh?"

"Be quick about it."

"Too bad you will not be able to taste the fruits of real men. Maybe another time, señora," the second man said as he grabbed the doorknob, flung it open, and slammed it shut behind them.

Antonia breathed a sigh of relief and laid the pistol down on the dressing table. She ran to the door and turned the lock. Still trembling, she went back to the bed and sank onto the mattress. For a long time she just sat motionless, trying to digest everything that had happened.

Chapter Twenty-three

Dominguez awoke shortly before the cool gray dawn of morning replaced the night. He shifted up onto his elbow and studied his bride. Antonia had been sound asleep when he joined her. No matter how hard he tried, he had not been able to awaken her last night; the stupid servant must have given her a sleeping potion. Her long golden curls were spread out in disarray on the pillow, creating a sunrise effect around her lovely face. Deep in sleep she was almost as beautiful as her *madre* had been so many years ago.

Antonia's thin nightrail had fallen off one shoulder, exposing creamy white flesh. Her slender hand lay resting on the pillow, entwined in her curls. Dominguez set aside the golden strands. He gently took his bride's hand and lifted it to his lips, brushing his mouth across her palm.

Antonia did not stir.

"My bride, I shall allow you your dreams for now. But this evening after the guests have retired, you will really know what it is to taste a man. I have waited years to possess Rafaela's child. I may have to wait a little longer to possess you, my flower, but now I own you," he whispered. He studied her delicate features before leaving her side to join his guests.

Houseguests began rising and making their way to the courtyard to partake of the magnificent buffet consisting of hot, steaming trays of *huevos rancheros chiles rellenos,* ham, fruits, and other delicious dishes. Dominguez joined his guests and devoured a large platter heaped with delicacies.

"I hope you and your bride slept well last night, El Señor. Where is the lovely young señora this morning?" the man seated across from Dominguez inquired.

"I fear she has not risen as of yet."

"She must not have gotten much sleep last night," another man commented.

Chuckles, snickers, and further congratulations echoed around the table as the men seated near Dominguez voiced their envy of the big man.

As Antonia was rounding the corner to join the others on the courtyard, an arm snaked around her waist and pulled her into the massive *sala.* "Oh!" she gasped before turning to see Michael's smiling eyes gazing down at her.

"Good morning, Princess," he said, and kissed her.

"Buenas días." She giggled and, after making certain they were not being observed, slid her arms up his chest to toy with his earlobes.

"Careful or I might forget where we are," he

196

playfully warned, and nibbled at her neck. He then held her from him as his face grew serious. "Are you all right? He didn't try to touch you, did he?"

"No. And I am fine. I pretended sleep last night. He was furious, and ranted and raved before storming out for a while, but when he returned he let me be."

"The man I had stationed outside your window reported Dominguez's ravings."

"I can handle El Señor."

His brow rose up into a skeptical line. "Like you did after he escorted you before the friar last night?"

"The man was not a friar. He was your coxswain, you said so yourself."

"And what about Dominguez's men? You didn't seem to be managing that pair with particular finesse."

"A mere oversight. The man you have commissioned to watch over me will see that I do not come to harm."

Michael huffed out a breath of frustration with her reasoning. "This is madness, woman. I don't want anything to happen to you. Even with one of my men trailing your shadow I don't like it."

"Nothing is going to happen to me. Now shh, I hear someone coming. I had better go play my role. Will you be joining us?" Antonia asked, hopeful that Michael would be nearby.

He rubbed the back of his neck, shaking his head. "I wouldn't miss it."

"Good." Antonia straightened her gown, peeked around the corner, and hurried through the double doors before Michael could change his mind about letting her help.

Michael cursed under his breath and followed her at a respectable distance out onto the patio.

Antonia painted on her brightest smile and took a seat a decent distance from Dominguez. *"Buenas días."*

"You look beautiful as always, my flower." Dominguez nodded, and spying Michael acknowledged his presence. "Join us, *capitán.*"

"Thank you, I will." Michael cast a sly wink at Antonia and sat down next to her.

Antonia looked the picture of the blushing bride as she demurely began eating her meal. But she had to make a conscious effort to keep a straight face when Michael's foot slid up her calf and sent her senses reeling.

"Antonia, my flower," came the gruff voice, jolting her from her reverie.

Antonia looked up sheepishly. "I am sorry. Did you say something?"

"Thinking about her wedding night, no doubt," a guest said.

Dominguez gave her a warning. "No doubt."

She held Dominguez's eyes until Michael's foot again slipped up her calf. At that a smile came to her lips. "It was a night which will remain in my mind for some time."

"Señora Dominguez, I believe your husband was attempting to gain your attention a moment ago," Michael said, concerned at the strange reflection in Dominguez's eyes over her all too gay remark.

A sheepish grin on her face, Antonia said, "I am sorry, El Señor. What was it you were saying?"

"Señor Mendoza was speaking to you," Dominguez said, his foot tapping his usual impatience.

Antonia turned toward the *ranchero.* "I hope you

198

will forgive a young bride's fanciful daydreaming, señor."

"Of course, señora."

"I was merely complimenting you on your gracious hospitality," the man with the bushy brows said, impressed and quite taken with Dominguez's bride.

"It is kind of you to say so," Antonia answered. She silently vowed to herself to be more alert so she could play an active role in Dominguez's downfall. She certainly did not intend to be a passive partner to Michael's scheme, especially after what that swine had done to her *padre*. Antonia was just about to ask after her *padre* when she was interrupted.

A frantic Señora Pica flew into the courtyard, wringing her hands. She questioned several servants and guests concerning the whereabouts of her daughter Rosa. As her fears mounted, she approached Dominguez. "El Señor, you must help me. My Rosa is missing. You must help me," she beseeched.

Dominguez looked pointedly at Michael. "I am certain your Rosa will make an appearance soon. She probably was up celebrating quite late last night and overslept."

"But she was not in her bed."

"Perhaps she did not want to wake you and so spent the night with one of the other young ladies at the hacienda."

"She has always been a thoughtful girl, I suppose that could account for her absence," she said, and cast Michael a quick glance.

"Of course it does." While Dominguez continued to soothe the worried *madre,* pounding footfalls were heard coming from the entrance of the hacienda.

"El Señor! El Senõr!" Señor Martinez panted, having pushed past the servant to rush to Dominguez's side. "I was out taking an early-morning stroll when I happened upon the most horrible sight. A young girl. Murdered. She was murdered!"

Señora Pica's eyes widened in horror, and the courtyard grew deathly still.

Her voice shaking, Señora Pica barely managed to mouth the words, "A . . . young girl? Was she wearing a light-blue gown?" All color drained from her face and she struggled for breath.

Dominguez placed his arm around the distraught señora's shoulders. *"Por favor* Señora Pica, allow me to have someone escort you to your room. I shall personally look into this unfortunate incident and put your mind at ease."

"Oh, El Señor, you are truly a kind man," Señora Pica sobbed, trying to contain herself.

Dominguez summoned one of the female servants and ordered Señora Pica assisted to her room. After they left, the men began to file out to the scene of the crime.

While the men whispered among themselves, Michael turned to Antonia. "Stay here," he said through clenched teeth.

Antonia frowned but moved to comfort the disturbed women in the patio while the men hurried to the scene.

Horrified by the broken body, one man exclaimed, "It is Rosa Pica! This is an outrage! Who could have done such a thing?"

"Whoever did such a horrible thing, he is an animal," another remarked, his hand over his mouth for fear he would be ill.

Michael, who had stood in silent horror at the deed, removed his jacket and placed the dark-brown garment over Rosa's battered body.

Dominguez, an eloquent speaker who was capable of easily manipulating and inciting others into doing his bidding, sought to use the feelings of outrage to his advantage. "Whoever is responsible for Señorita Rosa's demise shall be punished," he pronounced. "Her murder must not go unavenged."

Californios were very protective of their women, and regardless of the actions, they were quick to defend a woman's honor and even quicker to avenge what they felt as a wrongdoing. Dominguez continued. "We all must band together to seek out and question everyone at the fiesta. Someone may have seen or heard the struggle. This I promise you all — justice will be harshly swift. The one who committed such a heinous act will be dealt with without mercy."

Satisfied that he had achieved the desired response, he ordered two men to assist him with the unfortunate señorita. The men carried her back to the hacienda while the rest of them headed toward the *carpa* to question the other guests. Dominguez ordered his manservant to fetch the doctor and commandant, and then went to inform Señora Pica.

In the confusion which followed, Michael pulled Antonia aside. "Meet me in your rooms in a half hour." An instant later he left her standing alone beside a stone bench.

The patio was filled with distraught women milling about, and Antonia moved quickly to take charge of the situation before it got out of hand.

201

"Ladies, I think it might be a good idea if everyone went to their rooms and calmed down. It will not help Señora Pica if we panic," Antonia advised, ushering the women back into the hacienda.

Once she had settled the women and ordered the servants to see to their needs, she hurried to her room to meet Michael. She was seated at the dressing table when Michael quietly slipped through the door.

"You're amazing," he said. "Most women would have panicked with the others, but you remained calm."

"I am not like most women," Antonia said, rising to go to him. "Do they have any idea who could have done such a terrible thing?" Her face pinched into concern.

"Not yet. Although I have a pretty good idea who it was." Michael's eyes hardened.

"You do not think Dominguez did it, do you?"

"As a matter of fact I do. She was burned and savagely beaten with a whip."

"Oh, no!" she choked, feeling sick. "Dominguez did leave the room for a while last night. But can you prove it?"

"Not yet, but I will." There was a strange look in his eyes which told Antonia something else weighed heavy on his mind, and she wondered whether she should seek the cause. She could feel the tension in his body and thought better of it. Now was not the time to share the soul's deepest secrets.

"Why did you want to meet me here?" she asked, knowing their time together was limited.

"First, are you sure you want to get involved in this? This is not a game. Dominguez is dangerous." Michael looked squarely into her eyes and Antonia could read his concern for her shining there.

Antonia firmed her jaw. "I intend to help you and my *padre*. There is nothing you can say that will change my mind."

"All right, I know when I'm beat. Sit down and I'll fill you in," he said, leading her to the edge of the bed and pulling her down onto his lap. "God, you're beautiful."

"Michael . . ." Antonia protested.

"All right, all right." He accepted defeat gracefully. "As I told you earlier, Mano and I devised a plan to destroy Dominguez. Until now everything had been going smoothly. I learned he has been stealing his neighbors' cattle for years—"

"What?"

"If you will stop interrupting and just listen. I don't have my much time."

"That is a shame," she mumbled, coyly lowering her head.

"By God, you are a wanton wench." He stroked her cheek. "Now let me finish. As I was trying to say, I only recently learned of his thieving from a loosed-tongued sailor off the *Sea Shark*. I met the man after he had had a few too many, and he unknowingly supplied me with information about his captain and Dominguez. It seems Dominguez uses Captain Brian Thomas to dispose of the evidence. It's quite a tidy operation.

"You remember when I stepped on the hem of your aunt's gown in front of all the guests?"

"*Sí.*"

"I was pretending to be drunk. In reality I had left Rosa sleeping soundly after I drugged her drink. While everyone thought we were engaged in lustful pursuits she was actually providing the per-

203

fect cover so Mano and I could ride out and alter a dozen of the brands on Dominguez's cattle. Then after we returned, I came downstairs to play the drunk in search of another bottle in front of witnesses so my alibi would not come into question."

She cocked her head. "I had wondered about you two. But do not Dominguez's vaqueros patrol the range?" Antonia asked?

"A jug of rum laced with sleeping powder took care of the men."

"They did not recognize you?"

"Mano played the perfect role of a drunk, and they were too busy calling him a 'digger' and making fun of him to even know what hit them."

"It is a shame my people seem to find it necessary to use such a simple word to signify such an ugly meaning for the Indian people just because they had a simple life once and dug roots for food."

"Yes, man can be a viciously cruel animal," he observed, thinking about the father he had never known. "But as I was explaining, since my cook had the run of the place preparing that special cake I told you about, he replaced the irons in Dominguez's room of pleasures when we were done. I had planned to stumble on the incriminating evidence tonight at the fiesta, but Rosa's murder has changed all that."

Antonia pursed her lips. "I will just have to try and think of another way."

"You will do no such thing. You're doing enough already. I don't want you hurt."

"I know . . . I know. You better leave now before you are missed. Michael, I—"

"There's no more time for talk now. Be careful,

Princess."

"Now who is interrupting whom?" She cocked her head coyly.

Michael grabbed her shoulders and silenced her with a searing kiss, then strode to the door. "I'll see you later. Remember, stay away from Dominguez."

After he was gone Antonia leaned her elbow on her knee, resting her chin on her palm, and searched her mind to make sense out of the tangle. Nothing materialized. She continued to fret. She had to come up with an idea to bring a speedy end to Dominguez.

Chapter Twenty-four

As Antonia passed the door to the library, her husband called to her. She suppressed the urge to ignore him and continue on her way. True to her role, she stopped to peer into the room but did not join him.

"My flower, *por favor,* do not just stand outside the door. Come, my dear." Dominguez rose from his chair and moved toward Antonia. She cringed from him, but he took her arm and ushered her into the room.

Once inside, he closed the heavy wooden doors and seated Antonia on the couch. Lowering himself next to her, he could feel her body grow rigid and shrink from him.

"Is there a problem, my flower? You look quite wilted in that wrinkled dress. Perhaps you might wish to change. You are now a married woman."

"I am comfortable in the clothing I brought to wear for the fiesta," she said without emotion, ignoring the fact that he had had a trunk full of fancy gowns brought from her *padre*'s home for her. "If you have nothing further to say, I shall be on my way. I have guests, as well as your newest business partner, to entertain."

Dominguez decided that this was his opportunity to crush the hint of feelings toward Captain Domino that he had noticed in his bride the night before.

"I am worried about you."

"You need not be."

"Oh, but I am. There is a murderer among us and I noticed that Capitán Domino has seemed to be watching you rather closely as of late."

She stiffened, yet refrained from comment.

"You are very fortunate, my flower. You might have been the victim instead of poor Rosa." He paused for a moment in an attempt to make the most from the situation. When her icy face began to register an uneasiness he proceeded. "As you are aware, she was brutally beaten to death last night. You know, the first night of the fiesta she was seen leaving with Capitán Domino and the next morning she was quite upset. I would hate to think you spent time in the company of a man who would viciously beat a young woman to death. While there is no hard evidence to accuse the *capitán* of such a crime, there is his past behavior as well as his close association with Rosa."

"I . . . I do not know what you mean," she blurted out, astounded at the nerve of the man. "Capitán Domino is your partner."

"You certainly would not want me to shield a murderer, would you?"

Antonia did not answer him. It was too disturbing that Dominguez planned to have Michael take

207

the blame for Rosa's murder.

Almost as if fate were on the side of evil, one of the houseguests knocked at the library door. Dominguez bid him to enter. The man escorted one of the vaqueros from a neighboring rancho into the library.

"El Señor, Señora Dominguez . . ." He nodded respectfully. "I beg your pardon for disturbing you, but I thought you would want to speak to this man immediately." He nudged the short stranger forward. "Go ahead, tell them what you know."

As he had been instructed, the vaquero told them the story of witnessing the captain murder the dark beauty. The expression of disbelief on Antonia's countenance warned Dominguez that he had better have the witness wait elsewhere for the commandant.

"As you may see, this has upset my bride. *Por favor,* if you would be so kind, take this man to the kitchen and see to his needs until the *comandante* can be summoned," the enormous man directed. "And alert the men to be on the lookout for Capitán Domino. No one is to rest until the man is captured."

After they were alone again, Antonia sprang to her feet, her eyes a smoky amber-green from simmering rage. "I do not know how you managed to obtain a false statement from that man, but it is a lie!"

"Why, my flower, one would think you had feelings for Capitán Domino, the way you are carrying on so." He twisted his brows into an accusative arch.

"Do not be foolish," Antonia gasped and stood motionless.

"Listen carefully, for I am not going to repeat myself. You may not admit what you obviously feel between your thighs for Capitán Domino, and quite frankly I do not give a damn what your personal feelings are as long as you are the devoted bride in public. I am certain you would not want your *padre* to come to any harm. In his present state of mind he could wander off. And who knows what could become of him. So if you care for your *padre*'s health, you will avoid our *capitán*. Do you understand?"

She looked at him with revulsion and horror. "You . . . you killed Rosa! You were the one."

"That is a very serious accusation. If I were you, I would be most careful what I said and to whom I said it. I would hate to find your *padre* at the bottom of the bluffs. Now, I hope we finally understand each other."

For the first time Antonia felt as if she really did understand. She had no choice. She had to protect her *padre*, and she had to help Michael. Not that she had ever considered leaving before, but now she knew she had to remain. There was no way she was going to allow the swine before her to destroy any more lives.

"I understand." Antonia swallowed the hard lump sticking in her throat and lowered her eyes in a gesture of feigned subservience.

"Ah, very good. I shall escort you to our rooms so you can make yourself presentable. I will not have my bride appear as a peasant before my guests," Dominguez said. He noted her meek stance and felt assured of her helpless compliance.

Antonia raised her chin and glared into his black, hungry eyes and she wondered how far she

209

would have to go to end this nightmare. She steeled her shoulders; she would do whatever was necessary.

Noting her change of expression, he said, "Do not concern yourself, I am not going to touch you . . . not now at any rate. There will be time for you to please me when I am ready. And please me, my flower, you will."

"What about my *padre?* I want to see him."

"Later, when I decide you may see him. Not before. Today you will entertain our female guests."

Dominguez took Antonia's arm and escorted her to his rooms. He selected a gown and ordered that in the future she was to wear only the ones he was having sewn especially for her.

The remainder of the day, Antonia was a most gracious hostess while she silently kept watch for Michael. He had seemed to disappear into thin air. She had to warn him. She also had tried to visit her *padre* several times but a guard had been posted at his door, blocking her entrance. In frustration she stormed out into the courtyard and brazenly joined Dominguez and a group of his business associates.

"Excuse me, gentlemen, for interrupting, but I must speak with my husband." She smiled innocently and twined her arm around his.

Dominguez freed his arm and wrapped it constrictively around Antonia's waist. The group of men with whom he had been discussing the unfortunate incident cast him knowing glances. An air of gloom had overshadowed the festivities, but the men had decided that the rest of the fiesta should not be canceled in spite of the murder.

"My flower, wait for me in our rooms, I shall

join you shortly," he said, dismissing her.

"I would like to visit with my *padre* . . . now," she insisted through gritted teeth.

Relenting in the face of the others watching them, he pinched her waist. "If you will excuse us? Come along, my flower." He led her past the guards toward her *padre*'s room.

As they started for Don Diego's chambers, Doña Maria interrupted them. "Antonia . . . what kind of an ungrateful daughter are you? You have made no attempt to visit your sick *padre* or seek information concerning his condition until this late hour. Such a disgrace!" Doña Maria's voice was cold and harsh as she stood with her hands on her hips frowning darkly from the doorway.

While Doña Maria viciously tonguelashed her, Antonia remained still. Her *tía* had little of the grace of human understanding in her soul, and always had proved harsh with her, even as a child. But deep down Antonia tried to hold the thought of how her *padre* had told her that Doña Maria was a good person and meant well underneath that stony shroud she had worn for so many years.

Once Doña Maria had finished berating her with a tirade of all her shortcomings—real and imagined—Antonia returned her eyes to the floor and continued on her way without offering so much as a word of defense. She knew she would have been wasting her breath; once Doña Maria made up her mind, there was seldom a chance of changing it. When she neared her *padre*'s door she heard Dominguez's honey-sweet voice turned on Doña Maria.

"I do not wish to intrude in private family matters, but since I am now part of the family I shall,

211

with your consent of course, offer a suggestion," Dominguez cagily said to the dour woman.

Doña Maria smiled eagerly, thinking about the money due her. "Your advice is always welcome, El Señor."

"Come . . ." Dominguez took Doña Maria's arm. "We shall converse while my bride atones to her *padre* for her thoughtlessness."

Antonia heaved a sigh of relief that she was being left alone to visit her *padre* and made no attempt to respond to their slashing remarks. She continued to remain stationary for a few moments after she was left standing alone outside her *padre*'s room. She took a deep breath, rapped on the door, and entered the room.

"*Padre*, it is Antonia." Her eyes searched the room; they came to rest on a stooped figure seated in a high-back rocking chair. She barely recognized the rocking figure to be that of her *padre*. Don Diego sat in the chair staring down at an object clutched tightly in his hand.

She moved to the chair and placed her hand on his shoulder. When there was no response, she kneeled down and covered his hand with hers. He continued to stare blankly toward his palm with hollow, unseeing blue eyes that once were full of life.

"*Padre*, I love you." A tear ran down her cheek and she wiped it away. "Dear God, I love you," she cried.

"Rafaela . . . I have done her a grave injustice. Rafaela, you are the most beautiful girl I have ever seen . . ." Don Diego had slipped in and out of reality since the wedding and continued to mutter mindlessly.

212

"Padre, I do not understand." Antonia looked toward the clenched fist. She brushed his hand with her lips and gently slid her fingers within his grasp to retrieve the object.

In her palm was the key to her *padre's* illness. Carefully, she studied the small hand-painted cameo. She noticed his empty eyes begin to fill with pain.

"I do not understand. This is a portrait of *madre?"*

Don Diego stared at the piece. Many years ago as a young sailor he had painted the same cameo of the beautiful Rafaela. The beauty had commissioned him to paint it. By the time the cameo was finished, he and Rafaela were in love. He had not thought of the brooch in many years. Once he had wondered about the cameo, but his beautiful Rafaela had told him that she had given it to her *novio* at his request. Rafaela had never disclosed the identity of the man she was to have married, for it had been an unpleasant subject which she had adamantly refused to discuss any more than to say he was an evil and cruel man. Out of love and devotion for his beautiful Spanish wife, he had not pressed her or their family and friends. Instead, he had let the existence of the cameo slip into the dark inner recesses of his memory.

Don Diego had had reservations about his daughter's marriage to El Señor Dominguez, even though Doña Maria had convinced him of the importance of securing his child's future after he was gone. Feelings he could not explain had continued to plague him. Although Antonia's resistance had been met with stubborn reserve and righteousness, in his heart he had questioned his own actions.

Her eyes had pleaded for understanding and rescue as she stood before the friar. But it was not until it was too late that the horrible truth was discovered: Antonia had been sentenced to a life of misery. It was too much for the proud *ranchero*. His mind snapped, causing him to withdraw from life into fantasy.

Don Diego continued to gaze at the cameo in his only child's fingers. Intense agony surrounded his heart. Pools of tears welled and threatened to spill down his cheeks.

"My daughter, the piece you hold in your hand is a miniature of your *madre*. I loved her so." He started to cry uncontrollably. "I loved her so."

"It was painted so long ago. I do not understand. How did El Señor Dominguez come to give you this?"

"*Niña, mi niña* . . . Rafaela . . . I cannot bear it . . . Rafaela you are so beautiful . . ." The pain of remembering had grown too great. To Antonia's dismay Don Diego returned to ramble within his own world where only memories of his choosing could enter.

"*Por favor,* you must tell me of this cameo," she pleaded. It was the key which could return him to the man he had been. She had watched as Dominguez had given the box containing the cameo to the friar with instructions for its delivery. But she could not comprehend what the enormous man had to do with the piece that it could cause her *padre* such insurmountable pain.

The knob on the door squeaked as it turned. Michael glimpsed into the room and then approached a kneeling Antonia. "I looked everywhere for you, and when I couldn't find you I thought you might be in here with your father. How is he?" he said softly, compassion for her bravery and her devoted love for her father overtaking the hard stance he had intended to take with her.

She glanced at her *padre* and sniffled. "He is very ill."

He gathered her into his arms. "Your father is a strong man, Princess. He will heal."

He was not so sure Don Diego would be all right, but his concern right now was for Antonia. He feared she was taking too many chances and he feared for the spunky señorita's safety. He wanted to shake her, to do whatever it took to convince her that she should take flight from this evil hacienda before it and its owner consumed and destroyed her, too. Instead, he held her quietly as she sobbed against his shoulder.

"What are you doing here?" she asked once she had recovered from the shock of seeing the extent of her *padre*'s illness. "You must hurry and leave before they catch you," she said frantically, scrambling to her feet and pushing him from the room.

"Before who *'catches'* me?" he asked, bewildered by her strange behavior.

"Dominguez and his men. He has accused you of killing Rosa. He even has a witness. I was there when the man told Dominguez it was you who killed Rosa. Oh, please, you must leave. I could not bear it if something happened to you."

"You really couldn't?" he jested.

"Do not make light of the situation. You must go."

"Then you will come with me? It's no longer safe for you here. We must alert Mano. If he and I work separately we can put this nonsense of my

215

guilt to rest before it gets out of hand. And while he begins ferreting out the truth, I can see that you are far away from here."

"I cannot leave. I have to remain near my *padre*; besides, you need someone who is close to Dominguez to keep you informed about what he is planning next. No one can do that better than I," Antonia said. "Tonight is the last night of the fiesta, and I can help keep him from inciting all the men against you before they leave." *As well as learn as much as I can to help you.*

That same determined stubbornness Michael had witnessed before dropped down over her features as hard as the granite boulders strewn on the hillsides of the rancho. He had to admit her presence within the household could be useful despite his trepidation.

"All right. I will concede to your wishes to remain near your father for the time being. But I do not want you near Dominguez tonight at the fiesta since I won't be able to be there to keep you out of trouble. Perhaps it would be best if you stayed in your room tonight."

"Need I remind you that I managed my own life quite adequately before I met you?"

"So well, in fact, that there is no need to remind you how we came to meet," he shot back.

The sound of footsteps outside the door broke into their escalating argument. Antonia rushed to the window and threw it open.

"Quick. Before Dominguez catches you in here. You must leave. Now!"

Chapter Twenty-five

Antonia stood like a fine porcelain statue at the entrance to the courtyard. In her glimmering emerald silk gown, stitched with golden threads the color of her curls, she resembled a delicate china doll. She knew as she thought of it, that not one of her houseguests would have surmised she had just spent the last hour before the fiesta was to begin in a heated argument with Michael.

"I told you earlier that I planned to attend the last night of the festivities," she insisted.

"I do not want you in any more danger than you're already in, and that's final. You will plead a headache and stay here where it will be easier to watch over you." He turned his back on her and strode toward the door.

Desperate to glean what she could at the fiesta tonight, Antonia picked up a half-full bottle of spirits and tiptoed up behind him.

"Michael?"

He started to pivot around toward her. "Nothing

you can say is going to ch—"

She broke the bottle over his head.

Michael looked astounded for an instant before he fell to his knees and collapsed at her feet.

A gasp escaped her lips at what she had been forced to do. "I am so sorry, Michael," she said to his unconscious body. "But you left me no other choice."

Without wasting time, she slipped a pillow under his head, threw on her gown, and bolted from the room before he could come to and stop her. He was certain to be livid. She had no idea what he would do to her, and she did not want to be anywhere near him when he awoke to find out.

More and more houseguests began making their appearances fresh from siesta and warm baths supplied by a staff of overworked servants. Antonia had left instructions earlier with the servants to begin serving drinks made from cactus juice, lemon and lime, and mixed with spirits distilled from oranges. It was a potent mixture, which Antonia believed would help ease tensions created by the untimely death of Rosa Pica.

As the courtyard filled with houseguests, servants mingled among them carrying large trays filled with salt-rimmed glasses. After all the guests were served, the servants continued to move about refilling glasses before they could be emptied. Antonia mingled about the crowd, making sure everyone was beginning to relax and forget the terrible tragedy, for the evening at least.

"Señora Dominguez, the courtyard is most attractive," the hunched-over old man leaning heavily on his cane rasped.

He had a strange look in his eyes, which caused Antonia to fidget with the column of her neck. *"Gracias señor,"* she said, and blinked several times to study those angry blue eyes closer.

His gaze bored into her. "Such a young beauty to waste yourself on the likes of El Señor Dominguez. To look at you, one would think you had more sense."

Antonia was shocked at the old man's unabashed candor, then her hand flew up to her lips and her eyes grew as big as melons. "Mi-Michael," she whispered in shock. "I left you—"

"You mean you thought you left me neatly tucked away in your rooms. I ought to take you over my knee and teach you a lesson for such a stupid stunt." He ground his teeth.

She hurriedly looked around and then whispered, "But I could not help you and my *padre* if I stayed in my room this evening."

"I don't want anyone to harm that beautiful neck, you stubborn little fool. Although I probably shouldn't worry." He rubbed the side of his head. "You pack quite a wallop."

"One would think I must mean a lot to you." She leaned near him with hope-filled eyes, praying he would speak of his feelings toward her.

"Look, Princess, I don't want anyone else to be harmed by that man, especially not you."

Her hopes that he would say more dashed, Antonia's heart sank, but she buoyed her resolve. Now was not the time to let personal concerns impede her determination. She turned her attention to his apparel.

"Is that white mustache from the head of the old doll I brought with me?" She tented her fingers over her nose and grinning mouth. She had often hugged that old doll, which she always kept with her for sentimental reasons.

"She'll never miss it."

"And your hair . . ." She reached out and hesitantly stroked his locks. "That is my powder." She stifled a giggle.

"Yes, I know I'm a sight. Thanks to you, I might add. It's a pretty good disguise considering the time and materials I had to work with." He pursed his lips. "Just don't lean too heavily on your dressing table." He held up his makeshift cane sheepishly.

Antonia choked as she tried to keep from laughing. "You are most resourceful, *capitán*."

"I have to be with you around." His face then turned darkly serious. "I want you out of here."

"No." Antonia twirled and linked her arm with a passing matron's before he could force her to leave the fiesta; she was not going to remain in her room tonight. "I am so delighted you are enjoying yourself, *señor*." She then threw back over her shoulder toward Michael. With a painted smile she strolled from him chatting with the guest. "Señora Mesa, I do hope your room is satisfactory."

Damn her! He could not go after her in this sorry disguise. His eyes narrowed as he watched her. At that moment, if he could have gotten his hands on her, he would have happily forgotten his concern about her beautiful neck and wrung it himself.

After the last of the guests had retired to rest before departing from the hacienda early the next morning, Antonia glanced about to see if Michael was still glaring at her, as he had from a safe distance all evening. Although at the moment she appeared to be alone with Dominguez, she knew Michael or the sailor he had commissioned to watch over her would not be far away. Impatient and eager to see the last of Dominguez, she decided to question him in spite of Michael's warnings.

Dominguez reached for her arm to escort her to bed. She flung it away from him and squarely faced him, her eyes flashing fire. Casting off the last restraints of caution, she removed the cameo from her pocket, and holding it in her outstretched hand, demanded an explanation.

"I saw you have this delivered to my *padre*. And I saw the effect it had on him. It is a portrait of my *madre*. I want to know how you came to possess it and what hold it has over my *padre*."

"My flower, you are not in a position to bargain. Need I remind you? Now come."

"No! I will know what you have done to my *padre* before I take another step." Her voice grew louder as she spoke; the anger in her face was unmistakable, and her brows drew together.

Dominguez's eyes narrowed in assessment. "Since you insist, come with me and I shall enlighten you." His voice was calm yet filled with foreboding.

Antonia felt a cold shiver go down her spine. But she had to know the truth if she was going to help her *padre* out of his living hell. She was a strong woman, and seeing her *padre* in such condition served to strengthen her will, her determination not to let anyone think they could control her life with threats.

Her eagerness to learn what Dominguez had to do with her *padre*'s illness caused her to nod her consent. Once in his private rooms, she seated herself at the dressing table, careful not to lean against it — as Michael had instructed her — and waited. Dominguez took the cameo from her and, fingering it, began to unravel the mystery.

"I was not always the man I am today." He paused and Antonia thought she noticed the reflection of a man holding back a dark secret in his eyes. "*Sí*, the reputation I hold has always been with me. But once in my life kindness and even love prevailed over my actions. That was all too soon changed by a beautiful young señorita.

"I see by your expression you find it difficult to believe me capable of such an emotion, but I once worshipped someone. I would have done anything for her — anything at all. Knowing of my love, my family arranged for us to wed. It would have been such an ideal match. Our families were rich and powerful, which would have added to our influence and wealth. But sadly, my *novia*," his face grew dark with bitterness, "fell in love with the common sailor who painted this object. They ran away and were eventually wed.

"I can see that you are beginning to comprehend. *Sí*, my flower, if it had not been for your *padre* — the sailor — you may have been *my* daughter. You should have been my daughter." The level of his rage rose higher, his eyes flashed with frightening madness, and he began to pace the floor breathing heavily.

"You see, your *madre* was the only woman I ever felt anything for. Your *padre* took her away from me. But now I have taken his most treasured possession — you — from him. Do you not see, justice has finally prevailed." Dominguez began to laugh evilly.

"You . . . you are mad," Antonia cried in no

more than a whisper, hardly believing such a wild tale. She glared at him, and, although he had just unburdened himself, she could have sworn his eyes continued to wear an unspoken hood of secrecy.

"Mad, am I? Mad, am I! No. I have patiently waited for years to have my revenge, and now after I have taken Don Diego's daughter,.my revenge will be complete. I own you. I shall possess you, and then maybe even share you with anyone who shows an interest in that most beautiful body of yours. Your *padre* shall know of your fate, and I shall soon have totally destroyed him. With my marriage to you, I shall at last control his vast holdings. Now, do you think that mad or extremely brilliant?"

"You are sick."

"Think what you will. But now I shall take my pleasure in carrying out the next phase of my revenge."

"No!" she screamed and tried to dart past him.

He caught her arm and dragged her kicking and struggling to the bed. He forced her down onto the mattress. Antonia fought with all her might, but she was no match for the man's strength and sheer bulk. Without bothering to remove her gown, he threw her skirts high. He pinned her down with his body and ripped the undergarments from her. Antonia watched in shock as he managed to remove his trousers. Then he forced her legs apart with his knee.

He took his huge member into his free hand and stroked it, preparing to consummate their marriage. "See it, my scared little flower? Very soon it will be inside you. You will feel it come alive within you. And I will have left my mark on you—as well as your *padre*—forever."

"No." Was all she could manage to mouth.

"You silly little bitch. You may be very beautiful, but there are many women willing and eager to please me. If it were not for your *padre*, I would not even bother with you," he spat, taking delight in her total anguish.

Positioned above her, he gave a short laugh before he collapsed along the length of her. She cried out in pain as his enormous body threatened to crush her beneath his weight.

Suddenly he was on the floor.

"I certainly hope you do not plan to make a habit of this. One of these times I may not be around to anticipate your follies and rescue you." Michael was standing over her, the dressing-table leg in his hand.

"I had the situation well in hand," she choked, clasping her hands together to keep them from trembling.

"Who had whom in hand? From where I was positioned . . ." He began to smooth and tuck her shredded gown back into some semblance of order.

"Just where were you *'positioned'?*" Antonia gave a huff of feigned impatience.

"Let us just say some might have thought me to be beneath you." He brushed off the dust motes, which had gathered on his attire while he was under the bed.

"Very amusing, *capitán*," she returned, remembering how she had called him a lowly sailor.

He shook his head irritably. "You are either going to be my salvation or my downfall."

Antonia gave him a sweet smile. "I would like to think the former."

"Yes, so would I, although I fear the latter. Now come and help me return this whale to your bed."

"Can we not put him elsewhere?"

"It has to look like he slept with you. When he awakes you must be convincing when you demand he never bed you again."

She moaned, thinking about his ugly hands and flesh on hers. "I do not know if I can."

"If you can't, then you're coming with me — now!"

"I will do it. Oh Michael, did you hear what he said about my *madre* and *padre*?" she said, hardly believing it still.

"Yes. It seems that many of us have our crosses to bear . . . even Dominguez."

Again a distant look sparked into the very depths of Michael's eyes; the same one Antonia had seen before when he had spoken of Man's cruelty. It was a look of sadness and hatred, of unquenched need and longing, of hunger and demons. It frightened her. This was a man with dark secrets of his own that he had not shared with her, and she desperately wanted to learn of them. At the same time, she feared the possible consequences such knowledge would hold.

Chapter Twenty-six

Dominguez awoke feeling mean. His head ached, and he was still partially dressed from the night before. He sat up and glared at Antonia, who sat across the room at her dressing table.

"So. You are finally awake," she snipped. "I do not care how much you try to frighten me in the future; if you ever lay your vile hands on me again and try do to me what you did last night, I swear I shall kill you!"

Dominguez rubbed his head. He did not remember satiating his lust on the girl. He narrowed his eyes. "Never threaten me again, if you know what is good for you. And do not try to play me for the fool, my flower. Nothing happened last night."

"What? You mean to tell me you do not recall your vicious behavior when you came to after I struck you with a vase?" She motioned to the shattered pieces, near the bed, thinking how Michael had thought of every detail. "I do not believe you! You were an animal," she raged.

"How am I to know I really had you? You could be making all this up to try to trick me."

She angrily hiked her skirts up to display the blood she had smeared on her thighs and sheets. Michael had provided her with evidence—in case she needed it—from a newly slaughtered steer. "Does this look like a trick?" she shrieked.

Dominguez looked doubtful but finally accepted her reconstruction of the evening. Every part of him aching, he rose and checked the sheets for blood before dressing. A crimson stain boldly blotched the bleached muslin. "I will accept your story . . . for now. But be forewarned, my flower, I will have you again and again. Whenever I so desire. You are always to be ready for me. Do you understand what I am saying?"

She raised her chin in defiance. "I do believe we understand each other."

"You never cease to amaze me. One would think you would have learned to hold your tongue." At her look of disdain, he added, "I assure you, you will learn. And if you ever strike me again, even in self-defense, I promise you will come to regret it. I will not be as lenient with you a second time. Now hurry and get dressed. We are having breakfast with the governor this morning."

By the time Antonia joined Dominguez and Governor Figueroa, the last remaining guest, under the grape arbor, they were already eating. *"Buenas días,* Governor," she said brightly, and took her seat. "Did I hear you correctly as I came out? Were you discussing my *padre?"* she asked.

"Señora Antonia, you are looking lovely as ever. Your husband and I were just discussing the benefits Don Diego might derive from being in familiar surroundings."

She leaned forward in her seat, an idea flashing into her mind. "You think that if I took him home to Rancho de los Robles he might regain his health more quickly?"

"The governor did not mean for you to accompany him, my flower. After all, you are still a bride," inserted Dominguez.

"And I shall miss you, El Señor," Antonia said. "But I know how much my *padre*'s health means to you; you told me so yourself last night. Surely we can both afford a few sacrifices if it will help my *padre*." Antonia forced herself to remain calm. The governor had just supplied her with the perfect excuse to take her *padre* safely home and away from Dominguez. And with the governor present there was nothing Dominguez could do about it.

"It is worth a try," put in the governor.

"*Sí, sí,* of course. Anything is worth a try," Dominguez conceded.

Antonia rose. "I shall order a carriage. The sooner I get my *padre* home, perhaps the sooner he will recover."

"My flower . . . wait. I will have a word with you before you leave," Dominguez said much too calmly, although silent fury reflected in his black eyes.

It was the governor's turn to rise. "I shall leave you two to your privacy. We shall continue our discussion another time, El Señor."

"Oh, no. Do not leave, Governor," Antonia said. "I know your business with my husband is important and your time with us will be brief. I am certain that what my husband has to say can be said in your presence, and then you two can continue your discussion."

"I had hoped to finish our discussion this morning . . ." added the governor. "If you have no objection, El Señor."

Dominguez sent Antonia a stinging look. "No. No, of course not. I merely wanted to tell my precious bride how much I will miss her and pray for her speedy return."

"Gracias," Antonia said, and suffered his kiss before hurrying to make preparations to leave.

Michael had traveled to the presidio to seek out confirmation of Dominguez's accusations that he had murdered Rosa, leaving Antonia only after eliciting a promise she would keep her distance from Dominguez. So what better way to keep her distance for a short time than by getting her *padre* away from Dominguez? she thought while she packed.

When the carriage arrived at the Rancho de los Robles servants rushed out of the hacienda to assist Don Diego inside. His sudden illness had been a topic of much gossip among the staff, since several of the Winston vaqueros had been present when Don Diego collapsed. And the servants who had attended the ill *ranchero* had carried stories of the man's unusual sickness of the mind to family and friends.

Don Diego was helped from the carriage and carried to his room. As he was assisted onto the bed, he sang, laughed and spoke to imaginary friends from long ago. Doña Maria, who had returned to the hacienda the day before, now trailed behind Antonia and her *padre*. She ordered a glass of warm milk and fussed over the *ranchero*.

"At least he is not aware of what a thoughtless child he has raised," Doña Maria huffed while she

229

plumped the thick down pillows.

"I thought *you* raised me, *tía* dear," Antonia said sweetly, barely able to refrain from unleashing her temper at her aunt's deliberate insult.

"Do not take that tone with me, young woman, after all I have done for you," Doña Maria sniffed.

"I know you have sacrificed much." Antonia sighed, swallowing the hard lump of defeat in her throat. She should have known better than to respond to her aunt's condemning chastisements, since the woman so obviously felt she was justified.

"Someday, when I am no longer around, you will come to regret those words, and remember all I have done for you."

Doña Maria stuck her nose in the air and exited. She stalked to her room, slammed the door shut, and went directly to her drawers. She lifted a bulging bag from its corner and set it down on the table. Removing its contents, she smiled to herself at the shiny gold coins.

"At last I can return to Spain and live the life I am entitled to. I will never have to depend on another's generosity again." She slowly counted the coins given her by Dominguez. Her thoughts wandered from her anticipated future to the part she had played in Antonia's marriage and Don Diego's illness.

Although Doña Maria had always been a stern woman, she did not consider herself a cruel, totally unfeeling person. She was convinced that Antonia would be well provided for by Dominguez. She had known Antonia would fight against the union but would never want for anything. For Doña Maria, there had been nothing worse than living off what she considered charity from her dear, departed sister's husband. Dominguez had enlisted her aid, professing his love and desire to care for the young señorita. He had watched Antonia blossom into a beautiful young woman, and said he would never be happy with anyone but Antonia for his wife.

When Doña Maria had first returned from Spain to help care for the motherless child, she had questioned her dead sister's choice of a husband. Don Diego was English, and she had heard many stories of such men marrying prominent Spanish señoritas for the status it brought them. Determined not to like the recently widowed man, she closed her mind to the love and devotion he had felt for her sister.

It had taken Don Diego years of patience, understanding, and determination to change her opinion. Yet their alliance had been one of mutual need rather than genuine affection.

She had needed a home and support after her family had left everything to the daughter who had chosen to remain in California, and he required someone to care for his daughter after his wife's death. Years had caused their relationship to mellow, but she had always desired to be independent again.

When Dominguez had come to her with his proposal, it seemed to be an excellent idea, one which everyone would prosper by. Dominguez would gain a wife, Don Diego would never have to worry about his daughter's future and gain a powerful partner, Antonia would marry someone of Spanish heritage and wealth, and she . . . well, she would gain her long-awaited chance to return to Spain an independent woman.

Even when Don Diego had hesitated, she never imagined that her persistence would have such dire consequences. She could not understand his sudden illness but knew it had something to do with Anto-

231

nia's wedding. His ramblings had told her that much. And Antonia's behavior had surprised her. The girl, who had always worshiped her *padre*, did not even bother to visit him until late the following day after he had been overcome.

"What is done is done," she said to herself and finished greedily counting the coins. The gold pieces reflected the sparks of independence in her dark eyes. Smiling, she lifted two neatly stacked rows and let them slip between her fingers. The coins tumbled to the floor while she repeated the gesture again, holding the pieces even higher. She took delight in her new wealth, caressing the coins against her cheeks and spreading them along her arm before sending them to join the other shiny gold pieces. When all the coins were strewn about the thick handcrafted rug, she fell to her knees and began laughing openly.

"Well, James Diego Winston, I no longer need you. I am free . . . free . . . do you hear me? Free at last!" She laughed and cried hysterically as she lifted the coins again, letting them clink freely about her skirts.

She planned to leave on the first ship available. She would travel to Boston where she would be able to transfer to a ship sailing for Spain. Soon she would be back in the country of her ancestors. There she would purchase living quarters near the seaport of Barcelona, so she would no longer suffer the cultural depravation she had experienced for so many years at the isolated rancho.

She summoned one of the male servants she thought she could trust.

"I want you to hasten to the harbor and inquire after all ships as to their departure dates and destinations. If you do not mention your mission to anyone, you will be generously rewarded, do you understand?"

"*Sí*, I understand. You need not worry."

"Good. Here is enough money to secure passage on the earliest vessel departing for Boston. There is a little extra for you as well. And there will more when I am assured that you have kept our little secret."

After the man left, she retired to her room and began preparing for her journey.

Chapter Twenty-seven

Antonia finished her toilette, smoothed her gown, and left her room. Living in the same house with El Señor Dominguez was beginning to wear on her, but she was determined to help Michael now that she had seen her *padre* safely home and out from under Dominguez's immediate threats.

"Antonia, my dear . . ." Governor Figueroa hailed her from the grand *sala* as she passed the open doors. "I have been hoping to speak with you. Join me, won't you?"

She entered the room. "What do you wish to discuss with me?"

"I spoke with El Señor earlier and was delighted that you two have accepted my invitation to accompany me to Monterey," Governor Figueroa said.

"Invitation?"

"*Sí*, the invitation I extended to El Señor to sail with me back to Monterey. Surely he discussed it with you."

"Naturally."

"A trip is just the thing you need to bring the color back to your pale cheeks."

He rose and strode to her to gently brush her cheek with the back of his hand, then escorted her to the velvet settee. "You have looked so drawn since your return from settling your *padre*. His illness and the unfortunate events involving that *capitán* and señorita seem to have placed quite a strain on you."

"Your concern is appreciated, Governor. But I am merely a little tired and much in need of rest."

"You are fortunate to have such a wonderful woman as Doña Maria to look after your *padre*." The governor sensed Antonia's underlying distress and attempted to cheer her with his dry humor. "You know, with someone like Doña Maria nursing Don Diego, he would not dare remain ill—she would never allow it."

Antonia forced a smile. Doña Maria had continued to be her rancorous self, even when Antonia was forced to leave her *padre* and return to the Dominguez Rancho. "How true. When do you plan to leave for Monterey?"

"I had planned to leave within a fortnight, but with so many loose ends to attend to I have postponed my departure date."

"What is this?" Dominguez deceptively chuckled when he entered the massive *sala*. "My flower, the governor is a very busy man. We must not put him in a position of feeling the necessity to engage in idle chatter just because you are his hostess." The enormous man lightly chided his bride as if she were a child. When he was certain the governor could not see, he cast her a warning with his cold black eyes.

"Nonsense," the governor responded. "I can think of no better way to while away the time than with a beautiful woman. In fact, it is such a beautiful day I would be delighted if you, señora, would consent to accompany me while I ride this morning."

"*Gracias.* I would be delighted." Antonia accepted the man's invitation before her "husband" could object.

"Then I shall clear my schedule and ride along as well," Dominguez offered, not wanting Antonia alone with the governor.

"I shall not hear of it. You have many business matters to attend to before we leave. And besides, what better opportunity do I have to spend some time alone with your lovely bride." Governor Figueroa slipped his arm about Antonia's waist in support as he spoke. His dark eyes smiled down at her, and he grinned at Dominguez, although he noticed her tense.

Dominguez wanted to protest, but the governor was an important man. Although Dominguez was not pleased that his wife was going riding with the governor, he planned to take steps to assure her silence.

"Alas . . ." Dominguez's lips curled upward into a feigned smile. "I have been outnumbered and must concede. You two shall enjoy your day alone while I think of nothing but the return of my beautiful flower."

Dominguez accompanied the pair outside. His arm around Antonia's waist, he drew her near and warned her that she was to be the devoted bride and not give the governor cause for concern.

"Do not worry, I shall take very good care of her, and shall see that she returns in plenty of time to rest before the evening's meal," the governor said.

Dominguez's face reddened and a muscle below his right eye twitched as he glared at Antonia. But he bent over and lightly brushed his lips near her ear.

236

While his mouth was close, he whispered to her, "Heed my words." He then smiled at the governor. "Do not allow my flower to travel too far."

"Come, my child, we shall select our animals. We shall see you after our ride, El Señor."

"Indeed you shall," Dominguez muttered as he watched them head toward the stables.

"I . . ." Antonia wanted to thank the man for coming to her aid, but she feared her words would be met by questions she could not yet answer.

"We shall speak later," he interrupted. "Now, let us ride."

The governor selected a spirited gray steed. He mounted and waited for Antonia, who was offered a slow, old roan. A sidesaddle shipped from Europe was already strapped to the beast's back.

Antonia bristled with indignation that she should be offered such an old nag by the stablehand. "This horse will not do. I am certain you are aware I am an accomplished equestrienne." She pointed to the sorrel. "I shall have that one."

"Sorry, señora, but El Señor, he order the roan days ago. Old Lady, she fine, gentle animal."

"He wasted little time," she muttered under her breath.

"Beg your pardon, señora?"

"Oh . . . it is nothing," she said, resigned to ride the nag.

The young man helped her to the top of her mount, and she rode over to join the governor.

She was sorely disappointed and she chided herself for not realizing that Dominguez would move swiftly to control every aspect of her life. Well, she'd make the best of it and enjoy her ride in spite of her mount. She was grateful to be away from the rancho again. Dominguez had allowed her barely three days with her *padre* before he had come to collect her. At least the governor's presence had made her return tolerable, and Dominguez had not tried to approach her again. And she still had to help Michael, although she worried about his absence.

It was another warm, sunny day, and the sky was a brilliant shade of royal blue. The gently rolling golden hills were dotted with gnarled and twisted oaks. Squirrels perched erect on massive boulders, and birds sang their sweetest songs. How could the world look so right when everything was so wrong? she wondered. Why did the sky have to match the color of Michael's eyes and the sun remind her of his smile? Her expression faded and her mouth dropped. Memories of his caress, his lips, his body flooded through her thoughts.

"Antonia," the governor shouted.

The sharpness of his voice startled her, and she grasped the reins to steady herself.

"Are you all right?"

"Ah . . . *Sí, sí,* I am fine. I am afraid I was daydreaming," she too quickly offered.

"Why not rest here for a moment." He dismounted and helped her down. "I feel there is something we need to discuss. You are not the happy bride."

"I . . . I am merely upset by my *padre's* illness and Rosa's murder, that is all." She bit her lower lip to keep it from quivering. She wanted to confide in him desperately, but now was not the time . . . not yet.

Placing his hand on her arm, he spoke in a soothing voice. "Your *padre* is a strong man. He will heal. But it is a pity that Rosa will not. That *capitán* seemed to be a good man. I suppose one can be misled by appearances. Do not worry, though. I shall see that justice prevails. The *capitán* will be caught and rightfully dealt with."

"No! He did not . . . it was not . . ." she blurted out, unable to contain herself.

The governor had been scrutinizing Antonia closely as he spoke. He was a man who did not miss much, and he had expected her response.

"Antonia, is there something I should know before I speak to Comandante Velasco?"

"No . . . *sí* . . . I can only tell you that Capitán Domino did not commit such a monstrous act. Now *por favor,* I must return before my husband is upset," she stammered, fearing the governor's delving questions.

"*Sí,* of course, but we shall speak another time." The governor could see she was distraught and unnerved by his questions. He decided not to press her. There would be another opportunity. Meanwhile he planned to learn what he could from the commandant. There was more than met the eye happening right under his nose, and he was going to get to the bottom of it.

"If you do not mind riding on ahead, I could use some time alone," Antonia ventured. "Not that you are not excellent company, Governor."

"Think nothing of it. I understand perfectly. Everyone needs time for themselves now and then. I shall see you back at the rancho."

"*Gracias.*"

Antonia remounted and wheeled her steed around. Watching the governor disappear ahead of her, she began a slow-paced ride back to the hacienda. Michael had been gone too long, and she worried for his safety, since Dominguez had spread his lying story.

Michael was coming to mean more and more to her, a fact she no longer attempted to deny. She wondered of his intentions. He certainly made no secret about desiring her physically and had exerted no minimum amount of energy to stave off the unwanted attentions of Dominguez and his men. But he had not given her cause to hope he had any other plan than destroying Dominguez before he harmed anyone else.

"Well, if it isn't the world traveler," called Michael, standing on a distant rock and waving his arms.

Antonia's heart skipped a beat when she saw the massive man silhouetted against the sun. Just seeing him sent her entire being soaring. "Michael!" She waved and rode toward him.

"You're the most difficult women to keep track of. I pity the man who falls in love and marries you," he jokingly chided.

His words were like sharp prongs skewering her heart clean through. Antonia braced herself. Her mouth dropped for an instant before she caught herself and forced a smile.

"Days ago when I returned I heard Dominguez's servants gossiping that you had gone with your *padre*. When I went there looking for you, you had already returned to Dominguez. Of course, by the time I reached the hacienda, you were nowhere to be found. It was only pure luck I heard the stableboy mention the 'nag' you had been forced to ride." His brows pulled together into a serious line. "I thought I told you not to take chances."

"You told me to stay away from Dominguez. That is exactly what I have been doing," Antonia protested.

"Yes, you certainly have; my man watching you reported that much. But now, why not dismount. We can make ourselves comfortable over there." He motioned toward an inviting grassy knoll under the spreading branches of a mighty tree. "And you can bring me up to date."

Antonia shifted uneasily in her saddle. His remark about pitying the man she would marry caused her to question giving herself so willingly to him. From what he had said it was obvious he was merely gratifying his animal pursuits with her while he sought to heap his revenge on Dominguez. She had no intention of being cast off like an old horse after he had tired of her.

"I think I had better be getting back."

Michael's smile faded at the sudden change in her demeanor, but he casually strode nearer her mount and easily swung up behind her. "I hope this sad excuse for a horse can carry our weight."

She stiffened under his embracing arms. "Maybe you would be wise to walk."

Michael straightened his back and silently slid his arms from around her waist. "If you insist."

"*Sí*, I do," she said, biting her lip.

"Did something happen while I was gone?"

"No. Why do you ask?"

He shrugged and jumped to the ground. "No reason." Without another word he slapped the horse on the rump and sent it trotting toward the hacienda.

Antonia had not ridden far when she glanced back over her shoulder. Michael had flipped his waistcoat over his arm and was trodding along as if he had not a care in the world.

"Damn you, Capitán Michael Domino," she mumbled under her breath. Trying to convince herself she was being foolish, she reined in the animal and cantered back to him.

"Have a change of heart, Princess?"

"It is obvious you have not," she said through tight lips.

He looked up at her, a strange undefinable glint

mirrored in his eyes.

"I just thought we should try the nag," she lamely offered.

"No, I think I'll walk." He waved her off. "See you back at the hacienda."

"You are insufferable," she snipped, and left him shading his eyes and staring after her.

Antonia was feeling totally deflated by the time she reached her rooms. She felt little better than the *putas* in town who gave themselves to the soldiers. At least they made gain from it. What had she gained? Her self-respect was waning, her *padre* was ill, and she had shattered all her ideals in a few moments of heated passion. She sank to her bed and remained there with the shutters closed for some time until it dawned on her that self-pity never solved anything. She was moving to fling the shutters open and allow the sun's rays to warm and revitalize her when Michael's fingers suddenly closed around her arm.

"Ohh!" she started and swung around.

"Tonia." His voice had a deep intensity to it. "I think it's time we had that talk."

Antonia's breath caught in her throat, and her pulse drummed in her head. A few hours ago she would have eagerly anticipated his words, but she was a proud California Lady and had no intention of being the one jilted.

"I am glad you have the time. I have been wanting to tell you that from now on I think we should keep our relationship strictly platonic. I admit I made a foolish mistake, but I realize it now."

"Hmm, you actually think so," he said blandly, crossing his arms over his chest.

"*Sí*, I do." Antonia's voice was grimly serious. She tilted her chin upward in a show of determination.

242

"All right, señorita, you can rest assured that I will not forget myself again," he said coldly.

"*Gracias.* Now what was it you wanted to speak to me about?" Antonia asked, her voice void of the tumultuous emotions running rampant inside her.

"I have figured out a new plan. If you are still interested, I want to discuss it with you."

"Of course I am interested. I want to see Dominguez destroyed as much as you do. There is no reason we cannot continue to work together toward a common cause," she replied softly.

Impersonally he said, "No, of course not. Sit down and I'll tell you what I have in mind."

Chapter Twenty-eight

Antonia sat on the edge of her seat waiting to hear how they would proceed to destroy the evil man who had tried to ruin her *padre* and marry her as part of his plan for revenge and power. At the same time her heart ached, for no matter what she had said to Michael she could not deny what she continued to feel. He had awakened wild undeniable desires, longings, cravings, for which she still hungered. But he did not want her, and she would not be just a plaything for him to use. She folded her hands in her lap and determined to hold fast to her resolve to keep him at arm's distance from now on.

"You remember how I had planned to discover the branding irons the night of the fiesta when Dominguez held one of his special little entertainments in his cellar room?" he began, settling down too near Antonia for comfort.

She cleared her throat and edged away. *"Sí."*

Michael cast her an amused glance and continued to unravel his plan. "Since all Dominguez's illustrious guests are gone, that is not possible now, but the governor remains at the hacienda. I've heard Governor Figueroa is a fair and honest man, and if I can get him into that room—"

Antonia looked doubtful. "Dominguez never would take him down there."

"Maybe not, but if they thought I was hiding in the cellar, and the commandant just happened to be summoned out to the rancho at that time, Dominguez couldn't stop them without drawing undue attention to himself."

"They are not going to be looking for branding irons, though," worried Antonia.

"No. But if they just happened to fall from his cupboard, wouldn't it seem a strange place to keep such pieces which should be stored in a barn? It would arouse curiosity and with a little shove in the right direction, Dominguez would be caught in his own web of deceit."

"It all seems so complicated. Why not just confide in Governor Figueroa. After all, he is the most capable governor we have ever had. You know we have had four governors since 1831 with the internal strife ignited by secularization of the missions and the problems between the north and south. Governor Figueroa cares about California and will do what is right. He even has been working to alleviate the plight of the Indians. I think we should confide in him."

"There has to be proof, not just suspicion, and I don't want to give Dominguez the chance to garner an explanation or spirit away the evidence I planted."

"All right." Antonia sighed, conceding his plan was feasible yet dangerous. "What part do I play?"

"Your part, Princess, is to get yourself back to your father's hacienda. It's going to be too risky here for you from now on, and I don't want to have to worry about you. I might have to move fast and you will only slow me down."

"So, I shall only slow you down." Antonia grinned impudently. "I do not think I have slowed down so far, have I?"

"You haven't? If it were not for you I probably would be done with my plan and on my way back to England by now."

She gave an impertinent shrug of her shoulders. "I beg your pardon, *capitán.* I truly apologize if I have caused you any inconvenience."

"God woman." Michael dragged his fingers through his hair and stalked to the shutters, throwing them open and staring out without a thought that he might be seen. "If you were a sailor on my ship, you would have been flogged long ago."

"Then I am indeed fortunate, as are you. If I were a man I would have called you out and thoroughly thrashed you," she snapped.

"I don't see why being a woman has stopped you." He turned and strode over to stand in front of her, his hands on his hips. "The fact that you are a woman has not halted you yet from thinking you can do everything a man does." His brow shot up in amusement. "At least *almost* everything."

"You truly are insufferable."

"So you have said. Are you going to follow my instructions this time?" He thinned his lips to glare at her.

"Who do you think you are, my husband?" Antonia snarled.

"Heaven forbid. If I were, you wouldn't be involved in this at all," he said flatly.

"Oh?"

"I would keep you at home flat on your back."

"If I were your wife I would be at your side," she retorted.

"You probably would." He sighed his frustration at the beautiful vixen's stubborn streak. "We best get back to your father's ranch."

Antonia was determined not to be sent away like some nun to a convent. She leaned her hands back on the bed and jutted out her chin. "Dominguez will never stand for his 'wife' to be out of his sight," she argued.

"No, I am certain he would much prefer to have you gracing his bed instead. Is that what you want, to lie beneath him? You already had a taste of what it would be like. And if you will remember, I stopped him none too soon. Furthermore, Dominguez may not like you leaving his side, but since he is trying to maintain some semblance of the doting husband, with the governor here, he can hardly refuse a distraught daughter wanting to be near her ailing father."

"I do not want to leave," Antonia said, feeling she was losing ground. "I can help. I can make sure the governor and the *comandante* are led to the cellar at the right time."

"I said no. Try listening for once . . ." Michael began darkly. He did not have the opportunity for further argument as an impatient knock at the door interrupted them.

"Hurry! Get under the bed." Antonia jumped up, bent over, and lifted the spread.

"Oh, for Chrissake, not again." Michael rolled his eyes and slid beneath the large bed.

Dominguez was tapping his foot with his usual impatience outside the door when Antonia slipped the lock and opened the heavy barrier.

"Why, my flower, is it really necessary to barricade

yourself in our rooms? I told you that you need not concern yourself of my touch—not at the present anyway. I got what I wanted, and I am sure you noticed I had my clothing removed from the wardrobes. You are no further use to me now. Not until your *padre* has recovered." He grinned evilly.

"Then what do you want?" Antonia said curtly.

"I brought this note from your *tía*. I thought it might be of some importance." He strolled past her and plunked down on the bed, sagging the mattress dangerously close to Michael underneath.

Antonia's eyes rounded and she rushed to drag a chair from the corner of the room. "Would you not be more comfortable here?"

"I told you, you have nothing to worry about at the moment. But if you insist." He groaned and lumbered to his feet. Michael breathed a sigh of relief when the bulky man moved to sit on the now straining chair.

Anxious to see the last of Dominguez, Antonia said, "You said you have a note for me?"

"Ah, *sí*." He held out his hand containing the flowery, pink stationery. The flap hung free from the envelope. He had read the missive and, no doubt, after finding it amusing, sought the pleasure of watching her discomfort when she read it. "The message was delivered after you and the governor left for your ride earlier."

Antonia snapped it out of his hand. "It appears you already know of it contents," she said caustically, and drew the note from its encasement. She read it to herself.

Antonia—
    While my heart arches for Diego's untimely illness, my job in California has come to an end

with your marriage. I have seen you safely wed and now feel free to return to my beloved Spain. I only wish you could have come to realize how fortunate a match was made for you before I departed—maybe in time. I took only what was rightfully mine, the jewels which Diego long denied me. They will provide me the opportunity to live a life long overdue me. Until I entered Diego's locked room to retrieve the jewels and saw for myself his mementos of love for my dear departed sister, I had felt him not deserving. I pray he will forgive me for thinking the worst of him. I was wrong. He has indeed suffered long for his sins, and I no longer bear him ill will. Know only that God has found it in his heart to deliver me from a life of isolated deprivation.

Doña Maria

After Antonia read the note she neatly tucked it into the pocket of her skirt. Without a show of feelings, she looked Dominguez straight in the eyes and answered flatly. "My *tía* is a woman free to stay or leave by her own will."

"As well as by the help of my pocketbook."

"I do not know what are you talking about."

"I am talking about paying her handsomely for you, my flower. How else do you think it would have been so easy to have claimed you as a bride?"

"I do not believe you!"

He smiled, for in spite of the girl's denial, he could see by the crushed expression on her face that she realized it was true.

Antonia kept up a brave front, but the recollection of Doña Maria's insistence that she marry Dominguez haunted her; she recalled the special gown and how the two had left her in front of her *padre*'s door and went into Doña Maria's room together. In an attempt to change the topic, she said, "Now, if you will excuse me, I wish to rest."

"Of course, but you must inform me of your *padre*. When you hear of his condition, that is."

Antonia attempted to control her growing anger, but her feelings were becoming all too obvious. Her chest began heaving, and her neck and cheeks reddened. Her response to his last request was short and curt. "El Señor, I am certain you are most aware that my *padre*'s condition remains unchanged. Now, if you will please be good enough to leave." Antonia turned and proudly moved to fling the door crashing against the wall. *"Adiós, señor."*

Once alone again, Michael slithered from underneath the bed and rose to his feet, brushing the dust swirls from his breeches. "I'm willing to bet no one has dusted under your bed since the last time I was there."

"The servants may not be as meticulous in cleaning there, since I usually do not entertain guests under my bed, *capitán*."

"Just see that you don't start 'entertaining guests' on top of it, either." A crooked grin captured his lips. "Unless I'm the guest, of course."

"You need not worry. I have no intention of inviting anyone into my bed."

Michael frowned but did not make further comment. "You must agree it's time for you to go to your *padre* after what you learned about your aunt."

How could Antonia argue with him now? Doña Maria had left without even saying good-bye. For a moment Doña Maria's actions caused a sadness to come over her. She put it from her mind, realizing from the note that Doña Maria, in her own twisted way, had only done what the woman thought was best for her.

Antonia had lost this round, but she was not about to concede the battle. One way or another she was bound and determined to help destroy Dominguez.

After Dominguez left Antonia, he went to Figueroa's room and invited the governor to join him in the library. Unaware that the governor had visited the presidio and learned much from the commandant, Dominguez expressed his concern for Don Diego and his wife's health. He discussed his plans to alleviate the burden of running the vast Rancho de los Robles while Don Diego convalesced and talked of plans to introduce his wife into society in Monterey and Mexico City. Of course, he planned to provide for Don Diego's care while they were away. Pretending humble innocence to the intricacies of government, he offered to assist in any way he could but stated unequivocally that he was not interested for himself.

Governor Figueroa listened politely to the man while carefully observing his newly discovered adversary. With Dominguez content that the governor was an ally, it would be easier to look into the rumors and other interesting statements about Dominguez, which he had learned while at the presidio. And his presence would also ensure Antonia's safety.

The men spent the afternoon and into the evening discussing plans for the future of California; the governor quietly drawing Dominguez out. After a servant inquired as to when the evening meal should be served and the time set, the men parted to dress for the evening.

Dominguez opened the connecting door to Antonia's rooms. She was reclining on the bed, lost to troubled dreams. Before he awakened his sleeping wife, he stood over her admiring his possession.

"What a pity that you could not have been your *madre*," he sneered. He then roughly shook Antonia with enough force to startle her. She bolted upright and pulled her knees protectively into her chest.

"It is time for you to get ready for the evening meal," he said dryly. He walked over to the door, then hesitated and ordered over his shoulder, "Wear the beige lace gown tonight." Not bothering to wait for a reply, he snapped the door shut.

Antonia took a deep breath and walked to the wardrobe. She took out the beige gown, but, spurning his demands, returned it to the rod and slipped into the pale yellow.

Tonight, in front of the governor, she would announce her intentions to travel to her *padre*'s rancho to care for him. But she would return to help destroy Dominguez—that she vowed!

Chapter Twenty-nine

Much to Dominguez's dismay, the governor had decided to extend his stay in San Diego indefinitely. Dominguez had hoped to sail for Monterey with the governor soon in order to broaden his contacts and seek support for his ambitions. And he was tiring of playing the perfect host and devoted husband.

He longed to be free to entertain in his room of pleasures without the presence of watchful eyes nearby. He felt the uncontrollable tension building in his body, and knew he soon would be forced to seek its release or take his frustrations out in front of his guest—an act which would be viewed with great displeasure and seriously jeopardize his plans.

His thoughts turned to his favorite instrument of pleasure. It was such a small, slender riding whip, but in his hand it became a powerful precision tool with which he crafted his superiority.

Unfortunately for Antonia she had not left to care for her *padre* that morning as she had announced the night before. Dominguez had been forced begrudgingly to allow her departure at the urging of the governor at dinner. Governor Figueroa even suggested he accompany her to visit his ailing *amigo*.

They were to leave before sunrise, and after she had informed Michael of that, and he had obtained her promise that she would keep to her rooms until she left, he had felt secure enough to leave her while he and the man he'd had watching over her sought further information to tighten the noose around Dominguez's neck.

After the governor had begged her indulgence to wait until he returned from an unexpected but necessary trip to the presidio, Antonia had grown bored and anxious waiting in her room so she had haplessly ventured into the library to select a book while Dominguez was engaging in one of his favorite perverted fantasies.

"My flower, I thought you and the governor would be on your way to care for your ailing *padre* by now," he sneered. "Why is it you are not?"

Her pulse raced and her eyes widened upon hearing her husband's question. Caught off guard, she mumbled her response and took a seat.

"Speak up, woman," he impatiently thundered.

The fierceness in his face caused her hands to tremble, but she was not about to let him know her state and seated herself quietly.

"Well . . ." came the fury of his words like the hiss of a snake about to strike.

"He . . . ah, the governor was unexpectedly called to the presidio," she whispered through quivering lips. It became difficult to hide her growing fear that learning she was alone would lead him to forget the facade of gentleness he had shown her in the governor's presence. And Michael was not nearby this time.

"We are alone?" She had pricked his interest, and his brow flew upward. "When will Governor Figueroa be returning?" The intensity in his black eyes sharpened.

Antonia took a deep breath, closed her eyes, and answered his questions. "Very soon, I am sure. Now, if you will excuse me."

She proudly rose, attempting an air of bravado in hopes it would serve to give her enough time to escape his presence. Had not her *padre* once told her the best defensive pose was an offensive one? She felt like one of the desert lizards which puffed up and stood its ground in an attempt to outwit its enemies with a feigned display of forcefulness.

Before she had reached the wide double doors, he was behind her and grabbing her arm. Antonia swung around, not attempting to conceal the distaste for him in her eyes.

"My flower, you are trembling. Come, I have something in the cellar that will remedy your condition." He smiled.

She had tried to outwit him, but her shivering body had betrayed her. Panic began to overtake her, and she attempted to keep her wits by rationalizing he was just going to take her to select a bottle of spirits from the cellar. Then the thoughts of what Michael had told her of Dominguez's secret room surfaced. She could not allow him to force her into that room. She started to fight his efforts.

"Let go of me!" She struggled in earnest.

Her attempts at release were met with steely determination by the enormous man, who was enjoying his wife's panic; it spurred him to tighten his grasp.

"You will enjoy this, my flower." He laughed sadistically.

Antonia screamed, hoping the servants would hear

her cries and investigate.

To her utter dismay no one came.

"I am afraid no one will come to your aid, my flower. The servants learned long ago to turn a deaf ear when I am entertaining."

Without another word he forced her down the stairs.

Once in the room of pleasures, he paused deciding what would be the most appropriate method to introduce his wife to the true joys of his life.

Antonia stood still, terror and disbelief etching her face as she surveyed the room. She had never seen anything like it. There were so many strange evil-looking instruments positioned about the room.

"My flower, if you will be kind enough to disrobe, we shall begin," he said with a strangely calm intonation, which emphasized the half-crazed look in his eyes.

Antonia turned and sought to flee but found he had blocked the door. There was no escape. She faced him silently with her chin held high and her arms stiff at her sides.

He moved ever so slowly toward his victim-wife. There was no need to rush. No one would come to her aid; besides, no one could hear her cries down here. Excitement coursed through his veins at the total power he had over her. He felt the mighty cat which had cornered a helpless mouse; the victor, his wife the spoils.

He methodically reached out and placed his sweaty palm on her trembling shoulder. His touch repulsed her so, she sought the sanctity of oblivious darkness.

When she returned to consciousness, she found herself strapped to a table, her ankles tied widely apart. He was seated on a chair next to her patiently sipping a glass of wine.

"Did you have a pleasant rest, my flower? I would invite you to join me in a toast, but you appear to be unable to tear yourself away." He gave a short laugh.

He finished the spirits and began to search the room. She watched in terror as his ire grew when he seemed to be unable to locate what he was looking for. After a string of curses he settled for a small whip and placed it on the chair in full view of her helpless form.

"You have been such a naughty girl not disrobing for me. Now you must pay." He smiled with vicious intent.

Antonia bit her lip, determined not to give him the satisfaction of her screams.

His eyes narrowed in annoyance at her silence, and he picked up the whip and slowly fingered it over her head, delighting in the feel of the leather against his skin. Then swiftly he raised it high over his head and brought it down with a stinging blow on the table next to her.

She flinched but did not cry out, biting deeper into her lip until she could taste her own warm, sticky blood.

He had no intention of striking his wife until the governor left. But he was enjoying the afternoon. It served as a sample of what he would delight in when they were finally alone.

Their eyes locked, hers in terror and hatred, his in crazed desire. For what seemed to Antonia an eternity she held her stare, unyielding, afraid to look away for fear the consequences would somehow be worse if she did.

"You are your *madre*'s child," he snarled, breaking the stalemate of their eyes.

"And you . . . what are you?" she said in more of

a disgusted than frightened tone.

"Me? I am the one who controls your fate. I own you and do not ever forget that." He let out a heinous laugh.

Antonia was sagely silent. She had already dared more than wise. And now her breasts heaved as her body increased the flow of air to accommodate the blood rushing through her veins.

Just as he hefted the whip high again the air was filled with the sharp sounds of a choking cough and a wine bottle shattering to the floor outside the door in the cellar. Antonia deemed the sounds were from an embarrassed servant who sought her aid the only way possible. Unbridled hatred etched Dominguez's face, and he began loosening her bonds.

"You may be brave this time. But there will be another time when the governor is gone and there will be no one to question the kiss this, instrument of love," his lips twisted with sinister self-satisfaction, "will leave on such soft sweet flesh." Despite the tensions still striking him, he removed her bonds.

Antonia was grateful for the governor's presence and thankful to whomever had rallied to her aid. But the fear she felt of Dominguez reached new heights, and she vowed that he would never force her to undergo such horrors again.

He straightened her golden curls and escorted her to her rooms. There he opened the door but did not enter. Bowing widely, he grinned. *"Gracias señora,* for a most pleasurable afternoon. May we have many such encounters. I shall send your servant with hot water so you may refresh yourself before the governor returns."

"You *bastardo,"* she spat, and flung the door shut in his face. The shrill of his evil laughter assaulted her ears before the sounds faded as he moved away.

Still shaking, she jumped when Michael put a hand on her shoulder.

"I cannot leave you for even a second." He brusquely flung the words at her. When she turned he saw the terror in her eyes. "Oh, Tonia." He sighed and folded her into his embrace.

"It was terrible." She began to sob. "I thought he was going to . . . to—"

"It's all right, Princess, I know," he said soothingly.

She choked back another sob. "How do you know?"

"Because I was the one who broke the bottle in the cellar."

"You?"

"Yes."

"Then why did you not stop him?" she cried.

"I had only returned to the hacienda moments before. I nearly rode my horse into the ground to return after hearing the governor tell the commandant you had postponed your return to your *padre*. I searched the whole damned house looking for you. It was only a stroke of luck I went down into the cellar and found the door ajar. If he had seen me all my plans would have been for nothing, so I merely interrupted him without presenting myself."

"You should have killed him," Antonia said, surprised by her own venomous feelings.

"Nothing would have made me happier. Except I want him to experience how it feels to be destroyed. It took me long, hard years after he beat me and I missed my ship to overcome the taint of being branded a deserter."

Antonia closed her eyes and listened to the beat of his heart as he held her. It was thudding nearly as rapidly as hers, and she wondered if it was because

259

he spoke of revived memories of what Dominguez had done to him. For a second she had hoped it was something else—a small feeling for her—but that was too much to ask.

Michael stroked her silken hair and rested his chin on the top of her head. Oh, how he ached for her. She was so proud, so spirited, and still so innocent. He found himself thinking of more than just his physical desire again. If she belonged to him he would protect her with his life; no harm would ever befall her while there was still a breath left in his body. *If she belonged to him?* The thought rattled his usual unshakable manner and he stepped back from her. "Get ready. I'm going to personally see to it that you reach your father's ranch without further delay."

Antonia did not argue this time, and began changing her gown while Michael graciously consented to turn his back.

"Does Dominguez have any weapons in the house?" he asked. "I want to be prepared just in case we encounter any of his men. And I want you to have a weapon."

Antonia hurriedly slipped into the white-patterned gown. "He is an avid collector. Come and I will show you."

"Just tell me. I want you to stay here."

"It makes more sense for me to go with you. If we run into anyone, I can help."

"Don't you ever give up?" he groaned.

Moments later they quietly left her rooms and made their way toward the formidable collection. The specimens of destruction were magnificent. The room was filled with long arms, powder horns, bullet horns, and priming horns, swords, crossbows, knifes, and a variety of pistols. Each item was hung or laid in deliberate fashion to display it properly.

Antonia stood inside the door for several moments, taking it all in as Michael quickly moved about the room from item to item. He wanted something which she could easily conceal and carry with her at all times. Those needs immediately disqualified the long arms, swords, and crossbows.

He turned his attention to the smaller weapons, hoping to find a pistol she was familiar with and one which would not readily be missed. On his way to the pistol collection he stopped at a Spanish stiletto with an ivory handle, inlaid on the hilt with precious stones, and gold-plated scabbard. Next to it lay a leather sheath. The perfect size. He scooped up the knife and handed it to Antonia.

"Put it in your skirt pocket," he directed, then neatly rearranged the nearby weapons and continued his search for a pistol.

His quest for another weapon Antonia could easily conceal was about to come to a fruitless end when Antonia spied a percussion-lock pocket pistol with silver-plated handle. Upon closer examination she found it was a new type she had never seen before. Afraid she might not be able to load the weapon, Michael set it aside and handed her a flintlock pistol he had found. It was slightly larger, but small enough so she could still hide it from view. Michael quickly grabbed several lead balls. He flipped out a handkerchief from his pocket and poured as much powder from a horn into so it that would fit without spilling and tied it securely. Without further delay they left the room and slipped back into her rooms unnoticed.

"Thank God," she said, panting from the suspense of being a thief of need.

"I hope you know how to load this," he said. He

looked over the gun and then handed it back to Antonia. "Explain to me how you load it. And show me."

"Let me see, I should cock it first. *Sí*, that is it." Her fingers trembled as she went about the task. "Then, pour powder into the pan. Oh . . ." She pursed her lips and hurriedly brushed the spilled dust from the carpet. "Lower the hammer next and then what?" She knitted her brows together examining the pistol and trying recall the next step. "Oh *sí*, the barrel. I have to put powder into the barrel and then the ball, and push it down with the ramrod. There. It is ready. All I will have to do is pull the hammer back and squeeze the trigger," she said triumphantly.

"I'll be damned." He chuckled. "You not only know how to shoot a gun, you really know how to handle it as well." His expression suddenly turned serious. "We best get going," he said.

Chapter Thirty

"Hurry up and leave Dominguez a note so we can depart," Michael prodded.

"Why should I give him any information about my whereabouts?" Antonia protested.

"Because you don't want him sending out his vaqueros to look for you, do you?"

"You're right." Antonia sighed and quickly scribbled a few lines across her stationery, explaining that she felt an urgent need to visit her *padre* since Doña Maria had left. She slashed her tongue across the flap of the envelope, pinched it shut, and propped it against the gown she had been wearing when Dominguez had forced her into his room of pleasures.

Once outside, Antonia headed toward the stables.

"Where do you think you're going?" Michael's voice stopped her.

"To get a horse," she said as if it was too obvious to even question.

"Don't you think Dominguez may have spies watching out for you, should you try to leave without his consent?"

Antonia frowned and thought of the nag he had forced her to ride, and how he had arranged it in advance. "How do you propose we get to my *padre*'s rancho then? Walk?" She threw her hands on her hips and stared at Michael.

"Exactly. We'll head out to the coast and then back inland just in case Dominguez has other plans for you."

"It is an awfully long way," Antonia moaned, her eyes dropping to the delicate slippers she wore. "Why did you not tell me we were going to walk?" She looked dismayed.

"Don't worry, Princess, we'll make it even if I have to carry you." Michael snatched her hand into his and began the trek west toward the coast.

All day Antonia strained to keep up with Michael's swift pace. He stalked along practically dragging her, and never once asked if she wanted to stop and rest. Although Antonia did not complain, her temper was simmering near the surface as she trod alongside him in the blazing summer heat.

Michael tightened his grip on her slender hand. Just the thought of her closeness warmed his heart. She was having difficulty keeping up with the grueling pace he had set, but she was resilient and determined. She did not complain like most women would have, and he respected her for it.

Once on the coast Michael squinted out to sea while Antonia plunked down on a nearby rock.

"What are you looking for?"

"My ship, if you must know. If you'll remember, it was forced to leave the harbor after I was accused of murder and found it necessary to stay out of sight."

"I thought we were going to head inland toward my *padre*'s rancho?"

"I've had a change of heart. If I can locate my ship I'm going to deposit you where you won't be able to get into any more trouble."

"Why you . . ." Antonia hissed, "you are not—"

"Oh, yes I am, Princess. Now get up. There are signs of a white mast on the horizon a short way north, and if it's the *Áureo Princesa* we're in luck."

"You mean *you* are in luck, do you not?" Antonia ground out. She jutted out her chin and crossed her arms over her chest in a gesture of defiance. Just let him try to make her rise to her feet!

"Are you going to get up?"

"I am not."

"All right, my clever little wench," he said with resolution. "Have it your way."

Without another word he swooped down on her and scooped her over his shoulder.

"Put me down," Antonia croaked, mad as a flagged bull. She struggled but he held her fast, his boots sinking into the soft sand as he quickened his pace north. "If you do not put me down, I will—"

"I just bet you will." He chuckled and whacked her buttocks with a stinging wap.

"Oh!" Antonia's eyes flicked wide at the sharp swat which had just assaulted her bottom.

"Are you ready to walk yet?" Michael snorted after lugging her for some time.

"No." Antonia wriggled, trying to struggle free.

"I would stop that if I were you before you give me less than honorable ideas, Princess."

Antonia pressed her lips together in exasperation, but the feel of his hard shoulders rubbing against her belly was not easy to endure. Despite her efforts, the friction was arousing her, and she had to fight the sensations of her own body. "All right," she finally cried, "I shall walk. But do not talk to me."

"At last. You're not as light as you look, you know."

"I am, too," she protested.

Michael set her down and cast her a wicked grin. "Actually you are just right—in all the right places."

"I will thank you not to discuss my anatomy," she huffed.

"As you wish." He turned and strode off.

Antonia hiked her skirts and struggled after him.

Not more than a half hour later Michael stood on shore, waving out at the bobbing vessel. A longboat was sent ashore, and Michael lifted Antonia over the side, and they were rowed aboard.

"Cap'n, where by thunder have ye been?" Thadius's bushy brows arched in disapproval toward Antonia.

"It's a long story. I'll tell you about it later. But right now we need something to fill our bellies, right, Princess?" Michael looked over at Antonia, who just glared back at him and refused to answer.

"I'll see t' some food." The chief mate frowned. "What's this we be 'earin' 'bout ye bein' wanted fer murder?" Thadius abruptly asked.

"I thought you were seeing to the needs of our stomachs," Michael said flatly.

"Aye," Thadius grumbled.

"Come on, Princess, let's go to my cabin."

"Some people might call this kidnapping," she chirped, still angry at being spirited away.

"Yes, some people might. Are you going to walk or am I going to be forced to carry you again?" He took a threatening step toward her.

"I shall walk," she snapped, then refused to say another word.

They had barely reached his cabin and stepped inside when the Indian was spied through the glass.

Michael ran out on deck followed by Antonia and was joined there in moments by Thadius. They stood at the rail, the breeze whipping their hair as they waited for the Indian to come aboard.

"What took you so long, my friend?" asked Michael, casually leaning his elbow against the rail while Antonia stood silently nearby.

"My brother, you wasted little time while we were apart," Mano observed, glancing at Antonia.

Antonia bit her lip and lowered her eyes, remembering the last time she had seen the Indian.

"Aye, 'tis true. But they only be arrivin' a short time before ye, but he seems t' 'ave got 'isself a clam, that one," Thadius said, arching a glowering brow at Antonia.

"That is enough, man," Michael warned.

Antonia bit deeper into her lip, and for a moment considered blurting out the reason for her refusal to respond earlier. What was the use? It was obvious these were Captain Domino's men, and not a one would rise to her aid.

Thadius's words struck a sharp chord with Michael, too. He had at first thought his idea of safely depositing Antonia out of Dominguez's reach would be appreciated, but when she refused to barely speak to him he wondered at his own folly. Yet he still desired her as much—if not more—than he ever had. With a sigh he turned his attention to the young boy who had boarded with Mano and was now standing mutely behind several of his crew.

"And who might this one be?" Michael questioned, and Thadius grabbed the boy by the arm and dragged him from the rear of the crew. The youngster did not look up, remaining with eyes fixed on the deck of the ship. Mano stepped to the young Indian and put his arm around his lean shoulders.

"A scrawny one, this one." Thadius chuckled and pinched the boy's upper arm. "Not much meat or muscle on 'em bones."

"Why don't you take him below and fill his belly," Michael suggested. "We'll talk later."

Mano nodded his agreement, took the youth below, and summoned Mr. Russell to bring a hot and hearty meal. Then he requested the cabin boy to fetch clean trousers, a shirt, and shoes for the youngster. The cabin boy looked him over and scurried off to seek garments of a suitable size. Before the boy disappeared down the passageway Mano called for him to fetch hot water, too.

A short while later, not only steaming water arrived but a tub as well. Suitable clothes for the young Indian were draped over the edge of the tub. Mano stripped off his dust-ridden clothing and, after pouring the buckets of steaming water into the tub, sank into the hot liquid.

When he was through with his bath, he stepped from the tub, met with a large drying cloth. Mano dressed and then turned to the young Indian who had accompanied him in his search for clues to aid his captain.

"Well, my filthy brother, now it is your turn. Remove those rags and climb into the tub. It will soothe you as well as clean the dirt from your body."

"No!" the boy shouted, and crouched in the corner like a bobcat ready to fight. "I wash later, no sit water."

Mano sensed a fierce, unnatural uneasiness in the youngster. But if he were going to bunk with Mano a bath was in order.

"If you do not want to go to the mission, and wish to remain on board this vessel as you told me, you must not smell of old animal hides. Now come."

268

The young boy did not budge.

Mano knew he would not be allowed to remain unless the odor of many days' traveling was washed away. With determination lining his lips, his eyes like hardened obsidian, he strode over to the boy, roughly hauled him off his feet, and with his arms and legs flailing desperately, dumped him headfirst into the tub. The young Indian came up sputtering, brown streams of water running down his face mingling with straggly black strands of hair.

"To clean yourself properly you must remove those rags," Mano said flatly.

"No! You go!"

The youngster fought like a wild animal but was no match for the older Indian. After Mano had completed ripping the clothes from the boy's back his mouth dropped open in total surprise. All words left him and he remained stationary, staring in disbelief.

Finally finding his tongue Mano said, "Why did you not tell me you are female—a young girl?" Mano was amazed with himself that he had been with the young Indian for days and had not discovered the truth.

"I not girl. I woman. I have much children someday. I lived at mission with grandfather, but he called to spirit world. He dead now, murdered by *bandidos* and I no return to mission. I stay. You say I boy, no me," she said, speaking more in the last few minutes than she had since Mano rescued her from a bunch of vaqueros.

Mano's face softened and a gentle smile took root. He understood all too well. The friars meant well, but their treatment of the Indians was often less than kind. He knew the punishment meted out for leaving the mission without consent would be harsh, consid-

269

ered cruel if directed toward a white man.

He looked toward the young woman who proudly stood unclothed before him—with no shame. He felt a strange sensation, and wondered if it were a sign. He dismissed it for the time being. He had a responsibility to his captain, his brother. Later he would think more of this young woman.

Mano moved to the door. Before he left to fetch her proper attire, he turned. "What are you called?"

This time she did not hesitate as she had after he had rescued her days earlier. "My people Juañeo indios. I White Dove. No call that now. I go by name you give. You call Juanito."

"Juanito, no," he said. "I shall call you Juanita."

By the time he returned with a gown, Juanita was dressed in the trousers and shirt delivered with the tub. They hung loosely around her small frame. She had secured them with a length of rope found in the cabin. Mano handed her the gown, but she laid it aside.

"No time pretty dress. I work. Earn way."

He frowned his displeasure but left to speak with Michael.

Michael was standing on the quarterdeck talking to Thadius, and Antonia was sitting glumly on a cask nearby when Mano strode up.

"I be wonderin' when ye be up t' speak t' us. How's the lass farin'?"

Mano remained stoic, but a faint glint in his black eyes gave way his astonishment at the chief mate's perceptiveness, and Michael's brows shot up in amused surprise. Antonia's head bobbed up, but she continued to remain mute.

"Laddie, I may be just an old sea dog, but I be knowin' the difference betw'n lad and lass." Thadius gave a hearty, belly-rolling chuckle. "Ye may be a wise one in many ways, but like yer cap'n 'ere, ye have much t' learn of women."

"How right you are, Thadius," Michael said sadly, turning a somber gaze to Antonia. "Later you'll have to fill us in on how you came to bring her on board, but now we must retire to my cabin. I want to hear if you have learned anything of use while we have been separated. We have decisions to make. Tonia, go below and join our other female guest. I'll have that food we talked about earlier sent to you."

Antonia raised her chin high and swallowed hard. He had called her Tonia and it ripped at her heart, but she was not going to be softened from her decision. Still refusing to talk to Michael, she directed her answer to Thadius. "I would prefer to remain here."

Michael stepped over to her and placed his hand heavily on her shoulder. Antonia stiffened at his touch.

"Very well, señora," he said flatly, "have it your own way . . . for now. But sooner or later you're going to have to talk to me. And until you do, you're welcome to remain topside. I must warn you, it does tend to get a little cool and damp up here at night." He then turned from her, but knew he could not carry out his threat. If only she was not proving to be so stubborn. At that moment he wished he was not a man of his word, for he would have liked nothing better than to gather her into his arms and carry her directly to his bed.

The word "señora" stung, and caused tears to well in her eyes as she stared blankly out to sea. He knew she was not actually married to that swine. Why had Michael called her señora? To antagonize her, no doubt.

Thadius scanned the open sea, furrowed his

brows, then entered Michael's cabin behind him. Mano, too, glanced out to sea following Thadius's lead and then joined them inside.

They had just seated themselves to bring each other up to date when they were interrupted by the gruffly rasping voice of one crewman.

"Sail ho," a sailor shouted from high aloft.

Michael grabbed his eyeglass and immediately ran on deck. He put the cylinder to his lashes to get a better look at the ship sighted, and then handed the glass to Thadius right behind him.

"Looks like it bein' the bloody *Sea Shark*. I must say her cap'n, that scoundrel Brian Thomas, give her a good name, he did. Those pirates, damn 'em, been followin' us fer days. I be thinkin' they just waitin' their best shot t' make away with our cargo. That bein' why, laddie, we been sailin' up and down the coast a bit more than we'd planned."

Antonia strained her eyes. The words *Sea Shark* assaulted her memory, and she recalled Michael telling her about the captain of the vessel having dealings with Dominguez.

Michael studied the ship through the glass for some time. He knew Thadius was probably right, and he knew of Brian Thomas. To make matters worse, he knew the *Sea Shark* meant only one thing: trouble.

Chapter Thirty-one

"Drop anchor and furl the sails, mates," ordered Captain Brian Thomas. He had sighted the *Áureo Princesa* days ago, and was not in any hurry to move closer to the brig.

The *Sea Shark* and *Áureo Princesa* were merchant brigs sporting square masted sails and a gaffsail on the mainmast. Thomas knew the only real difference between the two was that the *Sea Shark* boasted four guns on each side of its deck while the *Áureo Princesa* totaled four guns.

His ship was so armed due to the nature of the activities he carried out. Obtaining coin from smuggling, trading illegally in hides and other goods, hunting sea otter illegally, and, of course, pirating were frowned upon by men who labored for an honest day's wage. Fortunate for him there was little the government in California could do as long as his ship remained a distance from shore.

Captain Thomas, still a dashing dark-haired man in his forty-fifth year, used his leonine appearance to his distinct advantage with the ladies. He was considered to be a complete rogue and blackguard without an ounce of human kindness or loyalty in his soul. He was only interested in easy profit and would do business with the highest bidder or prey upon vessels which could not be well defended.

The rumors were that the man had escaped a date with the hangman in a London prison by trading places with a prisoner about to be impressed into the Royal Navy and shipped out to sea. He had cleverly organized a mutiny on board. Anyone who had hesitated to follow him, then and there met his end. Captain Thomas did not believe in leaving witnesses or loose ends untied.

From that time on, he sailed along the Pacific Coast, being careful to stay a long ways away from an English gibbet. Taking care had paid off, for he had accumulated quite a treasure for himself and his scurvy lot of cutthroats.

"Captain . . ." The sailor saluted, a custom Thomas had insisted upon. "When are we going to finish her?" He nodded toward their opponent ship. "The men are ready and waiting."

"In due course. Tell the men to relax and provide them with an extra keg. We'll celebrate our victory first. Then we'll take care of Captain Domino's ship."

"Aye, aye, sir."

Captain Thomas had many spies throughout California and was known to pay handsomely for useful information. He had heard of Captain Domino's troubles and thought the captain of the *Áureo Princesa* was not on board his vessel, making it ripe to be plucked clean without effort.

He looked through his eyeglass; a smirk came to his lips. "The ship's riding low in the water, filled to near capacity, I'd say. There'll be a tidy profit in tomorrow's work."

"The crew will be glad to hear it. They are getting restless. We've been off the coast for some time without the warmth of female companionship," the sailor said.

"You can tell them once we capture the *Áureo Princesa*, we'll sell the hides to the first Yankee trader we encounter, and then be on our way to the Sandwich Islands. There should be plenty of women there to ease their needs," Thomas boasted, sure of his victory. After dismissing the sailor, he took one last long look at his opponent, and retired to his cabin to enjoy a tankard of ale and await the most opportune moment to attack.

Michael and the chief mate had returned to the captain's cabin after spying the other ship and promptly became embroiled in a heated argument over tactics to be employed in light of their present, rather dubious position with the authorities in California.

"I be sayin' we avoid 'em by weighin' anchor and sailin' along the coast," Thadius argued. "We be no match fer a vessel with twice as many guns as we 'ave. Thomas, he respects ye cap'n an' might not take the chance at a run with us. So if 'n we stay clear of the *Sea Shark* we won't 'ave t' test our lot of untried mates."

While Thadius usually was wise in judgments of the sea, this time Michael felt he was wrong. "You have a point, man. But I don't think Thomas knows I've returned to the helm of the ship. One thing I'm sure he does know, though, is that the ship's stores are running dangerously low. Soon we'll have to send part of the crew ashore to replenish them. If we follow your advice and sail along the coast, it won't be long before others sight us, then we could have even more trouble. No. I think our best chance is in the element of surprise. If we take the offense, then Thomas will be forced into a defensive position."

Thadius was not one to insist on a course of action when he was shown there might be a better way. While Michael had not a manner in which they might proceed, Thadius was beginning to admit his error in judgment. The scoundrel Thomas would not allow them to slip away from him.

Being an old sea dog, Thadius was familiar with naval strategies. "If'n we could get a shot at 'em devil's stern, rightly aimed it could put 'em blasted guns outta workin' order and be causin' enough damage t' the devil ship t' force it into land where the soldiers would handle 'em."

Michael's eyes reflected an approving glint.

"Of course, we just might fire a few shots into the ship's bow over the beakhead since the forecastle don't offer much protection. But they'd have t' be well shot. If'n we hit the side of 'er, the oak timbers wouldn't budge, they bein' so thick, they be."

"It sounds as if you have a plan," Michael said, the look of him clearly mirroring the wheels turning in his mind like the fine movements of a watch.

"The only trouble bein' gettin' her in position without the bastard knowin' we'd be comin'." Thadius frowned his troubling thoughts.

Michael, too, drew his brows together in disturbing contemplation.

"It bein' too risky, lad. I be sayin' we weigh the anchor until we can be comin' up with something a bit more likin' t' be puttin' us out on top," Thadius urged.

Thadius filled their tankards and lifted the giant mug, draining half the contents in one gulp. He then rose and began uneasily pacing the room, picking the grime from underneath his fingernails. His steps were heavy, ladened with the burden of his responsibilities.

Neither man came up with an alternative. The day was growing dim, and the spirits were nearly gone when they left the cabin.

"I better be seein' t' me duties. And ye, lad, 'ave a lass t' look after," Thadius said.

"We shall meet again later after our bellies are full."

"Aye, lad."

After Thadius left, Michael walked over to where Antonia had remained seated and clamped his fingers around her slender arm. "Dammit! I cannot let you stay out here."

"Por favor, just set me ashore," she said sadly, peering into his blue eyes.

"Even if I wanted to, I can't with that other ship breathing down our necks. Come in and at least have something to eat. You look like you haven't been eating well lately."

"If you insist, but I have nothing to say." She relented as she reaffirmed her earlier position.

"Yes, I know, the proverbial cat has got your sharp tongue." He sighed, grasping her waist to lift her from the cask.

After a stony silence during their meal Antonia cleared her throat and asked, "What are you going to do about that other ship, since you said it was following you?"

"Well, she's finally speaking to me." He rolled his eyes. "But to answer your question, right now I don't know."

"Certainly you are not afraid to turn the tables on them."

"Hardly, but we're slightly outgunned, and I have no desire to take the chance of handing my ship over to that pirate until I've come up with a plan to out-maneuver him."

Antonia shrugged her shoulders at the simplicity of the solution. "Well then, attack them tonight."

Michael pondered her simple idea for a moment and then jumped up and bolted from the cabin, knocking the chair over and leaving a bewildered Antonia staring after him.

Thadius was enjoying his evening's meal when Michael, followed by Mano, abruptly entered his cabin. He swung around in astonishment at the intrusion, licking his fingers.

Michael excitedly explained the idea, giving full credit where due. Thadius did not like the plan but agreed that there was a slim chance it might be possible, since the breeze continued to hum across the sea.

A half hour later the crew was assembled on deck, the plan was described, and everyone began carrying out their orders. The cabin boy was sent to fetch Antonia and Juanita.

"Here they are, Cap'n," the boy said, and left Antonia and Juanita standing topside.

"I'm sending you both ashore," Michael announced. "But don't get any ideas. A guard will keep watch over you."

There was the smell and taste of excitement in the air; that spark of tension one feels just before going into battle. Antonia found herself getting caught up in it. "No. I am going to stay," she was prompt to say.

Michael threw up his hands. "Listen to the lady! One moment she's demanding I put her ashore, the next she refuses to go. I'm afraid that the choice is not yours this time, Princess."

There was a determined twinkle in his eyes, causing Antonia to take a step backward. She glanced around swiftly, calculating her options. There were none. She raised her chin. "I refuse to be shuffled about at will."

He arched a brow. "Is that so?" He took another step toward Antonia, hating to do what he was about to do. "Sorry, Princess," he murmured, and swept her up into his arms. "Get the gig into position," he ordered.

"Put me down," Antonia demanded.

"You have only to ask," Michael said, and plopped her down into the bobbing boat next to Juanita, who had already wished the Indian success and taken her place. "Get these ladies to shore without delay," Michael ordered the waiting sailor. "And don't let them out of your sight."

Michael stood for a moment and watched the oars cut a smooth path through the water until the darkness of night enveloped them. Antonia sat erect, her arms crossed over her chest in silent fury, and refused to look at him.

With Antonia to safety, Michael, Mano, and the chief mate checked and rechecked the guns and coverings that had been hastily tacked over the portholes to dash all light. Now all they had left to do was wait until the crew of the *Sea Shark* settled in for their usual evening of hard drinking. Tension ran high on the *Áureo Princesa*, and no one was allowed to ease it with spirits. Michael had ordered that the spirits would flow freely only after they won victory and not before.

"The lights, they be dimmed on the *Sea Shark*," shouted the sailor on watch.

This was what they had been waiting for. It was

time to attack.

The hour was late, for the moon had already traced a path across the ebony sky. Only the brilliance of the twinkling stars was left to light their way. Eyeing their target, Thadius, his old heart pumping wildly, gave the order for all men to report to their stations at once.

"Weigh anchor," Michael ordered.

With the anchor hoisted and secured to the cathead, and the sails set, the *Áureo Princesa* silently inched closer to their unsuspecting prey. The men were so quiet that the pounding of their hearts sounded a drumming between their ears. Had a light been cast upon their faces, signs of fear-tinged excitement would have reflected off each man heading toward his first battle.

Michael and Thadius stood at the helm exchanging the use of the glass to eyeball their closing distance to the target. Soon they were nearly five hundred yards off the stern of the gently rocking *Sea Shark*. They slowed their pace until they were positioned a half pistol shot away.

At that time, an angry shout streaked through the air. Lights flashed on, casting an eerie glow upon the dark violet waters. Men frantically yanked on their shirts, scurrying about like ants toward their stations, but it was too late. The hinged lids of the gunports were already open on the *Áureo Princesa* as she eased into position.

"Fire!" Michael shouted.

A billowing cloud of thick black oily smoke from the gunpowder filled the air. There was no turning back. Whatever the outcome, the lines had been drawn indelibly. The men rushed about to reload the cannons, and within minutes another charge was in place. The fuse was lit, sending another stream of black smoke puffing skyward, scenting the air with the smell of battle. Twice more, fuses crackled and sparked to their destination, echoing thunderous explosions. Tensions erupted as the taste of victory touched their lips.

Their deadly aim had hit the bull's-eye, direct shots. The twenty-four-pound guns shattered the *Sea Shark,* which was enveloped in a heavy shroud of confusion and panic. Through the smoke, a white, tattered flag waved with a frenzy, held by a bloodied arm.

"All hands on deck," Thadius ordered. "Draw yer weapons, laddies. We be ready t' board."

Michael swung the *Áureo Princesa* alongside the *Sea Shark*. The men at once leaped on board the smoldering, splintered deck of the brig ready for blood, only to find their enemies sorely disabled from an evening ladened with too much rum.

Thadius, with gun drawn and sword dangling at his side, gave a hearty roar. "It appears the rum has gone 'n done our work fer us."

The defeated crew was rounded up and bound with heavy cotton ropes. All were accounted for except Captain Thomas. Thadius frowned over the man's absence. He started below but was halted by Michael.

"You're needed on deck with Mano to direct the men. I'll see to the infamous Captain Thomas," Michael said.

"Then ye'll be needin' this, laddie." Thadius drew his sword and tossed the treasured piece to Michael. Thadius had obtained the magnificent weapon in a dubious manner which he had flatly declined to disclose. It had a double-edge blade, silver guard, and wood grip. But what distinguished the weapon most was an arm emerging from clouds with a sword in the hand that was engraved on the blade. The arm bore the words: "The arm of a mighty God."

Michael nodded his acceptance and flew below in search of Thomas.

Brian Thomas was determined that no one would take his ship, or ever send him to prison again. When he realized all was lost he rushed to the store of powder and methodically emptied a line of the black substance from the door to the stacked kegs. He was nearly finished with his final deed when he came face-to-face with Michael Domino. Thomas was an extremely skilled swordsman, and thought it a fitting end to amuse himself one last time before igniting the powder.

The black-hearted captain whipped out his sword. "I hope, my illustrious captain, that for your sake, you know how to use that weapon in your hand, or have made your peace with your God." His full lips twisted into an evil grin.

"Don't count this your victory too soon" was the flat reply.

Swords struck with hard swift blows, crossing in a deadly dance. Captain Thomas had not given thought that Michael, too, was an accomplished swordsman, but he soon learned differently. Kegs and boxes were overturned, furiously crashing against the bulkheads and thudding to the floor in a jumbled maze as the men faced each other, death encircling them, waiting to take its due.

Captain Thomas swung around and viciously slashed Michael's left arm, turning his white sleeve a bright, oozing crimson. Thomas jumped to the fore and thrust a bloody signature across Michael's chest. The sight of blood began to taste inviting on Captain Thomas's lips, and he could smell victory's sweet embrace. Viciously he thrust forward, but Michael par-

282

ried his attacks again and again.

Panting, Captain Thomas said, "I grow tired of toying with you, Captain Domino." He boldly gave a short laugh. "Now I'll send you to meet your Maker."

Captain Thomas had backed Michael to a wall with his circling thrusts and lunged to finish him. He pivoted forward to sink his sword through Michael's heart.

"No!" Antonia screamed in terror.

Michael jumped aside, causing Thomas to plunge his evil sword deep into the soft timbers lining the bulkheads. His face dropped in utter shock, his eyes as big as cannons, and he spun around just in time to feel his opponent's double-edged blade ripping and slicing through his gut. He grabbed his belly, the blood gushing out between his fingers as his expression faded to utter horror at the deeply buried sword.

Feeling no sense of victory, Michael withdrew his weapon silently and turned to Antonia. "What the hell are you doing back here? And how did you get here?"

"I stole the gig from the beach while the guard was busy watching the battle. I guess in all the confusion I rowed to the wrong ship," Antonia explained, struck by the vehemence in his voice.

"That was a stupid stunt. The devil could have claimed you with the rest of us had we lost. You could have been killed, or worse. You could have become a most delectable prize," Michael snapped, then softened. "I hate to admit it, but I have to thank you. If you hadn't screamed, the outcome might have been reversed."

"Then you are glad to see me?" she ventured, and flung herself into his arms. "Do not be too harsh on the guard. It was not his fault."

Michael took her chin in his hand. "How well I know," he said.

Blood trickled onto her arm from Michael's wound. "Oh, no, you are hurt!"

"It's just a scratch; I've had worse."

Captain Thomas twisted his lips into an ugly smile as his breathing became ragged and labored. "I hate to interrupt this tender little scene. But I now am forced to believe that the best man does not always win the spoils," he choked in Antonia's direction. He managed to climb to his feet, garner a feeble bow, and stagger up on deck before collapsing.

"Stay here," Michael advised, and followed Thomas topside.

Antonia was still too frightened from what she had just observed to retort. Instead, she ignored him and went up on deck to stand quietly in the background and take in the horror of all the destruction.

Thadius calmly walked toward the lifeless body and nudged Thomas over with his boot. He cast a glance at Michael, who had just emerged from below. "Me thinks it be a fittin' end fer the likes of 'im."

A triumphant blue sky was dawning through the thin layer of remaining black smoke, and gulls soared overhead and screeched in search of a morning's meal. The sweet taste of victory curving his lips, Thadius strode over to the rail and gazed into the dark sea. As if they could sense the smell of death, sharks circled below—waiting, watching. Without ceremony Thadius ordered Brian Thomas's body delivered to a watery grave.

The rest of the crew of the *Sea Shark* was herded into longboats by the Indian and Thadius and rowed ashore. "It won't be takin' ye long t' free yerself," Thadius said to one of the men as he loosed his bonds. "Then ye can set the rest of yer scurvy lot free. When ye be free ye will be at the mercy of the people who ye 'ave taken from fer so long. Don't count on 'em bein' forgivin'," Thadius added.

Thadius and Mano left the men of the *Sea Shark* and set out to hurry Juanita and the sailor into the longboat. They climbed in after them and shoved off over the cresting waves.

By the time they returned, the men were celebrating.

"It appears as if we were more successful than planned—our fleet has increased thanks to Antonia," Michael said, grinning. He walked over to Antonia, who was standing at the porthole silently gazing out from Michael's cabin. He placed a mug of ale in her hands. "Here, Princess, you look as if you could use a drink."

"Michael . . ." she whispered in a pleading voice. She had feared for his life earlier, and now she had to explain that she had to return to her *padre*. She had agreed to move back to her *padre's* rancho, that now that Doña Maria was gone she was needed there. He had to understand that!

"Not now. When we are alone," he returned just as Thadius and the Indian joined them.

Thadius slapped Michael on the back with the chuckle of success still fresh on his lips and turned to Antonia. "It was your victory, lass. All will agree ye are quite a scrapper after all. Ye might just make a fine first mate fer me cap'n."

Antonia wistfully looked up at the crusty old sea dog and then over at Michael. For her, Thadius's words held a much deeper meaning.

Chapter Thirty-two

Much of what once had been the proud *Sea Shark* was stripped away by the well-directed blows of four cannons. Michael, accompanied by Thadius, surveyed what now belonged to him by right of conquest. A blow to the sternwalk had caved in a portion of the planks, and the splinters of once-stout wooden boards lay scattered about the deck and passageways.

In order for the two men to continue their survey it was necessary to push the rubble aside with their boots. As they made their way to the lower deck, the damage sustained to the deck beams became visible. Part of the lower deck was exposed to the elements, and the guns had been dislodged from their mountings, rendering them useless.

"Aye, 'tis no wonderin' why we didn't 'ave a time of it. Look at 'em cannons, will ye, laddie? 'Em scurvy dogs didn't 'ave a chance t' fire 'em. We musta got 'em first shot." Thadius was beaming with pride as he pointed out the disabled guns.

Once they had finished checking the damage and returned topside, they began to lay out a schedule to repair the vessel.

"We'll be doin' what we can out 'ere t' patch 'er up. But I be fearin' she won't be goin' far without 'er mizzen mast. I be supposin' I done me job t' well. Yer vessel ain't no more seaworthy than a landlubber. But let's see what we can do fer ye."

Thadius turned toward the crew. "Lay to, there's much t' be doin'," he ordered, before he turned back to Michael with a grin. "Ye be needin' t' do some thinkin' on rechristenin' 'er, laddie. And ye'll be needin' another crew."

When Michael finally returned to his cabin, Antonia was asleep on his bed. She lay on his bunk with her hair spread out across the pillow. Her long tresses shone like magnificent golden nuggets, their brilliance emphasized by the flickering lamplight.

The coverlet had fallen from her, exposing shadowy peaks of her full inviting breasts straining through the flimsy fabric of her simple white-patterned gown. He rubbed his chin and slowly smiled with an inviting intensity which could not be denied. Unable to restrain himself, he blew out the light and walked over to her with slow, deliberate steps.

"You are so beautiful, Tonia," he whispered, and tenderly ran the back of his hand along her cheek.

Antonia opened her eyes and stared up at him. She reached up to touch his face. He caressed her fingers twined in his and pressed a kiss to the inside of her wrist.

"Michael—"

"No, don't speak," he murmured, bending over to kiss her.

His kiss was overwhelming, and she put up no resistance. Maybe it was his near brush with death with that pirate, or her untenable circumstance. But whatever the reason, her burning body desired him. With that realization, the fire within her exploded away all her previous resolve. Her arms slid around his neck and she pulled him to her. Her thighs willingly parted under his weight and their clothes seemed to melt away.

"I want to possess you," he breathed against her ripe breast as he squeezed and kneaded the satiny sphere. "I want all of your sweetness."

Her body temperature rose to a fever pitch as his lips moved lower and his tongue dipped into her to savor the taste of her. Antonia moaned and arched against him at the exquisite agony with which he stroked and lapped. Her fingers curled into his shoulders and she began to writhe in earnest, feeling herself near release.

"I hunger to feel you inside me," she moaned, lost to the abandon of his devouring mouth and hands.

"There is no place I would rather be," he breathed.

He ached to feel the moist tightness of her surrounding him like a warm glove, and raised himself up on his elbows to slide deeply into her.

Antonia wanted to scream, the sensations were mounting so rapidly, so exquisitely. She writhed wildly, bucking with complete abandon as he rode her, full force, toward that pinnacle of release.

As the moon rose to cast its silvery beams through the porthole, all that could be seen was the silhouette of two bodies entwined in love's passionate embrace.

When Michael awoke, Antonia was gone.

Hurrying his arms into his shirt, he charged out

on deck and began questioning the crew on watch.

"Aye, we seen 'er take a gig. Waller even offered t' row her t' shore." At Michael's dark frown, the man added, "Only after she told him of her plans to search for herbs."

"How could you believe such an outrageous story without checking with me first?" Michael demanded.

"Sorry, Cap'n." The men's shoulders slumped and they dropped their eyes to study the deck.

Without so much as a word hinting that his rage was not directed toward them but inward for letting her outsmart him, Michael jumped into the jolly boat and doggedly rowed to shore.

The sun had just begun to break through the morning fog when Antonia reached the beach. She cast a sad, backward glance over her shoulder at the ship before beginning a trek which would take her back within reach of the one man whom she despised: the man she called husband.

All the while Antonia trudged along the road, thoughts of Michael surrounded her. Haunted memories. Visions of the time they had shared, the words left unspoken, the broken dreams. To keep from sinking in her pain she had to remind herself that she was a Winston. She was strong. Life went forward.

She stopped to rest once but not for long, since she feared Michael's wrath and knew he would follow once he awoke. She prayed he would not think she would leave the beach and journey inland; it was her only hope.

If Antonia thought she could outwit him she was sorely mistaken. He had watched her in action before and learned her ways well enough to practically read her mind. He immediately stomped up to the road at a record clip.

Antonia was hiking along an incline when she heard angry, crunching footfalls behind her. She threw a glance back over her shoulder and then flipped up her skirts and began to run; it was Michael.

Michael caught up with her at the base of the incline and swooped her off her feet. "Not so fast, Princess. You left without even saying good-bye."

"Just let me go!" She struggled.

"I had hoped you changed your mind after last night," he snarled, grappling with the wildcat until they tumbled to the ground.

"Last night has not changed anything." She kicked at him.

"That's not very ladylike." He grabbed her ankle. "Are you going to cease your futile attempts or do I have to bind you like a packing crate?"

Antonia was winded and finally stilled her fight for freedom.

"If I let go of you will you promise not to try to run?"

"*Sí*," she snapped.

Michael dropped his arms, and she jumped to her feet to glare at him. "I have to get to my *padre*," she insisted. "He has no one there to look after him since Doña Maria left."

He climbed to his feet. "Your *padre* will be all right. I'll even send a member of my crew to see to it if that'll put your mind at ease."

Antonia pursed her lips. "Are you going to let me go or not?"

"I think you know the answer to that question." He grabbed her arm and forced her to walk back to where he had left his boat on shore.

Antonia returned to the ship more sullen than before, shooting daggers at him whenever he attempted to speak to her. Finally conceding defeat in his attempts to talk to her, he sent her with Juanita back to his cabin. He and Mano then retired to Thadius's cabin for some peace, and to hear the Indian's tale of how he had met Juanita.

"After we parted to seek information to prove your innocence, I happened upon Juanita and her grandfather, an old indio shaman, as they were being attacked by *bandidos* along the trail," Mano said. "The old man was mortally wounded, but before he died, he begged me to care for her. At the time I thought her a boy since she was dressed as one."

"I be knowin' right off she be no lad," Thadius reminded the pair.

"Probably because you have had more experience with the weaker sex," Michael put in, enjoying the camaraderie of male companionship.

"Enough to know, laddie, that ye got yerself one ye ought to hang on to," Thadius advised. "And weaker sex, laddie? Señorita Antonia?"

Michael sent the old sea dog a disgruntled grunt. The old man's perception was far greater than Michael cared to think about at the moment. "Why not let our brother continue without further interruption," Michael said darkly.

Mano caught the unease in his captain and refrained from comment on the young señorita. He continued. "I helped Juanita send the old medicine man to the land of his ancestors, and then offered to return her to the mission from which they had come. She violently refused, and I knew the harsh ways of the mission friars toward indios, so I relented and thought to make a sailor out of the young indio. It was not until I dumped her into a cleansing tub that I unwittingly learned the truth, my brothers."

"Aye, 'tis a true romance I be hearin'," Thadius chimed in.

Michael leaned back in his chair enjoying the story.

"I have spent many suns away from my homeland and have traveled far with you, my brothers," Mano said, his face lacking all humor. "But as it is for most, there is a time to roam and a time settle down, a time to taste many fruits, and a time to pick one from the vine and savor it. It is my time to pick one. I made a promise to Juanita's grandfather, and although our time together has been short, I have chosen her."

Thadius's eyes widened. "Ye mean ye aim t' be marryin' the mite of a lass?"

"Yes, my brothers, I do. Juanita has given her consent. We will be wed in the morning," Mano said solemnly.

"You didn't waste much time," Michael said, disbelief clouding his face.

"When one knows his own mind and heart much time is not needed," Mano returned, casting Michael a look of understanding of deeper knowledge.

At the Indian's meaningful comment Michael's mouth cracked into a thoughtful line, and for an instant disturbing visions of Antonia and marriage flashed through his mind. It was the first time in his life that he had ever given rein so such thoughts, and he moved quickly to brush them from his mind. He turned his attention back to Mano.

"California is my home," Mano added, "the land of my people; I am a man come home. Be happy for me, my brothers."

They sat up into the wee hours of the night reminiscing and discussing their plans until the first slivers of light shimmered through the porthole.

The day was just beginning to dawn on this, Mano's and Juanita's wedding day.

Chapter Thirty-three

To celebrate the upcoming nuptials the crew had taken the opportunity to enjoy the flowing tankards of rum offered to them. It allowed them the chance to relax after the tenseness of the sea battle and the long hours working on the other vessel.

Thadius had rummaged through the sea chests in the hold until he found the pale-yellow gown that one of the crew had purchased in Boston for his wife. Since the man's wife was near Juanita in size, he had gladly donated it for such a special occasion. Thadius had also come up with a brilliant green creation for Antonia. While Antonia had cordially accepted his offering, she glared past him at Michael.

After Thadius left Michael's cabin, she swung on Michael. "Why did your chief mate supply me with this?" Antonia asked, touched by the gruff man's gift.

"I think he wanted you to look your finest today," Michael said without further remark.

Antonia furrowed her brows. "What is so special

about today?"

Michael pushed back from his desk and walked to the porthole, gazing out. Without looking at her he said, "Mano and Juanita are getting married today."

"I am really happy for them," she said softly. She carried the gown to the bunk and set it down. At least Michael's companion had found happiness. "They have not known each other long, have they?" she addressed his back.

"No."

"I did not know they were in love. How can she marry someone she hardly knows?"

"That's their business."

"*Sí*, well I suppose it is. Where are they to be wed?"

"We're going to travel to the Mission San Juan Capistrano as soon as they're ready."

"May I go along?" she asked hesitantly. "Juanita has been very kind to me, and I would like to help them celebrate their happiness."

Michael jerked around to face her. "I don't want you to ruin their wedding day."

"Do you believe I would do that?" she asked, incredulous.

His eyes bored into her. "Wouldn't you, if it met your need to escape back to your father?"

"No. I promise not to try to escape," Antonia stated flatly. "Furthermore, why did Thadius bring me this gown if I am to remain on board?"

Michael stood staring at her for a moment, his expression unfathomable. Antonia locked into those piercing blue eyes and silently returned his gaze. Although she could not deny her continuing desire for him, she wondered if her life would ever be the same.

A scratching at the door broke the moment. "Laddie, we be invited t' toast the couple in Mano's cabin before they be leavin'," Thadius rasped through the door.

"We'll be right there," Michael shouted. He then turned to Antonia. "You may go with us. But I warn you, you will be well advised to keep your promise. Now hurry and get ready. I'll wait for you."

"There is no need," she said coolly.

"I know. But I will nevertheless."

Antonia slipped into the gown, and stroked a brush through her hair with due haste. Without delay they went below to Mano's cabin.

Michael brightened as he followed Antonia into Mano's cabin. "I have never seen you look better, my friend."

"I have never felt better, my brother."

Juanita stood by Mano's side and accepted congratulations. She glowed with pride at how handsome her man was in his dark-brown trousers, cream-ruffled shirt and brown cutaway vest. Wanting to gift him, she removed a necklace of shells from around her neck and held out her hands for him to take it.

"Here. I give. You wear."

Mano slipped the necklace over his head. It had been a long time since he had worn the jewelry of his people, but he would wear it on this day to please Juanita. He glanced in the mirror at the cone-shaped horn shells which hung loosely around his neck, reminding him of his people's heritage.

"It is good," he said, and brushed a kiss across her cheek.

After a toast the bridal couple emerged on deck to cheers and applause from the crew. Thadius was so pleased that he decided to accompany them to the mission. He wanted to be present at the nuptials of his Indian friend.

"Lay to, Mr. Russell," Michael called to the steward, "Since Thadius will be accompanying us ashore, you will be in charge of the ship."

Mr. Russell was an able seaman who could be counted on to handle a difficult situation, and while Thadius in particular did not like leaving the vessel, Michael knew they would not be away long. But as an added precaution, after Thadius had gone below and changed his clothes, he assembled the crew and roughly barked a few last-minute orders while Michael looked on and chuckled.

Thadius's weathered fingers yanked at the collar of the ruffled shirt and jacket he saved for special occasions. He looked nearly as uncomfortable as he felt. Having never been one to dress in what he considered foppish clothing, he did not enjoy starting now, and silently longed to be done with the business as expediently as possible so he could again don his easy-fitting sailor's rags.

The trek to the mission took most the rest of the morning. Mano and Juanita walked hand in hand with Thadius alongside Juanita and Michael and Antonia behind.

When they first began the trek, Juanita was hesitant. She had thought they would be traveling to the Mission San Diego de Alcalá not Capistrano. But Mano reassured her no harm would befall her. Michael and Mano were known in San Diego, which might have proved dangerous with the murder charge hanging heavy over Michael's head and caused unnecessary delays.

The ocean breeze cooled the hot journey, and sang to them through the trees along their way. Gulls soared freely overhead squawking, and curious ground squirrels, sunning themselves upon the rocks, sat upright like miniature fence posts to watch the small wedding party.

Antonia was grateful for the respite the day offered. It seemed so long ago that she had been happy and carefree. Her burdens as of late weighed so heavy on her shoulders that sometimes she wondered whether life would ever again return to normal. She reminded herself that she was determined to help Michael destroy Dominguez.

Antonia stumbled when her foot wedged beneath a rock. Michael caught her. Instead of removing his hands, he slid his arm around her shoulders.

"Are you all right?" Concern echoed in his voice.

Antonia started to offer a sharp reply but thought better of it. There had been no sharpness in his question, only genuine concern. "*Sí,* I am fine," she said softly.

His touch plagued her with the feelings that jolted through her, but she made no attempt to pull away. Could he be softening? Or was it just because of the circumstance and Mano's and Juanita's love that seemed to encircle all who were near them on this special day. Whatever the cause, it was infectious, for Antonia, too, felt it. She gave a short sigh and relaxed as they walked along the El Camino Real.

Just when Thadius thought his legs would give way a rickety wagon rumbling down the trail behind them drew up and stopped. The drivers, of Indian and Spanish ancestry and moderate build, smiled broadly.

They tipped their worn sombreros. "*Buenas tardes,* señores and señoritas."

"Where do you travel?" the elder of the two asked,

fingering his thick handlebar mustache.

"To Capistrano. Is it bein' far?" Thadius questioned hopefully. " 'Avin' lived me life on board a ship, it is not used I be t' makin' long treks ashore and me legs ache."

They were kind men, and when they noticed Antonia and Juanita holding their skirts away from the dusty road, they offered them a ride. Thadius readily accepted for the party and hopped on board. Michael encircled Antonia's waist and lifted her to the back of the wagon where he joined her. Mano followed suit.

A crack of the whip started the animals along the trail at a brisk pace. The old wagon jerked, causing Michael to grab Antonia to keep her from tumbling out. He leaned her against his shoulder, sliding his arm around her. Antonia settled against him and silently stared out the back of the cart. Their feet dangling from the back of the wagon, they watched the dust swirl from the trail as they rambled along, each lost to their own thoughts of each other.

Thadius struck up a pleasant conversation with the men up front. "We be merchantmen tradin' along the coast. My friend in the back met the lass up the coast a bit, 'e did. And this bein' the first shore leave since then, they be gettin' wed t'day."

He slyly eyed them, as he spoke, drawing out any information they had of Captain Domino. They asked Thadius whether he had seen any other vessels during his journey. It seemed they were particularly interested in a ship named the *Áureo Princesa*. When he heard the name of the ship, he maintained only passing interest and told of hearing there had been trouble, asking if the captain had received his just rewards.

The men chuckled at his interest in seeing the captain brought to justice, and let their tongues wag freely. Michael appeared to show no interest in the conversation, but listened intently. Antonia, too, paid close attention.

By early afternoon the wagon came to an abrupt halt. The men pointed along a small trail, explaining that once around the bend, the mission would be in sight. The wedding party thanked them, received well wishes, and jumped from the wagon.

When they reached the mission, an old rotund friar welcomed them. He did not recognize Juanita in her fine gown, nor did he recognize Antonia, hardly expecting to see the bride of El Señor Dominguez accompanied by two common sailors and two Indians.

"And what brings you here today, my children?" the friar asked.

"My friends here . . ." Michael motioned toward Mano and Juanita, "have come to be married."

The rector smiled his blessing. "It will be my pleasure. *Por favor,* follow me." The small party was shown into a spare room where the friar seated himself behind a desk, removed a book from the drawer, and dipped his pen into the inkwell to scribble a record of the ceremony.

The friar rang a small bell, bringing an old shriveled woman into the room and sent her to fetch refreshments for the travelers. Moments later a young girl not more than fourteen appeared carrying a tray. She placed the platter on the desk and turned to leave. Suddenly a familiar light flickered into her eyes, and she spun around and rushed over to Juanita. She threw her arms wildly around Juanita's neck and sobbed with long-held joy. Antonia bit her

300

lip and held her breath fearing recognition.

The friar, who had witnessed the untimely reunion, raised his brows in a questioning gesture, and moved closer to the pair. The girl cowered, sorry she had not remained silent, as had Juanita.

"What is this display of affection about?" the friar demanded of the cringing girl.

"It is nothing, *padre.*"

"Nothing? If you wish to save your soul you best be out with it. Now. How do you know the bride?"

The girl looked imploringly at the others, then dropped her eyes. "She and her grandfather lived at the mission."

Upon learning Juanita's identity, the friar's attitude became hostile. "One of the mission indios, eh? Surely you must realize I cannot marry one of the Church's indios to a stranger until I have had ample time to thoroughly check into this man's background and judge him suitable."

Mano's eyes narrowed dangerously hard, and black anger began to overtake the usually stoic Indian. He took one darkly foreboding step toward the friar, his fists clenched in an attempt to restrain himself.

"My good friar," he said sharply, "my Juanita does not belong to the mission. Maybe you forget the missions are no longer the center of power in California." He gnashed his teeth furiously.

The friar puffed out his chest and stood his ground. "Maybe so, but she is a ward of the Church and I will see her properly married!"

"She will be properly wed!" Mano shot angrily back. "Now, shall we proceed?" he said through gritted teeth.

"I am sorry, but I shall not perform the ceremony," the friar returned stubbornly.

In an attempt to forestall an ugly confrontation between Mano and the friar, Thadius stepped in between them.

"Friar, I bein' a friend t' this lad I can swear t' his character," Thadius said, a hint of annoyance in his gruff voice.

"It does not matter. I have my responsibilities to uphold. Now, girls, get you to the kitchens," he ordered sanctimoniously.

Juanita defeatedly lowered her head, and took a step to do as bid when Mano caught her arm to storm out with her. Eyeing the situation with heightening anger, Thadius drew in a deep breath.

"Friar!" he boomed with a deadly note to his voice, "I be tellin' ye the lad is of a good breed who'll be takin' good fine care of the lass. Now me, I be comin' a long way with 'em t' see 'em married off proper-like, and me and me friend here," Thadius slowly parted his coat and patted the exposed pistol, "we would be a might bit unhappy t' see 'em disappointed. Ye understand?" He narrowed his glaring eyes until they were mere slits of serious intent.

"And if he did not convince you maybe I can," Michael said menacingly, stepping to Thadius's side.

Antonia had moved to Juanita, and silently slid her arm around the trembling maiden in an attempt to comfort her. Antonia had heard of the harsh treatment tendered by the mission friars toward the Indians, but she had never glimpsed it face-to-face before and was ashamed for her people.

"Well, I never!" The friar started and huffed. He was about to refuse until Thadius closed his hand around the butt of the pistol to remove it from its resting place. The friar had had occasion to encoun-

302

ter unscrupulous men before. He could do more for the rest of his flock alive than to test the old seaman's ire. He swallowed the hard lump of indignation in his throat and said dryly, "Come with me."

The friar stiffly ushered the couple, followed by Michael, Antonia, and Thadius, into the chapel. Silently glaring his disapproval, the friar donned his vestments and joined Mano and Juanita in marriage before God.

Antonia stood solemnly by Michael's side during the ceremony, and glanced up at him as the Indian couple was pronounced man and wife. For a moment she envisioned herself and Michael standing before the friar and had to bite her lip. It was a foolish thought, she reminded herself.

Michael, too, felt a twinge watching Mano and Juanita. But he had a score to settle first. He would have to be out of his mind to want such a troublesome wench. But the fact was, Antonia was weighing more heavily on his mind all the time lately.

The ceremony concluded, Mano's new bride stepped to the friar and fell at his feet, kissing the bottom of his robes and pleading forgiveness while at the same time thanking him for her happiness and begging his blessing.

The pious old friar, seeing the futility of further protest, relented and blessed the union. Thadius stepped up to him and gave him a hard slap on the back.

"Ye done good, man."

Michael clasped Antonia's hand as they offered their congratulations. Without releasing her, Michael moved to the friar. He curtly thanked the man, and then reached deep into his pocket and placed a few coins in the friar's hand for the mission while Anto-

303

nia remained mutely compliant.

Their goal accomplished, the newly wedded couple and their party began their trek back to the vessel. The sun had sunk far into the sea, leaving the sky the deepening color of a maiden's blush on her wedding night as Michael and Antonia quietly walked far behind the others along the trail.

Chapter Thirty-four

After they had reached Michael's cabin he bent over and dropped a chaste kiss on her forehead.

"Thank you for keeping your promise today, Princess."

"I gave you my word I would not ruin Juanita's wedding," Antonia said somberly.

He scratched his head and gave her a searching look. "Every time I'm with you, you never cease to amaze me. You're a hundred women all rolled into one."

"Is that good or bad?" she ventured.

"I'm not sure. But I've decided to take you to your *padre*. But this time, please stay there so I don't have to worry about you."

Antonia flashed an innocent smile up at him, but a wicked grin lurked just behind her lips. She did not want to cause him concern, but she was going to help destroy Dominguez—whether he asked for her aid or not.

The trip to her *padre*'s rancho was uneventful. Michael stopped near the wooden post at the entrance of the drive leading to the main house. Rancho de los Robles was nestled deep into the woods and rose tall and straight — a perfect representation of the man who had built it.

"I'm going to leave you here. You will go straight to the hacienda," he said, clutching her shoulders.

"What makes you think I would not?" came the guileless reply.

He gave a hearty laugh. "I can't begin to imagine." Then he grew serious. "Just stay out of trouble. I'll sneak back later after I've checked out the situation and find out what has been happening since you left Dominguez."

"You do not have to sneak," Antonia protested.

"Until there is no longer a murder charge hanging over my head, I have to be cautious. No pun intended," he said, thinking of the hangman's noose which awaited him.

"All right. But be careful." Antonia reached up on her tiptoes and pressed her lips to his. The sensations caused her to part her lips and slip her tongue into his mouth.

Michael cupped her buttocks and ground her against his hips. "You drive me mad," he breathed into her mouth.

Antonia sighed and pulled away. "I have to go now." She gave him a troubled smile and turned to walk silently toward her *padre's* hacienda.

"Damn sorceress," Michael groaned. She was weaving her spell around him, and he was helpless to stop her. Regardless of how he had tried to deny it, he was sinking deeper and deeper.

Antonia was brimming with the bitter and the sweet. She ached with emotions. Was this what love

306

was all about? Give and take. Push and pull. Happiness and sadness. Pleasure and pain. Antonia smiled to herself. Her childhood fantasy of a rescuing vaquero was fading, and was being replaced with the image of a real man—a man with good points and bad points, strengths and weaknesses; a man filled with passions; a man she was determined to help clear his name.

Before she reached the hacienda she slipped into the stables. *"Padre*, forgive me." She mouthed the words while she saddled Oro. "Before I come home I must help Michael. I fear he may need me far worse than you right now." She mounted the spirited golden filly and raced toward the Dominguez rancho.

By the time Michael reached Dominguez's rancho it was a beehive of activity. He left the horse he had taken from the range at the Rancho de los Robles tied to a creosote bush and crept through the underbrush on foot past the vaqueros and household staff.

As he passed the garden just outside the hacienda, a small Indian child looked up from her weeding. Michael smiled and lifted his index finger to his lips in a gesture for silence. The little girl hunched her shoulders and giggled, but did not utter a word when her mother shook her shoulder to reprimand her wandering attention.

With little difficulty Michael slipped into the hacienda through the kitchens. He had nearly reached the private rooms when he heard loud, angry voices coming from the library. He recognized Dominguez's gruff voice, but could not identify the other men. Hoping to learn more of their conversation, he carefully glanced around the corner through the massive doors. He did not know the other men by sight, yet had seen them somewhere—where he could not recall.

"I told you two never to come here unless I sent for you," Dominguez spat viciously. "And you especially, what are you doing here? You are supposed to be keeping watch on what is going on over at Winston's rancho. I do not pay you to sit in my library."

"Listen, El Señor," the squat man with the bushy mustache retorted, "I would be more careful if I were you, or do you have such a short memory that you do not recall our agreement of long ago?" His black eyes flashed barely concealed fires at Dominguez.

"It appears I may be forced to recall our agreement all too well. But let us speak of this later after I hear what better be important as to bring you," he swung on the other man, pointing an accusing finger, "all the way over here at this time of day."

A servant girl with a large tray of refreshments had just rounded the corner on her way to the library when her eyes widened in surprise at Michael, and she drew her breath in to scream. The tray slipped from her fingers and crashed to the floor, causing her to clamp her hand over her mouth to muffle her cries. She did not want to call attention to the shattered dishes, which lay about her feet, since her fear of El Señor Dominguez was greater than of any stranger.

Michael dashed into the formal dining room to conceal himself just as Dominguez stormed from the library and closed the doors behind him, before stomping over to the girl in a rage. He roughly drew the frail girl from her feet and shook her by the collar. He was just about to strike her when Antonia and the governor appeared from the courtyard.

"Tonia, you stubborn little vixen," Michael muttered under his breath. He had only left her a short while before, and already she had managed to put herself in the middle of his plans—again.

Governor Figueroa uneasily cleared his throat. "El Señor, is there a problem?"

Dominguez glanced up over his shoulder at his wife and the governor, a frown snarling his lips, but he released the servant and lowered his hand. "There is no problem. The clumsy girl merely dropped the tray. Do not let yourselves be concerned with such trifles," he said in a most matter-of-fact manner.

When Dominguez turned to look at the trembling girl his eyes were filled with the flames of unfulfilled vengeance. "I shall see you later—in the cellar," he whispered to her. For the benefit of those looking on, he painted a false smile. "Clean this up and see to another tray."

The girl said not one word. Trembling, she quickly bent down and began to clear away the wreckage.

"If you will excuse me." Dominguez nodded, and returned to the library, shutting the doors after him.

The governor did not make mention of the incident, but escorted Antonia to her rooms and retired to finish the papers he had been working on.

Antonia sighed heavily and leaned against the inside of the door. Her heart ached for the young servant girl who had regularly seen to her needs since her "marriage," but there was nothing she could do to help—not yet. Dominguez had made it very clear when she had returned that if she displeased him again with one of her stunts of running off to her *padre* she would suffer the consequences regardless of who was in residence.

By the time Michael crept into her rooms she had fallen into the exhausted world of sleep. Without a sound he turned the lock in the door and propped a chair against the door leading to Dominguez's connecting rooms. He stealthily padded to the side of her bed and sank to the edge. His weight on the mattress jolted Antonia to consciousness, and she swung into action to defend herself. Michael pounced on her and, pressing his weight against the length of her, clamped his hand tightly over her mouth.

Her eyes were wide with fright until she focused and looked into the face of the man who gazed angrily back at her. As Michael removed his hand, Antonia's expression faded into an impish grin.

"Michael, what are you doing here?" she asked.

"I just might ask you the same question," he said through angry lips. "I thought I left you at your *padre*'s rancho."

She shrugged. "You did."

"Well, why aren't you there?"

"I told you I wanted to help. You are a wanted man and I can move about freely," she offered.

"And you certainly do, too, don't you?" he said, chagrined. "You didn't waste any time at it, either." He grew serious. "Antonia, this is not a game. Dominguez is a very dangerous man and, if you get in his way, he will not hesitate to do the same thing to you that he did to Rosa. He has already demonstrated that to you. Can't you get that through your beautiful head?"

"What if someone saw you come in here?"

He expelled a sigh. "Were you listening to me at all?"

"Oh, of course. But why not let me take some of the risks? I am involved in this, too, whether you like it or not. Look what he did to my *padre*, and tried to do to me."

"And would have succeeded in doing to you if I hadn't come along," he reminded her. "I have a score to settle with my ex-partner and you are in my way," he said without the torrent of emotion he was feeling. His eyes turned to cold blue Arctic chunks of glacial ice.

"Michael . . . I . . ." she began. She wanted to convince him that it was her fight, too, but she dared not speak the words which burned on her lips. It was apparent he had no intention of listening to reason.

"There is nothing you can say to make me change my mind." He frowned. "I should have left you in chains on the ship."

"I am sorry, but—"

"No more buts. I'm getting you the hell out of here." She was totally exasperating, but he wanted her; he could not deny it as he suddenly could not deny that to himself, in spite of all the trouble she was causing him, he loved her.

He rose and held out his hand to Antonia. She gave a small pout but offered hers in return. It was vital to be gone as quickly as possible. Michael grabbed a cape from the wardrobe and draped it over his arm. He carefully creaked open the door and scanned the hallway before they slipped out and headed toward the kitchens.

Governor Figueroa left his room just as they neared a corner in the rambling hacienda. He abruptly stopped when he sighted Antonia with the man thought responsible for the demise of the poor unfortunate Rosa. He shot Antonia a mildly surprised look and cocked his brow. Remembering her protest when he had mentioned the captain before and her silent expression now pleading that he not try to stop them, as well as a conversation he'd had with the commandant, he smiled his understanding.

"Such warm weather for an afternoon's stroll. But you are a wise young lady, Antonia to take a cape for when the weather turns cool. Oh . . ." his eyes sought Michael to offer a wise word, "you may find the foothills much more pleasant at this time than the coast." He then silently nodded his approval and stepped back into his room.

Antonia patted her skirt. She had slipped the weapons she and Michael obtained from Dominguez's room into her pocket. One never knew when they might come in handy.

The governor's message about the foothills was not lost on Michael. He would heed the advice offered by him, for it was said the governor was a fair and honest man.

Cautiously they sneaked past the library, through the kitchens, and into the burning sun. Before they made their way from the rancho Michael led Antonia to the open window just outside the library.

Crouching below the window, Michael whispered, "Listen, do you recognize any of the voices?"

She craned her neck and set her ear close to the bottom of the sill. She could not believe what she heard. The angry men inside were arguing over why Rosa's murderer had not been apprehended at the Rancho de los Robles where he'd been spied earlier. Dominguez then ordered the man to return to the rancho and not allow such stupidity to overtake him again. The door slammed with a bang and then only two voices could be heard.

Michael and Antonia moved behind a dense juniper and watched as the man stomped from the hacienda, his silver rowels clanging with each step, mounted his horse and dug his spurs into the animal's sides.

"Did you recognize him?"

"*Sí.*"

"Who is the man?" Michael asked impatiently, knowing time was of the essence.

"Pedro Montoya, a vaquero who has been with my *padre* for many years. I do not understand. What was he doing here?" A puzzled expression crossed her face. "Why," she wondered, almost afraid to finish her question, "was he reporting to El Señor?"

Michael drew her to him in an effort to calm her fears and keep her from losing sight of the task at hand. "Just be thankful he didn't report to Dominguez that you actually hadn't been with your father during your latest absence. There'll be time to sort through all your questions later, but now please, do you recognize the other voice?"

"No." She shook her head. "It is vaguely familiar, but I do not recognize it."

"Stay here while I make sure it's safe." He motioned for her to crouch further into the shrubbery and rounded the corner of the hacienda. Her heart pounded with fear, but she sank back into the juniper as directed. Not seeing anyone, Michael swiftly returned for Antonia. Without wasting another moment, they made their way quickly from the rancho.

"*Sí*, I received your note," Sanchez angrily shot back at Dominguez. "Why do you want to meet with me while the governor is here?"

"And why do you so soon forget our arrange-

313

ment? It has been profitable for both of us until now, has it not?" Dominguez spat out.

"I take care of the unpleasant details for you. You do not have to worry unless you forget how you came to be in your present position. I know all about you and your past. Need I remind you?"

"I suggest you watch what you say," Dominguez retorted, barely able to contain himself.

The two men faced each other with murder in their eyes. Dominguez quietly placed his hand on the drawer of his desk, concealing the small pistol he kept hidden there.

Sanchez narrowed his eyes, watching like a hawk in anticipation of his opponent attempting something rash. The tenseness of the moment was alleviated only when the servant girl arrived with another tray.

Realizing he still required the man's assistance, Dominguez sought to relieve the tension. "I shall call my lovely wife to join us," he said politely, as if he were entertaining an honored guest.

Sanchez, stroking his bushy mustache, was amused by Dominguez's sudden change of heart but did not argue at the opportunity to see such a vision of loveliness as was the new Señora Dominguez. "She will make a delightful addition."

"If you will excuse me for a moment, I shall request my wife's presence."

"I get if you want," the servant girl meekly chirped in a mere whisper as she finished setting up the cups. She hoped to placate his anger of her earlier accident with the tray.

"No. You attend my guest while I see to my wife," he said with authority, as if he were speaking to a cur.

314

Dominguez left the library and stopped outside Antonia's door. He circled his hand around the knob and turned just as Governor Figueroa stepped from his room and started down the hall.

"El Señor," the governor said when he saw he was about to enter Antonia's rooms, "I have been hoping to speak with you. I wonder if I may beg your indulgence now for a few moments."

Dominguez withdrew his hand from the door handle and turned toward the governor. His feelings of annoyance were well hidden as he greeted the leader of California.

"Of course, Governor. I can always spare a few moments for one such as yourself."

"I am grateful; besides, I believe Señora Antonia mentioned something about resting after a most tiring journey returning to the rancho."

"I suppose she does need her rest. The visit to her *padre* has left her looking pale. But a sea voyage would undoubtedly do much for her," Dominguez said, knowing the governor might consider wrapping up his business sooner if he thought it would put the color back into Antonia's cheeks.

The governor had only taken two steps toward the library when Dominguez caught his arm. "Come, let us speak in your room. I want to devote my full attention to what you desire to say without servants interrupting or the noise from the kitchens disturbing our conversation." Dominguez was pleased with himself for so easily convincing the man to follow his lead. He was prepared to be more insistent if necessary to keep the man from the library and Sanchez.

After a long, conversation of little substance, Dominguez managed to excuse himself, and annoyed with such a waste of his time, lumbered back to the library to finish his business with Sanchez.

When he entered the room, Sanchez was standing by his desk sipping a glass of fine spirits.

"I did not think you would mind, but I found this . . ." he raised the glass of aged brandy, "more to my liking."

"Of course not, I shall join you since Señora Antonia is resting from her tiring journey and will not be joining us." Dominguez's hatred silently grew deeper for the man who would even dare to help himself to his private stock of spirits. Maintaining an air of nonchalance, he poured himself a glass. "Forgive me, I was detained by Governor Figueroa, the fool. But now, let me explain why I sent you the message. I need to make arrangements with Captain Thomas to dispose of some more cattle." He lifted the glass to his thick lips.

Chapter Thirty-five

When Michael and Antonia reached the horse tethered in the thicket of brush not far from the Dominguez rancho outbuildings, Antonia wound her arms around the animal's neck and hugged it. The stallion was her *padre*'s pride and she had always cared for the formidable horse.

"Where on earth did you get Lobo?" she asked in astonishment, knowing her *padre* had not let the animal off the rancho but once.

"Tonia, we can stand here and discuss my methods and why I'm forced to be here with you now, or we can put as many miles between us and Dominguez as we can before he discovers you're gone," Michael said, frustration with all her questions beginning to gnaw at him. "You didn't leave a note this time, and I doubt if he will believe another story that you felt the sudden urge to visit your *padre* right after you have just returned. Here I am risking my life to see you safely away from here, ignoring my own mission once more, and you stand there with your hands on your hips, your lips in a pout, demanding answers."

"I must know where you got this horse before I move from this spot."

"My God, why do I bother with such a troublesome wench? I could have been done with my mission long ago and been back safely on my ship," he said with an exasperated sigh. Time was of the essence. "Woman!" The fires flared as all patience dried on his lips. "We'll speak of this later, unless you wish to remain here and discuss it with your 'husband.' "

"He is not my husband."

"He thinks he is . . . Are you coming or not?"

Michael swung his leg up and over the animal's back, settling into the saddle. Antonia was perturbed with his seeming lack of concern for her need to learn how he had obtained her *padre's* animal, but she feared Dominguez and his madness. He had not exactly welcomed her back with open arms upon her return. She quickly extended her hand and was helped up in front of the man who had changed her life.

Michael turned the horse east, toward the foothills.

No time was spent on further conversation. They rode the animal hard until it was lathered and strained to continue. Michael then jumped from the saddle and reached up to grasp Antonia's waist, helping her down. He loosened the bellyband from the saddle and tossed it from the animal's back. Like many such animals belonging to Californios, it galloped off to find its way home after a swat to its rump.

"That is my *padre's* prize horse," Antonia cried in horror as it ran free.

"What's more important, the animal or our lives? And besides, horses sell for only a little over one gold piece," he snapped, growing weary of her poor sense of the true value of things.

"I am sorry, I know you are trying to help," she admitted.

Antonia was tiring but labored to find strength to keep pace with Michael as they trudged along the winding path. Her cloth slippers were no match for the rocky terrain and she stepped on a sharp twig. Her ankle turned to the side, sending her tumbling to the ground.

Her throbbing ankle, coupled with the events which had occurred during the last two months, caused tears to trickle down her dust-smudged cheeks. She tried to rise, but before she could, Michael was there, gathering her into his arms. He gently carried her to a large tree and set her down beneath its shading branches. Joining her on the ground, his fingers pressed at the swelling ankle.

He grinned up at her. "This somehow has a familiar ring to it. I surely hope you don't intend to make a habit of it," he said, thinking of his first encounter with the young señorita.

"Por favor, capitán." She pretended righteous indignation. "It is how I attract strong, handsome men to carry me in their arms," she said straight-faced.

"And what do they extract for payment? A kiss perhaps?" Michael puckered his lips expectantly.

"Only for the most deserving," she said, fluttering her long lashes coyly. She was delighting in the brief respite from the seriousness of their circumstance.

Behind her smile she wondered if the two of them would be dubbed runaway lovers. This caused her fear for Michael's safety to rise to greater heights, since it would only serve to turn away any of the *rancheros* still believing in the possibility of Michael's innocence.

The Californios were such proud men. She, too, would be branded little better than a *puta*. Although adultery was not unheard of, it was usually handled with the utmost discretion, with care to not openly cause a husband to lose face.

"Am I deserving?" he asked, jarring her back to the present.

"Oh, Michael . . ." She threw her arms around his neck, seeking an end to their game. Turning the moment from merriment to a more serious note, she said, "I cannot deny my feelings any longer, and I cannot keep them hidden inside me. No matter how hard I have tried to ignore them, and then convince myself it did not matter if you did not care for me—I have not been able to. I have tried to stay away from you—I cannot do that, either. You have risked your life for me. But even before that, I have fought with myself—since that first night when I . . . when we . . . made love." She lowered her head and bit her lip. It was not easy putting into words all the conflicting emotions which ran rampant inside her. With trembling lips and searching eyes, she murmured his name.

Before she could say all the words held in her heart, he grabbed her and held her tightly pressed to him. Then he lowered her backward to the leaf-strewn ground and put his finger to her lips.

"My little sorceress," he said, tenderly gazing into her amber-green eyes. "I was wrong. I know now you didn't try to trick me on the ship. I, too, had feelings for you even then, and you recognized what I feared to admit. I was such a fool. But caring for a woman is foreign to me, and it was not until I found that I might never see you or hold you again that I discovered there is more to life than I had ever hoped to dream. And, my God . . ." He squeezed her to him again before he held her from him to gaze at her with a troubled question on his lips.

Her face pinched and her voice cracked, trying to blink back the tears. "I—"

"Oh, Tonia . . . my Tonia." His voice was soft, gen-

320

tle, suddenly caressing as a morning breeze.

Disappointment scratched at her. She had hoped he would say more, but he had not.

Michael released her and rose from the ground. He walked to the edge of a jagged cliff. He stood there with his back to her, gazing out over the valley below them.

She tried to rise to her feet, to reach out for him, but a sharp pain caused her to shrink back to the ground.

He was so attuned to her that he knew of her pain before he turned to see her slumped against the earth. He immediately erased the distance between them while silently loving all of her with caring eyes.

"Tonia, soon we'll speak of many things. Now you must get some rest. You will be able to walk in the morning. We have a long journey ahead of us." He made her a simple bed from bunched leaves and the cape and settled her onto it. "Close those beautiful eyes and do not worry, I'll be nearby." He brushed her hair back from her forehead and dropped a kiss near her ear, restraining himself from asking more of her now.

She felt worn, and fluttered her eyes closed. But behind her lids she was afire with unresolved emotions. And she worried, for she knew he would never leave California until he destroyed Dominguez.

Michael had spirited her away and by now Dominguez probably knew. The enormous man had a vicious temper and would undoubtedly increase his efforts to locate them and have Michael murdered. They were like two hunters each stalking a deadly prey. And despite what happened between Michael and her, Antonia feared for Michael's fate should Dominguez manage to emerge the victor.

Chapter Thirty-six

Dominguez and the governor stood on the veranda, the fragrant wisteria draped low, teasing at the heavy silver streaks striping El Señor Dominguez's hair. When the evening's meal was announced, Dominguez's face glowered that his wife had not joined them yet.

"Your wife has looked so drawn as of late and just returned from her ailing *padre*. Why not allow her the luxury of keeping to her bed tonight" the governor said.

"You are too kind. I am afraid you would spoil her. But all she needs is time to adjust to the responsibilities of a señora of such a rancho as this."

"*Sí*, but—"

He sharply cut the topic short with, "It is her duty."

Dominguez excused himself, and moving to the door, hailed a nearby servant. He ordered the man to see that his wife was not tardy for dinner. The humble man took one look at the ugly expression on Dominguez's face and skittered off to do his bidding.

After searching her rooms thoroughly, the man hesitantly returned to the veranda to whisper into Dominguez's ear. The enormous man leaped to his feet crazily, ignoring the governor's presence, and stomped to her rooms.

Ranting and raving for his vaqueros and household staff to assemble just outside the kitchens if a thorough search of the hacienda did not locate his wife, he stormily returned to his guest.

"Will your lovely wife be joining us shortly?" the governor asked in feigned innocence.

Dominguez's lip twitched and he stiffened. "It appears she will not. But we shall not delay any longer." He swept his arm toward the door. "After you, Governor."

After the meal Dominguez escorted the governor to his room, and returned to Antonia's rooms seeking a clue to her whereabouts. As he angrily paced the floor, his hands jammed into his pockets, he thought he had made his position clear earlier. But it seemed she needed something more to make a lasting impression on her. He had evidently been too lenient and would not make the same mistake again. In a rage he tore the rooms apart, overturning the tables and chairs and ripping the gowns from the wardrobe. Not yet satisfied, he made his way through the hacienda like a cyclone to where the staff had been assembled.

"Is everyone here?" he snarled. His eyes flashed over the motley assortment of peasants he had so generously provided with work. Maybe he should send them all off the rancho and let them starve; it would not be a loss, he thought. He paced back and forth in front of them, his hands clasped menacingly behind his back, his cheeks sucked in, hollowing his face in disgusted assessment of the huddling group.

"What a pathetic lot of *cholos*," he spat. "As I am

certain your filthy, wagging tongues have already spread the gossip that my wife is nowhere to be found within the hacienda, we shall dispense with the need for preliminaries. Has any of you seen Señora Dominguez since she returned this afternoon?" His nostrils flared as he hissed, much like an animal's.

For a moment there was total silence. A cricket chirped off in the distance, and an old barn owl hooted from its high perch in a nearby oak tree waiting for an unsuspecting rodent to make the mistake of wandering by. Dominguez crossed his heavy arms over his chest.

"*Madre, Madre,* . . ." A small child tugged on her mother's skirts. "I no see señora, but I see *hombre* go back of big *casa.*"

"Hush." The little girl's *madre* grabbed her and pulled the child behind her, trying to protect her.

Dominguez heard the child, causing the fires of hell to turn his ears scarlet. He grabbed the little girl, ripping her from her mother's arms. The frightened woman hurriedly formed the sign of the cross over her breast.

Dominguez crouched down in front of the child, dwarfing her wee body next to his huge bulk. He grasped her shoulders and demanded she describe the man. When the child stuck her tiny finger in her mouth and glanced back over her shoulder in the direction of her *madre,* he shook her viciously. The little girl whimpered but managed to describe the man and what she had seen.

"Capitán Domino," he muttered between gritted teeth. "I should have known." He gave the little girl a hard shove toward her mother and rose to command one of the men to ride to the presidio and alert the commandant. "So many men, and you idiots cannot stop one *capitán* from entering the hacienda and taking my wife. Get on your damned horses and start combing the countryside for them. They better be found soon or there will be hell to pay for such stupidity."

Before he whirled around to leave, he pointed a foreboding finger at the remaining assemblage of cowering workers. "Since you now are all aware of what has happened, there will be no need for anyone to speak of this further. I hope I have made myself clear." He grabbed a branch from a nearby tree and crushed it symbolically under his boot.

Inside the hacienda, he ordered a bottle of spirits delivered to him in his rooms.

Lying on his bed with the bottle tipped to his lips, he thought of the incredible ignorance of those surrounding him. "Such a pity, Capitán Domino, that you took such a liking to my wife. Next to myself, you are probably the most intelligent man in California. You should have been a Californio. You fool. I might of shared the bitch with you." He twisted his lips into a sadistic snarl.

Feeling even more rage fester inside him, he turned the bottle up and began madly gulping down its contents.

There was little else that could be done until morning, so he emptied the bottle and flung it viciously across the room.

Chapter Thirty-seven

The morning was cooler than usual, a sign that September had whispered past August and shortly would give way to the beginning of fall. Soon the days would grow short and the gray clouds of winter would hold the land tightly within its showery grasp. Michael leaned against the mighty tree trunk, his hands clasped behind his neck, his long legs spread out in front of him crossed at the ankles.

He knew he would have to leave California soon or be forced to remain until spring when the sea would prove a more hospitable host. A perplexed wrinkle crossed his face. He could afford to remain and brave the storms around the cape, and his men were a worthy lot, but what of Antonia? Until now, he had not thought that far ahead and it suddenly troubled him. He was a man of the sea; she was a *ranchero*'s daughter accustomed to a life of landlocked ease. They were worlds apart.

No time for those thoughts right now, he reminded himself. He had to settle accounts with Dominguez first. He squared his shoulders to shake the thoughts from his mind.

Antonia stirred beneath her cape. She squinted open her eyes to find herself gazing up at the handsomely carved, gentle face of the one man she desperately cared for. She inched into an upright position, and cuddled into his arms until she could hear his heart thudding against his chest. Her lips eagerly parted in anticipation.

"Tonia, my princess," Michael groaned. He needed no other prompting, and he covered her mouth in a full wet, exploring kiss, leaving no question of his desires.

His hands flowed down her neck, over her shoulders to rest at the top of her breasts peeking from the low décolletage of her pale-green gown. Just as smoothly as the current carries a river along its course, his lips meandered gently along behind his hands.

The sun rose over the ragged hills behind them, sending streams of golden light weaving through the branches, which had sheltered them from the morning mist. The warmth of the sun on his back further sent Michael's hungers demanding release.

Antonia strained toward him, experiencing heated slivers stirring her to the boiling point, her body permeated with need. Urgently she tugged at their clothing. His swollen shaft stood free and pressed at her belly, demanding entrance into her feminine core. By its own volition, her body opened to him while her breasts became hot, peaked buds.

Michael's thumbs and index fingers pinched and circled around the hard tips before his palms took over and rubbed and kneaded the soft swells. Then he blazed a trail to her spread thighs and settled questing fingers deeply within her.

"I cannot stand it any longer," she moaned as his fingers seemed to vibrate to her center. "I have to have you. I have to." She thrust her body against his hands, grinding helplessly, straining for release. "Oh, Michael, please," she practically screamed.

Michael nipped her shoulder. "God, woman," he muttered, and descended into the very depths of her.

Her womanhood surrounded him, encased him, and begged him to lose himself further within her. With long, slow strokes he claimed her. In and out he slid, grasping her buttocks to draw her even nearer. He wanted to devour all of her; he had to claim her, indelibly mark her as his. Then the tension strained and he began to pump harder, faster, lost to all but the sensations.

Antonia, too, was lost. She met his every stroke, kept pace with the crescendoing rhythm, the intensity threatening to explode within her. The swirling culmination whirled and whirled about her, and her entire being became a mass of sensation, glorious fingers of torture taunting and teasing until her body could stand no more and thrust and shuddered against him.

Then there was only the sounds of the wilderness, the rustle of trees, the songs of birds, the heated grass beneath her, and the still weight of his drenched body pressing against hers. She felt a momentary peace so long unknown.

They remained quietly joined until their heartbeats slowed, each lost to mindless contentment.

"You make it difficult to want to leave here. But if we don't go now, I'll soon find myself needing to make love to you again," he finally said with regret, breaking the spell to rise and gather their clothing.

Antonia's heart cried, for she wanted him again. But she reined in her feelings lest she neglect the seriousness of their circumstance. "We better go," she

328

said forlornly, accepting his offer of clothing. Following his lead, she quickly dressed.

His hands slid along her ankle. "All the swelling is gone. You'll be fine now," he said, and helped her to her feet.

His touch was more than she could bear, and she fought to hold in the words she longed to say. He was so close and something could happen which would not allow her another opportunity to tell him that which burned on her tongue.

"Michael . . ." She raised herself up on her tiptoes to lessen the disparity in their height. "I know there is far to go and we must be on our way. But I must say something while there is time."

He brought his fingers to her lips in an effort to silence her, for he felt the intense tension in her fingertips and the pulsing beat of her heart as she stood wrapped about him. "This is not the time or place," he moaned.

"No." She shook her head from his finger. "There are words I must say—now." Her eyes flickered into his, silently begging him not to reject her. Her voice was unsteady, cracking with emotion as the words "I . . . I love you" came tumbling out.

"My God," he said in anguish. A floodgate of emotions opened, and the urge to hold her, to make love to her again, overflowed in him. He pulled her flush against him and caressed her lips with his, nibbling at the corners.

She could hear his breath grow into shallow pants and feel the hardness of his need. Her thoughts raced. She wanted him as he did her, as much as a woman ever wanted a man.

"I cannot . . ." She drew her hands up and pushed herself from him with all the inner and outer strength she could muster. She had told him she loved him, and he had not returned her words of love.

"What's wrong?" he asked. A look of consternation slid deeply between his brows, creasing his face.

She trembled, losing control of her emotions. "Oh, Michael, I do want you, I do."

"Then don't stop me, my golden princess," he breathed softly, nuzzling her hair. His hot, probing tongue darted out to explore her ear, tracing circles while his lips nipped at her lobe. "I want you. I need you," he murmured against her temple, his moist breath caressing her skin.

Unable to offer further resistance, Antonia succumbed to a desire as old as time. She weaved her arms around him, her thoughts fading into a distant, deepening maelstrom of emotions.

Ardently searching, he parted her lips to learn all the secrets of her tantalizing mouth. Antonia shivered. Lightning waves struck through her entire body, and she responded naturally with trembling fingers splaying in his hair and down his back.

She was helpless to resist. Although he had not returned her words of love, in her heart she knew she belonged with Michael; she had belonged with him after that first night. He had awakened an untamed part of her which had lain dormant and now cried out to be satiated again and again by the union of their bodies.

"Oh, Tonia," he groaned against her lips in a husky voice, "tell me what you want; what will please you; what will set you afire for me and only me."

"I want it all. I want to experience everything you have to offer. I want to return everything I have," she whispered, trembling with passion.

"We shall know it all—together. I shall teach you." He took her into his embrace. His fingers stroked her body as a musician would play a finely crafted instrument. She moaned her desire. He pushed her bodice aside and toyed with her full, ripe breasts, and she arched her back to him. Where his hands left off, his mouth took over and suckled at her enflamed breasts. In response, she raked her nails inside his shirt and along his sides.

Her body cried out for his in the unashamed rhythm of primeval mating. She no longer thought or cared what anyone said. Her love needed no dried ink stains on paper to bind her to him; she was bound, with her heart and soul.

They tore at their remaining clothes until they were again gloriously naked. He made his way lower along her softly rounded curves until his hand came to rest on the thickly furred mound of her most intimate of treasures. He was breathing heavily, ragged with desire. The muscles in his chest contracted and begged for release.

Antonia tensed, her body tingling with untapped longing as he dipped searching fingers into the dark, warm moistness of her. Finding her ready for him, he joined their bodies and they sought release.

Spent, she expectantly lay in his arms, glistening with beads of their passion. He kissed her but remained silent.

He wanted to speak of his love for her, but the words stuck as dry boards of balsa in his throat. Those were words that could not be spent until he was free of the demon's debt which, until now, had totally imprisoned his heart.

"We must leave, Tonia," he finally said, tearing himself away and gathering up their clothes once again.

She bent over and picked up the remaining scattered articles of clothing on the ground, then turned her back to dress.

"I am ready," Antonia said, feeling dejected that he

had not declared himself.

She followed him into the jagged foothills. She had hoped so desperately that he would have responded to her statement of love with one of his own. But he continued to remain silent. She felt the prick of despondency. She requestioned whether she had been foolish to suddenly hope he wanted more than her body, which she had given all too freely already. She gulped another breath of the sage-laced air and forced the doubt-ridden thoughts from her mind.

As they were beginning their ascent they ran into three men in ponchos and wide-brimmed hats heading toward San Diego. Their dark eyes shifted slyly over Michael and Antonia. They did not attempt even a simple greeting, preferring instead to lower their dark heads. Michael shot a glance back over his shoulder and led Antonia around a sharp bend in the trail.

"Get behind that boulder," he ordered after they were out of sight.

His strange behavior confused her. "What?"

"Don't question me, just move!"

She caught the seriousness of his expression, and the lines of tension that deepened across his face. Without another word she lifted her skirts and hurried to follow his directive. She watched him weigh and gather two rocks and a fallen tree limb. Understanding spawned a sickening jab in her stomach. Reality hit her, cold, hard. They were not merely two people on an adventure; they were fighting for their very survival.

Antonia did not have long to ponder their circumstance. One of the men, seeming to come out of nowhere, grabbed her around the waist and swung her off her feet. The man attempted to silence her by placing his hand over her lips. He was clumsy in his haste and received the full force of her teeth sinking into his flesh.

"Damn you, you little wildcat," he swore and dropped her to the ground, sucking on his throbbing hand.

Michael heard the scuffle and whirled around to rescue Antonia. He was halted by the man's two companions, who jumped him from behind. The three entangled men lost their footing and tumbled against some rocks. Michael, his fists swinging with such great force, managed to free himself with a swift, well-placed jab to the jaw of one. The man fell against the other causing them to stumble again.

They were thrown off balance just long enough for Michael to grab one by the front of his poncho and smash a crashing right to his face. The man's jaw snapped as he crumpled to the ground from the impact. The other man picked up the limb Michael had dropped when he heard the scuffle. He swung viciously at Michael but was too slow; Michael jumped clear. The man furiously threw the limb aside and pulled his knife, swinging and waving the piece wildly.

The sun reflected off the blade and temporarily blinded Michael. He threw his arm over his eyes. Thinking he had the advantage, the man lunged. Michael grabbed his wrist, sending him sprawling to the ground. Not giving the man time to orient himself, Michael flew at him, bunched his fist, and sent a striking blow into his nose. The man reeled and slumped back, an unconscious mass against the dusty earth.

After recovering from the nasty bite on his hand and bloodied head, the third man angrily grabbed Antonia's retreating arm and threw her to the ground. He raised his fist high and was just about to strike the flailing woman when Michael scrambled around the bend.

"Arrgh." The man gave a strangled cry. He whipped

his head around just in time to catch sight of a gigantic fist slammed into his face. Shrieking and clutching his bleeding lips, he sprang to his feet and madly rushed to join his companions, who had already realized they were no match for the wild man of a captain and were beating a hasty retreat.

"Are you all right?" Michael asked Antonia, frantic with concern.

"*Sí*, they are just lucky they knew when to run. Another moment and I would have had to hurt the big one," Antonia said through tears glistening in her eyes.

He pulled her shaking body against his. "I'm lucky to have you here to protect me."

After she stopped trembling, he attempted to right the top of her torn gown which hung immodestly low over her bosom.

His eyes smiled, thinking of how many times he had helped readjust her torn gowns. "One would have to be very wealthy in order to keep clothing on your back."

"The right man would not have to," she said, a playful glint streaking her face.

He devilishly cocked his brow. "Oh?"

She was proud she had held her own until Michael could finish the man. But beneath it all a sadness lurked, for she so hoped to hear that he loved her as she did him.

Michael walked over to where the man had dropped the knife and picked it up. "This may prove useful should we encounter any more suspicious characters. Although you will not have to concern yourself about any future encounters."

She shot him a quizzical glance. "I do not understand." Fear struck at her that he had decided to send her back.

"I couldn't help but notice the wound you inflicted upon your attacker, as well as the virtual arsenal we borrowed from Dominguez, which you have donned since this morning."

She blushed and smoothed the gown down over the gun and knife strapped to her leg. "I started wearing the weapons for protection when I returned to Dominguez's rancho but removed them last night. It was not until after we . . . ah . . . after I put on my dress just before we left this morning that I remembered to strap them to my leg. I guess in all the confusion I completely forgot I even had them."

His eyes shrank to angry slits. "If you thought it was so dangerous to go back to Dominguez that you needed to arm yourself, you are more foolish than I realized."

"I am not foolish," Antonia protested. "I just felt the need, that is all. There is enough to think about now without starting another argument."

Michael looked her squarely in the eyes. He knew she was going to keep interfering, and he bit his lip. She was a thorn in his side—a beautiful desirable thorn.

As they resumed their trek, Antonia sighted one of the men's bundles a few yards from the trail and climbed down to retrieve it. Inside were at least three days' provisions of breads, cheeses, dried meats, fruits and a neatly folded paper. She unfolded the wrinkled sheet she had found in the bottom of the pack. Her eyes darted across the Wanted poster. Her face sketched lines of distress, and she drew her hand across her lips as she held out the sheet to Michael.

He shrugged it off. "It doesn't resemble me in the slightest."

"Be serious. That drawing is a close enough resemblance to cause those men to attack you." She chided him for flamboyantly brushing aside the seriousness of it.

He dropped his eyes to the rendering again. "I think I'm worth much more than this offers, don't you agree?"

He cast her a sly grin as she snatched the paper out of his hand and tucked it into her pocket.

"You cannot be serious for a moment. They tried to kill you — no doubt because of the reward on this poster."

"But they didn't succeed, now did they? Come, we must be on our way before those men decide a return match fitting. After we are far enough away from here, we'll stop and picnic on the food they were kind enough to leave."

"You are impossible!"

"No, Tonia." The mischievous smile slipped from his face. "Nothing is impossible if you strive hard enough for it."

His words gave her reason for pause. Could there be a chance for them? As they climbed deeper into the foothills she wondered exactly what had brought him to say such a thing, and with such deadly seriousness.

Chapter Thirty-eight

Dominguez awoke well after the sun had risen. His head felt as if an Indian had shot an arrow through his temples, a signal his mood would be as black as the day was bright. He grumbled as he readied himself to visit Don Diego, and bellowed for a servant to be quick about his morning's meal and see to a carriage within the hour.

"Buenas días El Señor, I hope you are feeling well this morning." Governor Figueroa smiled broadly, joining the enormous man, who was sitting in the sun. "Ah . . ." he took an inviting breath of air, "it is such a pleasant morning, *sí?"*

"Would you care to join me?" Dominguez grudgingly invited the fool to breakfast with him, when the last thing he wanted was to listen to such inane ramblings.

"Gracias no, but perhaps I shall have a glass of the juice of oranges," the governor said cheerily to the servant. "Will your lovely wife not be joining us this morning?"

337

"Governor Figueroa! I am indeed astounded that you remain uninformed of the circumstances preventing my wife's presence at the table this morning," Dominguez said all too calmly.

An idea sparked into his head. "It seems that one of the young children observed a man fitting Capitán Domino's description enter the hacienda and emerge a short time later with my unwilling wife. As you may know, I had been thinking of withdrawing the reward I offered for the man's capture, but since he has seen fit to add the crime of kidnapping to his other offenses, I am afraid that is out of the question now."

The governor was amazed by the man's resourcefulness at inventing tales to cover himself and proceeded to display nothing but surprised shock. Behind the facade, the governor silently added the lies told him to the other accusations already leveled against Dominguez by the people he had been talking to at the presidio.

"Your carriage is ready, El Señor." A meek, aging servant bowed.

"Do you travel to the presidio to inform the *comandante* of your dreadful loss?" queried the governor.

"No. I have already sent a vaquero to inform the *comandante*. I must journey to tend to the needs of my poor *amigo* and relative. The least I can do is attempt to cheer him. It will ease the burden of waiting for news of my beloved flower." He hung his head mournfully.

"You are a most kind and generous man. *Por favor,* allow me to accompany you. I did, after all, promise Señora Antonia I would visit her *padre*. It is the least I can do."

"It is not necessary."

"But I insist. I could never forgive myself if I, too, did not make an effort to lighten your load during this most unfortunate time."

Dominguez ground his teeth. He was left with no choice but to accept the man's offer.

Much to his dismay, Dominguez did not add, as he had hoped, to his wealth of information during his visit to Don Diego. The governor's presence further hindered his efforts, since he was unable to question Don Diego as he had planned.

Instead he was forced to remain seated, sipping weak coffee, watching for the *ranchero* to mistakingly gesture or present some other indication, however slight, that would give away his true condition.

Don Diego's state remained unchanged; he sat still, staring into space. In disgust Dominguez had withdrawn from Winston's rancho and was forced to suffer the heat of the return journey, as well as the governor's idle prattle.

With footsteps which rumbled like an angry bear, Dominguez walked through the hacienda and into his library to plop himself down at his desk. "The imbecile!" His fist slammed hard into a stack of papers, sending them scattering about him. "Meddling fool!"

"El Señor," Commandant Velasco clicked his heels together, nodded, and entered the room. Behind him were three bedraggled excuses for men. "I am sorry to arrive so unexpectedly, but I thought you would want to hear what these men have to say."

The strangers stood gawking, their mouths open and their eyes darting from item to item of priceless furnishings.

"Well! Spit it out or have you lost your filthy tongues?" Dominguez snarled.

The three men, who had proudly boasted earlier to the commandant of their near victory over Captain

Domino, now humbly told their tale. When they had finished, Dominguez tossed them a skimpy handful of coins and ordered them sent on their way.

"Velasco, I pray you have been paying close attention to the location where you and your 'soldiers' should be directing your efforts." Dominguez's voice was full of contempt for the commandant.

After the room had been vacated Dominguez flew into a rage and kicked at his desk. Still seething, he ripped a vase from a nearby table and sent it shattering to the floor. He then stormed to the door and leaned out. "Send that clumsy young girl Lupe to me!"

Lupe trembled as she meekly entered the bookfilled room. Her face was red and swollen with a trail of tears left on her cheeks by her fearful cries upon learning the evil *patrón* had summoned her.

He smugly motioned for her. "Come over here, Lupe."

Lupe fought to swallow the dry, hard lump of fear in her throat and did as ordered. Her hands were trembling and she clasped them tightly behind her back in an effort to hide her fright.

"Did you think I would forget your name and the promise I made you after you broke those dishes outside my door?" he snickered.

When the girl remained silent, biting her lip, her wide eyes staring at the floor, he pushed his chair back and moved beside her to lift her chin.

"What is this? You cry that I may have forgotten you?" he tormented. He squeezed her arm painfully. "Come, Lupe," he said with deadly calm, "it is time for you to pay for displeasing me. But do not let it worry you, you may also learn how to please me."

Her eyes darted around the room, but there was nowhere to run. She meekly allowed herself to be led to his room of pleasures as a steer is to slaughter. When he turned the lock in the door she suddenly struggled free and bolted toward the stairs. In her haste she caught her foot underneath an open plank, causing her to tumble to the floor. She scrambled to her feet, but his foreboding shadow blanketed her.

The twisted grin widened as he scooped her to her feet and dusted off her skirt. "Here, allow me to assist you. I do hope you were not harmed."

"Por favor El Señor, *por favor . . ."* Her voice was frayed about the edges with a hoarse, dull ring.

He did not hear her. His thoughts were on Antonia and Captain Domino. Enveloped in a blistering hatred, all he could think of was Antonia, who, in his warped mind, became transformed into his lost Rafaela. Instead of Antonia he envisioned Rafaela entwined in the arms of a common sailor, giving herself willingly, freely to him. With each picture, his anger grew until it leaped off the edge into a bottomless crater of insanity.

With eyes of fiery glass he dragged the girl into the room and clamped her arms and legs to the wall. "You have been a naughty girl, my love. Why did you want to marry another, and then run off with that sailor while I waited for you. I would have given you everything you ever desired, Rafaela." He crazily paced back and forth before the panicking girl.

"El Señor, *por favor,* my name Lupe. I no Rafaela. *Por favor* El Señor, I Lupe." She frantically screamed, shrieking for help, begging, pleading.

"Lupe? No! You try to trick me, Rafaela. But you will not succeed. You are mine! And I shall have anyone who may think differently know you are mine!" He gave a heinous laugh, then stormed over to an old iron container he kept for warmth in the winter. Viciously tossing split wood into it, he struck a match and flipped it onto the wood. Soon a crackling blaze flared from the center. His eyes mirrored the fiery fingers hypnotically mesmerizing him.

"Are you more comfortable, Rafaela?" His face had lost any semblance of sanity, and he became little more than a rabid beast.

"El Señor, *por favor,* I Lupe," she piercingly shrilled.

After the fire had burned into a red-hot bed of coals, he moved to the storage cabinet like a revived corpse and removed a branding iron. He placed the iron in the glowing embers, staring blankly ahead. When the long, slender rod was aglow, he closed his fingers around it, his eyes bulging madly from their sockets as he slowly carried it toward the girl frozen with fear.

"No!" she cried hysterically. *"Por favor,* no! *Díos mío,* I Lupe."

Her blood-curdling screams resounded about the room.

Chapter Thirty-nine

Commandant Velasco and his men rode hard in the direction of the foothills. But once out of sight of the hacienda Velasco raised his hand for the men to halt.

He was a sly man who made it a point to be prepared for emergencies, so he ordered his men to draw in close so they could clearly understand his orders. He had his own reasons for finding the captain and señora, as well as long-held debts of his own to repay.

"El Señor is not at all pleased with us failing to apprehend Capitán Domino. Now it appears he has taken matters into his own hands. We are to join his own men in the foothills at the base of the mountains. He demanded that should Capitán Domino be apprehended, we take steps to assure his safe passage to a cell. He warned that his men may become over zealous in their efforts, and we, as trained soldiers, must prevent the situation from getting out of hand. And of course, Señora Dominguez, who is believed to be his captive, is to be treated in only the most ladylike fashion. Do I make myself clear?"

His orders delivered, he wheeled his horse about and thrust his heels into its sides. When they caught up with the vaqueros from the Dominguez rancho, Velasco quickly singled out the leader and nudged his horse in the man's direction.

Chico Lima was a lean man in his fortieth year. His hair had just begun to gray at the temples and his sun-drenched face reflected a life of one accustomed to the rigors of hard living.

"Buenas tardes, Comandante Velasco. You come to join in the hunt?"

"My soldiers and I shall be here to aid your efforts," Velasco answered, careful to give the impression that Lima was in command of the search. "Have you found any trace of them yet?"

"No. But this is where we found three men who almost killed the *capitán.*"

Velasco chuckled. "Judging from the state of the men when they came to me, it might be said the *capitán* nearly killed them."

"They were fools. We know how to deal with him."

"That," Velasco said with all due seriousness, "is one of the very reasons for which El Señor requested my soldiers join your men . . ." He presented the same speech which he had to his men.

Lima rubbed his chin, contemplating the commandant's words. He knew Dominguez's methods and thought it strange that he would want the captain alive until the commandant convinced him of the enormous man's desire to personally supervise Michael Domino's sentence.

Velasco had a way with words and was pleased with himself that he so easily convinced the man to summon his men and give strict orders that Captain Domino was not to be harmed. Michael Domino had visited Velasco on several occasions and they had

344

come to be comrades of circumstance; each had his own reasons for wanting Dominguez destroyed.

With his most pressing task accomplished, Velasco shifted in his saddle and squinted his eyes over the terrain. "If I were Domino, what would I do?" he mumbled to himself.

To the east the mountains rose sharply only to drop to the desert floor below. To the south lay Dominguez's grazing land. To the north they would have to cross another rancho, and west Domino would rendezvous with his ship but could encounter Dominguez's men. After much consideration Velasco suspected the captain would sneak past the men and get Antonia far out of Dominguez's reach once and for all. That could only mean the captain would be circling and heading west.

"Scout the area south of us," Velasco recommended, and left his men with Lima in charge. After he was out of sight, Velasco headed north and came around a ridge just behind the camp.

The campfire had died down to smoldering ashes and by the time Lima returned from his search and climbed into his bedroll. The men had finished the chores of cleaning away the remains of the evening's meal, made preparations for the morning, and had seen to the needs of their steeds before bedding down for the night. He felt secure in his position of leadership, and was certain no one would dare to challenge such an impressive lot of men, so he foolishly ignored suggestions of a guard.

The men were weary from the long day and welcomed a full night's sleep. The horses whinnied and tugged at their ropes, causing one of the men to grumble and crawl to his knees to check on the restless animals.

"Do not worry about the nags. The big cats and

coyotes they scare them. Go back to sleep," another grunted at his companion's efforts.

After another confirmed the reason for the animals' restiveness, the men settled back down and were soon so sound asleep that they did not hear the crickets cease to sing their songs.

A twig snapped with a crunch. Velasco, who had dozed, bolted upright. Slowly, he gained his feet just in time to sight a shadowy figure near the animals. He strained his eyes and recognized Michael Domino but did not see Señora Antonia.

Crickets resumed their chirping as Michael silently slipped the reins and threw saddles on the backs of two horses. His nimble fingers untied the knots securing the steeds, and he shooed all but two from the herd. He was thorough in his task, making certain the men would be unable to follow them immediately.

Michael led the horses clear of the camp and fanned his hand toward a clump of cresote bushes, whispering, "Hurry, so we will have time to gain a comfortable lead before the men collect their horses."

Antonia's heart was pounding so loudly between her ears, and her breath was so ragged as she darted from the thicket, that she failed to notice a brawny soldier who had just stepped from behind a tree after tending to his body's needs.

She ran right in front of him. He grabbed her and swooped her from her feet. "Nooo!" she instinctively screamed.

The men sprang to their feet and scrambled for their weapons.

Michael drew his knife. He was about to challenge the entire camp when Velasco suddenly stepped from a bush.

"Capitán Domino, do not be a fool. You cannot help her if you are dead or captured," Velasco said, glancing at the captain's lone weapon. "How could you do her any good with only one knife against forty men?"

"Why aren't you with them?"

"I have my reasons. Trust me. I am on your side, do you not remember?"

"Then prove yourself. Join me and help me free her."

Michael's face was seamed with angry determination. He had not spoken the words of love he felt in his heart, and he could not bear to lose her—not now that they had truly found each other.

Velasco's eyes shifted from the knife to the soldiers scattered in a frenzy, scrambling to dress and running after their horses. "All right, *mi amigo,* I am with you."

Michael was blinded to everything except rescuing Antonia and bounded toward the soldiers ahead of the commandant.

Velasco, close behind, caught Michael's shoulder. *"Capitán?"*

Michael swung around.

"Lo siento, capitán, truly sorry." The commandant swung back his balled fist and sent a crashing blow to Michael's jaw, causing him to collapse in the commandant's arms. Velasco then dragged the unconscious captain beneath the dense brush.

A paunchy soldier ran toward the commandant with his pistol pointed at Velasco's heart.

"Soldier!" Velasco shouted.

The man came to an abrupt halt and clicked his heels in attention, his pistol dangling at his side. "Sorry, *comandante,* I did not realize it is you."

"Of course it is me! Who did you think I was? Capitán Domino? I was afraid something like this might happen, but it looks like I returned too late." He scowled, pointing an accusing finger at the vaquero responsible. "Where were the guards?"

"All sleeping," the soldier said, and hung his head.

"Humph! Well, get busy and look for Capitán Domino, although he is probably long gone by now."

The soldier swallowed hard, saluted, and skittered off to search for the captain. Once Velasco was sure he was alone, he checked on Michael, who had not moved, and turned toward the camp. He shouted orders, directing the men to cease such a futile search without benefit of horses and prepare to return Antonia to her husband.

While the men rushed to do as directed, Velasco casually strolled over to Antonia. With her arms held tightly across her chest, she was seated between Lima and the soldier who had captured her. Pouting, she refused to answer any of their probing questions.

"Leave us. I shall take full responsibility for Señora Dominguez," Velasco said with authority.

Lima opened his mouth to protest, but clamped it shut and moved off after he was assured he would not be left to shoulder all the blame for failure to capture the captain.

"Can I do anything for you, Señora Dominguez?" Velasco offered, folding himself onto the log next to the distraught young woman.

She glared at the man. "You can turn your back and let me go."

"You know that is not possible."

"And Michael thought you might be someone I could go to if I needed help. Why, you are nothing but an opportunist," she spat.

Velasco pressed his finger to her lips in an effort to silence her, but she slapped it aside and screamed at him.

"Don't touch me! *Bastardo!*"

348

"Señora Dominguez," he said in hushed tones. "I *am* your friend. I cannot speak now, but trust me." He rose as her eyes burned with hatred and called two men to escort her to one of the horses which had been rounded up and saddled.

When the ragtag band of men was ready to leave, Velasco ordered, "Do not to waste time returning Señora Dominguez to her husband. I shall be along shortly." He then stood and watched as they put the lash to their horses and moved out.

Antonia was on her way back to the one man she despised most. Surrounded by soldiers and Dominguez's vaqueros there would be no chance to escape. She wondered of her fate. More than her concern for herself was her worry for Michael.

Through hot, angry tears she quietly lifted her head to the heavens and prayed he would be safely delivered from the misfortunes which had befallen him since their first encounter. And while she desperately wanted to be with him, her mind was already swirling with plans to help him.

Velasco stood alone in the clearing, which had been a camp just an hour before. After building another fire, he returned to the brush and helped the still-dazed captain to his feet.

Michael rubbed his aching jaw and staggered to the fire to take the night's chill from his aching bones.

"My *friend*, I want to thank you properly." Michael tore back his hammered fist and, with brute force, smashed the commandant in the jaw, sending him sprawling on the ground.

When Velasco awoke he remained prone, massaging his face until Michael walked over and stood darkly over him. His legs were spread and his hands were on his hips. Michael cocked his brow, cracking the hint of a smile. "No hard feelings, Juan." He held out his hand to the commandant. "I have to admit you were right; I could not have rescued Antonia by myself."

Velasco returned the grin and accepted his offering.

"We are *amigos* then, *sí?*"

"We're *amigos*. Now, let's get going. I have to free Antonia once again before Dominguez harms her — the troublesome wench," he grumbled.

Chapter Forty

Antonia was welcomed back to the rancho as if nothing had happened. Dominguez entered her rooms only once after she returned.

"My flower . . ." he said casually, standing at the foot of her bed like a forbidding mountain. "I pray you are well."

"Get out!" Antonia demanded through angry eyes. "I have nothing to say to you."

His eyes grew cold and his lips taut. With deliberate, controlled words, he said in a dangerously low voice, "You continue to be fortunate that Governor Figueroa is our guest. I warned you once before, but I tell you now, this is your last chance. If you care at all for your *padre*, you will say nothing of your foolishness. I will handle all the necessary explanations. And do not try my patience further." He did not wait for a response but turned on his heel and left her staring after him.

Antonia declined to accept visitors for two days; instead she remained in bed, claiming exhaustion and the need for rest. She had hoped Michael would come for her. When he did not, she spent the time trying to figure out a way to unmask Dominguez in front of the governor.

On Antonia's third day of isolation a servant meekly hobbled into her rooms and reached up to remove her beige gown from the wardrobe. "Where is the girl who usually serves me?" Antonia asked, arching a brow. "I have not seen her since my return."

The old woman forced a weak smile. "Señora, Lupe much sick. El Señor, he say help you get ready for tonight. People come soon, celebrate you return. I get bath."

Antonia sighed her frustration, wanting to defy Dominguez's command, but overwhelming concern for her *padre* and hope she might be in a better bargaining position if Michael were caught, caused her to relent.

The courtyard was lit with brightly swaying lanterns. Mariachis sang and strummed their guitars while the guests proposed toasts of congratulations to the bride for her safe return. Antonia was forced to remain by Dominguez's side the entire evening, not allowing her the opportunity to speak alone with the governor or the commandant, who had tried several times without success to draw her away from Dominguez.

The hour was late and the guests were preparing to depart when Dominguez escorted Antonia to the door. They began bidding farewell to the celebrants.

"Señora Dominguez." Velasco took her hand in his and lightly brushed his lips across the back of it. "I cannot tell you how I feel to see you here."

She retrieved her hand and did not answer.

The governor was directly behind the commandant and stepped up to join in the conversation. "My dear, we have not seen much of you as of late. I do hope you have recovered, although you do look rather pale. You must spend some time in the sun."

"My wife has had a terrifying experience, gentlemen. It is a wonder she looks as lovely as she does." Dominguez crushed her hand in his in warning before releasing it. "I think we must allow her to retire for the evening and seek her rest," he said, drawing the tiresome conversation to a close.

Antonia had remained quietly mute, but her eyes now pleaded with the governor and commandant. She had to know of her *padre* and Michael. When the men made no effort to move on but remained still, Dominguez began to tap his foot in an impatient beat.

Governor Figueroa took Antonia's hand briefly in a display of reassurance and sent her a nod of sympathy before Dominguez began to lead her away.

They had taken no more than a few steps when Antonia yanked her hand free and rushed back to Governor Figueroa. "Forgive me, but I must know of my *padre*. Has there been any change? Is he all right?"

Dominguez bristled and quickly attempted to disengage Antonia from the governor again. "Antonia, my flower, why did you not ask me about your *padre*'s condition? Come, I shall inform you of his health."

"No," she cried, then calmly added, "I shall only require a few moments of the governor's time, then I shall be able to rest."

Dominguez had no other choice but to relent, and he simmered beneath his cool exterior. "Very well, but we must not linger. You do need your rest." He snaked his hand around her waist and held her securely.

"I think it might be best if you visited your *padre* and saw for yourself, my dear," the governor suggested. "But do not worry, I have been spending some time with your *padre* in your absence."

"It would ease her mind, El Señor," put in Velasco.

Michael paced impatiently in the commandant's quarters where Velasco had recommended he hide out. Velasco had convinced him of the prudence of assessing the situation before trying to rescue Antonia again. But Michael did not like waiting and contemplated riding out to the rancho until a tap at the shutter took him to the window.

It was dark, but the moon cast just enough light for him to see the large square form of a man outside. He flipped the latch and swung open the shutters to find Mano standing there.

Mano climbed over the ledge and into the room. "My brother, I have been worried about you. I expected you would have rejoined us by now. Thadius was prepared to send the entire crew out after you."

"I'm glad you're here. With your help we can be finished with this business once and for all."

They seated themselves and brought each other up to date. Each listened intently to the other.

"You have been busy. But what of the beautiful Spanish woman? Do your feelings still run deep for her?" It was not the Indian's custom to pry, but much had changed since returning to the shores of California.

Michael cast his companion a sideways glance but determined to answer him. "As you know, she has greatly troubled me. But much of that, too, has been resolved. I care for her more than I thought I could care for a woman. And after I destroy Dominguez . . ." Michael reached out and fiercely grabbed the leather rod which he had found in Dominguez's room of pleasures during the fiesta, his eyes icing over to turn as cold as a glacier, "we'll all be free."

At the creak of the door opening their attention snapped toward the doorway.

"What did you learn of Antonia?" Michael asked when he spied Velasco. He was anxious for news of her, and did not give the commandant the chance even to seat himself.

"Although words have not been spoken directly, I believe Governor Figueroa is wise to Dominguez. He has been asking many questions lately. And he is very protective of the señora. You need not concern yourself for her safety while the governor is a guest at the rancho. But that is one important piece of information of which I must speak. The governor plans to sail back to Monterey shortly, and Dominguez and the señora are to accompany him, so if you do not wish to suffer the inconvenience of following them, we shall have to speed things up a bit."

Michael's spine stiffened against the back of the chair as he listened to Velasco. Fire sparked from his eyes and he clenched his fists.

"Señora Dominguez quite skillfully manipulated Dominguez, with the governor's help, to allow her a visit to her *padre* before they leave." Velasco chuckled. "She certainly is giving him more trouble than he bargained for."

"How well I know about the trouble that wench can stir up." Michael shook his head. "While she's visiting her *padre* would be a good time to see that she does not return to Dominguez once and for all," Michael said coldly, the wheels churning in his mind like a runaway cart.

"I thought it might," Velasco slyly put in.

"That would leave us free without her interference to see to Dominguez," the Indian chorused.

"I wouldn't count on it," Michael grumbled under his breath.

"Then shall we drink to Dominguez's final downfall?" Velasco offered, and grabbed three mugs and a bottle from the shelf. He poured the last of the dark liquid, and they tipped their mugs in unison. Velasco smiled to himself. He was glad he had listened to the captain's explanation after Rosa's murder. And gladder still that he had decided to join forces with Captain Domino. It was the best way to at last see his own long-awaited desire for revenge against Dominguez come to fruition.

Chapter Forty-one

The old servant hobbled into Antonia's rooms. She set a tray of *ranchos huevos* and coffee on the table by Antonia's bed, and with great effort moved slowly for the door.

"Wait! Where is the girl Lupe?" Antonia called out.

The old woman hesitated and turned, a pained expression on her face. "She still sick. I help."

Antonia noticed the old woman's words possessed a certain uneasiness about them. She was concerned for the young girl. "Send Lupe to me," Antonia directed.

"But she much sick, señora."

"I will judge Lupe's illness for myself. Now, send her to me," Antonia insisted with a growing feeling that something was amiss.

Trepidation crossed the old woman's face. "*Sí, señora,*" she muttered in defeat as she hobbled from the room.

While waiting for the girl, Antonia went to the window. Only remnants of the gray morning remained. A haze which had settled in a distant valley lingered.

Soon it, too, would give way to the warmth of the day, robbing the land of its moisture until the ground added yet more hairline faults across its dry terrain.

She felt as if she were one of the many parched shrubs begging that her thirst be sated. Like the evening's moisture, Michael Domino had awakened a thirst within her heart, and somehow she would see it satisfied.

It seemed an eternity before the door slowly squeaked open and Lupe slipped inside. Her head hung below her shoulders and she spoke in no more than a whisper.

"You want see me, señora?"

"*Sí*, I have been concerned about you."

"I sick, no come." Lupe did not look up or attempt to approach Antonia but kept her distance, remaining in the shadows of the room.

"Is there something else you may wish to tell me?" Antonia pressed.

Antonia could tell by her actions that she was lying about something. The girl was acting very peculiar, and Antonia was determined to find out why.

"I much sick, no more," Lupe said a little too quickly.

"I am sorry." Antonia was taken aback by her tone. "I did not mean to pry. If you are feeling well enough, I would like you to be my personal servant from now on." Antonia moved to her and dropped her hand on the girl's shoulder.

Lupe flinched and shrank away, nervously picking at her fingers. "I like, but go now."

At the door of the library, Dominguez stopped the young servant returning from Antonia's room. "*Buenas días,* Lupe, I pray you have seen to the needs of the señora?"

She trembled and her voice quivered, remembering

the terror she had suffered at the big man's crazed hand. *"Sí,* señor."

"Do not worry, child." His lips twisted into a snarl. "I will never forget you, Lupe."

"Gracias, señor," she barely mouthed the words through her fright.

"Will my wife be joining me soon?"

"I no know."

"Very well," he frowned darkly, "you may go."

With a bated sigh of relief, Lupe fled from his sight.

Dominguez turned to the governor, who had been seated with his back to the library door.

"It does not appear that my wife will be gracing us with her presence soon. Perhaps it would be wise to wait for another day to visit Don Diego. With the *capitán* loose, travel is not safe at this time."

"You are right of course, El Señor. I shall travel to see Comandante Velasco today and make arrangements for an escort to ensure our protection. In the morning we will be able to get an earlier start." He picked up the package he had brought into the room with him. "I had meant to present this gift to you and your delightful wife as a small token of my appreciation for your hospitality. But since she is not present, I shall offer the gift to you." The governor presented six fine embroidered handkerchiefs. "They were hand-sewn by the villagers near Monterey. *Por favor,* accept them as a symbol of brotherhood and unification between north and south California."

Dominguez took the offering and tossed it down on his desk. "My wife and I thank you and the people of northern California," he returned indifferently.

"Then if you will excuse me, I shall inform Señora Antonia of our decision, then be on my way."

* * *

Antonia rose early the next morning eagerly looking forward to the day. After readying herself, she stepped to the wardrobe and removed a small enameled box she had carefully placed in the corner of the cabinet. She held the box tightly and carried it to her dressing table. She seated herself in front of the silver-framed mirror. Within the satin-lined box were numerous treasured pieces of jewelry she had saved from childhood. She picked through the items looking for the special piece her *padre* had given her shortly after her *madre* died.

It was a simple necklace made from the acorns of the oak tree. Antonia continued her search, remembering its history. Her *madre* had crafted it as a child, and had lovingly saved it as if it had been made of precious stones. Before her *madre* died, she asked that it be given to her daughter as a symbol of the humble beginnings of the great oak. She had said that she wanted her child to grow strong as the tree and always to remember that in spite of the many obstacles life presented, a strong person would survive and grow from the experience.

At the bottom of the box Antonia found the necklace. She removed it and fastened the clasp around her neck. She ran her fingers lightly over the brightly stained acorns and silently prayed it would jar her *padre*'s memory when he saw it.

"You up early," Lupe said, coming into the room. She stepped to the wardrobe and slipped a cape from the rod. "It turn cool today. Winter come soon. You need." She moved to the door expecting Antonia to follow. When Antonia remained rooted to the floor, Lupe said, "It long way. You eat."

"I will have a tray in my room. I shall not be joining my husband this morning. And Lupe, I want you to travel with me. You may be of help once we reach my

360

padre's rancho."

Lupe pressed her lips into an understanding line, nodded, and disappeared to fetch a plate.

Antonia returned the small box to its place in the wardrobe and sat down to wait until it was time to depart. She did not leave her rooms until she heard the clopping hooves of the carriage team beat against the ground outside her window. As she ran her hand over her gown to brush the wrinkles from her skirt before joining the governor, she heard additional horses' hooves mingled with the sounds of soldiers' gruff voices. An escort had arrived to protect her from the one man she loved and wanted to be with more than anything.

Chapter Forty-two

The journey to the Rancho de los Robles proved un-eventful. Lupe sat on one side of the carriage humbly gathered into the corner. Governor Figueroa and Antonia traveled across from the girl. When the governor's efforts failed to put the girl more at ease, he clapped her knee in understanding and turned his attention to Antonia.

"Thank heavens. You come home at last." Josephina welcomed Antonia and ushered her into the house. "Your *padre*, he get well now you here."

"*Sí*, I pray he will," Antonia said with a catch in her voice. "Has there been any change?"

"You go, see for yourself."

Leaving Josephina and Lupe, Antonia and the governor hurried to Don Diego's room.

Don Diego remained seated, the cameo in his hand.

Antonia joined him, hoping he would see the necklace and show even a faint glimmer of recognition. She fingered the acorns, speaking softly as if he were not ill and unhearing. "*Padre*, I am here now. I love you. And my love will help heal whatever pain you have locked inside you."

When she received no sign that there was life behind his hollow eyes, she craned her arms around the back of her neck and snapped open the clasp on her necklace. Sliding the necklace into her hand, she folded her *padre*'s fingers around it.

"Do you remember what you said when you gave this to me?" Tears threatened to sting her eyes and overflow down her cheeks as she half pleaded, half sobbed. "You, too, are like the mighty oak, and you are strong and will be well again soon — I know you will."

"Antonia," the governor interceded, "you must not upset yourself. Your *padre* will heal. Now come and wipe your eyes, my dear." The governor wound his arm about her shoulders and led her toward the door.

Close to being overcome with emotion as pain filled Don Diego's eyes and welled in his heart, he forced himself to remain mute. In an effort to keep Antonia from seeing his heartache he turned his head and slipped the cameo into his pocket. Keeping his gaze averted, he stared out at the empire he had built and would throw away in a second to erase the part he had played in causing Antonia's marriage to Dominguez.

Listening to her sobs as she was leaving the room, Don Diego could no longer endure seeing his only child so unhappy while he maintained the pretense of being ill.

"Antonia, my child . . ." Don Diego reached out splayed fingers to her. Briny tears spilled down his face, overcoming his efforts to stem the flow.

Hearing his voice, Antonia spun out of the governor's embrace and ran to her *padre*. She threw herself down upon her knees at his feet and laid her head in his lap, weeping openly and clutching at his hands.

"You are well," she sobbed.

"*Sí,* child, I am well. I regained my health a short time ago." Don Diego closed his fingers under her chin and gently raised her head until their tear-filled eyes met. "My daughter, I have caused you so much unhappiness."

"José,"—Don Diego motioned for his friend, the governor, to join them—"and I spoke when he last visited, and we felt at the time your interests could best be served if I remained ill to the world. Will you ever forgive me?"

She smiled up at him through the prisms of her tears. "There is nothing to forgive. I am only happy you are well."

"Your *padre* and I hoped to gain proof that the *capitán* is innocent. And I have been spending many hours talking to the other *rancheros,* the *comandante,* and reviewing certain records of business transactions Dominguez has been involved in," Governor Figueroa explained.

"Unfortunately we have not yet been able to obtain proof of the man's dubious business dealings. It had been our hope that by delaying my departure and then suddenly changing my plans he would be forced into some careless action."

The two men sat with Antonia and poured out all they knew of Dominguez and Captain Michael Domino, no longer holding anything back. Josephina entered the room while they were speaking and dropped her tray, so overwhelmed was she by the don's miraculous recovery. Freshly squeezed juice splashed across the floor mingling with soggy pastries and broken glass.

"Oh, Señor Winston, I so happy!" she rambled between sniffles.

"Josephina, would you be so kind as to fetch more refreshments. Our tongues are parched from much conversation." Don Diego spoke calmly, the authority returning to his voice.

"I send Lupe. She clean floor."

"Lupe?"

"She is my personal maid," Antonia explained. "I brought her along to help out."

Josephina rushed through the kitchen like a tornado, and ran out into the yard with the good news. Anyone within earshot of the old woman's tongue now knew Señor Winston had suddenly regained his health.

The old woman's information was of particular interest to one of the vaqueros who had patiently watched and waited. Upon hearing the news, Pedro Montoya stealthily left the rancho, viciously digging the rowels of his spurs into the flesh of the unsuspecting animal he had mounted. The horse reared up and thundered toward the Dominguez rancho.

After arranging another tray, Josephina handed it to Lupe and gave her a nudge toward Don Diego's room. Lupe delivered it as instructed and set about picking the broken pieces of glass from the floor.

Lupe gathered slivers of strewn glass fragments and placed them on the empty tray. She had nearly completed her task when she noticed a large chunk near Don Diego's chair. Not wanting to interrupt the conversation, she crawled along the floor to retrieve it. As she stretched out her arm her peasant blouse slid off her shoulder. Don Diego glanced down at the girl to move his foot from her way. She quickly retreated and rose to leave.

"Lupe, *por favor,* come here," Don Diego suddenly called to her.

She set the tray down and hesitantly went over to them. Her eyes were wide with terror. "Señor?"

"Do not worry, my *padre* will not harm you." Antonia went to her and closed her fingers around Lupe's hand to reassure her. "He is not at all like El Señor Dominguez."

"What is that mark on your shoulder?" Don Diego questioned.

"It is birthmark." Her voice cracked and she chewed on her fingernail.

"Would you allow us to examine the mark?"

Lupe did not respond. Antonia, noting the girl's fear and wondering at her *padre's* reasoning, shot a questioning glance to the governor, who raised his brows quizzically.

"Por favor, would you face the door for us? We shall not harm you." Don Diego's deep, soothing voice was reassuring, and the girl turned.

She held her breath as the mark on the back of her shoulder was closely scrutinized by Señor Winston, and then the governor and Antonia.

Antonia knitted her brows in dismay. "I do not understand?"

"Lupe, child, how did you get this mark?" Don Diego pressed.

"He . . . he kill me," she stammered, her eyes pleading.

"No one is going to kill you. Now, where did you get the mark?" Don Diego asked again.

"No one will harm you," reinforced the governor.

"I noticed the mark when the girl reached for the sliver of glass under my chair," Don Diego said, "but the significance of it eluded me until she had nearly reached the door. The mark is actually a brand used by Dominguez to identify his cattle. I did not realize the real importance of the mark until I had a chance to examine it closely. It is the Dominguez D brand, but it has been cleverly altered from the brand of one of the neighboring ranchos and is only recognizable by a well-trained eye."

Antonia slipped her arm around Lupe's trembling shoulders. "You must tell us the whole story, Lupe. It is vitally important."

After Lupe had forced herself to relive every nightmarish detail of how she came to have the brand on her shoulder, Don Diego suggested Antonia settle her into one of the guest rooms. Nodding, Antonia, who did not inform them of her knowledge of the altered brand, led the distraught girl from the room.

"José, that girl bears the proof we seek," Don Diego said. Explaining the full significance of the discovery, he added, "During the insanity of his rage, Dominguez not only selected one of the branding irons he uses in the theft of neighboring cattle, like those we discovered among his own herd, he unknowingly chose one which would finally provide proof that the man is a thief. Lupe is living evidence of Dominguez's guilt."

"We must protect the girl, Diego, until Dominguez is imprisoned and on his way to Mexico to the work in the silver mines. Or until we can prove he is responsible for Rosa Pica's murder and see justice done."

"I shall keep her here and station one of my vaqueros outside her door for protection. We can trust Pedro Montoya to watch out for the girl."

Antonia returned from settling Lupe just in time to hear the name of Pedro Montoya mentioned to shield Lupe. Her eyes widened at the mention of his name, and she rushed forth to relate what she had seen and heard while hiding outside the library with Michael.

"It appears that the eyes and ears of Dominguez reach even farther than we had suspected. Pedro Montoya has worked for me for many more years than I care to mention. Of all men, I never would have suspected he would betray me." As he spoke, Don Diego remembered how he had treated the man like a brother, and his face fell despairingly.

Antonia, her *padre*, and the governor spent the remainder of the afternoon sharing memories of times past and enjoying the newfound bond between father and daughter.

"*Padre*, what of Capitán Domino? I know he did not kill Rosa."

"With all I know of El Señor Dominguez, I, too, believe the *capitán* is telling the truth. But we need proof." Don Diego gently patted her hand.

"I know he did not do it!" she beseeched, her heart pounding with the thought of the man she loved.

"I am sorry, Antonia. More evidence is needed than your word. The *capitán* did not come forward to proclaim his innocence. He ran. That made people think him guilty," put in the governor.

While Antonia understood the governor's dilemma, she desperately prayed Michael would soon be cleared of the charges. He had to come back for her before leaving California, for she knew she would never find true happiness without him. Silently, she vowed to wait for him no matter how long it took. If he never returned, she swore to herself that she would grow old on her *padre*'s rancho cherishing the memories of the time they had shared together—those precious intimate moments known and treasured only by lovers.

Chapter Forty-three

Before his horse could come to a skidding halt, Pedro Montoya flung his leg over the animal's back and leaped to the ground. Not waiting for a servant to offer him entry to the Dominguez hacienda, he rushed inside to the library, his spurs noisily clinking his arrival. A curious servant, hearing the sounds, cautiously crept from the kitchens to investigate, only to be grabbed by his collar by the anxious vaquero.

"El Señor Dominguez, where is he?" demanded Montoya, his eye nervously twitching.

The flustered servant hesitated too long to suit the vaquero.

He shook the hapless man. "I asked you where El Señor is?"

"But señor . . ." the man gasped when he found himself tumbling backward to the floor.

Montoya grunted his disgust and started through the hacienda. Before he had gone very far an angry voice rang in his ears.

Dominguez appeared in the doorway of one of the rooms. "What is the meaning of this outrage?" His black eyes flashed with fire and he stood with his hands on his hips.

"El Señor, I am sorry, the man entered—"

"Return to your chores, I shall handle this!" the enormous man bellowed.

The servant skittered back to the kitchens while Dominguez ordered Montoya into his library and slammed the door.

"I warned you."

"But my information is of great importance to you." Montoya swallowed hard, since he knew what Dominguez was capable of, although he expected to be generously rewarded once he delivered his news.

"It better be, for your sake."

"While I watched at the Rancho de los Robles, the old woman Josephina rushed out of the hacienda and announced that Señor Winston has recovered from his sickness. I thought you would want me to come right away because your wife and the governor are there."

Dominguez did not respond to the information immediately. His thoughts had turned to the possible consequences of the *ranchero*'s recovery. His contemplative expression held for a moment, then changed into a deepening frown.

He shook his head as if to clear his mind.

"Gracias, you have done your job well. Now get out. I have a work to do."

"But El Señor—"

"I said get out!"

Montoya's mouth fell into a bewildered line. He had anticipated a generous reward, and would have liked to protest. But the mad glint in the enormous man's eyes reminded him of a rabid coyote he had come across on the range once; he had no desire to further tempt the fates. Without another word he realized his usefulness would best be served far away from there. There was no telling what Dominguez would do in his present state of mind, and Montoya wanted no further part of it.

Dominguez angrily summoned a servant and ordered his favorite black stallion, Fuego del Diablo—Fire Devil—saddled. He then hastily scribbled the last entry in his ledger and tucked a pistol snugly into his *bolero*.

Fire Devil snorted and pawed the ground impatiently. Dominguez hefted his bulk into the saddle and rode with lightning speed toward Winston's rancho. As he traveled, his thoughts raced as rapidly as the hooves of his horse.

He reached the rancho in time to spy Don Diego dismissing the soldiers who had escorted his wife to her *padre's* rancho. He viciously reined in his horse and waited behind some nearby sumac bushes until the soldiers had departed. He knew that something had gone terribly wrong when the soldiers left. Quietly he sneaked around behind the hacienda.

Josephina was busy in the kitchen, and did not hear the thumping sounds of carefully placed footsteps as they passed by the door and continued through the hacienda.

When he reached Don Diego's room he discovered the door had been left ajar, simplifying his task. Three voices drifted from the room.

"There is so much to make amends for," Don Diego said. "And to begin with, I shall instruct Josephina to ready your old room. You will not be returning to your husband."

"I believe that is a very wise decision," seconded the governor.

Antonia smiled mutely. This was what Michael had wanted; she was not to go back to Dominguez. She could remain with her *padre* and be safe and protected. But Michael might need help, she worried.

"You know, if it had not been for Capitán Domino,

we may have never known the truth about Dominguez. We owe the *capitán* a great deal. I am glad you decided to share his plan about the branding irons with us, Daughter. I only pray he can be cleared of Rosa's murder," Don Diego said on a hopeful note. He liked the captain and was certain his daughter, too, felt deeply for the man.

"I am certain the truth will become known," the governor replied.

"*Sí,* I shall use all the resources available to me in order to aid the *capitán*. After all," chuckled Don Diego, "I do not want my future son-in-law to be a fugitive."

"*Padre!*" Antonia blushed with embarrassment. "He has not even spoken the words of love, let alone mentioned marriage vows." She lowered her eyes, not wanting them to glimpse the sadness etched on her lips. Nor did she tell them that her marriage to Dominguez had been staged.

She loved Michael Domino, of that there was no doubt. She had told him as much. She had given herself to him without the sanctity of the Church, so why would he feel the need to legalize what he had already tasted? Yet hope lingered. He had shown he cared in so many ways. He had risked his life to save hers, set aside his own plans, been accused of murder, and nearly lost his ship.

"My dear, you are young, such words do not come easy to many men. There are those who speak their feelings through actions. Capitán Domino has spoken most clearly of his. And as for that 'husband' of yours, I am certain there will be no problem freeing you from him once the truth is known. I will travel to Rome if necessary to get you released from the vows you took before the eyes of God." Don Diego patted her shoulder reassuringly. "It is a pity your *tía* could not have been here. I believe in her own way, she only wanted what she thought best for you. I pray she finds in Spain what it was she felt lacking here," he reflected sadly.

"*Sí*, I, too, pray she finds happiness," Antonia said wistfully, and decided to always keep secret Doña Maria's collusion with Dominguez. She did not want her *padre* to learn how his generosity had been repaid; sometimes secrets were better kept than shared. She smiled, and her thoughts turned to her feigned marriage. She wondered what her *padre* would do when he found out.

"I will call Josephina. I want you settled in your room before evening. And we shall need to provide a room for you, too, José. You both must wish to rest." Don Diego rose and stepped toward the door.

"Wait. You and Governor Figueroa have much to discuss. I will speak to Josephina. After all, this is my home, and as lady of this rancho, it is my duty to see to the needs of my guests," Antonia announced.

"One cannot argue with the lady of the rancho," Don Diego said.

The governor chuckled. "Certainly not."

Antonia raised up on her tiptoes and lightly kissed her *padre* on the cheek before leaving the room. She closed the door behind her and headed for the kitchen.

She was excited about returning home, and so lost to her own thoughts that she failed to notice the hulking, shadowy figure pressed against the doorframe. Like a flash, a hand curled around her waist cutting off her oxygen and tearing her off her feet. Another hand clamped over her lips like a vise. Utter panic pervaded every inch of her being, and her heart beat like a drum between her ears. She stood motionless, suspended in a frightening purgatory. She could feel hot, sticky breath on the back of her neck, and her captor tightened his grasp around her.

"If you do not wish to join Rosa, you will remain completely silent. Do you understand?" Dominguez whispered with such deadly venom that Antonia could barely control the shudders waving through her body.

Fighting for all the control she could gather, she managed to nod her acceptance. As if a sudden decision had been made, she felt a thick handkerchief snake around her head and gag her mouth. Both his hands free, he swung her around to face him. Terror filled her wide eyes when she saw his crazed glare.

"My flower . . ." His lips twisted like a merciless messenger of death. "I have come to escort you back to where you belong." Without further delay, he pressed the cold, hard steel of his pistol into her ribs and forced her to move through the hacienda like thieves in the night.

Once outside the main house, he removed the gag. Antonia thought of crying out as she rubbed her lips, but the pistol reminded her his punishment would be swift and deadly. She could see vaqueros in the distance busily engaged in their trade. One even waved to her, and she was forced to return his greeting.

When they reached his stallion, Antonia was forced to sit astride in front of him. While he seated himself in back of her, a branch caught his coat pocket. He swore menacingly, painfully digging his fingers deeper into Antonia's soft flesh. Furious, he gored his heels into the animal, sending it wheeling toward his rancho with only the sound of its hooves to break the sickening silence between them.

"You will not get away with this," Antonia said when they reached the rancho.

"No? No one will even know you are here."

"The servants will see me."

"We are not going in the front door. And no one will find you where I plan to take you." He dragged her around the outside cellar door to ensure they would not be seen.

Dominguez roughly threw Antonia into his room of pleasures. She tried to fight but felt like a puppet forcefully locked in his painful grasp until he slammed her against the wall. He snapped an iron chain around her wrist as she slid, dazed, to the floor. Antonia opened her mouth to scream but realized no one would even hear her. In his demented state it would probably drive him totally over the edge to insanity.

He stood over her like a massive volcano ready to erupt at any moment. "Such a pity I shall not have the opportunity to fully savor your delicious body," he spewed forth hotly. "You would have learned the real pleasures of life."

His deranged laugh caused Antonia to shrink tightly against the wall.

"What is wrong, my flower? You have not spoken for some time. Are you not glad to be home again?"

"You . . you will not get away with this," she stammered, unable to control her proud tongue.

"I fear my plans have changed. But I shall take from your *padre* the one thing he treasures most. That, my flower, is you. It is a shame I cannot have you accompany me, but I am certain you will understand. I shall attempt not to make your departure from this life overly painful." He smiled cruelly. "Now, I must leave you to ponder your fate while I pack for a most untimely journey. You will wait for my return, will you not?"

The heinousness of his laughter stabbed at Antonia's ears as he swung the door shut behind him, leaving her sequestered in the throes of a living, hellish nightmare.

Chapter Forty-four

Michael wheeled in his animal behind a thick sumac bush and slid from the saddle. As he knotted the finely braided leather reins, he plucked an errant handkerchief stuck to a nearby branch and wiped the sweat from his heated brow. He waited until no one was in sight before sneaking inside the hacienda to Don Diego's room. He rapped on the door lightly then entered.

"Capitán Domino, do come in," startled Don Diego, remembering him from the fiesta. "We were just speaking of you."

"You are well," Michael said, astounded.

"*Sí, capitán.* But, *por favor,* I do not believe you have been formally introduced to my guest. *Por favor,* join us, and allow me to introduce Governor Figueroa."

"We did meet briefly, Diego," corrected the governor, who nodded in Michael's direction.

The two men rose from their chairs. Michael, who had been closely studying the governor, offered his hand as he moved to take their hands in turn and take a seat next to them.

"I have heard much of your exploits, *capitán*," the governor said warmly.

"And I've heard and seen for myself that you're a fair and just man who can be trusted," Michael returned.

The governor was impressed with the captain's courage and candidness in the face of such adversity and favorably assessed Michael Domino's character further as he talked of the last few months.

"Capitán Domino . . ." Don Diego cleared his throat as he often did when he was about to seek information of a delicate nature, "you have risked much by remaining in California to assist my daughter. Although it is of a personal nature — your relationship with my daughter — I must ask exactly what are your plans in respect to the girl?"

"Señor Winston, I could sit here and pour my heart out to you, but there are other reasons for my presence in California. Reasons I cannot at this time totally divulge to you."

Michael's steel-blue eyes were met by Don Diego's delving eyes of a similar hue. Two men from the sea — they were so different yet so alike, just like the sea's color changes at its depths.

Governor Figueroa leaned back in his chair and rubbed his chin, watching in amusement at Don Diego's less than forceful efforts to clarify the young man's intentions toward his daughter.

"I assure you I shall not ask of any of your motives other than those which involve my daughter. Am I correct in assuming that my daughter is at least in part the reason for your presence here now?"

"As I have just told you, your daughter is very much a constant companion to my thoughts. In fact señor, a short time ago I would not have admitted as much — even to myself."

Don Diego turned toward the governor, a hazy triumph flitting about him. "José, do Capitán Domino's intentions satisfy you?"

The governor shook his head in amusement. "I am assured the *capitán's* intentions are strictly honorable. But it is·not for us to judge. I learned long ago that affairs of the heart are best left for the two directly involved and do not need the assistance of well-intentioned friends and family."

"Well said, José." Don Diego smiled, admitting defeat. "I shall leave Antonia to you, *capitán*. As a matter of fact, she is here now. If you two will entertain each other for a few moments I shall call her." He rose and started for the door, then thoughtfully pivoted. "Capitán Domino, *por favor,* be patient with Antonia. She has suffered much due to an old man's stupidity."

"Don't concern yourself, I'll not cause Tonia to suffer any anguish, although I have to say she is quite a resourceful and capable young woman in her own right."

Don Diego knew when he heard his daughter called "Tonia" he had no need for concern. He grinned. "I think what you are politely trying to say is that she is stubborn and sometimes too proud for her own good."

Michael chuckled and the governor cleared his throat at Don Diego's observation.

"Well . . ." Don Diego opened the door, "I will go fetch my daughter now."

A knock at Antonia's door received no response, so Don Diego slowly nudged open the door and glanced inside so as not to disturb her if she were resting. When he saw the room was untouched, his brow shot up.

He moved through the hacienda peeking into rooms

378

and keeping his ears peeled for the sound of her velvety voice until he neared the kitchen. Josephina was warbling brightly while she worked, which brought to mind all the times as a young child Antonia had to be literally hauled from the old woman's side to begin her lessons. A smile crept up his face as the memory lit a corner of his mind.

Josephina was busy in the kitchen and did not hear Don Diego enter. His chiding voice abruptly ceased as she startled and looked up from the chopping block, a shiny butcher knife pressed nimbly in her hand.

"Now, now Josephina . . ." his hands popped up and fingers splayed wide in a motion to stop. "There is no need for that. I have only come to fetch my wayward daughter. There is someone I want her to see. Now tell me, where have you hidden her?" He chuckled at his own attempt at humor.

When Josephina suddenly realized she had been pointing the threatening blade, she dropped it on the table and wiped her stained hands on her bibbed apron.

"You surprise me, señor. When Señora Antonia little *muchacha,* you come much to get her. But she no here. I no see her but with you."

Don Diego thanked the woman and walked outside to look for his daughter. When he did not locate her, he was puzzled. It was such a beautiful autumn day, and Antonia so enjoyed strolling about the grounds that he assumed she must be out somewhere enjoying her rediscovered freedom.

He returned to his room and took his chair near the small table. "Antonia was not in her room; she must be out enjoying the warmth of the afternoon sun. I left word with Josephina to send her to us when she returns," he informed Michael and the governor.

Don Diego lifted the acorn necklace from the table and smiled tenderly.

"I want you to return this to my daughter, *capitán.*" Don Diego held out his hand, the acorns draped limply through his fingers. "It is very dear to her, and will mean much if, when you return it, you remind her how the oak survives many adversities and becomes stronger because of them."

Michael accepted the necklace. He smiled to himself, thinking of how their relationship had been anything but traditional and had grown from the seeds of hardship. Theirs had not been a customary courtship—only a series of tumultuous encounters. Yet out of the ashes of such a fiery relationship a bond had been forged. He gazed down at the simple necklace, and vowed that their love would grow strong as the oak tree. He then yanked a handkerchief from his pocket and began to wrap the piece carefully within its folds.

The governor had watched quietly as Michael removed the handkerchief from his pocket, but when the captain began to encase the stained kernels in the bit of linen, the governor leaned forward in his chair, his brows quizzically knitting together.

"Pardon me, *capitán,* but that handkerchief, may I examine it?"

"Of course." Michael dropped it into the governor's hand.

The governor frowned. "Where did you get this?"

"I found it in the bushes outside the hacienda."

"José, why do you inquire after such an article?" Don Diego questioned, taking a puzzled interest.

"Because this is the very same handkerchief I myself so recently presented to El Señor as part of a gift for his hospitality. I saw it in his possession just this morning at breakfast." He handed it back to Michael.

"Are you certain?" Michael said darkly.

"*Sí*, it is the very same one."

The three men looked mutely at each other.

Antonia had been nowhere to be found. Without a word the dark shadow of foreboding drew over them like a black raincloud about to open and send forth its destructive force.

Michael sprang to his feet, firebrands burning in his eyes.

Don Diego spun around. "*Capitán,* where are you going?"

"I think you both know the answer to that question," Michael tossed back over his shoulder, the outline of his mouth determined and set hard as cold steel.

"Wait! We shall go with you."

"No! Someone is needed here to search for Tonia in case we are mistaken. If not, Commandant Velasco must be summoned and sent to Dominguez's rancho."

"Capitán Domino. *Vaya con Dios.*"

The door slammed behind Michael before the words were barely out of Don Diego's mouth.

Michael raced to his waiting horse and jumped into the saddle. He drove the mighty animal to its very limits.

He reached the Dominguez rancho in record time, cautiously slithered inside, and began checking the rooms. As he was coming out of an empty guest room a servant sighted him and demanded he leave, since neither El Señor nor Señora Dominguez were at home.

While the servant was bravely challenging Michael, Dominguez, who had started out of his room, heard the exchange—and slunk back behind the door. He knew the captain would not leave until he tore the place apart, and it was just a matter of time before he made his way to the cellar.

Dominguez's lips snarled into a vicious grin. "Now I will be able to take care of them both at the same time." If he disposed of his wife and the captain, then returned to the Rancho de los Robles to kill Winston and the governor, he would not have to leave. He could point the blame at the captain. He would then be free to inherit Winston's rancho, doubling his empire and wealth, which would put him in an excellent position to carry out his plans to control the government of California.

Michael shoved the servant out of his way, sending the man scurrying back to the kitchens. As he was about to resume his search, something drew him toward the cellar. To his surprise the door to the secret room had been left open a crack. He quickly dropped to his knees and crawled along the dusty floor until he reached the door. He put his ear to the door and listened. Not a sound left the room. He slid his fingers around the bottom of the door and pushed it open just far enough to peer in.

Thinking it was Dominguez returning to torment her, Antonia screamed. At the sound of her distress Michael flew open the door and rushed to her side.

"Michael, oh, Michael, in my heart I knew you would come! I knew it. But you must not let Dominguez take you. You must leave." She sobbed as he enfolded her within his arms to comfort her.

"Don't worry, Tonia, we'll both be long gone before Dominguez returns. Haven't I accomplished that feat before?" he reassured her.

Michael yanked at the chains, but they held fast. Without the key, he was forced to hammer at them with a branding iron he had taken off the shelf in hope of dismembering one of the links. As he hurriedly worked, a vision of Rosa in similar circumstances flashed into his mind. He dared not leave Antonia for more appropriate tools, for he feared she would be left to suffer a similar fate.

In an attempt to calm her trembling body, he ceased his efforts and tenderly pressed his lips to hers, whispering into her mouth, "Don't worry, everything'll be all right."

"How touching," Dominguez spat, towering over them like a treacherous precipice. In his hand he held a pistol aimed with deadly precision.

"You! You—"

"Keep your tongue, Wife, or I shall be forced to silence it before I am ready," he raged insanely.

"I am not your wife," Antonia hissed.

Michael touched his finger to her lips. "Hush, Tonia. Do as he says."

"But—"

Michael shot Antonia a deadly look. "Shh, I said."

Antonia ignored Michael. "No. I am not your wife, Dominguez!"

Michael grimaced and rolled his eyes. "Women," he grumbled.

"Oh?" Dominguez questioned. "Tell me more."

"Michael suspected you might try to force me to marry you, so he substituted one of his crew for the friar," Antonia spat and proudly jutted out her chin.

Dominguez gave a short laugh. "Why, *capitán*, I must give you credit, you are quite resourceful. But it really does not matter now," he said as his eyes settled on Michael's gun lying on the floor at his side. "Now, slide your weapon to me carefully, *capitán*. My trigger finger itches, and I would hate to scratch it just because you try something foolish."

Michael leaned over slowly, closing his fingers around the barrel of the pistol and eased it toward the enormous man. If he had been alone he would have lunged at Dominguez, and squeezed the life out of him with his bare hands. But he could not take the chance of anything happening to Antonia because he had not waited.

Antonia watched Michael surrender the pistol and knew it was on her account. If only he had gone when she had begged him to, but he had stayed with her. He had sacrificed his safety; had put his life on the line for hers. She wondered if they were destined to be ill-fated lovers, star-crossed as lovers she had read about such as Romeo and Juliet or Antony and Cleopatra. While the means were not the same, the ending still bespoke of the finality of their deaths, irrevocably intertwined, indelibly woven in tragedy. She bit her lip to keep from crying out to him; she clasped her hands to keep from reaching out.

"Had it not been for your interference, Capitán Domino, I would not be forced to do what I now must. It is such a pity you happened to sail your ship to these shores. And even more unfortunate that we happened to meet."

"Are you so sure that I merely *happened* to meet you by chance?" Michael's face burned dangerously close to the boiling point, and he glared at Dominguez with such hatred that Antonia could feel his entire body tense.

"Do you attempt to tell me something, *capitán?*"

"Oh, yes, Dominguez." Michael's hand slowly moved from Antonia's shoulder down her back and thigh, hesitated, and slid over to his side until his fingers closed around the leather riding quirt hanging from his waistband.

"Be careful, *capitán,*" Dominguez warned as he watched Michael's hand move.

"You needn't fear, it's simply something of yours I found here and want to return to you. I've been waiting years for this moment to repay the debt this"—he held out the small whip—"incurred at your hands."

Dominguez furrowed his brows at the whip in the captain's hand. He had wondered what had happened to his favorite piece. He had been unable to locate it when he'd first brought his wife to this room, but then had dismissed it from his mind.

"What meaning could it have for you?" He gave a short laugh. "Am I supposed to remember you?"

"Perhaps not, but I have never forgotten you." Michael's fingers closed so tightly around the quirt that the veins stood out white on the back of his hand.

"You have stirred my interest," Dominguez said with indifference. Then he dragged a chair in front of the couple and seated himself, carefully keeping his pistol trained directly on Antonia who quietly huddled next to Michael. "Before we continue . . ." he waved the gun toward a nearby ankle chain, "if you would be so kind as to put the bracelet on. And do remember, at this distance I cannot possibly miss such a lovely target, so do be quick about it, *capitán.*"

Michael glanced at the iron anklet for a moment, then gazed into Antonia's terror-filled eyes before he slowly began to do as ordered.

"You swine!" Antonia screamed in an outburst of overwhelming emotion.

Dominguez curled his lip toward her. "You are fortunate, my flower. If I did not wish to first hear the *capitán's* tale, I would have sent you to join your lovely departed *madre* just now."

Michael pulled her even closer to him. "Shh, Tonia. I don't want anything to happen to you."

"*Por favor.* Such a display of emotion," Dominguez

385

said with a casual roll of his eyes. "Now, get on with it. I do not have all night — and neither do you."

"Think back about a dozen years to a young sailor who mistakenly attempted to ride across your property. That young man was severely beaten, then left for dead by a wealthy *ranchero* who took pleasure in inflicting pain on others.

"If you don't recall that incident, perhaps you'll remember that at about the same time a young Indian was caught and his hand held over an open fire, his only crime being that he accompanied another who had an appetite for the taste of horseflesh." Michael's breathing was slow, but he took deep, deliberate breaths like an animal poising itself to strike. His face burned crimson with hatred, and only the blazing thoughts of revenge entered his mind as he watched Dominguez.

Dominguez snorted in amusement. *"Por favor, capitán,* do not tell me that you have spent years waiting for an opportunity to avenge a mere beating and burned hand? How utterly absurd!" He ceased his laughter when he saw the cold-blooded hatred in the eyes of the man who stared back at him. He studied the captain and then glanced at Antonia, who remained motionless, frozen with fear.

"Strange is it not, what one can be driven to by a beautiful woman." Dominguez noticed the captain's hands clench, along with his hatred climb toward new heights. "Could it be that I have touched upon the real reason for your desire for revenge? No woman is worth your life. But then again, it is a lesson I, too, have had to suffer." He sighed a quick reminiscent thought of Rafaela and the need for revenge, which had driven him for over twenty-five years. "Such a pity."

"While I would like nothing better than to kill you if

just for Antonia's sake, I've waited many long years for this moment I promised myself as a boy," Michael returned.

"A boy?"

"Yes. If you'll but look closer at the object in my hand and remember where you obtained it, I believe it will be self-explanatory."

Dominguez glared. "What meaning could this simple whip have for you?"

"Don't you recall where you purchased this?" Michael held out the short-handled quirt, laced with heavy silver threads, the "D" brand for the Dominguez rancho adorning the rawhide lashes.

Dominguez's lips twisted into a vicious grin as he scanned the riding quirt more closely, searching his memory. For a few moments he said nothing, but did not take his eyes from the whip. Dominguez's glance darted with intensity from the quirt to Michael and back again.

A light began to glow in the distant dark past of his memory. "Now I understand. I recollect thinking of the coincidence that our names should be so strangely similar when we first were introduced."

Antonia barely mouthed the words, "As did I," remembering her first encounter with the captain. She clamped her lips together, a strange feeling creeping into her bones.

"Of course, I have not used the name Miguel for years, preferring *El*, which added a note of distinction. Miguel always seemed to lack something, and it was so easy to train the filthy peasants to use a more suitable title — one that would always be remembered." Dominguez hesitated to study Michael again.

"Since you understand, how do you propose I address you during the time remaining for one of us?

387

Would "Father" or the Spanish '*padre*' be more appropriate?" Michael spat with disgust.

"Oh, no!" Antonia gasped in horror, throwing her hand over her mouth as her wide eyes stared in shock. She could not believe her ears. She wanted to question Michael about such an astounding revelation, but the deadly seriousness of their exchange caused her to think better of it. Thoughts of Michael and Dominguez clouded her mind, and she fought with herself to absorb the horror of it all.

"I see the resemblance now, but if you will forgive me," Dominguez snickered, "I do not recall the *puta* who named you so closely after your *padre*."

Michael had all he could do to contain himself. He wanted nothing more than to slit the enormous man's throat. With great presence of mind, he silently reminded himself to wait; there would come a moment . . .

"It's not important that you recall my mother, only what you did to her." Michael increased the pressure of his grasp even tighter around the smooth leather handle until his fist shook with the force of his hatred.

As Michael slowly raised himself to his feet, Antonia's eyes filled with heightening terror. All color suddenly had left Michael's countenance, and he was strangely calm. But within the very depths of his cold blue eyes, which never once left the evil man, the fires of hell raged with a need for vengeance out of control.

"After you remember your deed, I'm going to repay a long overdue debt; I am going to kill you." Michael's lips were chiseled into a taut line of inflexible marble as he spoke without display of emotion.

Watching Michael, Antonia feared he was giving up control to the madness of hatred. Although she hated Dominguez almost as much as Michael did, he was Michael's *padre*, and she could not banish the thought — no matter how horrifying. He was Michael's *padre*.

"Humph! You forget you are chained, *capitán*. But I am forced to respect a man who stands tall to meet his fate. There have been so many who pleaded, groveled before me, so you, *capitán,* are a refreshing change." He put his finger to his lips in contemplation.

"Let me think, where shall I begin? Ah *sí,* my companion and I were on our tour of Europe. And it was in London, was it not?" He smiled at the recollection. "We had been enjoying a few too many Scotches. On our way back to our apartments, my companion spotted this pretty young thing walking the streets alone, and so late at night too. Tch, tch, tch, a pity.

"Well, my man, what else could we do? I remember what a pleasure she was to my companion. She fought like a wildcat. Oh, very much like you, my dear." He turned to Antonia briefly then returned his attention to Michael. "It is amusing, you showing your face after all these years. You see, I had thought that riding whip in your hand had settled the issue of your birth."

"Obviously you were mistaken." Michael was seething, barely under control beneath his cold exterior.

"Dios mío!" cried Antonia in utter disgust. "El Señor, he is your son. What kind of a creature are you?"

"Do you not already know, my flower?" he answered in crazed jest. He then grew serious again.

"That old man Dominguez said he or his issue would someday come back to haunt me. Ha! How convenient at least that his prophecy should occur in such a way as to cause me little more than a small annoyance — a thorn in my side." He glanced at Antonia and back at Michael.

"You look puzzled, *capitán*. Allow me to clarify what I have just said. It is such a pity that for all these years you have been driven by your hatred of a dead man. You see, I am not your *padre*—or father, whichever you prefer. Your *padre* has been long dead, near thirty-four years I believe. You see, I merely found it convenient to assume the real Miguel Dominguez's identity after I killed him." He gave a heinous roar of laughter. "I actually did you favor.

"You see, I was your *padre's* companion at the time; Carlos Chavez was the name, a mere orphan, servant to a spoiled young Spaniard sent on an adventure through Europe by his *padre*, hoping he would become a man. It was he who abducted your *madre* as a prank, a jest. And it was he who in a fit of drunken rage beat her when she told him she was with child.

"Sadly, he did have a liking for the bottle; adeptly developed by my own hand. The poor fool would never have overindulged and beat her if he had not been drunk. Anyway, that is of little interest. After he left her and arrived at my apartment he was remorseful. Said he had fallen in love. He planned to return and marry the pitiful wench and bring her home to California.

"I tried to reason with him, tell him she was nothing but a *puta*. She was nothing like Rafaela—Rafaela left me for your *padre*, my flower. Oh, yes, I loved her, too, more than anything," he rambled, explaining his obsession with the dead woman, and how he'd had to stand on the sidelines while she chose a lowly sailor. His eyes glazed over and insanity seemed to reach his very soul, and in his mind he became the jilted fiancé again, as he told of his reasons for hating Antonia's *padre*. After a moment he snapped his head back and forth, returning him to reality.

"Let me see, where was I? Oh, yes, your *madre*, *capitán*. I called your *madre* a *puta* but your *padre* mumbled something of her being of gentle birth. He refused to listen to reason. Said he was going back for her. So I struck him to keep him from returning to her. He was such a weak *bastardo* that he fell after only one blow and hit his head.

"I was strong and deserved to be the son of such a powerful family, so I assumed his identity. I remained in Europe several years, five to be more exact, hoping that our similar appearance, a beard, and time would keep his *padre* from learning the truth. I had them all fooled for a while. But old Dominguez somehow learned the truth; he knew, the stupid, old fool. I was strong and would have been the son he always desired, but he refused to understand it was an accident. He was going to have me jailed—hung, he said. Those were his last words. I squeezed the breath from his body with my bare hands. And with his death I inherited all this, an empire—all mine! There was not even any other relatives to get in my way; it was so easy.

"Now you must understand why I cannot allow anyone else to get in my way. Not him, not Rosa or all the others, not you, not even the governor. I have earned my destiny. I have earned my heritage to be a Dominguez," he said, a streak of madness engulfing him again. He then stepped forward in preparation to finish the messy business. "Now I shall—"

Michael interrupted the crazed man before he could finish his sentence. "Now, you shall die."

Michael swung his arm up, a pistol in his hand, and squeezed the trigger.

The tremendous blast of the pistol shot echoed through the room as a cloud of smoke rose from the singing weapon. Within seconds, Dominguez began to crumble, his face white as he slumped to the floor. Calmly, without a word Michael dropped the pistol, removed the chain from his ankle, and walked to the body. He ripped the key to Antonia's chains from around the neck of the still form and released her.

Once Antonia was no longer held by her chains, she tried to step into Michael's arms, but she sank to the floor numbed with fear and shock. Michael kneeled down and gently folded her into his embrace.

"It's over now, Tonia." He spoke softly. "It's over now."

Tears of relief flowed freely down her cheeks as she clamped herself to him, never wanting to let go.

"I do not understand," she said after she had calmed. "How did you . . . where did you get the pistol? I thought he took your gun. And your chains, I saw you put them on." She was bewildered and could not grasp all that had just happened.

"It actually is not complicated. Don't you recall when and where I obtained the pistol?" Michael picked up the gun from the floor and showed it to her. "Don't you recognize it?"

Antonia stared down at the weapon, then ran her fingers along her thigh. Still puzzled, she returned her gaze to Michael.

"*Sí*, it is the one I—"

"The one you had strapped to your thigh." He finished her words. "You do not remember when I took my hand from your shoulder right after Dominguez entered the room? At the same time I removed the pistol and tucked it into the back of my belt. You proved to be helpful when you screamed at him after he ordered that I lock the chain around my ankle. His attention was diverted just long enough that he failed to notice the links were not secured." Michael tenderly pressed a kiss to her temple.

"Oh, Michael, it is so terrifying and happened so

ast that I do not remember any of it—not even the cream."

Michael smiled at her innocence. He had thought he knew when he looked into her eyes before he lipped the bracelet around his ankle.

He then removed the acorn necklace from the handkerchief neatly folded in his pocket. Fastening it round her neck, his eyes smiled. "Your *padre* said you vould understand its meaning."

Antonia did understand as she ran her trembling finers over the acorns . . . she did understand. "*Sí*, hrough adversity comes strength."

"We have both learned something and are stronger or it," Michael whispered.

"*Sí*," she murmured back. "But my *madre* and that nan?"

"Don't let it concern you. Your mother probably ever even knew of his obsession. He had been Dominuez's companion. The dead man probably had conided in him. In his madness—after he killed the real Dominguez—the man not only assumed Dominguez's dentity, but in his mind became Dominguez, complete vith his passions and hatreds. He was crazy, Antonia."

"*Sí*, you are right. But all those years—"

"Don't think of him anymore. It is over now. Come, Tonia, I'll return you to your *padre*'s rancho."

Antonia looked quizzically up at Michael, her face uddenly filled with sadness. She lowered her eyes to he floor and prepared to follow him from the cellar.

"Don't be afraid. I still have unfinished business. I continue to be a man wanted for murder," he said in answer to her silent questioning.

Michael's words provided little consolation, for he had not said the three words she so desperately needed o hear. In an attempt to be strong, she fingered the

393

necklace as she began to move toward the door. Sh
stopped and turned slowly near the body of her tor
mentor. Glancing down, she solemnly repeated th
words he had spoken to her once:

"You see, there comes a time in everyone's life whe
debts must be paid. You have paid yours."

Without another word, Michael opened the door fo
her, and they left the motionless Carlos Chavez, alia
El Señor Dominguez, alone in his room of pleasures.

Chapter Forty-five

Commandant Velasco and his men left the presidio shortly after they received Señor Winston's urgent message. The sun had set and a few scattered stars sparkled through patches of clouds in the deep purple sky when the soldiers finally reached the rancho.

Don Diego hurriedly informed the commandant of his suspicions directing him to Dominguez's rancho. Velasco reassured the distraught don that he and his soldiers would waste no time in reaching their destination. Before he left, Velasco had hinted that there might be new information concerning Rosa's death and the cattle stolen over the past years, but would say no more than to mention that the Indian, Mano, was on his way to deliver some witnesses.

Michael and Antonia did not arrive at the Rancho de los Robles until early the next morning. After they had left the cellar, Antonia collapsed. Thoughts of the harrowing ordeal had overwhelmed her suddenly. It was late into the night, so Michael had scooped her into his arms and carried her to a guest room within the hacienda.

Once she had been nestled beneath the coverlet, Michael settled into a nearby chair. He was drained and near exhaustion. But with the weariness in his bones was a strange inner feeling of peace. The demon that had driven him had been exorcised. His eyelids grew heavy, and he, too, dozed, his long legs sprawled out in front of him.

Not more than fifteen minutes after he had fallen asleep he was awakened to screams of anguish. He leaped from the chair to find Antonia writhing on the bed, lost within a terrifying nightmare. He rushed to her side and gathered her into his arms, gently kissing and stroking her sweat-drenched brow. "Tonia, it is all right, you are safe with me."

After awakening and realizing it was a dream, she glanced around the room and flung her arms about his neck.

"Oh, Michael, I want to leave this place—now. The hacienda is only filled with unhappiness. I cannot bear to spend another moment under this roof."

"You need to rest. Now, lie back. I'll not leave your side."

"If we cannot leave here now, then make love to me," she whispered against his cheek.

Her sultry, passionate words awoke a raging fever in him, and his mouth crashed down on hers. Grinding and devouring her lips and the satiny inner recesses of her mouth, he strained to release the hidden tension which had suddenly exploded to the surface.

It was a torrent, a driving lust to reaffirm that they had escaped death's bid that grasped the pair and drove them with such urgency. This time there was no gentleness or tenderness, just the animal need to release all the pent-up emotion. Each one understanding the other's frenzy, the compelling rush to relieve the bur-

396

eoning tension, they stormed forward at a mad, ravhing pace.

Michael demanded and manipulated, too ravenous ） control his growing rampage.

Antonia responded with her own wild ardor, greedy feasting and beguiling him with her mouth and finers.

In a torrid whirlwind of motion arms and legs wisted and flung until they had gorged themselves on ach other. Only then did Michael mount her. Shamess, unbridled movements seized them in untamed gyations until they erupted and were carried together to hat burning, fiery end.

Their need satiated, they stilled. Antonia could feel he moisture of his life-giving seed overflow within her. and she took an exhausted pleasure in knowing there ad been no pretense between them, only a display of onest feeling. She felt a pleasant drowsiness overtaking her and a sense of peacefulness invade her body, ausing her to drift off toward sleep.

Michael held her slender fingers in his until her reathing slowed to the shallow, even rhythm of slumer. After his own heart slowed, he wiped the sweat rom his brow and settled down beside her. His body ressed reassuringly warm against the length of hers, ue soon followed her into the world of dreams.

When they arrived at the Rancho de los Robles, they vere greeted by a much-relieved *padre*. They were soon oined by the governor, Josephina, Lupe, and a whole rray of vaqueros who had been searching for them.

Don Diego rushed forward and threw his arms round his daughter. "Are you all right?"

"Señora, señora . . ." Josephina stepped up, wringng her hands. "You pale. Señor Winston, bring her inside and him, too. I fill them with much food." Josephina turned and marched toward her kitchen.

"Come along," chuckled Don Diego, "or we shall really have trouble. Josephina is not one to have her orders about food ignored." Don Diego swung his arms around them, and with one on each side walked blithely into the dining room.

After Michael and Antonia finished the hearty meal provided them by Josephina and Lupe, Don Diego insisted they be allowed to rest before describing their harrowing experience. Antonia sighed her thanks for the opportunity to relax and bathe before having to relive those terrifying moments. Michael, too, expressed the desire to freshen up in a hot tub.

By the time Michael was shown to his room, hot water, fresh cakes of lavender-scented soap, and recently laundered linens had been delivered.

Without bothering to knock, Josephina flung Michael's door open and barged into the room.

"What the hell?" he roared as, with awkward amusement, he slunk down to his neck in the steaming soapy water.

"I bring clean clothes. Man close your size, he give." Josephina grinned, standing near the tub ignoring Michael's discomfort at her presence.

"Thanks. Now if you don't mind, I would like to finish my bath." He inched down into the water to his chin.

She pooh-poohed his efforts at modesty. "Ha! You no hide. I see much *muchachos'* bottoms. I raise much babies."

"You win, Josephina." Michael chuckled, and started to rise.

"Dios mío!" She threw her hands up and barreled from the room, his laughter surrounding her.

Antonia received similar treatment. Josephina had

ummaged through some of Antonia's old gowns to
nd a fresh garment, and when she spotted the pale-
reen silk, she removed it from the trunk. It had been
ne of Antonia's favorites, and the old woman grinned
er approval as it was pressed and delivered to Anto-
ia. Antonia was pleased with Josephina's selection
nd promptly slipped it over her head.

"It is a perfect fit, Josephina. *Gracias.* I was afraid I
ould not be able to squeeze into it," she said, twirling
1 front of the mirror.

"You get skinny, but I feed," clucked the old servant.

Antonia giggled, and hugged the aging woman.

"You sit. I put ribbons in you hair."

Antonia watched in the mirror as Josephina brushed
er long thick tresses and threaded the emerald ribbons
1rough her golden curls adeptly.

When Antonia reached the door to the study, Mi-
hael was already there engaged in conversation with
er *padre* and the governor.

When Michael glanced up and saw her in the door-
vay, he jumped to his feet and offered her his arm. "To-
ia?"

With her lips drawn into her brightest smile, she
·laced her hand on his arm without taking her eyes
rom his. "It is an honor, *capitán.*"

"You are very beautiful," he murmured in her ear as
e escorted her to the settee.

Antonia's pulse threatened to leap into her throat,
nd she blushed as her eyes darted to the others who sat
vatching them.

Once seated on the sofa, Michael did not take his
1and from hers while they told of their experiences,
ight down to the smallest detail, including the mock
vedding. Michael poured out the story of his mother,
1is childhood, and the search for his father as he
ought revenge.

He went on to explain fully every detail about his partnership with Dominguez and described how he had sought revenge, even telling about his efforts with the branding irons. When he felt her body begin to tense or her voice grow shaky as they answered every question, he quietly squeezed her hand to reassure her.

Although he had not yet had the opportunity to say all the words he felt in his heart, he thought of her as his woman. He wanted to protect her, to cherish her, to hold her and never let her go. A heavy lump settled in his throat, and his heart swelled when he imagined her always by his side.

Antonia was also brimming with emotions. She loved Michael, of that there was no doubt. But did he love her? Or had he wanted her because she had belonged to the one man he sought to destroy.

Shortly before they had finished their tale, Commandant Velasco arrived and was shown into the study. He quietly seated himself and listened to the final details.

"Ah hmm . . ." Velasco cleared his throat and hunkered up stiffly on the edge of his chair. "Excuse me, gentlemen, señorita, I have just come from the Dominguez rancho and I fear they have not told the entire truth."

All eyes widened and stared at the commandant. Pleasant expressions faded to frowns, and a sense of well-being fell into deepening glares, as if a wet blanket had been thrown over them.

"Comandante Velasco, perhaps you had better explain your meaning immediately." Don Diego's eyes narrowed to angry slits at the question of his daughter's integrity.

Velasco turned to Michael. "I am afraid, *capitán*, that you left behind a rather, shall we say, messy situation."

Antonia was furious. She did not completely trust the commandant. And since one of his soldiers had captured her that night in the foothills, she had been even more leery of him. She jumped to her feet, her eyes flashing steely darts.

"Why you are no . . . Oh!" she yelped as Michael grabbed her arm, startling her, and pulling her down by his side.

"Tonia, I want to hear what Juan has to say," Michael stated flatly.

"All right, Comandante Velasco," Don Diego said in a serious tone, "we are listening. Say what you have to say."

"*Gracias,* I shall be completely honest with you in spite of the consequence."

Antonia glanced worriedly at Michael. What could Velasco say that they had not already spoken of? Michael gave her knee a reassuring clap and squeezed her closer to him.

Michael, too, was wondering what the commandant had to add. Had the man actually been working for Dominguez? Was he going to fabricate some lie for his own gain? Michael stared intensely at the man as he rose to his feet.

Velasco leaned over the nearby table, took a large gulp from the glass of spirits he had been served when he arrived, and began to unravel his tale. For the commandant, his words came vividly alive and in his mind he began to experience it all over again.

Chapter Forty-six

Velasco looked around the room. All eyes were intently staring at him. He took another gulp of the fortifying liquid, and began to tell his tale . . .

"My soldiers and I reached the Dominguez rancho just before dawn. We awoke the servants and questioned them at length. They had not seen Dominguez, and the only thing they could add was the argument with the *capitán*. Knowing the fear instilled into the hapless household staff, I ordered my men to search the hacienda thoroughly."

"We must have left already," Antonia said.

Velasco paused, studying the angry faces, expecting the worst before continuing. "I had known of the room of pleasures, so while the men began combing the many rooms, I sent one man to guard the cellar door outside the hacienda. Not knowing what to expect, I drew my pistol and carefully descended the steep stairs. An oil lamp was lit and swung gently from a hook at the bottom of the stairway, casting an eerie yellow light about the dusty room. I walked around the shelves. My heart was pounding as I surveyed the dank, musty storage area. To my left a shelf stood out at an angle and lent a strange shadow. I slowly crept toward it and leaned around the corner, my finger on the trigger. My breath caught in my throat when that room came into focus. It was the secret room of pleasures.

"My heart was throbbing, and my pulse pounding wildly when I stepped into that room. I had never seen such an evil array of chains and whips. The sight caused an anger buried deep within me to overflow until I burned with unspeakable rage. On the floor, not more than ten feet to my left, crumpled into an enormous heap was the gruesome form of a man. In three strides I was across the room and held the lantern high over the lifeless figure. With my boot I shoved the body over until the twisted face became visible. It was the horribly knotted features of El Señor Dominguez. When I leaned over for a closer inspection I saw blood slowly oozing from a wound in his chest."

"Are you not being a little melodramatic, *comandante?*" Antonia asked. "Why not just come to the point."

"Let the man tell his story," Michael said, noting the tension in the soldier's lips.

"Josephina," Don Diego said, "get Comandante Velasco another drink."

"Gracias, señores," Velasco said, and accepted the bolstering liquid. He took another drink. His eyes seemed faraway as he continued.

"My heart sank. Being within those walls after so many years caused all the anguish and hatred I had once felt to resurface all over again.

"I set the lantern and pistol down on a nearby table

and sank to a chair close by. I then couched my head in my hands and wept openly.

"Memories of my one, true love—my young wife—filled me and tore at my broken heart."

"We did not know you were once married, *comandante*," Don Diego put in.

"Oh, *sí*. I had been a young, ambitious soldier at the time I met Yolanda, a young *indio* maiden. It was not long before she had stolen my heart. But I knew if I married her, my career would be ruined. Marriage to an *indio* is not viewed favorably for one interested in rising through the ranks. Unable to relinquish my career aspirations or Yolanda, we were wed secretly up the coast. She desperately wanted to live as man and wife, but I convinced her to wait, often visiting her at her peoples' camp in the foothills.

"On one occasion I was forced to remain at the presidio for several weeks. Unable to get a message to her, Yolanda grew worried, and against her family's advice, left to travel alone to the presidio in search of news of me, her cowardly husband." He gave a derisive laugh.

"She never reached her destination. Her bruised and battered body was discovered in a ravine not far from the borders of Dominguez's rancho a week later. There was no doubt a whip had been used. There were rope burns on her wrists and ankles, and she had been savagely violated. There was not proof to link her murder to El Señor Dominguez except the common knowledge among the *indios* and some Spaniards that Dominguez often forced unsuspecting young women to submit to his perverted desires in a specially equipped room.

"Dominguez was a rich and powerful man, which kept me from seeking him out and killing him at the time, as I should have. Instead, I waited all these years to catch Dominguez. Although I knew in my heart the *bastardo* was guilty, I had hoped that when Dominguez married you," he nodded toward Antonia, "the daughter of an equally powerful *ranchero,* he would make a fatal error in his desire to force his perverted desires upon you. When Don Diego summoned me, I was elated. Dominguez had done just as I had hoped, but I did not arrive in time.

"After I composed himself, I began to search the room. Visions of my helpless wife within those walls filled my consciousness as I scanned all the items of torture. Finding it impossible to remain much longer, I was about to leave that evil place when I stepped on several keys attached to a gold chain. I leaned over and picked them up and began unlocking the cabinets and drawers I had been unable to inspect earlier. I found the assorted branding irons used to alter the brands on stolen cattle. I discovered various whips, chains, leather pieces, and other sundry items used to satisfy the *bastardo'*s sick needs. Repulsed, I was about to leave without completing my search. But for some reason I could not fathom, I unlocked the final two drawers.

"Within the last drawer was a thick red leather-bound book. I opened it and began to leaf through the pages. Reading the nauseating scribblings made me ill. But I forced myself to continue, until what I read made me lose all that had been in my stomach.

"While wiping my mouth, I heard a faint groan. I grabbed the lantern and rushed over to Dominguez's body. To my total surprise, Dominguez feebly opened his eyes and made an attempt to speak. But there was not enough breath within him to utter more than the captain's name. His weak black eyes pleaded with me for help as I stood over him."

Velasco's eyes glazed over, and in his mind he was transported back to those final moments . . .

"I thought Capitán Domino had denied me the privilege of killing you, Dominguez," Velasco said emotionlessly. "You may not remember a pretty young *indio* woman from long ago who was with child when you beat her, causing her to lose the child and bleed to death. But that woman was my wife. And the child was the unborn flesh of my body, who until this very day, when I read your diary, I had not known existed." A single tear welled in Velasco's eye at the thought of the loss of his child.

Dominguez vainly tried to reach his splayed fingers out to the commandant.

"This room is a fitting end for one who ended the lives of countless others here. You will cause no more suffering."

Velasco picked up his pistol and fired point-blank.

The echoing blast brought the soldiers running. When they arrived and spied the body, they looked at Velasco with troubled, questioning expressions.

"You need not concern yourselves. I merely repaid in full the payment he owed for but two of his debts." Velasco calmly handed his pistol to one of the soldiers, tucked the book into his jacket, and quietly left the room.

Velasco shook his head to bring himself back to the present. "I came here directly from the Dominguez rancho. I wanted to be certain that you knew who was actually responsible for the man's death. If there are any questions from Mexico, Governor Figueroa, they are for me to answer, not Capitán Domino."

Antonia rose and rushed to the commandant, reassuringly placing her hand on the man's shoulder.

"I am so sorry," she said in a low, comforting voice.

The mood within the room drifted to one of sorrow for the commandant.

"Por favor, do not pity me. It has been many years, and at last I have been granted the fortune to avenge my wife and unborn child. And I am happy to be able to present to you," he walked over to the governor, removed the book from his jacket and handed it to the seated dignitary, "Governor Figueroa, this book. It is a diary detailing the horrors that occurred in that room. I have removed one page, but the rest of the book is intact. You will find, written in the man's own hand, proof of the *capitán's* innocence. Now, if you will excuse me, I am much in need of rest, so I shall be returning to the presidio. If there are any further questions, you know where I will be." Velasco turned laboriously, and with memory's pained steps, began to leave.

"A moment Comandante Velasco. You need not concern yourself about any questions regarding the man known as El Señor Dominguez."

"I beg your pardon?"

"This book will serve as the last nail, closing the coffin on many years of injustices which now may be buried . . ." Governor Figueroa began, informing Velasco of the truth about the man known as El Señor Dominguez. "And you need not worry, there will be no additional questions asked of you."

"Comandante Velasco, I insist you remain and accept the hospitality of my hacienda, and later we can all celebrate the end of a nightmare," Don Diego urged.

"*Gracias,* it is a long way back to the presidio, and I am feeling quite exhausted." Velasco sank weary bones back into his chair.

Antonia immediately left to request that Josephina ready another guest room. While she was gone, Michael and Velasco explained the remainder of the unpleasant details left untold in Antonia's presence. Just as they concluded their tale, Josephina entered the study and led a totally fatigued commandant to his room.

A short while later, Father Manuel and his Indian escort, accompanied by Juanita and two crewmen, were shown into the study. Mano introduced his Indian bride, then handed the governor the two confessions he had gotten from Dominguez's other partners and proceeded to add his piece of the puzzle to the story. All listened intently as he brought them up to date on further events.

"You mean Sanchez, that man we heard with Dominguez in his library that day, had actually known El Señor was really a man named Carlos Chavez all these years and never divulged the information?" Antonia asked, astounded, as she rejoined them.

"I asked Mano to do some checking on the man that night in your office, Commandant," Michael said. "It seems Sanchez had much to hide as well, so they formed a rather tenuous partnership. But the most ironic part of it was Sanchez was planning to dissolve their dubious relationship after one last transaction. It seems he'd had enough. But fate stepped in and he ran into Thadius, expecting to find Captain Brian Thomas on the *Sea Shark* and make one last deal for another bunch of stolen steers to help Dominguez raise the extra cash he needed when he traveled to Monterey with you, Governor," Michael explained from what he had gleaned from the confession and Mano's story.

"You had already captured Thomas's ship, is that correct, *capitán?*" Don Diego asked, attempting to keep it all clear in his mind.

"Here food. You all eat," Josephina entered with trays of tender morsels neatly arranged like clusters of garden flowers. Behind Josephina, Lupe carried glasses and several pitchers of beverages stacked neatly on another tray. Josephina was pleased to see so many visitors milling about in clusters again at the rancho, just as it had been before Antonia had become betrothed.

After filling their plates, the governor and Don Diego moved to speak quietly with Father Manuel. They had been surprised to see him, and wondered why he would arrive at this time escorted by Mano and two crewmen.

When Michael noticed that the men's expressions began to grow serious, he excused himself and joined Father Manuel and the others. Antonia, too, wondered about the friar's presence and worried if it had something to do with her wedding to Dominguez. She tried to focus her attention on what Juanita was saying, but under her long lashes, she watched Michael cross the room and continued to wonder.

Late in the afternoon Don Diego requested everyone present remain at the rancho for the night. It had been an exhausting day in which the miseries, misfortunes, and burdens of many had been finally brought to the forefront and forever laid to rest.

Josephina, who had anticipated Don Diego's invitation, had already prepared the needed guest rooms and had moved Lupe to quarters nearer her own. When Antonia entered the kitchen to ask Josephina to make arrangements, the old woman looked up from her chores, laughed, and informed her of her belated request.

Antonia returned to the study.

"All the rooms await your pleasure. If you will allow me, I shall show you to your rooms so you may refresh yourselves before the evening's meal." Antonia motioned for the guests to follow her and turned to leave.

"Antonia, child, wait," Don Diego said. "There is something of importance I must discuss with you."

Governor Figueroa cleared his throat. "If you will permit me, I think I know the hacienda well enough to escort everyone to their rooms."

"Gracias, José," Don Diego said.

Michael and Father Manuel remained, seated on the settee. Don Diego moved to stand near his desk, as all eyes fastened on Antonia, who stood silently uneasy, questioning them with apprehensive amber-green eyes.

"Come here, Daughter. There is something of importance which cannot be delayed any longer."

As Antonia hesitantly crossed the room, she recalled the earlier conversation her *padre* had had with the friar. From their expressions at the time, she knew whatever they had been discussing was of a serious nature. And now they wished to speak to her without the others present.

She took a seat, but remained on the edge of the chair. With her hands nervously pillowed in her lap, she glanced into the eyes of the men watching her.

"Well, *padre,* what is it you have to say that involves Friar Manuel?" she asked nervously.

"As you may have noticed, we spoke with Friar Manuel earlier. Our conversation, my child, was regarding the recent events in your past as well as plans for your future. You have been through much pain during the last few months, and it is my desire to seek only your peace and happiness. I believe that we, with the assistance of Friar Manuel, have found a desirable solution to end your heartache."

The seriousness of her *padre*'s words caused Antonia to envision a convent. Father Manuel must have been summoned without even consulting her.

"Did you summon Friar Manuel here?"

"No. He came here out of concern."

Her mind began to spin. Her *padre* had spoken of her finding peace and happiness. She had previously heard of young women being sent by their families to convents in faraway countries.

Michael had not spoken of love, so she concluded that he would be relieved to be part of their solution — maybe even to provide her transportation. Could they be condemning her for acting the part of Dominguez's wife? Her mind raced frantically with churning thoughts until finally, in a panic, she bolted from her chair and shrieked.

"No! I shall not be sent away to a convent!" She lifted her skirts and raced from the room like a frightened rabbit.

Michael jumped to his feet to go after her, but Father Manuel grabbed his arm. "My son, she has been through much. Allow her time to settle her thoughts."

Michael released his arm. "I know your intentions are well-meaning. But Antonia is a resourceful young woman and will not return if she fears such a fate."

Michael ran to the front of the hacienda just in

time to catch a glimpse of her golden curls billowing out like frothy waves upon an angry sea behind her as she disappeared in a cloud of dust.

Antonia had raced as fast as her feet could carry her from the hacienda to the horses tethered nearby. She selected the first animal she came to and, without a thought to her attire, mounted the animal astride, urging the steed on to ride like lightning away from the rancho.

Michael quickly leaped on a horse and rode after her. He was rapidly erasing the gap between them until all of a sudden her horse spooked, snorted, and sped ahead.

The animal seemed to sense Antonia's panic and moved like the flight of eagles along the rolling hills. In her state of mind, she began to lose control.

Antonia's horse became lathered, slowing its pace just enough to allow Michael the opportunity to come within a short distance of her. When she glanced over her shoulder and saw him, she reined in the tiring animal. Jumping from the steed, she scrambled toward the heavy underbrush hoping to successfully lose him, but Michael was a breath behind her.

Just as she was about to disappear into the tangled brambles, Michael caught her leg. They fell to the ground and, in an effort to calm her, he pinioned her to the earth beneath his weight.

"No! I am not going to let them send me away." She continued to struggle to free herself until she was totally exhausted.

"Tonia . . ." Michael tried to explain, "no one plans to send you to a convent."

In her panicked state she did not hear him. Finally, in an effort to subdue her, he grasped her face toward him and forcefully kissed her until he felt the tension nwillingly leave her body.

Michael gazed deeply into her eyes. The eyes which
tared back were angry, searching, questioning, seek-
ng. Yet she remained silent.

"Oh, Tonia, I promise you, no one is going to send
ou away. I swear to you. Now please, return with me
nd allow your father to finish what he was trying to
ay."

Michael's soothing voice calmed the distraught
oung woman and she reluctantly nodded her agree-
ent but stubbornly maintained her silence all the
vay back to the hacienda.

Chapter Forty-seven

Seated again in the same room with her *padre*, Michael, and the friar, Antonia waited with trepidation to hear what they had in store for her.

"Antonia . . ." Father Manuel rose from his chair. He uneasily cleared his throat several times in search for the right words.

When Michael noticed that Antonia was starting to twitch nervously, he interrupted the friar.

"Excuse me, Father, Don Diego, but I believe the quest for appropriate words may be causing undue tensions. So if you will allow me, I shall simply explain."

The two men were happy to turn over the responsibility to the captain, and seated themselves on either side of Antonia.

"You know the day of your wedding Father Manuel was not in attendance because I had replaced him with a member of my crew."

"*Si.*" She quizzically arched her brow, for she had known that for some time. Antonia thought about it for a moment, then responded. "Since the man who

414

as not actually my husband is dead, why do you tell e now there is a serious matter which must be dis-ssed?" Her voice was filled with annoyance.

Stepping in to finish what he thought his duty, Fa-er Manuel turned to Antonia. "It was my . . . ah . . . ur, concern that caused us to speak with you. Since ou were never legally married but indeed did live with e man," the friar uneasily cleared his throat again ver the delicate nature of the conversation, "the possi-ility does exist, my dear, that you may be with child. I . . we, thought something should be done to protect ou and your name."

Don Diego, in an attempt to put an end to his daugh-er's agitation, continued. "Antonia, Friar Manuel and are merely concerned for your reputation."

"My reputation? My reputation!" she shrieked, ooking directly at Michael. What was his role in this istasteful discussion? she wondered.

"*Por favor*, allow me to finish what I had begun to ay." Don Diego waited until he was certain there vould be no further outbursts. "Now, as I was saying, ve were only concerned for you and the child you may ave conceived. But Capitán Domino has laid those concerns to rest by graciously consenting to marry ou."

Antonia's face turned a raging crimson. She had oped Michael would someday want to wed her, but he ad never returned the words of love that she had so lesperately longed to hear.

Ignoring her churning inner emotions, she calmly aid, "Let me see, since I may be with child, Capitán Domino has agreed to make an honest woman of me and give my child a name—that is, if I am indeed ex-pecting a child. Is that correct?"

"Well, *sí*. I suppose that basically is correct," Don Diego answered.

Attempting to stem the flow of her temper, Antonia took a deep breath and slowly rose from the settee. She calmly walked to the window and hesitated before she turned toward the expectantly waiting men.

"*Padre*, Friar Manuel, Capitán Domino." She stiffly nodded to each one in turn. "I am deeply touched that you should choose to be so concerned about my reputation and the possibility of a child conceived outside the sanctity of the vows of the Church." She spoke with such deliberately measured calmness that her words had them squirming in their seats.

"Capitán Domino, I am particularly overwhelmed by your self-sacrifice. But since it is going to be my decision and mine alone, I have chosen against your most generous offer. If I am with child, I shall simply have to accept the consequences that being in such a circumstance may bring. Now, if you will excuse me, I am most weary and desire to rest."

Michael could not believe his ears after she had confessed her love for him. He had risked prison and even his life for her; he could have just as easily left California safely many times. And now she so casually rejected him. His face heated to a color matching hers and his blue eyes turned to cold blue steel.

Don Diego, who had been closely scrutinizing Michael as well as his daughter, took Father Manuel's arm. "Come, Friar, I am suddenly very thirsty. Josephina will have coffee ready, and I know how much you like her coffee." He turned to Michael and Antonia. "Excuse us, won't you?" Sagely, Don Diego and the friar did not waste time retreating from the room.

The *ranchero* and friar had just barely shut the door behind them when Josephina appeared carrying a tray.

"Why you stand there? Open the door. I have work to do."

"I believe it would be wise if you did not go in there.

416

right now, Josephina. My daughter and the *capitán* are quite busy discussing their marriage plans, and I think it better if they were not disturbed," Don Diego advised.

Angry voices stabbed through the door.

She chuckled. "You wise man, señor."

"*Sí*, well, I do hope so."

Father Manuel made the sign of the cross as the sounds of anger grew louder. He then took a cup of Josephina's coffee.

Lingering near the door, Josephina mumbled, "Sounds like going to be wedding. I prepare. This time good," she clucked and leaned nearer the door.

"How dare you!" Antonia screamed, and sent a glass hurling toward Michael.

"I thought my offer was most generous!"

"Generous? After what you did to me!"

"What I did to you?"

"*Sí!* What you did to me! Why didn't you just tell them that if I were going to have a child, it certainly would not be that swine's issue! I lived in that house to help you. You know he never touched me."

"Do I?"

"How dare you!" she choked. "I would have killed him first," she raged on.

"Yes, just like you did in his cellar."

"Oh, do not be so conscious of details. And why did Friar Manuel get involved?"

"He was merely concerned for you, Princess, after your father explained about your marriage to Dominguez."

"Do not call me princess," she hissed.

Don Diego requested that Josephina show Father Manuel to his room since he would be staying the night, but Don Diego remained outside the door. He had convinced himself that he did not wish the others to overhear the angry exchange occurring in his study. Secretly, he wanted to be certain that neither his daughter nor the captain left the room until they had set a wedding date. He knew they loved each other, and he was prepared to arrange a wedding with rifles, if need be, before they tried to leave the room if they did not come to the same conclusion he had.

Within the study the argument continued to rage.

"Men do not want to have known their wives before marriage," Antonia snapped.

"For the last time, it does not matter. If there's a child, it will be mine."

"But Doña Maria said—"

"Hang what Doña Maria said. If you want me I'm all yours," Michael said calmly, a smile flickering in his eyes.

"Oh, no, I would not ask for so much of your anatomy!"

"Let me guess, you want my head on a silver platter."

"Your head, *sí*. But I would not be so rude as to demand the platter."

When Don Diego heard the captain's acknowledgment that he would be the father if a child were conceived, Don Diego truly understood what he had suspected all along—his daughter and the captain had been together. Don Diego remained silent, waiting outside of the door.

"Why do you sacrifice yourself then?" she demanded, her fierce pride continuing to erupt with frustration.

Michael dodged a flying vase and positioned himself in front of her, his legs spread wide. He reached out, grabbed her shoulders, and stared into her stormy amber-green eyes. As he gazed at her, his anger began to melt. He knew she was the woman for him, and he would always want only her—meddlesome temper and

418

all.

He no longer desired to continue to fight. He felt the overpowering urge to hold her to him and say the words which he had been unable to say until now — until freed from the demons which had so unrelentlessly driven him. Now he no longer feared those words. And he would never again hesitate to tell her what she meant to him.

Antonia, too, suddenly no longer wanted to fight. She did not want to lose this man. She had waited all her life for him, and knew she would never want another. As her eyes stared back into his, she searched for unspoken words.

Tenseness and anger drained from their bodies as if a plug had been pulled. Time stood still, and their eyes spoke for them; their hearts beat together in unison with a quickening pulse. For a moment they stood lost in each other until Michael broke the silence.

"Tonia . . . my Tonia, I love you. Will you marry me?" he murmured.

Michael's simple declaration brought tears of joy to her eyes. As he took her into his arms their bodies melded together, and he gently lowered his lips to hers.

Don Diego could no longer tolerate the sudden silence. He quietly opened the door and stepped inside. Josephina, who had walked by the door on her return to the kitchen immediately after Don Diego had slipped into the room, returned to the door and glanced past him.

"Well, it about time," she cackled. "It about time."

"I am most pleased you two have finally reached an equable agreement," beamed the proud *ranchero,* startling the embracing couple. Not giving them a chance to reply, Don Diego walked over to them, hugged his daughter and pumped the captain's hand.

"Congratulations. Now, before you two have the opportunity to start another argument, let's all retire to our rooms for a much needed rest before I make the happy announcement this evening."

After a few moments' conversation, Don Diego watched them separate and enter their respective rooms. He had assured them there would be plenty of time to speak alone — after they were wed.

It was Don Diego's home, and he soon would be Michael's father-in-law, owing the man respect, but Michael was not in need of rest. As soon as he closed his door, he left his room through the window to appear in Antonia's room moments later.

She giggled like a child when she saw him. Lying on the bed, she motioned for him to join her. "What took you so long?"

"So you knew I'd come, did you?"

"Why do you think the window was open? If you did not come soon I was prepared to go to you."

Michael laughed at her daring. "It's a good thing you agreed to marry me. After you, my princess, I could never settle for your everyday girl. Life would be too boring." He paused and winked at her. "Might be less complicated, though."

"Just get those thoughts out of your mind. You have already made your selection."

"Yes, and soon you'll belong to me," he said in a serious murmur, changing the tone of their encounter.

"I love you *mi capitán,* and I give my love freely to you to share your life." She rose on her elbow and kissed his lips as she unfastened the buttons from his shirt and slipped it off his shoulders.

"Your chest is so hard, so muscular," she cooed, and nipped at the wiry hairs covering his flat belly.

Michael encircled her within his embrace and began to nibble at her neck.

"No." She sighed and tickled his sides.

He coiled at her teasing touch. "What? You seek to deny me?"

"Never. This afternoon *I* want to make love to *you*. Lie back."

Michael cast Antonia a glance filled with smoldering embers as he leaned into the soft feather bed, and watched her remove his breeches.

"Relax," she murmured, and pushed him against the fluffy pillows, resting his head on his hands.

She poured lotion from her dressing table into the palm of her hands and warmed it, rubbing her hands together before massaging and kneading his ankles, calves, and thighs. Michael groaned his approval and turned onto his stomach. Using the lightly lilac-scented lotion, Antonia straddled him, her fingers working magic, soothing all the tenseness from the muscles in his shoulders and back.

"You're a passionate woman, my wanton princess," he said with pleasure and flipped over to reach out and tweak her breasts through the flimsy low-cut gown. He then pulled her down to him and savagely kissed her as he separated her from her garments.

When Antonia lay atop him, she could feel his rising desire pressing hard against her thighs. She moved down to lean over him and, taking him between her fingers, she caressed and kissed him until he groaned. With each stroke she knew she brought him dangerously closer to the brink of release.

She took delight in giving him pleasure. He was her man—the man who had awakened her and taught her to revel in the joys of the heart and body. She gave freely, knowing she always would, as she positioned herself over him and guided him into her.

Time stopped, suspended in the endless river of their love until their passion burst forth in sweet release. Afterward they lay, threaded arms and legs entwined until they fell into a restful slumber.

As evening fell everyone assembled at the dining table. Don Diego held his glass high and proposed a toast to his beautiful daughter and future son-in-law before the men retired to the study, since the fall weather had turned too cool to spend evenings on the veranda. Don Diego offered the men his finest cigar while they discussed many of the events of the last months.

Antonia took Juanita and Lupe to sort through her old gowns. Don Diego had sent several of his men to fetch Antonia's and the governor's personal items so by morning, Antonia would no longer have to rely on the old trunk.

The men Don Diego had sent to locate Pedro Montoya returned and were escorted to the study. The leader stepped forward. "I am sorry. We were unable to locate Montoya or any of the vaqueros working at the Dominguez rancho," the spokesman said.

"No doubt they sagely chose to leave the area to escape the consequences of their deeds," Michael said.

"*Sí*, Montoya is now reaping his just reward for his loyalty, Don Diego. Your influence reaches far, and Montoya will have difficulty finding a hole wide and deep enough to accommodate him. Do not worry, he will be caught eventually," Velasco assured Don Diego.

Don Diego thanked his men and directed them to remove a keg from the storehouse so all could celebrate the good news of his daughter's happy betrothal to Captain Domino.

Heading toward the study, Antonia overheard her *padre's* men discussing Montoya while they filed out of the hacienda. The last man stopped to offer the group's

422

ongratulations, and then hurried to catch up with the others.

Michael spied Antonia and rushed to her side.

"Your *padre* is interested in knowing how long he has to prepare for our wedding," Michael said, slipping an arm around Antonia's tiny waist as he ushered her and Juanita into the study to join the men.

"And what was your answer?" she purred.

"I told him I would only wait until tomorrow to wed you," he whispered in her ear.

Antonia giggled, covering her lips and glancing around as she blushed, wondering if anyone had overheard him.

Don Diego joined the radiant couple. "I have spoken with Josephina and Friar Manuel." He glanced at the friar before continuing. "I fear we shall not be able to complete all the preparations and publish the banns for a wedding by tomorrow. But if you will be patient, we shall work as rapidly as is humanly possible," he offered.

"Señor Winston, thank you for your generous offer. But as I said, I'll only wait until tomorrow, banns or no banns."

Antonia had learned to read Michael's expressions well and knew he was serious.

She grinned mischievously. *"Padre*, you do remember speaking of the possibility of a child born out of wedlock, do you not?"

Don Diego understood, and raised his palms, "I concede, you two win. One way or another there will be a wedding tomorrow."

He moved to his desk and rapped his knuckles on the hard wood. When he obtained everyone's attention he raised his glass.

"I want all of you to be my guests tomorrow evening to witness the nuptials of my daughter, Antonia

423

Rafaela Winston y Ortega and Capitán Micha Domino."

For the remainder of the evening there was muc merriment — and dizzying preparations.

Chapter Forty-eight

Antonia looked at her reflection in the mirror as she completed her toilette prior to the wedding ceremony. Her long golden tresses hung in shining ringlets. She felt beautifully radiant. Soon she would slip into her gown, and Josephina would place her *madre's* traditional Spanish comb and lace mantilla on her head.

Attired in an undertunic and wrapper, she began to shift from foot to foot as she waited for Josephina to deliver the gown she would wear on this special day. Despite her insistence that the gown was of no importance, Josephina had steadfastly insisted that she would have a special gown to wear for her wedding.

"Lupe, I think I should select one of my gowns from the wardrobe. It is getting late, and I shall never be ready on time if we wait much longer," Antonia fretted.

"No. We wait. Josephina come. You see."

Just when Antonia could bear to wait no longer Josephina scurried into the room with a gown draped over her arm.

"Señorita Antonia, come put over you head."

Antonia donned the gown, and moved back to the mirror. Tears of joy brimmed in her eyes, and she whirled around to hug the old woman.

Antonia forced back a sob. "This was my grand mother's bridal gown."

Josephina bent down and fussed with the hem. "*Sí, señorita*. Work all night. But it ready."

Antonia looked down at the corded red silk gown designed to accentuate the high neckline edged with lace flouncing. The sleeves were three-quarter length, ending in lace. The skirt was full and fell into a graceful train with large billowing quantities of flowering lace. Antonia glanced at herself in the mirror again. Her tiny-heeled kid slippers fastened by silk ribbons crossed over her insteps peeked from beneath the hemline.

"You sit, I put on mantilla now."

Antonia did as bid, wishing her *madre* were alive to see her happiness.

"You much beautiful. Like you *madre*. She wear too, when she and you *padre* take vows in church."

"Josephina, *gracias*," Antonia barely held back her tears and embraced the old woman again.

"Not now. You wrinkle gown. Later," she scolded.

Michael knew he looked every bit like a member of the *gente de razón* in the raiment hastily acquired for him. He shifted in his short blue silk

426

acket, waistcoat and pantaloons laced with gilt be-
ow his knees. The white stockings presented a
triking contrast against his dark-brown deerskin
hoes.

Mano stood with his arms folded across his
hest. "You look as if you are a successful *ran-
hero,* my brother."

"I think it is one of Don Diego's subtle hints,"
Michael said as they left the room and made their
vay toward the spacious *sala* used to entertain large
umbers of guests.

When Michael and the Indian entered the room
hey were greeted by Governor Figueroa and Don
Diego, who had spent a harried day directing prepa-
ations for the joyous event.

Guests, who had been hastily summoned that
norning using a dozen of the swiftest riders, began
rriving. Don Diego smiled at his work. Antonia
vanted to be married here instead of in the church
lespite his objections. The room was filling with
eople from neighboring ranchos. Wooden tables
nd benches lined the walls, leaving plenty of space
or dancing later. Large bowls of fruits had been
ositioned among platters of tortillas, cheeses, and
liced meats.

As the four men moved to stand at one end of
he room, the governor glanced at Michael and re-
narked, "Capitán Domino, it appears that we may
ave made a real Spanish gentleman of you."

"In appearances only, Governor."

"But you are of Spanish ancestry. It is the land of
our people."

"A seaman calls many ports his home, and his
eople are his crew," Michael answered.

Governor Figueroa cleared his throat. "True, I

suppose."

Accepting defeat gracefully, he patted Don Diego on the shoulder. *"Mi amigo,* we have accomplished much together in one day." He glanced around the room, proud of the part he had played in the preparations for the wedding.

Father Manuel joined them. *"Capitán,* I have returned after gathering my vestments at the mission with someone who is most anxious to see you before you are wed," he said.

Father Manuel stepped aside. Directly behind him, with his hands on his hips and his bushy red brows drawn together in a formidable frown, stood Thadius.

"Cap'n, me lad, when I hears from the friar here that ye be takin' the Spanish lass t' wife, I had t' come and see fer meself," Thadius snickered and shuffled his foot along the floor like an embarrassed cabin boy. "An' besides, ye been like a son t' me."

"And you have been my family, you old sea dog. I'm glad you are here." Michael put his hand on Thadius's shoulder. "I would be proud if you would join Mano and be part of the wedding party. Then I'll have two best men at my wedding."

He chuckled. "Aye. An' I be thinkin' ye'd never ask me."

"Well then, what are you waiting for? Take your place," Michael advised.

"Never seen anythin' like it—a man bein' so anxious t' put the weddin' noose round his own neck.'

"That's because no one you've ever known has had the good fortune to marry anyone like Antonia."

Don Diego beamed. "What did I tell you, Friar'

knew I'd find the right man for my little girl."

"*Sí,* Don Diego," Father Manuel agreed indulgently, refraining from mention of El Señor Dominguez.

Josephina appeared in the archway, causing a hush to fall over the room. She nodded to Don Diego, signifying that Antonia was waiting just outside the door.

Upon seeing the old woman, Don Diego hurriedly ushered everyone to their places. He then joined his daughter.

Tears brimmed in Don Diego's eyes when he saw his daughter. "Next to your *madre,* Daughter, you are the most beautiful woman I have ever seen. That is the gown your *madre* had always dreamed you would wear on your wedding day. She would have been so pleased to see you this radiant." Sniffling back tears of joy and pain, he took her hands in his. "Antonia, I was so foolish. Can you ever forgive me? I —"

"*Padre,* there is no need. The past, with all its hurt and suffering, is over and what really matters is now and the future."

"*Gracias,* Daughter. You have made me the proudest man alive. At least let me give you this." Tears flowed down the aging *ranchero*'s cheeks, and he fastened the hand-painted cameo of his Rafaela round Antonia's neck. "She would want you to wear this today," he said, his voice breaking. "It brought your *madre* and me together."

"*Gracias, mi padre,*" she whispered through tears of joy. Her heart bursting with love, Antonia fingered the treasured piece hanging next to the acorn necklace.

"I love you, Daughter," he choked out.

She answered him with all the love in her sparkling amber-green eyes as they made their entrance, her hand wound lovingly within his.

"I love you, too."

Chapter Forty-nine

It was a misty gray morning when Michael joined Don Diego and Antonia for breakfast. Giant billowing clouds, the shape of mighty anvils, threatened to release their wrath down upon San Diego as a signal winter would soon be upon them. It was a long voyage to Boston to unload the hides filling the ship's hold, and the crew was anxious to sail from there homeward to England. Michael, too, was growing anxious to feel the roll of the sea beneath the decks of his ship.

"It was wise of the governor to grant you the old Dominguez rancho," Don Diego remarked, lifting his cup.

"Michael is the blooded grandson," Antonia put in.

"There are advantages to being a wealthy and powerful member of the *gente de razón*," Don Diego added.

"I am sure there are," Michael said, thinking of hiring a *mayordomo* — a manager — to run the rancho under Don Diego's watchful eye until he made a final decision of what to do with the land.

"*Sí.*" Disappointment creased Don Diego's face.

"More coffee?" Antonia offered.

"Yes. Thank you." Michael took a sip and gazed listlessly out the window toward the stormy sea.

Antonia could not help but notice her husband's restiveness grow as she watched him daily pace their room. Each day he climbed a nearby rise overlooking the vast ocean. Once at the crest, he positioned himself atop a rock and stared longingly out toward his moored ship.

After they had finished the morning's meal, Michael rose.

"I shall be gone for the day."

"Wait a few moments; I shall go with you," Antonia offered.

"No. I am going to visit Mano and Thadius. The weather is threatening and you should stay inside."

"I have not seen Juanita for sometime; besides, do not want to be left alone without my husband for the entire day." She smiled coyly, expectant of getting her way.

"What can I say?" He threw up his hands in defeat. "You really are a sorceress who has me under her spell. Go get ready," he relented.

"But the weather—" interjected Don Diego, protesting.

"*Padre,* I have been exposed to worse."

"But—"

"She'll be fine, sir. I'll take good care of her."

"*Sí,* while I look after you." Antonia grinned a wicked smile, and spun around to hurry from the room.

Michael waited until Antonia was out of earshot

and then said, "I know you have hoped we would settle on the Dominguez rancho and someday . . . well, who knows. But Antonia married a sea captain. It is my way of life as it will become hers." Michael hesitated to give Don Diego time to fully absorb the significance of what he had said. "It is time for Antonia and me to leave. I have a hold full of hides which I must get to market."

"While I cannot put into words how disappointed I am to lose my daughter from the rancho, I must admit I understand your love of the sea and the need to return to it. But, Son, do not let the sea come between you." Don Diego smiled sadly. "You will bring my daughter back from time to time with the children so they will know their grandfather, won't you?"

"Children?"

"But of course. I expect a houseful to visit so I can properly spoil them," Don Diego said.

Michael chuckled. "We'll do our best."

Don Diego grew reflective again. "At least Antonia will see England, and I hope come to know her English relatives." His thoughts drifted to his childhood and a country he had not seen in nearly thirty years. Accompanying them and personally escorting his daughter around his homeland was a thought, but only fleeting, and Don Diego blinked his lids to sweep it from his mind. California was his home, and this was where he belonged.

"I'll take good care of her, sir. You'll not have cause to worry."

"*Gracias,* Son. I know you will. Now, how about another cup of coffee before Antonia returns?"

Antonia appeared in the doorway. She had bundled herself in layers of warm apparel in anticipation of the cold journey. Michael glanced at her and smiled. He had planned to ride the magnificent stallion given to him as a gift from the governor—until he saw his wife. He could not force her to endure the same hardships he had accustomed himself to years ago.

"I'll order a carriage."

"I require no special treatment," she argued.

"Listen to your husband, child," advised Don Diego.

Michael ignored her, and hurried off to summon a coach.

"Do not tell Michael, but I am glad he did not indulge me this time," Antonia said when she and her *padre* were alone.

Don Diego rolled his eyes, hugged Antonia to him, and laughed. "Indulge you? Somehow I have the feeling Capitán Domino has yet to find out exactly to what extent you will go to get your desires gratified."

"After all that has happened I think he has a pretty good idea."

"*Sí*, I fear he does. And to think I told *him* to take care of *you*. I wonder who is going to protect him from you?"

Before they reached the coast, raindrops began furiously pelting the coach as the wind howled through the trees. As they were rowed to the ship, the angry sea tossed the longboat about like a mere twig, causing Antonia to clutch Michael's arm in order to keep from being thrown from her seat.

Antonia was soaked to the bone by the time they reached the ship. Thadius greeted them and hurried Antonia to Michael's cabin while Michael went to check the ship's stores.

"If'n ye be me missus, I be takin' better care of ye," he said, helping her off with her dripping cape.

"Thadius," Antonia's expression grew serious, "you have been with the captain for many years. And next to Mano, you must know him better than anyone."

"Aye, I knows him long"

Her eyes silently beseeched him. "Then please help me."

"What bein' it that causes ye t' seek ol' Thadius's help, lass?"

"I had hoped . . . ah . . . *thought* Michael would be happy here. But he has become so restless."

"Me girl, he has been a man of the sea fer many years, he has. The sea is part of 'im. It's in his bones. But be sured, the cap'n, he chose ye."

Before Thadius could continue, Michael entered the cabin carrying a pale-green cotton gown. He took one glance at his wife still wearing her soaking-wet garments and chided Thadius for allowing her to remain in such a state. Thadius attempted an explanation but soon conceded and shrugged his defeat.

"I be goin' now. Ye's don't be needin' me here." Before he left he winked at Antonia. The old sea dog had grown fond of the spunky golden-haired woman who had captured his captain's heart. He had started to tell her of the captain's love for the sea, but soon after Michael's untimely arrival, Thadius knew his advice was not required.

The moment they were alone Michael moved to stand directly in front of her. "Here, let me help you out of that gown before you catch your death."

Antonia let out a throaty giggle. "Is that all you are concerned about?"

435

Michael feigned surprise. "Surely you can't think I'm possessed of ulterior motives, can you?"

"I certainly hope so."

"Who am I to deny a lady?" he returned innocently with a deep bow.

"Well then, what are you waiting for?"

Michael did not waste another second. He pulled her to him and peeled off her wet clothes. He wrapped her in his arms and cupped her buttocks hard against his throbbing sex while his lips captured hers. He nibbled and tasted and savored the taste of her, all the while rocking his hips against hers.

Antonia broke their kiss. "You undoubtedly know what you are doing." She laughed, as her agile fingers went to work and released Michael from his clothing.

"You strip me bare, wench."

"Better to touch you, here and here and here," she said, exploring all his contours. "And lastly, here," she added as she encircled his stiff maleness.

"Ahh," he groaned with pleasure. "You don't play fair. I am your servant; your desires are my commands."

She drew his hand to her breast. "Then I command you to feel me here."

Michael took a breast in each hand, and lifting them to his lips, each one in turn, he kissed and caressed, fondled and suckled until Antonia thought she was going to scream out her joy.

"Do not forget about the rest of me," she managed to moan in between gasps.

"Never!"

Michael carried her to the bed and lowered her gently before joining her. He levered himself into a position to devour her and set about ravishing her.

"Oh, Michael, I can stand no more," she panted. "Join me, please."

"Soon, Princess. Soon," he whispered and proceeded to work his fingers and tongue together.

Antonia was straining harder and harder against him until he withdrew and positioned himself between her ready thighs. He stroked his finger along her cleft and drew it, glistening with the moisture of her arousal, to his lips. "You are a feast, my love. And I shall never get enough of you."

Her hands encased him and glided him into her, and their movements became powerful spiking thrusts. Harder and faster he plunged; she met each stroke with a strength of her own. The intensity grew to a mighty force, and wave after wave of pleasure so extreme was unleashed that they strained their release.

For the longest time they remained quiet, reveling in the wonder of each other. Then Michael took up a towel and bathed and dried her lovingly.

"You best get dressed now before my need rises again and we're forced to quench it," he said, looking down at himself.

"It would be my pleasure to help out whenever the need arises," she offered devilishly.

"Such a brazen wench." He threw his hands in the air. "Get dressed before you convince me to change my mind."

"Speak and it shall be done." She giggled. Donning the gown, she dried her tresses and settled down at the desk to comb the now-limp curls.

"This truly is cause for celebration. The wench is actually following my command."

Antonia tossed a pillow at him, then returned to fashion her hair.

Michael watched her before the mirror, thought of her beautiful body tempting him until he was forced to shift his thoughts to his ship and how he had come to name her the *Áureo Princesa.*

"You seem to be deep in thought," Antonia said, noticing his faraway look.

"I was just thinking of my ship and you."

"Oh?"

"Yes, my golden princess. You see, I had been on my way to a gaming house in London when an old woman dressed in colorful scarves and beads stopped me in the street and offered to tell my fortune.

"The Gypsy foretold of a voyage to a faraway land and of a beautiful woman with hair the color of sunlight who would change my life forever. I scoffed at her. But when I won the ship I renamed vessel the *Áureo Princesa*—Golden Princess; the Hispaniciled form because of the Gypsy. Then, my love, you came into my life."

Antonia rose and walked over to him. She placed her arms around his neck and gently kissed his brow.

"We were fated to be together," she whispered, and nibbled on his ear.

Her kiss made him silently thankful for his luck — or fate, whatever the cause which had brought him his own real live golden princess. As he held her, distant thoughts of England crept into his mind.

Although he held her, she could feel his withdrawal. "My love, what is it that takes you so far from me?" She stepped back, seeking the truth. "Is it the sea which beckons you?"

"Tonia—" He swallowed, preparing to inform her of his decision.

"No, my love," she pressed a slender finger to his

ips, "allow me to finish before you speak. You have called this ship your home for many years. And while you have pledged your heart to me, I know that part of your heart shall always be here. I realize that where your heart is, is where I, too, want to be. So," with tears of joy and sorrow forming behind her lids, she announced, "I, too, wish to call this ship my home."

Michael was gratefully surprised. His heart swelled inside his chest until he felt he could burst with love that he had been so blessed to find such a wife who would stand beside him no matter where life took them. He silently vowed to never disappoint her and cherish the gift of her love always.

His eyes glistened. "You never cease to amaze me," he said. "I had planned to tell you that we will be leaving soon. But, as usual, you beat me to it."

He enfolded her in his embrace once again and gently kissed her. Then he spoke of his plans and all the exotic faraway places they would visit.

While she listened and took delight in a childhood dream coming true, she also reveled in the joy in his eyes as she watched him while he spoke. A momentary twinge of regret pricked her when she wondered if she would ever return to her beloved California again, but she had considered the thought before. At last now she truly knew that it did not matter where she lived as long as she was with the man she loved.

Michael gazed out the porthole and noticed Mano and Juanita approaching from the old *Sea Shark*.

Once they all were seated around a potbelly heating stove, they warmed their bellies with spirits while Mano and Thadius brought Michael up to date on the completion of repairs aboard the old *Sea Shark* and selection of a crew. As Mano spoke, Michael's excitement grew at the thought of returning to the sea.

"How soon can you be ready to sail?" Michael asked Mano.

Mano's face dropped into serious lines of etched stone.

"My brother, we have been together long and traveled many miles, but I have sailed my last voyage. We have settled the score which brought us together, and we have found homes in the hearts of two good women. California is the land of my people; it is the land of my woman's people. For me, my brother, I am a man come home. Juanita grows large with child. That child must know of its land and heritage, here, in the land of my birth," Mano stated simply. "But know, no matter where you travel, we shall always be as brothers."

"I understand," Michael said sadly.

Antonia, too, was saddened for her husband. She knew of the closeness of the two men, and she had grown to have a genuine fondness for Juanita.

"Aye, ye be a man finally come home, lad," Thadius added. "We'll all be missin' ye."

In the excitement, no one had given another thought to the old *Sea Shark* until Michael turned to Thadius and lifted his glass.

"Thadius, since I'll not be in need of a second vessel, and since we never would have taken it without your expertise, I want you to have the *Sea Shark*."

Thadius dropped his glass. "Me own ship?"

After the laughter over Thadius's surprise, Michael stepped toward Mano and Juanita. "I'm going to deed part of my holdings to you. As a matter of fact, my friend," he dropped his hand on Mano's shoulder, "I'm going to give you the east valley the

440

Indians call *Escondido*."

"The hidden valley," Juanita mouthed, ov[e]whelmed. She flew from her chair and threw her arms about Michael's neck. "You much good man. We name first man-child for you." She looked over her shoulder at her man. "If you want, Husband."

"I will be pleased to name my first son after my brother."

Michael turned to Thadius. "What are you going to christen your new ship?"

Thadius cast Michael and the Indian a sly grin. "I be thinkin' I've got the perfect name fer her. I be callin' her the *Indio*."

They joyfully raised their glasses in toast, and began making plans for their departure from California.

Chapter Fifty

December 1834

During the remainder of her last day in California, Antonia carefully packed the last of her possessions and sent them to the ship. She rode across the hills with her *padre* and stopped at her *madre's* grave.

"Oh, *madre,* I love you," Antonia said quietly, staring at the simple headstone which marked her *madre's* final resting place. "I shall miss you." Tears welled in her eyes, and she tenderly laid flowers near the plain cross.

Don Diego took out a handkerchief and blew his nose before settling his hand on her shoulder. "No, my daughter. You will not be without your *madre* because she lives in our hearts."

"Gracias, padre."

He kneeled next to Antonia and brushed the fallen leaves from the grave. "Thank you, my dear wife, for taking care of our Antonia. And please continue to watch over her." Lightly, he ran his fingers over the marker. "I love you, my beloved Rafaela. Someday we shall walk together again." He kissed his trembling fingers and tenderly touched the cold stone. Tears threatening to overcome him, he said, "Daughter, if you do not mind returning by yourself, I would like a few quiet moments alone with your *madre.*"

Antonia patted his shoulder, understanding his need. "I will see you back at the rancho."

Antonia was sitting in the study, waiting for him, when he returned. They spoke of many things. But most important of all, they spoke of the love between a father and daughter.

Michael, followed by Commandant Velasco, joined them late in the afternoon. Velasco helped himself to a refreshing drink, and then handed Michael the papers he had carried out to the rancho.

"Thank you, Commandant. Don Diego, if you will serve as witness, Mano's title to the land will be legally documented."

"Of course." Don Diego gladly affixed his signature to the documents and handed them to the commandant.

Before Velasco had a chance to quench his thirst, Josephina entered. "Put glass down! No time. I busy cook food all day. You come. Now!" When the commandant hesitated, she ordered, "You, too, Comandante Velasco. You come eat, too."

"Since they must leave before the January storms swing down from the north, we have decided to celebrate Christmas early," Don Diego explained.

"Por favor, do stay," Antonia urged. "We want all our *amigos* to celebrate with us."

"*Sí,* it is a pity the governor could not have stayed to celebrate with us as well. Of course, he had to return to Monterey," Don Diego added.

Thadius, Mano, and Juanita joined them shortly after they entered the dining room. Josephina, helped by Lupe, served a hearty Christmas repast of fowl, with all the trimmings. They spent hours enjoying the delicious fare and each other's company, along with a good measure of Don Diego's finest wine.

Thadius was the first to inch his way toward the door. "Juanita, me child, that husband of yers better be treatin' ye good or next trip he'll be answerin' t' Thadius, he will." he said as he embraced the Indian woman.

"Tadius, we name man-child for you, too." She hugged him warmly and planted a smacking kiss on his cheek.

He blushed and turned to Mano. "Don't ye be lettin' her do it. I'll be back this way t' be checkin' on ye." He smiled and embraced the Indian in a rare display of emotion. He then stepped to Don Diego and offered his hand. "I'll be watchin' over the lad and lass, ye needn't be worryin' none."

Don Diego grinned in return, administering a hearty slap to Thadius's back. "You are quite a man."

"And Commandant Velasco, without ye helpin' me cap'n, we might be singin' a different tune now, we might." The two men shook hands.

"I'll be seein' ye two soon," he said to Michael and Antonia.

"Will you not change your mind and spend your last night in California with us?" offered Don Diego.

"Not me, I've much t' see 't before we be leavin'. And besides, I'm not bein' one t' sleep on no land without the rockin' of a vessel t' lull me t' sleep."

Everyone chuckled.

"Very well, *mi amigo. Vaya con Dios,*" Don Diego

said.

After Thadius left the rancho, Velasco rose to depart. "Ah, *capitán,* I envy you your ship. But I shall see you off in the morning."

"Juan, my friend"—Michael halted the commandant's departure—"since you are so envious of me, and I am in dire need of a chief mate after losing Mano and Thadius, why not join Antonia and me? You have no ties here any longer, and I will be happy to teach you the life of a sailor. Perhaps you will come to learn it's not all soft pleasure as is the life of a commandant," Michael jokingly chided.

"Do you invite me to join you in the morning?" Velasco's brows shot up, and his eyes widened dramatically in an expression clearly showing his surprise as well as intrigue at the thought of leaving his post at the presidio.

"Yes, Juan, that's exactly what I'm proposing," Michael said.

"Well then, Capitán Michael Domino, your new chief mate will join you in the morning. I do warn you though, that while my heart is willing, my body is one used to the soft life and may require time to adjust." He cast them a wide grin.

"I assure you, Juan," chuckled Mano, "Captain Domino will have you whipped into shape in no time."

Everyone laughed at Mano's implication except Velasco until he thought about it for a moment and realized Mano was merely jesting. He then wished Mano and Juanita success. He turned over the papers to Don Diego with instructions for their delivery. After a few moments' conversation with the *ranchero,* Juan Velasco, chief mate, left to assemble his belongings.

After the rest of the guests retired for the evening,

Michael and Mano spoke as brothers for the last time. They relived old memories and vowed to never allow the miles between them to blur the meaning of brotherhood.

Long before the sun was due to peek over the majestic, violet mountains to the east, Josephina handed Antonia a basket of her favorite foods. She bid them a tearful *adiós* before the carriage and its occupants, lost in thought-filled silence, lurched forward toward the sea.

The carriage came to a jarring halt at the steep cliffs overlooking the great masted ships. On the damp sand below, Velasco and a longboat waited in the cold, misty morning to take Michael and Antonia on board ship.

Michael offered his hand to Don Diego. "Don't worry, we shall return."

The *ranchero* pulled his son-in-law into a warm fatherly embrace. Michael heartily returned the gesture, feeling a true family member. "I shall hold you to that."

Michael then gently embraced Juanita and kissed her forehead. Michael and Mano needed no further words. He nodded to the Indian who returned the sign. "My brother" were the only words spoken between the two men that morning.

Michael began slowly descending the steep path, giving Antonia a few moments alone to say her farewells.

Antonia pressed herself tightly into her *padre's* circling arms and kissed his cheek. "I love you, *padre*," she said, tears streaming down her face.

"And I you, Daughter," the *ranchero* returned, his heart filled with a sad joy.

Antonia then hugged Mano and Juanita. "We shall miss you both."

She smiled a last gentle smile of parting and hurried after Michael. As she reached him, he curled his fingers lovingly around hers. She paused to glance back over her shoulder at the three figures standing tall at the top of the bluffs.

"I love you, *padre,*" she mouthed the words. "I love you all."

As they were being rowed toward the ship, the sun was just beginning to rise over the dark, jagged peaks, hinting that the glorious pink hues of morning promised a bright day ahead.

Taylor—made Romance From Zebra Books

WHISPERED KISSES   (2912, $4.95/5.9.
Beautiful Texas heiress Laura Leigh Webster never imag
ined that her biggest worry on her African safari would b
the handsome Jace Elliot, her tour guide. Laura's guard
ian, Lord Chadwick Hamilton, warns her of Jace's dange
ous past; she simply cannot resist the lure of his stron
arms and the passion of his *Whispered Kisses*.

KISS OF THE NIGHT WIND   (2699, $4.50/$5.50
Carrie Sue Strover thought she was leaving trouble behin
her when she deserted her brother's outlaw gang to live he
life as schoolmarm Carolyn Starns. On her journey, he
stagecoach was attacked and she was rescued by handsom
T.J. Rogue. T.J. plots to have Carrie lead him to her broth
er's cohorts who murdered his family. T.J., however, soo
succumbs to the beautiful runaway's charms and loving ca
resses.

FORTUNE'S FLAMES   (2944, $4.50/$5.50
Impatient to begin her journey back home to New Orleans
beautiful Maren James was furious when Captain Haw
delayed the voyage by searching for stowaways. Impatienc
gave way to uncontrollable desire once the handsome cap
tain searched *her* cabin. He was looking for illegal passen
gers; what he found was wild passion with a woman h
knew was unlike all those he had known before!

PASSIONS WILD AND FREE   (3017, $4.50/$5.50
After seeing her family and home destroyed by the crue
and hateful Epson gang, Randee Hollis swore revenge. Sh
knew she found the perfect man to help her—gunslinge
Marsh Logan. Not only strong and brave, Marsh had th
ebony hair and light blue eyes to make Randee forget he
hate and seek the love and passion that only he could giv
her.

*Available wherever paperbacks are sold, or order direct from th
Publisher. Send cover price plus 50¢ per copy for mailing an
handling to Zebra Books, Dept. 3093, 475 Park Avenue South,
New York, N.Y. 10016. Residents of New York, New Jersey an
Pennsylvania must include sales tax. DO NOT SEND CASH.*